CONTEMPORARY AMERICAN FICTION

RIDE WITH ME, MARIAH MONTANA

Ivan Doig grew up in northern Montana along the Rocky Mountain Front. He has worked as a ranch hand, newspaperman, and magazine editor and writer. His 1978 book, *This House of Sky*, was a finalist for the National Book Award in contemporary thought. *Ride With Me, Mariah Montana* is the third novel of a trilogy about his fictional McCaskill family and their Two Medicine country. *English Creek* (1984), available from Penguin, was the first, and *Dancing at the Rascal Fair* (1987) the second.

. . . I determined to give it a name and in honour of Miss Maria W———d called it Maria's River. it is true that the hue of the waters of this turbulent and troubled stream but illy comport with the pure celestial virtues and amiable qualifications of that lovely fair one; but on the other hand it is a noble river . . .

MERIWETHER LEWIS JUNE 8, 1805

RIDE WITH ME, MARIAH MONTANA

Ivan Doig

PENGUIN BOOKS

PENGUIN BOOKS
Published by the Penguin Group
Penguin Books USA Inc.,
375 Hudson Street, New York, New York 10014, U.S.A.
Penguin Books Ltd, 27 Wrights Lane,
London W8 5TZ, England
Penguin Books Australia Ltd, Ringwood,
Victoria, Australia
Penguin Books Canada Ltd, 10 Alcorn Avenue,
Toronto, Ontario, Canada M4V 3B2
Penguin Books (N.Z.) Ltd, 182–190 Wairau Road,
Auckland 10, New Zealand

Penguin Books Ltd, Registered Offices:
Harmondsworth, Middlesex, England

First published in the United States of America by
Atheneum, an imprint of Macmillan
Publishing Company, 1990
Published in Penguin Books 1991

5   7   9   10   8   6

PUBLISHER'S NOTE
This is a work of fiction. Names, characters, places, and incidents either are the product of
the author's imagination or are used fictitiously, and any resemblance to actual persons,
living or dead, events, or locales is entirely coincidental.

THE LIBRARY OF CONGRESS HAS CATALOGUED THE HARDCOVER AS FOLLOWS:
Doig, Ivan.
Ride with me, Mariah Montana / Ivan Doig.
p.   cm.
ISBN 0-689-12019-2 (hc.)
ISBN 0 14 01.5607 0 (pbk.)
I. Title.
PS3554.O415R54   1990
813'.54—dc20   90-35834

Printed in the United States of America

To Wallace Stegner

one in a century

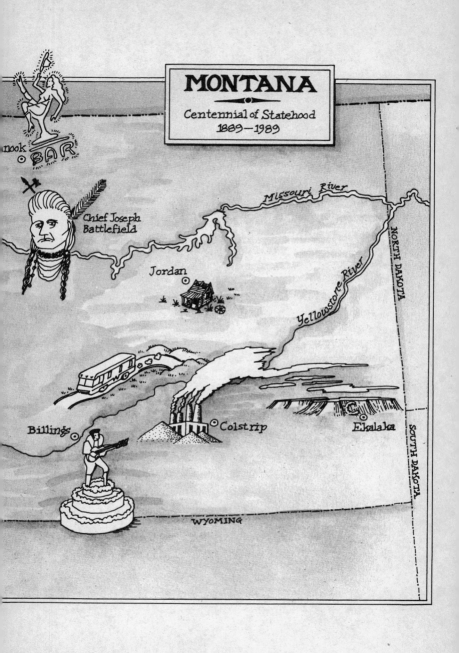

THE END TOWARD IDAHO

Well, old buddies out there the other side of the ink, I am not a happy camper this Fourth of July morn. What we've got here is the hundredth time the grandandglorious has turned up on the calendar since the U. States of A. decided to let Montana in, so wouldn't you think we could do the holiday with some hiss and vinegar by now? But no, it's going to be more of the lame old usual. From Yaak to Ekalaka today, we Montanans will bake our brains in the sun at rodeos, meanwhile consuming enough beer and fried chicken to cholesterate a vegetarian convention, waiting for dark so we can try to burn down our towns with fireworks. A centennial Fourth of the same old guff: hip-hip-hoorah, flap-the-flag-and-pass-the-swag. Maybe it is an American condition, in this strange nation we have become, all helmet and wallet and no brain or heart. But does Montana have to be in a patriotic coma too? Take it from Riley, friends: the calendar this morning says "Independence Day," but you can look high and low in the doings of this centennial year and nowhere find a really independent idea—like changing the name of this state of ours to something more appropriate, such as Destitution.

—"WRIGHT ANGLES" COLUMN,
MISSOULA MONTANIAN, JULY 4, 1989

CLICK. From where I was sitting on the bumper of the Winnebago I was doing my utmost to outstare that camera of hers, but as usual, no such luck. You would think, wouldn't you, that a person with a whole rodeo going on around her could come up with something more highly interesting to spend film on than me. Huh uh, not this cameraperson. No more than an arm's reach away she was down on one knee with the gizmo clapped to her eye like she couldn't see without it, and as soon as she'd shot she said as if it was something the nation was waiting to hear, "You're not such a bad-looking old coot, you know that?"

"The old part I do, yeah."

CLICK. Her next snap of the shutter caught me by surprise as it always did. After all this while, why didn't I know that the real picture Mariah wanted was ever the unexpected one, the one after you'd let your guard down.

She unfolded up out of her picture-taking crouch and stood there giving me a gotcha grin, her proud long mane of hair deeper than red—the double-rich color that on a fine horse is called blood bay—atop the narrow but good enough face and the figure, lanky but not awkwardly so, that somehow managed to be both long-legged and thoroughly mounded where the female variety is supposed to be mounded; one whole hell of a kit of prime woman suddenly assembled. I just sat there like a bumper ornament of the motorhome. What's a guy supposed to say, thanks ever so much for doing exactly what I wish to hell you would cut out doing?

Just then a sleepy *bleah* issued out of a Hereford calf unconcernedly trotting past us into the catch pen at the end of the arena. "AND KEVIN FREW HAS MISSED WITH HIS SECOND LOOP!" the announcer recited the obvious in that tin voice we'd had to hear all afternoon. By habit Mariah twirled a long lens onto her camera and in a couple of quick pulls climbed atop the arena fence to aim out at the horseback subject who was disgustedly coiling his pair of dud lariats, but then didn't bother to snap the scene. "FOLKS, WHAT DO YOU SAY WE GIVE THIS HARDLUCK COW-BOY A BIG HAND OF APPLAUSE! IT'S THE ONLY PAY HE'S GOING TO TAKE HOME FROM HERE TODAY!" My thumb found the Frew boy on the program. Christamighty, he was only the first contestant in the third section of calf roping. Down through all the Fourths of July, if I had a dollar for every guy who entered the Gros Ventre rodeo under the impression he was a calf roper I could buy up Japan.

Mariah was staying perched on the top fence pole while she scanned through that telescope of a lens at the jampacked grand-stand crowd across the arena. Involuntarily I found myself seeing the surroundings in the same bit by bit way she was through her picture-taking apparatus. What this was, the woven wire between the posts and poles of the arena fence sectioned everything in front of my eyes into pieces of view about the size of postcards. So when I gazed straight across, here would be a wire-rimmed rectangle of the rows of rodeo-goers in dark glasses and their best Stetsons. Seek a little higher and the green tremble of the tall cottonwoods along Gros Ventre's streets was similarly framed; like the lightest of snowfall, wisps of cotton loosed from the trees slowly posed in one weave of wire and floated on into the next. Farthest beyond, there hung the horizon rectangle, half sky and half cliffwall of Roman Reef and its companion mountains, up over English Creek where it all began. Where I began. Where she'd begun.

Everything of life picture-size, neatly edged. Wouldn't that be handy, if but true.

I shook my head and spat sourly into the dirt of the rodeo grounds. Blaze of the July afternoon notwithstanding, this was yet another of those days, half a year's worth by now, when my shadow would have frozen any water it passed over.

Naturally Mariah had come to the attention of young Frew, who halted his horse, doffed his rodeoing hat and held it over his heart in a mock pretty way while he yelled across to her, "Will this smile do?" Mariah delivered back to him, "The calf had a better one, Kevin," and kept on scoping the crowd. Young Frew shrugged mournfully and went back to winding up his spent ropes.

I regarded her there above me on the fence. That pert behind of hers nicely enhanced by bluejeans, and her snapbutton turquoise-colored western shirt like some runaway blossom against the sky. Mariah on high. Up there in sight of everybody for a mile, but oblivious to all as she waited for the next picture to dawn. Not for the first time, more like the millionth, I wondered whether her behavior somehow went with her name. That *eye* sound there in Mariah, while any other of the species that I'd ever encountered was always plain *ee* Maria. She was a singular one in every way I could see, for sure.

I stood up, partly to unstiffen but mainly to turn it into the opportunity to announce, "I've had about enough of this." Of course my words meant the all-afternoon rodeo and this perpetual damn calf roping, but more than that, too.

Mariah ignored the more. "What's your big rush?" she wanted to know, all innocent, as she alit from the fence and turned to face me. She made that gesture of swinging her hair out of her eyes, the same little sudden tossing way she always did to clear her view into the camera. As always too, that sway of her head fired off a flash of earrings, silver today, against the illustrious hair. As if just the motion of her could strike sparks from the air. No wonder every man afoot or horseback who ever saw her sent his eyes back for a second helping.

"Jick, somebody's going to use you for a doorstop if you keep on the way you've been," she started right in again as if I was running a want ad for advice. "I had to half-drag you here today and now you can't wait to mope off home to the ranch and vegetate some more. I mean, what is this, suicide by boredom? Before, you were never the type to sit around like you got your tail caught in a crack." Before.

"You know as well as I do that you've got to get yourself going again," she supplied in the next breath. "That's why I want you to pack your socks and come along with me on this."

I'd already told her no. Three times, N-O. Actually I guess it must have been four, because Mariah never starts to really listen until you say a thing the third time.

"Sitting sounds good enough to me," I tried on her now. "The world can use more people who stay sat."

Wouldn't you know, all that drew me was the extended comment that if such was the case then I might just as well plop my butt behind a steering wheel where I'd at least be doing somebody a minimal amount of good, hadn't I. She let up just long enough to see if any of that registered on me. Judging not, she switched to: "I don't see how you can afford not to come. The whole trip gets charged off to the newspaper, the use of your rig and everything, didn't I tell you that already? And if you think that isn't a real deal you don't know the bean counters they've got running the *Montanian* now." Before I could point out to her that free stuff is generally overpriced, she was tying the whole proposition up for me in a polka dot bow. "So all you've got to do is bring the motorhome on over and meet the scribbler and me Monday noon, is that so tough?"

Tough, no; impossible, yes. How could I make her savvy the situation? Before, I'd have said I could shoulder whatever was asked of me, this included. But everything changed for me on that night six months ago, none of it for the better. You can be told and told it will all heal, but that does not make it happen any faster.

4

Mariah wasn't waiting for my deep thoughts to swim ashore. Gathering her gear into her camera bag, a lightweight satchel made of some kind of synthetic but painted up to resemble Appaloosa horsehide, complete with her initials as if burnt in by a branding iron, she simultaneously was giving the rodeo a final scan to make sure there wasn't some last-minute calf roping miracle to be recorded and saying over her shoulder as if it was all settled: "See you in Missoula on Monday, then."

"Like hell you will. Listen, petunia—if it was just you involved, I'd maybe see this different. But goddamn it, you know I don't even want to be in the same vicinity as that Missoula whistledick, let alone go chasing around the whole state of Montana with him."

"Jick. If I can put up with Riley for a couple of months, it shouldn't be that big a deal for you to."

She had me there. Of all the people who'd gladly buy a ticket to Riley Wright's funeral when the time came, Mariah was entitled to the head of the line.

"You and him, that's up to you," I answered as I had any number of times before. "Though for the life of me I can't see why you'd hang around that joker Riley any longer than it takes to cuss him out, let alone all the way from now until the celebrating gets over." The rest of July, August, September, October, the first week of November: four entire months, Mariah's version of "a couple."

"Because this centennial series is a chance that'll never come again." She still was working me over with those digging gray eyes. "Or anyway not for another hundred years, and I'm not particularly famous for waiting, am I?"

"Christamighty, Mariah." How many ways did I have to say no to this woman? "Just take the rig yourself, why don't you?" I fished into my pocket for the Winnebago keys and held them out to her. "Here. The Bago is yours for however long you want it and I don't give a good goddamn how poor a specimen of mankind you take along with you. Okay?"

She didn't take the keys, she didn't even answer my offer of them. No, all she did was that little toss of her head again, as if clearing her firecloud of hair out of the way would clarify me somehow too. People either side of us on their perches of bumpers and fenders were watching the pair of us more than the rodeo. Swell. See the world champion moper Jick McCaskill and his girl while they duke it out on the glorious Fourth; we ought to be selling ringside tickets. I started to turn away and do what I should have done long since, stick the key in the ignition of the Winnebago and head home to the ranch. Try that, though, when the next thing you hear is Mariah saying ever so slowly, in a voice not her usual bulletproof one:

"Jick. Jick, I need to have you along."

Damn. Double damn.

Going Winnebagoing around the countryside with her and the other one was still the last thing on this earth I wanted to do. But *need* instead of *want*. Do people really know what they are trying to reach for with that word? I wasn't sure I could tell, any more.

I scrutinized Mariah. Her, too? Her own wound not yet scarred over, either?

Our eyes held each other for a considerable moment. Until I had to ask her outright:

"You're not just saying that, are you?"

A kind of crinkle, or maybe tiniest wince, occurred in her expression. Then she gave me that all-out grin of hers, honest as the sun, and said: "If I was it'd be the first time, wouldn't it?"

God, that grin. That world-by-the-tail grin that brought back with fresh ache what I was missing, these months since.

In back of Mariah, out in the arena dirt a grunting guy was kneeling on a calf, trying to collect three of its legs to tie together. I knew how that caught calf felt.

Christamighty. Four entire months of letting myself get just exactly where I knew not to get, between the pair of them. Mariah the newspaper picture-taker, my headlong daughter. And writing Riley Wright, my goddamn ex–son-in-law.

Missoula was sizzling. *93*, the temperature sign on top of the *Montanian* building kept spelling out in blinking lights, as if it needed any spelling out.

I still had the majority of an hour before noon when Mariah and Riley were to present themselves and I'd already used up the scenery from the parking lot. The *Montanian* offices fronted onto the Clark Fork River, in a building that looked as though it had been installed before the river—a gray stone heap with an odd pointy-topped round tower, turret I guess it'd be, bellying out over its front entrance. When the rooftop temperature sign wasn't broadcasting a terrible number, it recited in spurts. Or tried to. First:

RIDE WITH ME, MARIAH MONTANA

IF IT'S N WS

Next:

THEN IT' IN

And lastly:

THE MONTA IAN

Over and over again. I had to wonder what they thought
about that gaptoothed brag across the river where the other
newspaper, the *Missoulian*, was headquartered in a new low
building like a desert fort. Mariah had told me it is rare to have
two papers in one town any more, but who ever said Missoula is
your average place.

I'd acquired a discarded copy of today's *Montanian* when I
stopped at Augusta to coffee up before coming over Rogers Pass,
but purposely wasn't reading it because that'd have seemed like
giving in to the blinking sign. I figured it wouldn't count if I just
leafed through to see whether Mariah had any photos in. The
picture with her credit under it, though, I almost missed, not
expecting to find her handiwork in the sports section. A balding
softball player gasping on third base after running out a triple,
his stomach pooching out under a T-shirt which read KEEP MON-
TANA GREEN. SHOOT A DEVELOPER.

Since I had the newspaper open anyway, I took a peek at Riley's
column next. Same as ever, the *Wright Angles* heading and the all
too familiar Riley mug, so favorable a picture of him it surely had
not come from Mariah's camera, and then the day's dose of words.

*The year: back there somewhere. The season: youth. We are six
in number, three of each and much aware of that arithmetic.*

*Curlicues of drawl from the car radio. The girls sing along, and
prairie hills squat all around the endless highway. We are, as the
road-restless word that year says it, motating. Our green Studebaker
coupe motates to the music of time, "melodied radio-special" for
us, announces the disc jockey, "by the one and only Mr. Hank
Williams."*

*Fast miles of lost romance banner behind us, who still think
high school is the world. The gold-haired girl leans softly nearer
the radio and hums at the hills easing past. Mr. Hank Williams
echoes the wail life made as it happened to him, and might to us.*

7

And some more like that. Riley was working himself up into a road mood, was he. Probably he never had to exert himself to be in a girling mood.

What roused me from Riley, not that it would have taken much, was the heavy whump of a car door against the passenger-side of the Bago. A brand new Bronco had pulled into the parking space there, and a guy with a California look to him was squeezing out and frowning down at his door edge and what must have been the first paint chip out of his previously virgin vehicle. My sympathy was not huge. I cast him a go-eat-a-toad-why-don't-you glance to let him know so, then stuck my head back in the newspaper while he gave the dusty put-putting Bago—naturally I had the generator on to run the air conditioning—and me some eyeball time before he vanished into a side door of the *Montanian* building. I figured he must be a bean counter. During the energy boom when there were some actual dollars in this state, a big California newspaper named the *Globe*—unfondly referred to by Mariah and for that matter Riley as the *Glob*—bought up the *Montanian*. A person has to wonder: is everything going to be owned by somebody somewhere else? Where does that eventually end up, in some kind of circle like a snake eating its tail?

I checked the dashboard clock again; still half an hour till noon. Well, hell. Given that I'd already made a five-hour drive from the Two Medicine country to get here and there was no telling what corner of the state Mariah and Riley would want to light off to when they showed up, it seemed only prudent to stoke myself up a little. I went back to the middle of the Winnebago to the gas stove and refrigerator there and from what was available began scrambling a batch of eggs with some slices of baloney slivered into them for body.

To combat the stovetop warmth I put the air conditioner up another notch. Pretty slick, if I do say so myself; one apparatus of the motorhome putting forth hot and another one canceling it out with cold. Next I nuked myself a cup of coffee by spooning some instant into a mug of water and giving it a strong minute in the microwave. Looking around for anything else to operate, I flipped the radio on for dining company. And about lost my hand to the ruckus of steel guitars and a woman semishouting:

"Somewhere south of Browning, along Highway 89!

> *Just another roadkill, beside life's yellow line!*
> *But morning sends its angel*
> > *in a hawk-quick flash of light!*
> *Guiding home forever*
> > *another victim of the night!"*

Some angel, her. Leaving the music on but considerably toned down, I seated myself to do justice to my plateload of lunch and the question of what I was doing sitting here in a Missoula parking lot eating eggs a la baloney.

Every family is a riddle, or at least any I have ever heard of. People on the outside can only glimpse enough to make them wonder what in the name of Jesus H. Christ is going on in there behind the doors of their neighbors and friends, while those inside the family have times, sometimes lifetimes, of being baffled with one another. "Can this one really be *mine?*" parent and child think back and forth, eyeing each other like foreign species. Knots in the bloodline. The oldest story there is, and ever the freshest.

We McCaskills are far from immune. I still wished mightily that I had stuck with my original inclination and kept saying no, daughter or not, to Mariah's big thee-and-me-and-he-in-a-Winnebago idea. If that daughter of mine didn't want to ram around the countryside alone with Riley Wright while Montana went through its centennial commotion, let the newspaper dig down and hire her a bodyguard, why not. Preferably one with experience as a coyote hunter, so that he could recognize what he was dealing with in Riley.

> *"Up along the High Line, on Route 2 east of Shelby!*
> *The guardian in action is Angel Number Three!*
> *Now chrome collides with pheasant,*
> > *sending feathers in the air!*
> *But heaven's breeze collects them*
> > *with a whisper of a prayer!"*

"That was another oldie but goodie from Montana's homegrown C-and-W group, The Roadkill Angels doing their theme song for you here on Melody Roundup," the radio voice chirped. "The time now is eleven forty-seven. In the weather outlook, temperatures east of the Divide will hit the upper eighties the rest of this week, and in western Montana they'll continue to climb into the nineties. So, hot *hot* HOT is going to be the word . . ."

I shut the voice off. The hell with the radio guy and his word. I hate heat. Although, a week of scorchers would provide me a way to tackle Mariah about getting out of this trip, wouldn't it: "Sorry, petunia, but I'm allergic to any weather over ninety above—it makes me break out in a sweat."

But when I came right down to it, I knew I could not call things off that easily. Digest all my reasoning along with the pan of lunch and there still was the fact of Mariah and myself alone with each other, so to speak, from here on. She and I are the only Montana McCaskills there are now. God, it happens quick. My other daughter, Lexa, lives up in Sitka, married to a fellow with the Fish and Game Department there, both of them as Alaskan as you can get without having been conceived in an igloo. And Marcella, my wife . . .

I swallowed on the thought of her again and sat staring out the motorhome side window to Mount Sentinel and the University of Montana's big pale M up there, branded onto the mountain's grassy flank in white-painted rocks. Already the slope of Sentinel looked tan and crisp. By this time next week, wherever the Winnebago and I and Mariah and goddamn Riley might be, haying was going to have to get underway at my ranch by my hired couple, Kenny and Darleen. There was that whole situation, too. Even yet, in the worst of the nights when the question of what to do with the ranch was afire in my mind, I would turn in bed to where she ought to be and begin, "Marce . . ."

Her at every window of my mind. Ghosts are not even necessary in this life. It is hard facts that truly haunt.

I was not supposed to outlive Marcella. In just that many words, there is the history of my slough of mood, the brown trance that Mariah kept telling me and telling me I had to pull out of. But how do you, when the rest of a life together suddenly turns out backwards. Not that it ever can be a definite proposition, but any couple in a long marriage comes to have a kind of assumption, a shared hunch about who will die first, which is maybe never said out loud yet is thoroughly there. Our own fund of love, Marcella's and mine, seemed to have its eventual sum clearly enough set. My father died at sixty-five, and his father must have been a whole lot younger than that when the labors of

his Scotch Heaven homestead did him in. In both of them, the
heart simply played out. So, you didn't need to be much of a
betting person to figure I'd go off the living list considerably
before Marcella.

But cancer.

Only a year or so ago the two of us thought we were on the
verge of getting life pretty well solved. By then we had adjusted,
as much as parents ever do, to the breakup of Mariah and
Riley's marriage. We'd hired a young couple from down at
Choteau, Kenny and Darleen Rice, to take the worst of the
ranch work off our hands from here on. And we'd bought the
Winnebago, secondhand but with under fifty thousand miles on
it, to do the traveling we had always promised ourselves—Alaska
to see Lexa and Travis, and then somewhere away from Montana winter, maybe Arizona or New Mexico or even California.
The brunt of our forty years of effort daylight to dark on the
ranch seemed to be lifted at last, is what I am saying. And so
when Marcella went in to the Columbus Hospital in Great Falls
for that examination and there on the X-rays was the mortal spot
on not just one lung but both, it was one of those can't-happen
situations that a person knows all too well is actual. Six months
before this Missoula forenoon—six months and six days, now—
the air of life went out of my wife, and the future out of me. Her
death was as if I'd been gutted, the way a rainbow trout is when
you slit his underside all the way to the gills and run your
thumbnail like a cruel little plow the length of the cut to shove
the insides out.

An eruption of light where the side door of the Winnebago had
been. I jerked back, blinking and squinting into the bright of
noon.

"Hi, how many days you been here?" swept in Mariah's voice
and swiftly the rest of the swirl of her, led by the ever present
camera bag she hoisted with both hands. "You're the only person left in America who's always early."

"Gives people something to say about me, at least," I fended.

"You've got this place like an icebox, you know that?" As
usual, her attention was in several directions at once, roving the
inside of the motorhome as if she only had sixty seconds to
memorize it. Today she was equipped with two or three more
cameras and other gizmos than usual slung across her shadowplaid
blouse, evidently loaded for the road. None of it seemed to

weight her down any. A mark of Mariah was that she always held herself so straight, as if parting a current with her breastbone.

Her flying inspection lit on the frying pan with its evidence of recent scrambled eggs, and that brought out her grin. Which is to say, it brought Marcella into human face suddenly again, as if my thoughts of her were rendered visible. In most other ways Mariah was built McCaskill, but like her mother she grinned Withrow. So many times I saw it originate on old Dode Withrow whenever he and my father talked sheep in the high summer pastures of the Two Medicine National Forest, and it awaited me on his daughter Marcella my first day in the first grade with her at the South Fork schoolhouse—that grin, one hundred per-cent pure, which seemed to reach out from all the way behind the eyes, to tell the world *Pretty good so far, what else you got up your sleeve?*

Trying desperately to get myself off that remembering train of thought, I put into voice: "I wasn't actually all that hungry, but—"

"—you figured you'd better eat before you got that way," Mariah melodically finished for me with a laugh. With a quick step she closed the distance between us and leaned down and provided me a kiss on the cheek. Another of the things about Mariah was that she closed her eyes to kiss. I always thought it was uncharacteristic of her, but I suppose kissing has all its own set of behavior.

Her lips sampled my cheek only an instant. She pulled back and stared at me.

After considerable scrutiny of the scissor-eyed kind only a daughter or wife can deliver, she asked: "What, did you fall face down on a porcupine?"

"You never seen a beard before?" I said in innocence. I suppose maybe that was a generous description of the not quite week of snowy stubble on my face; but I was growing the whiskers as fast as I could.

"Beard?!? Jick, *beard* has always been next thing to a cussword with you! What brought this on?"

"What do you think did, the centennial, of course. They're having a beard contest for it, up home. I figured I'd get in the spirit of things." Actually I didn't know why, after 64 3/4 years, I suddenly was letting my face grow wild. All I can report is that the morning after the Fourth of July I took stock at the mirror and thought to myself, hell with it, let her sprout.

"Jick, you look like what's left of a wire brush."

"It'll get to looking better."

"I guess it's bound to." She gave me another stare almost strong enough to wipe whiskers away, then shook her head and said, "Listen, I just came to say I'm not really here yet." My impulse was to retort that I knew she wasn't *all* here or the two of us wouldn't be about to go gallivanting around the state of Montana with that Riley dingbob, but I abstained. "To stay, that is," she more or less explained. "I've got a shoot I have to do. The Rotary Club speaker. Big fun," she droned in a contrary voice. By now she was fiddling with the middle camera around her neck as if the orator already was barreled in her lens. "How about if you stock us up on food while I'm doing that, okay? Riley's finishing up another of those thumbsucker columns of his and he's supposed to be done about the time I am. He better be, the turkey." Mariah hefted her photographic warbag and spun for the door. "See you."

Off she vanished Rotaryward, and I drove the Winnebago over to the big Buttrey's store at the east end of town. One thing about having spent a lifetime tending camp for sheepherders is that you don't dillydally in the presence of acres of groceries. Pushing the cart up one aisle and down the next, I tossed in whatever I came to that I figured we might conceivably need in Bago living. Supper of course was closest on my mind, and at the meat counter I contemplated pig liver until I remembered Mariah's golden words: "The whole trip gets charged off to the newspaper." I threw back the liver in favor of the three biggest ribeye steaks I could find.

All the checkout lines were busy—I guessed this was city living, people buying scads of stuff in the middle of the day—so I parked my cart at the end of a line of four other carts at least as heaped as mine and settled to wait.

I didn't stay settled long.

Only the moment or so it took to study idly along my neighbors in front of me in the grocery line until my eyes arrived at the woman, about my age, being waited on by the clerk at the cash register. I was viewing her in profile and that snub nose told me with a jolt.

Holy H. Hell, it couldn't be her, out of a past that seemed a thousand years distant. But yet it indubitably was. I mean, I know what is said about why coincidences so often happen: that there actually are only twelve people in the world and the rest is done with mirrors. But magic dozen or no, this was her for real. Shirley. My first wife.

For the next several eternal seconds I wondered if I was having some kind of attack. My knees went flimsy, as if something was pushing into them from behind, so that I had to put a hand to the grocery cart to steady myself. Simultaneously my heart seemed stopped yet I could almost hear it butting against my breastbone. My guts felt snaky, my blood watery. Normally I do not consider myself easy to spook. But where was there any normal in this, coinciding in a checkout line hundreds of miles from home with somebody you mistakenly barged into marriage with so long ago?

That marriage had been committed right here in Missoula. I was at the university on the GI bill, my last year in forestry school when Shirley and I connected. Shirley Havely, as she was then, from the town of Hamilton down toward the south end of the Bitterroot Valley. In that college time her figure was more on the tidy side than generous and her head was actually a bit big for the rest of her, but it was such a terrific head no male ever cared: a black cloud of hair that began unusually high on her forehead, creating a perfectly straight line across there like the top of a full-face mask; then black eyebrows that curved winningly over her bluebird-blue eyes; then that perky nose; then a smile like a lipstick advertisement. She was a Theta and a theater major and ordinarily our paths would not have crossed in a hundred years, but Shirley had a taste for life on the edge of campus. As did I, in those afterwar years. I hung around with some of the married veterans who lived and partied in prefab housing called Splinterville and at one Saturday night get-together there the two of us found ourselves at the keg of Highlander beer at the same time and she tested me out in a voice as frisky as the rest of her, "You're the smokejumper, aren't you." I surprised myself by smiling a smile as old as creation and giving her back, "Yeah, but that ain't all I'm up to." It happened fast after that, beginning with an indelible weekend when a Splinterville buddy and his wife were away and Shirley and I had the privacy of their place. Then the day after graduation in 1949, we were married. We stayed on in Missoula while I smokejumped that summer, that wicked fire season; on the Mann Gulch blowup in August, thirteen smokejumpers burned to death when the flames ran them down one after another on a tinder-dry grassy slope; and ever after I carried the thought that I could have been one of them if I hadn't been out of reach of the muster telephone on a trail maintenance project that day. Whether it was the fever of living with danger or it simply was the temperature of being young, whenever I got home from a parachute trip to a forest fire, whatever time of day, Shirley and I plunged straight to bed.

When that wore off, so did our marriage. After I passed the U.S. Forest Service exam and was assigned onto the Custer National Forest over in eastern Montana, Shirley did not last out our first summer there. It tore us both up pretty bad. Divorce was no everyday thing then.

That was then and this was now, me standing in the land of groceries gaping at some grayhaired lady with whom I'd once popped into bed whenever it crossed either of our minds. I still was totally unlaced by coinciding with Shirley here. What was going through me was like—like a storm of time. A kind of brainfade, I can only say, in and out, strong and soft, like the surprise warm gusts that a chinook wind hurls down from the mountains of the Two Medicine country: a far-off roar, a change in atmosphere, a surge of thaw where solid winter had been minutes ago, but the entire chinook rush taking place inside me, forcing through the canyon country of the mind. Right then and there, I'd have stopped all remembering that the sight of Shirley was setting off in me if I could have; don't think I didn't try. But I couldn't make my brain perform that at all, not at all. Even the familiar way she was monitoring the clerk at his tillwork, keenly counting her change as he drew it out before he in turn would count it into her hand, I recognized all the way to my bones. Shirley always not only dotted every *i* and crossed every *t*, she crossed every *i* and dotted every *t*, too, just in case. With but one monumental exception; me.

I caught my breath and tried to think of anything adult to step forward and say to her. *Remember me?* logically invited some response along the lines of *I sure do, you parachuting sonofabitch.* Or *How you been?* was equally meaningless, for although Shirley was still attractive in a stringent way it was plain that the same total of forty years had happened to her as to me since that altar mistake we'd made with each other. No, search as I did in myself, there seemed nothing fitting to parley to each other now. While I was gawking and trying not to seem to be, Shirley did

give me one rapid wondering glance; but with my everyday
Stetson on and sunglasses and the struggling whiskers, I must
have looked more like a blind bum wanting to sell her a pencil
than like anybody she'd ever been at all interested in.

"There you go, Mrs. Nellis," the clerk said cheerily as he
positioned the final sack of groceries in her cart, and away
Shirley went, one more time.

"Get everything at Buttrey's?" Mariah asked when she and I
reconvened in the *Montanian* parking lot.

"Uh, yeah." Plenty. My mind still racing with it all as I
stowed canned goods and other belly ammunition in the Bago's
warren of compartments. Why were those married youngsters,
Shirley and me, back into my life? It wasn't as if I hadn't had
better sense since. After I found my way out of the Forest
Service and into ranching on the same land where I was born,
after I mustered myself and married Marcella in the springtime
of 1953, I put that failed first try with Shirley out of memory.
But now right here within sight of where that mutual wrong
guess began, where education took on a darker meaning than a
dramatic girl or a green punk of a smokejumper ever bargained
for, that long-ago error insisted on preening its profile to me.
What right, even, did that episode have to come swarming back
at me again? Doesn't time know any statute of limitations, for
Christ's sake?

Out of memory. Suddenly it chilled me, there in the blaze of
that Missoula day, suddenly to be aware that there may be no
such place.

"I can tell by looking that you're antsy to get going," Mariah
was saying over her shoulder as she busily stacked film into the
refrigerator. I admit I was about half tempted to respond, just to
see the effect on her beaverish activity, *By the way, I just met up
with the woman who could have been your mother.*

But the day had already had sufficient complication and so I
kept on with my storekeeping and just conversed, "How was
your Rotary shoot?"

"Same as a kabillion others. God, I can't wait to get going on
the centennial. Something realer than lunch faces."

This time she had shown up loaded for bear, equipmentally
speaking. As she continued to move gear in—black hard-sided
cases somewhat like those that hold musical instruments but in
this instance I knew contained her camera lights and stands,

then a suitcase-looking deal that she said was a Leafax negative transmitter, which told me nothing, and another case with portable "soup," as she called her stuff for developing proof sheets of her pictures, then a cargo of ditty bags which must have held all other possible photographic dealies—I was starting to wonder whether there was going to be room in the motorhome for human occupancy.

When she at last ran out of outfit to stash, Mariah gave a quick frown in the direction of the *Montanian* building and the prominently absent Riley Wright, then in the next second I and my unshaven condition were under her consideration again. Oh sure, you bet. Up to her eye leapt a camera.

"Mariah, don't start," I warned. "I am not in a photogenic mood."

She dropped the camera to the level of her breastbone, holding it in both hands while she gazed at me as if she couldn't understand what I could possibly be accusing her of. With a honey of a grin she asked, "Don't you think you're being unduly suspicious?" and right there under the sound of *icious* I heard the telltale *click*.

"Hey, damn it! I just told you—"

"Now, now," she soothsoaped me. "Don't you want the history of that beard recorded? If the world's supply of film holds out, maybe I'll eventually get a picture of you looking presentable."

I kept a wary eye on her, but apparently she was through practicing camera aggravation on me for a while. Now impatience simply was making her goosier second by second. Her hair swung restlessly. Today's earrings were green-and-pink half moons which I gradually figured out represented watermelon slices. "All we need is the scribbler," her one-way conversation rattled on, "but you know him, you'd have to pay him to be late to get him to be on time."

"The slanderous McCaskill clan," in through the motorhome's doorway arrived the voice, still as satisfied with itself as a purring cat. "Ever ready to take up the bagpipes against a poor innocent ex-husband."

So here he was, Mister Words himself. I had not laid eyes on him in, what, the three years since he and Mariah split the blanket. But ducking into the Bago now the sonofabitch didn't look one eyeblink older. Same slim tall build, an inch, maybe two, shorter than I am. But notably wide and square at his shoulders, as if he'd forgotten to take the hanger out of his shirt. Same electric hair, wild and curly in that color that wasn't quite blond and wasn't quite brown; more like applesauce, which I considered appropriate. Same foxtail mustache, of the identical color as his hair. A person's first glimpse of this character, hair seemed to be the main agenda of his head, the face and anything behind it just along for the ride. But the guy was slyer than that, a whole hell of a lot. I have seen him talk to people, oh so casually asking them this or that, and before they knew it they'd been interviewed and were about to be served up with gravy on them in the next day's newspaper.

He was studying me now. I stonily met his nearest eye, surprisingly akin to Mariah's exact gray, and waited for something wisemouthed from him, but all he issued was, "Managed to find your way to civilization from Noon Creek, hmm?" which was only average for him. Even so, up in me came the instantaneous impulse to snap at him, let him know nothing was forgotten, not a thing mended between us. Instead, for Mariah's sake I just uttered the one flat word of acknowledgment: "Riley."

Meanwhile Mariah looked as if there was a dumpload she wanted to deliver onto him, but instead she expelled a careful breath and only asked: "Did the BB have any last words of wisdom for us?"

"You bet. I quote exactly: 'Make our consumers sit up and take notice.'" Riley swung back to the doorway, stuck his head out and intoned to Missoula at general in a kind of robot voice: "CONSUMERS OF NEWSPAPERS. IT HAS COME TO THE ATTENTION OF OUR LEADER, THE INCREDIBLE BB, THAT YOUR POSTURE LEAVES SOMETHING TO BE DESIRED. SO SIT UP AND TAKE NOTICE." He pulled back inside with us and said with a sense of accomplishment, "There, that ought to do it."

Mariah regarded him as if she was half-terminally exasperated, half-helplessly ready to laugh. "Riley, one of these days he's going to hear you mouth off like that."

Riley widened his eyes under applesauce-colored eyebrows. "And demote me to a photographer maybe even? Shit oh dear!" Next thing, he was at the doorway again, sending the robot voice out again: "BB. I DIDN'T MEAN IT. MARIAH MONTANA MADE ME DO IT."

"Demote?" Mariah pronounced in a tone full of barbwire. "Listen, mittenhead. You can barely handle the crayons you write with, let alone a camera."

Uh huh. We hadn't so much as turned a wheel yet and the road war was already being declared by both sides. The two of them faced each other across not much distance there in the middle of the motorhome, Mariah standing straight yet curved in that wonderful womanly way, Riley cocking a gaze down at her from that wilderness of hair. An outside soul couldn't help but wonder how they could stand to work under the same roof, even though Mariah had explained to me that they didn't really need to cross paths all that much at the newspaper, Riley's column appearing as it did without photos except his own perpetual smartass one. So imagine the mutual nasty surprise when Mariah unbeknownst put in her suggestion to do a series of photographs around the state during its centennial celebration and Riley in equal ignorance put in his suggestion to write a series of stories about same, and their editor the BB—his actual name was Baxter Beebe—decreed that they were going to have to do their series together, make a mix. Likely that's how gunpowder got discovered, too.

Which of them relented now I couldn't really tell, but it was Riley who turned a little sideways from Mariah and delivered to me as if we were in the middle of a discussion of it:

"Still hanging onto the ranch, hmm, Jick?"

To think that he would even bring that subject up.

"How's that going?" he pressed, blue eye fixed steadily on me.

Him and his two colors of eyes. I don't know what that particular ocular condition is called, maybe Crayola in the genes, but on Riley the unmatched hues were damn disconcerting—his way of looking at you in two tones, flat gray from one side and bright blue the other. Rampant right up to his irises.

I returned his gaze squarely and gave the ranch answer I'd heard Marcella's father Dode Withrow give whenever my own father asked him that question during the Depression, the self-same answer that Montana ranchers and farmers must have given when times turned rocky for them in 1919 and the early twenties, and probably back before that in the crash of 1893. "Doing good, if you don't count going broke."

Brisk, or maybe the better spelling is brusque, Mariah passed between us toward the front of the motorhome, saying, "This isn't getting anything done. Let's head out."

"Mariah, you keep forgetting," Riley spouted in her wake. "Your license to boss me expired three years ago." At some leisure he proceeded to give himself a tour of the layout of the motorhome. The gateleg table where he'd have to write on his computer or whatever it was in the case he was carrying. The bathroom with its chemical toilet and the shower just big enough for a person the height of us to duck into. The kitchenette area with its scads of built-in cupboards all around the little stove and sink and refrigerator and microwave. Riley of course recognized the derivation of that condensed kitchen and delivered me one of his sly damn grins. "Jick, I didn't know you sheepherders have engines in your wagons these days." No, there was just a hell of a lot he didn't know. One silo after another could be filled with what this yoyo did not know, even though he did go through life as if it was all being explained through him.

"Tight goddamn outfit," I heard Riley mutter as he finished nosing around. I flared, thinking he was referring to the Winnebago, which was as capacious as Marcella and I had been able to afford; but then I realized from the note of resignation in his voice that he meant the management of the *Montanian,* who utterly would not hear of four months of travel expenses for Mariah and Riley until she came up with the frugal notion of using my Bago.

Something other than the fact that the newspaper's bean counters would sooner open their veins than their wallets seemed to be bugging Riley, though. He fixed a long look onto Mariah's camera bag as if the fake white hide with brown spotted pattern was in fact the rump of an Appaloosa. He'd had that equine paint job done and given her that bag the first Christmas they were married. I wondered if during the breakup of their marriage it ever occurred to Mariah to tell him he was the resident expert about a horse's ass, all right. Now he prowled some more, nosing into one end of the motorhome and then the other, until finally he turned to Mariah and asked: "Well, where do we sort out?"

"Sort out what?"

"Our bodies, Little Virgin Annie," Riley enunciated so elaborately you could all but hear his teeth click on that second word. "Where do we all sleep in this shoebox?"

Mariah sent him a satisfied glint that said she'd been waiting several thousand whetted moments for a chance like this. "I sleep here," she indicated the couch along the wall opposite the dinette area. Then with a toss of her head she aimed his attention, and mine, to the bed at the very rear of the motorhome, scrunched in behind the toilet amid closets and overhanging storage compartments. "You two," she gladly informed Riley, "sleep there."

"Oh, come on!" Riley howled, honestly aggrieved. "This wasn't in the deal, that I'd have to bed down with Life's Revenge here!" indicating none other than me.

"It sure as hell wasn't anywhere in my plans either," I apprised him.

"Then one of you delicate types sleep on the pulldown instead," said Mariah, which Riley and I both instinctively knew was a worse proposal yet. Guys our size, only a bare majority of the body would fit into the bunk that pulled down above the driver's and passenger's seats and the rest of our carcass would have to be folded up like an accordion some way.

"I wonder if it's too late to volunteer for the South Dakota centennial," Riley grumbled, but tossed a knapsack onto the rear bed as if deciding to stay for a while.

By default then, the wordbird and I unhappily resigned ourselves to being bedmates, and once Riley got his laptop computer and a fannypack tape recorder and a dictionary and a slew of other books and a bunch more kit and caboodle aboard, it finally looked like the historic expedition could strike off across Montana. Something was yet tickling at my mind, though. Here we were into the afternoon already and nobody had mentioned the matter of destination. Thus I felt compelled to.

"How far do we have to get to today, anyway?"

"Moiese," Mariah proclaimed, as if it was Tierra del Fuego.

She and Riley kept going on about their business as if that wasn't some kind of Missoula joke, so I had to figure it wasn't. "Now wait a goddamn minute here, am I right that Moiese is just up the road a little ways?"

"About an hour, yeah," Riley assessed, helping himself to a handful of the Fig Newtons he'd discovered in a cupboard. "Why?"

"Are you telling me I got up before daylight and drove my butt off for half a day in this rig just to chauffeur you two somegoddamnwhere you could get to and back in a couple of hours yourselves?"

It was Riley and Mariah's turn to look at each other, accomplices unhappily harnessed together. Riley shrugged and chewed a cookie. "Having you along as chaperone is strictly Mariah's idea," he pointed out. "I wanted Marilyn Quayle to come, myself."

"Shove it, Riley," he was instructed by Mariah. To me, she stated: "Moiese is where we both think the series ought to start. Begin the world at the right end, as somebody always said to me when I was growing up."

In the face of being quoted back to myself I surrendered quick and fished out the Bago's ignition key. "Okay, okay, Moiese it is. But how come there?"

Riley's turn to edify me. "Jick, companion of my dreams, we are going to see the ideal Montanans," he announced as if he was selling stuff on TV. "The only ones who were ever able to make a decent living in this state, before the rest of us came along and spoiled it for them."

Since I'd never been up into the Moiese country, I didn't have a smidgen of an idea what he was yammering about.

"Meaning who?"

Riley, damn him, gave me another sly grin.

"The buffalo."

Tracking buffalo from a motorhome the size of a small boxcar was an occupation I had never done, and so when we rumbled across the cattleguard—buffaloguard, I guess it'd be in this case— into the National Bison Range at Moiese, I didn't know how things were going to go. Especially when the Range turned out to be what the word said, a big nice stretch of rolling rangeland that included Red Sleep Mountain sitting fat and slope-shouldered across the southern end of the Flathead Valley, enough country for livestock of any kind to thoroughly hide away in. The best I could imagine was that we'd need to creep the Winnebago along the gravel road until maybe eventually some dark dots might appear, far off across the prairie. About as thrilling as searching for flyspecks, probably.

For once, I was short of imagination. Just a couple of hundred yards beyond the Park Service visitor center, all of a sudden here were a dozen or so buffalo lolling around like barnyard cows.

"How's this for service?" I couldn't resist asking Mariah and Riley as I braked the Bago to a stop within fly-casting distance of the buffalo bunch. But he already was intent on them, leaning over my shoulder with notebook and pen ready for business, and she long since had rolled down her window and connected her camera to her eye.

Their goatees down in the grass, the miniature herd methodically whisked at flies with their short tasseled tails. Huge-headed. Dainty-legged. Dark as char. I knew buffalo only from the stories which the oldest of Two Medicine oldtimers, Toussaint Rennie, held me hypnotized with when I was a boy, and so it was news to me that a buffalo up close appears to be two animals pieced together: the front half of a shaggy ox and the rear of a donkey. There is even what seems like a seam where the hairy front part meets the hairless rear half. But although they are a cockeyed-looking creature—an absentminded family where everybody had put on heavy sweaters but forgot any pants, is the first impression a bunch like this gives—buffalo plainly know what they're on the planet for. Graze. Eat grass and turn it into the bulk of themselves. Protein machines.

These munched and munched while we gawked. Digestion of both sorts until suddenly an old bull with a head big as a mossy boulder began butting a younger male out of his way, snorting ominously to tell the rest of creation he was on the prod, and of course at that exact same moment came the sound of the passenger-side door as Mariah went out it.

"Hey, don't get—" I started to yelp and simultaneously bail out of my side of the Bago to head her off, but was halted by the grip of Riley's paw on my upper arm.

"Far be it from me to poke my nose into McCaskill family affairs"—oh, sure—"but she generally knows what she's doing when she has a camera in her hand, Jick."

True, Mariah so far had only slipped her way in front of the Bago to where she could sneak shots at the bulls doing their rough stuff. But I was staying leery about how she was going to behave with that camera. Long lens or not, she had a history of getting right on top of whatever she was shooting. Years ago at a Gros Ventre rodeo, Marcella and I heard the announcer yap out, "FOLKS, HERE'S SOMETHING A LITTLE BIT DIFFERENT! MARIAH McCASKILL WILL NOW . . . " and we looked up to see this daughter of ours hanging sideways off a running horse, snapping the view a bulldogger would have as he leaned off to jump onto the steer. We counted ourselves lucky that at least she didn't jump.

These buffalo now were not anything to fiddle around with. Compact though they were, some of them weighed as much as a horse, a *big* horse; couple all that muscle and sinew to those wicked quarter-moon horns and you have a creature that can hook and rip open a person. The reputation of buffalo is that even a grizzly bear will back off from them, and for once I vote with the bear. My buffalo unease was not helped any by their snorelike grunts, *umhh . . . umhh,* which somehow kind of hummed on in the air after you heard them. I noticed even Riley keeping half an eye on Mariah despite his unsought advice that there wasn't anything in her picture-taking behavior to sweat about.

She did nothing too suicidal, though, in firing off her *click* as a pony-sized calf suckled on its mama or the proddy old bull laid down and vigorously rolled, kicking all four legs in the air as he took his dust bath. Up until the point where she climbed onto the top of the Winnebago to see how the buffalo scene registered from up there.

My heart did some flutters as Riley and I listened to her prowling around on that slick metal roof. I mean, oughtn't there be some kind of hazard rule that a photographer never do anything a four-year-old kid would have the sense not to?

My flutters turned into genuine internal gyrations as the old bull shook off the last smatters of his dust refreshment, stood for a minute with his half-acre head down as if pondering deeply, then began plodding directly toward the motorhome.

"It must take nerves of utter steel," Riley observed to me.

"What, to be a photographer?"

"No, to be Mariah's father."

Riley's mouthery wasn't my overriding concern by now, though. The buffalo bull continued toward us in a belligerently business-like way, horned head growing huger with every undeviating step.

"Hey, up there," I leaned out the Bago window and called nervously to Mariah on the roof. "How about coming down in? This old boy looks kind of ornery."

Answer from on high consisted of a sudden series of *whing-whingwhing*s, like a little machine going. It took me a bit—about four more paces by the inexorable buffalo—to figure out the blurty *whing* sounds, which kept on and on, as being the noise of a motorized camera Mariah resorted to when she wanted to fire the shutter fast enough to capture every motion. As now. "You've got to be kidding," her voice eventually came down but of course none of the rest of her. "When am I ever going to get closer buffalo shots than this?"

Only when skewered on a buffalo horn if she happened to slip off that roof. I had my mouth open to roar her some approximate version of that when I became aware of two dull pebbly eyes regarding me out of a mound of dense crinkly hair, around the front end of the motorhome. I yanked my head inside at record speed, but the buffalo was nearsightedly concentrating on the vehicle anyway. Experimentally he shifted his full weight sideways against the grillwork below the hood and began to rub.

The motorhome began to shake rigorously.

"I figured this rig must be good for something," Riley contributed as the buffalo settled into using the grill for a scratching post. Jesus, the power of that itch. The poor old Bago was rocking like an outhouse in an earthquake. *Umhh . . . umhh*, the three-quarter-ton beast grunted contentedly as he scraped and scraped. To look at up close, the hide on a buffalo is like a matted mud rug that hasn't been shaken out for many seasons, so there was no telling how long this bison version of housecleaning was going to go on. From my perch in the driver's seat, every sway of the Bago brought into view those up-pointing horns, like bent spikes thick as tree limbs. *Whingwhing whingwhingwhing* from above told me Mariah still was merrily in action, but my jitters had had enough. Without thinking I asked over my shoulder to Riley: "If you know so goddamn much about buffalo, how do we get rid of an itchy one?"

"A little noise ought to make him back off," Riley diagnosed with all the confidence of an expert on large mammals and reached past me and beeped the horn.

The honk did send the buffalo scrambling away, but only far enough to whirl around. Those dancy little legs incredibly maneuvered the top-heavy bulk of the creature, then propelled it head-on at us. Squarely as a pointblank cannon shot, the buffalo butted the grill of the Bago with a crunching *Bam!*

"Shit oh dear!" Riley expressed in something like awe.

"Hey, quit, you sonofabitch!" I shouted. Properly that utterance would have been in the plural, for I was including in it both the hornthrowing buffalo and goddamn hornblowing Riley.

Overhead there had been the sound of a bellyflop, a person hitting the deck. At least there hadn't been a photographer's body flying past.

"Mariah?!" I squalled next, mesmerically watching the buffalo back off with exact little steps, as if pacing off for another go at the grill. "Will you get yourself down here now, for Christ's sake!?" Riley was poking the upper half of himself out the passenger-side window to try and locate her, for all the good that did.

"No way," arrived the reply from the roof. "I know that buffalo can't climb up here. But into the cab with you two lamebrains, I'm not so sure."

"Then can you at least hang onto something while I back us out of here? I'll take it as slow as I can, but . . ." Butt was still the topic on the buffalo bull's mind too, from the look of him. As I eased the Bago into reverse and we crept backwards down the road with Mariah prone on the roof, he lumbered toward us at the same gait as ours, patient as doomsday. Not until the motorhome at last bumped across the hoofcatching metal rods of a buffaloguard and we were safely on the other side of that barrier and the massive fence, did our pursuer relent.

When we halted and Riley and I piled out, that daughter of mine relinquished her armhold around the rooftop air conditioning unit and climbed down perfectly unscathed. The Winnebago, though: its grill had a squashed-in dent as big around as a washtub. The abused vehicle looked as if a giant fist had punched it in the snoot.

Luckily the hood would still open, just, and as far as I could tell the radiator had survived. "How, I don't know," I stormily told the *Montanian* perpetrators and punctuated by slamming the hood back down.

"Honking the horn was a perfectly dumb-ass idea," Mariah rendered.

"Riley's who did it," I self-defended.

"Then that explains it."

"Don't get your kilts flapping," Riley told us soothingly. "A little flexible arithmetic is all we need." He flipped open his notebook and jotted the reminder to himself. "I'll just diddle the expense account for the cost of fixing the grill when we get a chance. The bean counters will never know they've been in the Winnebago repair business."

"Speaking of," I gritted out. "Now that the two of you are done with your goddamn buffalo business, let's get the hell out of—"

Riley stirred in a suddenly squirmy way, like a kid who's had an icicle dropped down the back of his neck.

Mariah jumped him. "You haven't got what you need for a story yet, have you."

He grounded her with an appraising look and the rejoinder, "And you've just been burning film without getting the shot you want yet, haven't you."

Christamighty, all that uproar and neither one of them had anything printable to show for it? They called this newspapering? I suggested coldly to the pair of them, "How about reporting a buffalo attack on an innocent motorhome?"

"BUFFALO BONKS BAGO," Riley considered. "Naw, the BB would only give that story two inches on the pet care page."

Their stymied mood prevailed until Mariah proposed, "Let's go up Red Sleep for a look around, how about." Riley said with shortness, "Good as any."

Red Sleep Mountain is not hospitable to long-chassised motorhomes, and so as far as I was concerned it was up to Riley and Mariah to hitchhike us a ride up the steep one-lane road with a bison ranger. Rather, it was mostly up to Mariah, because any ranger with blood in him would be readier to take along a red-haired woman of her calibre than mere Riley and me.

Shortly we were in a ranger's van, rising and rising, the road up Red Sleep coiling back and forth and around, toward the eventual summit of the broad gentle slopes. Although no more buffalo, other game more than abounded. We drove past antelope curious about us and elk wary of us and every so often sage chickens would hurl up into a flock of flying panic at our coming. At least here on Red Sleep my eyes could enjoy what my mind couldn't. I was thoroughly ticked off yet, of course, about the Bago's bashed-in condition. But more was on me, too. The morning's encounter out of nowhere with Shirley. The firefly thoughts of the mind. Why should memory forever own us the way it does? That main heavy mood I'd been in ever since Marcella's death now had the Shirley layer of bad past added onto it. Was I radically imagining or did life seem to be jeering under its breath to me *is that all you can do, lose wives?*

I shook my head against that nagging theme and while Mariah and Riley carried on a conversation with the ranger I tried to make myself concentrate on the land spreading away below our climb of road. Montana west of the Continental Divide, the end toward Idaho, always feels to me as if the continent is already bunching up to meet the Pacific Ocean. But even though this was not my preferred part of the state I had to admit that the scene of the moment was A-number-1 country. North from the buffalo preserve the Flathead Valley stretched like a green tile floor, farms and ranches out across the level earth in highly orderly fashion, while to the west the silverblue Flathead River curved back and forth broad and casual, and to the east the Mission Mountains tepeed up prettily in single long slants of slope from the valley floor to peaks a mile and a half high. Extreme, all of it, to an east side of the Divide inhabitant like me accustomed to comfortable intermediate geography of foothills and buttes and coulees and creeks. But extremely beautiful too.

The federal guy dumped us out at the top of Red Sleep where there was a trail which he said led shortly to a real good viewpoint. While he drove off to check on the whereabouts of some mountain sheep, the three of us began hoofing.

Out in the tall tan grass all around, meadowlarks caroled back and forth. Here atop Red Sleep the afternoon sunshine felt toasty without being overwhelming. I'd begun to think life with Riley could even prove bearable, if it went on like this, but I had another think coming. We were in sight of the little rocky outcrop of viewpoint when he stopped in the middle of the trail, swung around to me and asked right out of nowhere:

"What do you say, rancher? Could you get grass to grow like this on that place of yours?"

Well, hell, sure. I thought so, anyway. What was this yoyo insinuating, that I hadn't paid any attention to the earth under me all my life? Riley was truly well-named; he could rile me faster than anybody else ever could. I mean, I saw his point about the wonderful grass of this buffalo preserve. Knee-high, thick as a lawn, it was like having a soft thicket beneath your feet. Originally this must have been the way prairie America was, before farming and ranching spread over it.

"Yeah, my place could likely be brought back to something like this," I responded to goddamn Riley. One thing for sure, that mustache wasn't a latch on his mouth. The ranch. Why did the SOB have to keep bringing up that tender topic? On this grass matter though, I finished answering him with "All it'd take is fantastic dollars" and indicated around us to the tremendous miles of tight ten-foot-high fence, the elaborate system of pastures, the just-so balancing of how much grazing the buffalo were allowed to do before the federal guys moved them to fresh country. Sure, you bet, with an Uncle Sam—financed setup like this I or just about anybody else above moron could raise sheep

or cattle or any other known creature and still have knee-deep
grass and songbirds too, but—

The *but* was Riley's department. "But in the good old U.
States of A., we don't believe in spending that kind of money on
anything but the defense budget, do we. The death sciences.
Those are what get the fantastic dollars, hmm, Jick old buddy?"

Having delivered that, wherever it flew into the pigeonhole of
his brain from, Riley spun around again and went stalking off
down the trail. He all but marched over the top of Mariah where
she knelt to try a shot of how a stand of foxtail was catching the
sunlight—sprays of purplish green, like unearthly flame, reflecting out of the whisks of grass.

Riley, typical of him, had freshened another bruise inside of
me with his skyblue mention of my ranch. What in the name of
hell was I going to do with the place? I trudged along now trying
to order myself, Don't think about the ranch. Like that game
that kids play on each other: don't think about a hippopotamus,
anything but a hippopotamus is okay to think about, but if you
think about a hippopotamus you get a pinch, are you by any
chance thinking about a hippopotamus?

I am not as zippy on a trail as I once was, but before too long I
caught up with Mariah and Riley at the rock finger of viewpoint.
Below, Red Sleep Mountain divided itself judiciously into two
halves of a V, letting a small stream and its attending trees find
their way down between. Then beyond, through the split of the
V the neatly tended fields of the miniature Jocko River valley
could be seen, and immediately over the Jocko, mountains and
timber accumulated into long, long rising lines of horizon. By all
evidence, the three of us were the only onlookers in this whole
encompassing reach of planet.

Picturing that moment in the mind, it would seem a scene of
thoroughest silence. But no. Warbles and trills and solo after solo
of *sweet sweet* and *wheeep wheeep* and *deedeedee*: the air was
magically busy.

None of us spoke while the songs of the birds poured undiluted. I suppose we were afraid the spate of loveliest sound
would vanish if we broke it with so much as a whisper. But after
a bit came the realization that the music of birds formed a
natural part of this place, constant as the glorious grass that
made feathered life thrive.

I take pride that while we three filled our ears, I was the one who detected the promising scatter of dark specks on the big slope to the west; at least my eyes aren't lame. After I wordlessly pointed them out to the newspaper whizzes, those dots grew and grew to become a herd of a couple hundred buffalo. Bulls, cows, calves, by the tens and dozens, spread out in a nice graze with one of the stout pasture fences blessedly between us and them so Mariah couldn't caper out there and invite a stampede onto herself. Of course, even this pepper pattern of a herd across an entire mountainslope amounted only to a fingernailful compared to the buffalo millions back in the last century. But I thought them quite the sight.

Mariah broke the spell. "Time for a reality check," she levied on Riley. "So what are you going to do in your Great Buffalo Piece?"

Riley's pen stopped tapping his notebook. "I won't know that until I sit down and do the writing, will I."

"Come off it, Tolstoy," Mariah said as if telling him the time of day. "Since when don't you have an angle to pull out of storage? Here's-my-ever-so-clever-idea-about-buffalo, and then plug in the details."

"Oh, it's that christly easy, is it," he retorted, starting to sound steamed.

Mariah sailed right on. "So, what can I best shoot to fit with your part of the piece? Buffalo, or country, or grass, or what?"

He gave her a malicious grin. "The birdsong. Get me that, that'll do."

For half an instant, that put me on his side. I wished they'd both can the argument or discussion or whatever kind of newspaperperson conversation this was, and let the air music stream on and on.

But Mariah had on her instructive voice now, not a good sign. "Don't freak, Riley. All I'm asking is for some idea of what you're going to write."

"Buy a Sunday paper and find out."

"How crappy are you going to be about this? Let's just get down to work, okay?"

"I *am* working! At least when you're not yapping at me."

"Then let's hear some of those fabulous words. What's your buffalo angle going to be?"

"I'm telling you, I don't know yet!"

"Tsk," she tsked briskly. "A tiny wee bit rusty out here in the real world after all that sitting around the office dreaming up columns, are you?"

"Mariah, ring off. Shoot whatever the fuck you want and they'll slap it on the page next to whatever the fuck I write and that'll be that. Simplissimo."

"Two half-assed pieces of work don't equal one good one," she said, all reasonableness.

"We are not going to be Siamese twins for the next four months!" he informed her. "You do your job your way and I'll do mine mine!"

With equal beat she responded, "No! The series won't be worth blowing your nose in if we do it that way!"

It must have been some marriage, theirs. By now I'd gone off a ways to try and not hear anything but the birds and the breeze in the grass, but I'd have had to go into the next county to tune those two out. Quite a day for the *Montanian* task force, so far. Newspapering is nothing I have ever done, but I have been around enough work to know when it is not going right. Here at the very start of their centennial series, Mariah and Riley both were spinning their wheels trying to get off high center.

Does time make fancy knots to entertain itself this way, as sailors did when ships were vessels of wind and rope? Cause to wonder, for a centennial started all of this of Mariah and Riley. Not this one of Montana's statehood, of course, but a number of years ago when the town of Gros Ventre celebrated a hundred years of existence. That day Mariah was on hand in both her capacities, so to speak; as somebody who was born and raised locally, and for the *Gros Ventre Weekly Gleaner* as its photographer, there at the start of her career of clicking. Thus she was in natural orbit on the jampacked main street of Gros Ventre that centennial day, and it was Riley who ricocheted in—I would like to say by blind accident but there was more to it than that, as I suppose there ever is. Riley's mother's side of the family was from Gros Ventre originally and so it could be said he was only being a dutiful son by coming with her to the reunion. My suspicion, though, is that he was mainly fishing for something to write in his column. When was he ever not?

In any case, I was witness to the exact regrettable minute when Riley Wright hooked up with Mariah. Late in the afternoon, after the parade and the creek picnic, with everybody feeling gala and while the street was clogged with people catching up on years of news from each other, extra commotion broke out at the Medicine Lodge saloon. Young Tim Kerz, who never could handle his booze, had passed out drunk and his bottle buddies decided a ceremony was called for to commemorate the first casualty of the day. Scrounging up a sheet of thick plywood, they laid out Tim on it as if ready for the grave—*his beer bier*, Riley called it in the column he wrote—to the point, even, of folding his hands on his chest with a purple gladiolus clutched in them. Then about a dozen of the unsoberest ones began tippily pallbearing Tim out of the Medicine Lodge over their heads, the recumbent body on high like a croaked potentate. Somehow Mariah seems to sense stuff like this before it can quite happen. She had raced up into a third-story window of the old Sedgwick House hotel with a panoramic view down onto the scene by the time the plywood processional erupted out of the Medicine Lodge, singing and cussing.

And then and there I noticed the tall shouldery man with the notebook and pen, one intent eye gray and the other blue, lifting his gaze over the tableau of Tim and the tenderly held gladiolus to Mariah above there as she worked her camera.

I had skyhigh hopes for Riley Wright originally. What daddy-in-law wouldn't? Oh, true, matters between him and Mariah had taken a couple of aggravatingly slow years to progress toward marriage. First the interval until a photographer's job at the *Montanian* came open for her. Then after she moved to Missoula for that, a span when carefully nothing was said by either us or them but Marcella and I knew that Mariah and Riley were living together. On their wedding day in 1983 we were glad to have that loose situation ended. So then here Riley was, in the family. An honorary McCaskill, so to speak. In his own right a semifamous person because of his newspaper column, although some of that fame was a grudging kind from people who yearned to give him a knuckle sandwich for what he wrote. Just for instance, a few years ago when agriculture was at its rockbottom worst and corporations got busy taking each other over and hemorrhaging jobs every time they did, Riley simply ran a list of the counties in Montana that had voted for Reagan and put at the end, *How do you like him now?* Or the time he wrote about a big farming operator who was plowing up thousands of acres of virgin grassland in a time of roaring crop surpluses—farming the farm program, it's called—and then letting that broken earth sit fallow and victim to the wind, *When he becomes dust himself, the earth will spit him back out.*

But when Riley wasn't armed with ink, he truly looked like a prime son-in-law. Oh sure, even in his nonwriting mode, any moment of the day or night he was capable of being a smart aleck. But better that than a dumb one, I always figured. No, exactly because Riley was the kind of sassypants he was toward life, his natural Rileyness, call it, I made my offer. An afternoon in April three years ago, in the middle of lambing time, this was. He and I were sharing coffee from my thermos outside along the sunny south wall of the lambing shed. Bold black and white of a magpie strutted the top of a panel gate, and Noon Creek rippled and lulled, but otherwise just we two. A few minutes earlier when I'd seen Mariah and Riley arrive in his old gunboat Buick I momentarily thought it interesting that after we waved hello mutually, he headed straight down here to the shed while she went into the house to Marcella. Nothing major suggested itself from that, however, and so far as I knew, father- and son-in-law were sipping beanjuice companionably amid the finest of scenery. Spring can be an awful flop in the Two Medicine country. Weeks of mud, every step outdoors taken in overshoes weighted with the stuff. Weather too warm for a winter coat but cool enough to chill you into a cold. Then out pops a day such as this to make up for it all. Just west of us, seemingly almost within touch, the midair skyline of the Rockies yet had white tips of winter, sun-caught snow on the peak of Phantom Woman Mountain and the long level rimrock of Jericho Reef, but spring green colored all the country between us and the foot of the mountains— the foothill ridges where my lamb bunches were scattered, the alfalfa meadows pocketed away in the willow bends of Noon Creek, the arcing slope of Breed Butte between our ranch and those of English Creek, green all.

I recall that Riley looked a little peaked, like he was in need of a fresh turn of season right that moment. But then the stuff he and Mariah dealt with in their news life would make anybody ready for some recuperation by week's end, wouldn't it: a schoolbus wreck, or a guy getting high on something and blowing his wife and kids away with a deer rifle—Christ only knew what messes he and she just averagely had to write about and take pictures of, any given week. So Riley's expression of having been through the wringer bolstered my decision to speak my piece now. I mean, when better? Any number of times he had been heard to grouse about newspaper life and how he ought to just chuck it and go off and write the book he wanted to do about Montana, and equally often Mariah would wish out loud that she could do her own idea of photography instead of the *Montanian*'s, so I honestly and utterly believed that Marcella and I were handing them their chance.

The ranch was theirs to have, I told Riley on that pivotal day. Marce and I wanted the place to be his and Mariah's as soon as they liked. Maybe not the biggest ranch there ever was, but every acre of it financially clear and aboveboard; perfectly decent grazing land, a couple of sections of it still the original native prairie grasses that were getting to be rare, plus the new summer range we'd just bought on the North Fork of English Creek; every bit of it strongly fenced, which was needed when you neighbored onto a grass-sneaking cow outfit such as the Double W; irrigation ditches already installed to coax maximum hay from those creekside meadows; haying equipment that maybe was a little old but at least was paid for; decent enough sheepshed and other outbuildings, brand new house. Here it all sat for the taking, and at their ideal age, old enough to mostly know what they were doing and young enough that they still had the elbowgrease to do it, Riley and Mariah could run this place with a dab of hired help and still find time to work on their own words and photos, couldn't they? A golden chance for the two of them to try, at the very least.

But do you think goddamn Riley would see it that way?

"Jick, I can't."

"Aw, sure you can. I know this isn't your country up here" —Riley was originally off a ranch down in the southern part of the state, on the Shields River near the Crazy Mountains; the father in the family died some years ago but the Wright cattle outfit still was in operation, run by Riley's brother—"but the Two has got some things to recommend it, now doesn't it?" I held my thermos cup out in a salute to the royal Rockies and the sheep-specked foothills and the fluid path of Noon Creek. I don't care who you are, you cannot doubt the earth's promise on such a spring day.

"If it's the sheep that're bothering you, that's fixable," I splurged on. "This place has put up with cattle before." And for that matter horses, the original livestock my grandfather Isaac

34

Reese brought onto this Noon Creek grass almost a hundred years before; and hoofless commodities such as hay, those beautiful irrigated meadows created by my uncle Pete Reese before he passed the ranch to me. I am on record as having declared that in order to keep the ranch going I would even resort to dude ranching, although as the joke has it I still don't see why they're worth fattening. In short, three generations of us had contrived, and every once in a while maybe even connived, to keep this Noon Creek ranch alive, and all the logic in me said Riley was the purely obvious next candidate.

"It's not the sheep."

"Well, okay, the money then," I hurried to assure him. "That's no big deal either. Marce and I have hashed it over a lot and we figure we can all but give you two the place. We'll need to take out enough to buy some kind of house in town, but hell, the way things are in Gros Ventre these days, that can't cost—"

"Money either," Riley cut me off. He had a pale expression on him like he'd just learned he was a stepchild. Pushing away from the warm wall of the shed, he turned toward me as if the next had to be said directly. "You're a contradiction in terms, Jick. A Scotchman too generous for his own good."

"In this case, I got my reasons," I said while trying mightily to think what was the unseen problem here. It's not every day a guy turns down a functioning ranch.

Riley flung the cold remains of his coffee, almost the cupful, to the ground. "You really want to hear some advice about this place?"

"Yeah, sure, I guess."

"Sell it to the Double Dub," he stated.

I felt as if I'd been slugged behind the ear.

Offer after offer had been made to me by Wendell Williamson when he was alive and snapping up smaller ranches everywhere to the east of me into his Double W holdings; the Gobble Gobble You is the nickname that own-everything penchant so rightly earned for the Williamson outfit. The same appetite in my direction was being continued as WW, Incorporated, part of a big land conglomerate back east, now that the Double W and the rest of the lower Noon Creek valley with it was theirs, courtesy of a buyout of the Williamson heirs. Every one of those offers I had always told Williamson and the corporaiders to go stuff.

"Jesus, Riley! That's what I've spent the majority of my life trying not to do!"

"Jick, get out while you can. Ranchers like you aren't going to have a prayer. The pricks running this country are tossing you guys to the big boys like flakes of hay to the elephants."

I still didn't tumble. "I know I'm pretty close to being history, but that's just exactly why the place ought to go to somebody younger like you," I argued back to him. "You and Mariah could have quite a setup here, and the Double Dub and the rest of the world go chase their tails. Why the hell won't you give it a try, at least?"

He and I stood staring at each other as if trying to get through to each other from different languages.

"Jick," Riley blurted it, "Mariah and I are splitting up."

Whatever is the biggest size of fool, that was me, there in the spring sunshine of the ranch I had just tried to give him, as Riley dropped the end of their marriage on me.

I turned away from him toward the mountains, my eyes stinging. By God, at least I would not bawl in front of this person.

Three years that had been now, since everything went crash. And the memory of it festered just as painfully even yet, here on Red Sleep Mountain.

"What, you want to give the BB the satisfaction of telling us he knew all along we couldn't manage to team up for this?" Mariah's latest interrogation of her fellow employee pierced across the grass to me.

Riley delivered in turn, "If the choice is one honeybucketload of 'I told you so' from the BB or four months of this kind of crap from you—"

Just then the federal guy beeped the horn of his van, signal for our ride back down the mountain with him. Off we trooped to the trailhead, each of those two in their separate mads and me perturbed at them both. Was this what they called getting the job done, throwing snits?

Back at the Winnebago, silence now as sourly thick as their argument had been, I decided to use the chance to fill the air with what was on my mind.

"Too bad you two weren't hatched yet when there were people around who had really seen some buffalo."

As fresh as ever to me were those tales from Toussaint Rennie when I was but a shavetail kid, fourteen or fifteen years old, of having viewed buffalo in their original thousands and thousands when he himself alit in Montana as a youngster. "Before Custer," as Toussaint dated it, a chuckle chasing his words out his crinkled tan face. "Before those Indians gave Georgie his haircut, Jick. I was like you, young. My family came in from Dakota. We saw the end of it, do you know. Buffalo, then no buffalo."

"Yeah," I kept on remorselessly as I drove toward the original dozen dark grazers we'd encountered, who by now had drifted around a corner putting the high fence between us and any more possible butting of the Bago, "Toussaint said the Two Medicine country was absolutely buffalo heaven at first." I guess I was pouring it on a little, dwelling on Toussaint and what a sight the buffalo were to his fresh eyes, but damn it all, I did feel justifiably ticked off about having been enlisted into this big centennial journey that had petered out here in its first day.

Mariah eyed me severely from the passenger seat as if about to say something, thought better of it, then resumed a fixed gaze out the window. Behind her on the sidecouch where he was staring into his notebook as if it was in Persian, Riley stirred a little. "Geography time, class," he announced in a singsong schoolma'am voice. Then in his ordinary annoying one: "If this peerless pioneer of yours came from Dakota Territory, how come he was called Tucson?"

"That was the way it was pronounced, but spelled T-O-U-S-S-A-I-N-T," I took pleasure in setting him straight. "Nobody could ever get it out of him just what he was, but maybe French Cree. He's buried under a Cree cross up home, anyway."

"Métis," said Riley.

I glanced at him from the corner of my eye. The sonofagun did know some things. The Métis were Canadian French Crees who came to grief in 1885 when the Riel rebellion in Manitoba and Saskatchewan was put down and their leader, Louis Riel, was hung. Out of that episode, several Métis families fled south across the border into our Two Medicine country. But as I started to point out to Riley in case he thought he knew more than he did, "Yeah, but you see, by Riel's time Toussaint already had been in the Two—"

"Your guy Toussaint," Riley butted in on me. "How did he talk?"

"What the hell do you mean, how did he talk? Like any of the rest of us."

"Jick, I bet if you think about it, he didn't." Quick as this, Riley was in his persuading mode. "Do something for me a minute. Pretend you're him, tell me what Toussaint told you about the buffalo in just the words he said."

I gave the scribbler an X-raying look now. Which did everloving Riley want, a driver or somebody to play Let's Pretend?

"Stop! Right here!"

Mariah's urgent shout made me slam on the brakes, at the same time wildly goggling around and trying to brace myself for whatever national disaster this was.

After the scrushing noise of tires stopping too fast on gravel, in drifted the fluting notes of a meadowlark, answered at once by Mariah's quick *click*.

Daughter of my own loins notwithstanding, I could have throttled her. Here I figured the Winnebago was on fire or some such and she'd only wanted a picture stop.

I blew out the breath I'd been holding and with the last patience in me sat and waited for Hurricane Mariah to climb out and trigger off a bunch more shots at whatever she'd spied, but no. Our dust hadn't even caught up with us before she announced, "Okay," meaning *drive on*.

Meanwhile Riley wasn't paying her and our emergency landing any attention at all, but was back at me about how Toussaint talked. "Just in the way he said it, try to tell that story of him seeing those buffalo, hmm? No, wait." He scrabbled around, swapping his notebook and pen for his laptop computer. "From your lips to those of the *Montanian*'s readers, Jick. Ready?"

My God, life with these people was herky-jerky.

It is true that I have always been able to remember. I could all but see Toussaint Rennie of fifty years before, potbellied and old as eternity, by profession the ditch rider of the Blackfeet Reservation's Two Medicine irrigation project and by avid avocation the most reliable conductor in the Two country's moccasin telegraph of lore and tale. Could all but hear as real as the meadowlark's notes the Toussaint chuckle at life.

" 'I was young then, I wanted to see,' " I began, to the *pucka pucka* accompaniment of Riley typing or whatever it's called these days. Mariah for a change quit fiddling with her camera and just listened. The sentences surprised me with their readiness, as if I was being told word by word right then instead of all those decades ago when Toussaint was yet alive. As if the telling was not at my own instigation. " 'When it came the season to hunt, I rode to the Sweetgrass Hills. From up there, the prairie looked burnt. Dark with buffalo, here,

there, everywhere. It was the last time. Nobody knew so, but it was. The buffalo were so many, the tribes left each other alone. No fighting. Each stayed in place, around the buffalo. Gros Ventres and Assiniboines at the northeast. Piegans at the west. Crees at the north. Flatheads at the south. For seven days, there was hunting. The herd broke apart in the hunting. I rode west, home, with the Piegans. They drove buffalo over the cliffs, there at the Two Medicine River. That, now. That was something to see."

It was not seen again, by Toussaint's young eyes or any others. Killed for their hides or killed off by disease caught from cattle, the buffalo in their millions fell and fell as the cutting edges of the American frontier swathed westward into them. That last herd, in the last west called Montana, was followed by summers of scant and scattered buffalo, like crumbs after a banquet. Then came the Starvation Winter of 1883, hundreds of the Piegan Blackfeet dying of deprivation and smallpox in their creekside camps. A hunting society vanished there in the continent-wide shadow of a juggernaut society.

Say the slaughter of the buffalo, then, for what it was: they were land whales, and when they were gone our sea of life was less rich. The herds that took their place were manmade—ranch aggregates of cattle, sheep, horses—and to this day they do not fit the earth called Montana the way the buffalo did. In the words of the old man the color of leather:

"Those Indians, they said the buffalo best. They said, when the buffalo were all here the country looked like one robe."

This buffalo stuff of Riley's when it showed up in the *Montanian*, I read with definite mixed emotions.

I was pretty sure Toussaint would have gotten a chuckle out of seeing his words in the world, outliving him. That about the manmade herds, though. What, did goddamn Riley think I ought to have been in the buffalo business instead of the sheep business all these years? And Pete Reese before me? And my McCaskill grandfather, who withdrew us from Scotland and deposited us in Montana, before Pete? I mean, you come into life and livelihood with some terms set, don't you? The Two Medicine country already was swept clear of buffalo and thick with sheep and other livestock by the time I came along. So why did I feel the prod of Riley's story?

And, yes, of Mariah's photo along with. That one she'd shot, sudden as a fingersnap, out the window of the motorhome in our slam-on stop while Riley was trying to persuade me to Toussaintize. A high thick fencepost of the buffalo range enclosure, a meadowlark atop. The beautiful black V dickey against his yellow chest, his beak open to the maximum, singing for all he was worth. Singing out of the page to the onlooker. And under and behind the songbird, within the fence enclosing that wonderful restored grass, dark hazes of form which the eye took the merest moment to recognize as buffalo, dim but powerful, indistinct but unmistakable.

The next day after Moiese the famous newspaper pair had me buzz us back down the highway to Missoula and keep right on going—when I asked if they wanted to stop at the *Montanian* for anything, Mariah and Riley both looked at me as if I'd proposed Russian roulette—south through the Bitterroot Valley. Well, okay, fine; as we drove along beside its lofty namesake mountains and their attendant canyons, even I could see that here was a piece of country well worth shooting and writing about, fertile valley with ranches and residential areas nervously crowding each other for possession of it, and any number of times in our Bitterroot route I figured my passengers would want to pull over and start picture-taking and scribbling in earnest.

Wrong a hundred percent. "Old news," Mariah and Riley chorused when at last I politely inquired whether they were ever going to get their butts into gear at chronicling the Bitterroot country's highly interesting rancho de la suburbia aspect. Old news? If I was translating right, the Bitterroot and the way it was populating was just too easy a story for these two. I couldn't help but think to myself, what kind of line of work was this story stuff, that it was hard to get anything done because it was too easy to bother with?

The next thing I knew, the Bago and we in it were across

Chief Joseph Pass and over into the Big Hole. Well, okay, etcetera again. Now here was a part of Montana I had always hungered to see. The Big Hole, which is actually a high basin so closely ringed with mountains that it seems like a sudden grassy crater, has a reputation as a hay heaven and in fact the ranch crews were putting up that commodity fast and furious as we drove past hayfield after hayfield where beaverslide stackers, big wooden ramplike apparatuses which elevated the loads and dropped them like green avalanches onto the tops of haystacks, were studiously in action. Blindfolded, I could have told you what was going on just from the everywhere smell of new hay. You don't ordinarily see haymaking of that old sort any more, and I'd like to have pulled the motorhome over onto the side of the road and watched the scene of the Big Hole for a week steady—the new haystacks like hundreds of giant fresh loaves of bread, the jackstay fences marching their long XXXXXX lines of crossed posts between the fields, the timbered mountains like a decorated bowl rim around it all.

Yet the one blessed time we did stop so Mariah could fire off camera shots at a beaverslide stacker ramping up into the Big Hole's blue loft of sky, Riley chewed the inside of his mouth dubiously and asked her if she was sure she wasn't just juke-boxing some scenery. "Doesn't work," he dispatched her beaverslide idea. By the same token, when we hit the small town of Wisdom, far famous in the old horseworking days for the army of teamsters who jungled up in the creek willows there while waiting for the haying season to start, and Riley proposed doing a Wisdom piece of some kind, Mariah suggested he check the little filing cabinet he had up there instead of a brain and count how many *wistful little town off the beaten path that, lo, I will now discover for you* versions he'd churned out in that column of his. "Doesn't work," she nullified Wisdom for him.

So that was that for the Big Hole, too. Zero again on the Mariah-Riley centennial scoreboard.

Ditto for the Beaverhead Valley after that, nice substantial-looking westerny country that anybody with an eye in his or her head ought to have been able to be semi-poetic about.

Ditto after the Beaverhead for the beautiful Madison River, a murmuring riffle in its every droplet, classic water that was all but singing *trout trout trout.*

Ditto in fact for day after day of traipsing around southwestern Montana so that he or she but more usually both could peer out of the Winnebago, stew about whether the scene was the one that really truly ultimately ought to be centennialized, and decide, "Doesn't work." Doesn't work? Holy J. Christ, I kept thinking to myself, don't you pretty soon get to the point in any pursuit where you have to *make* it work? At this rate it was going to take them the next hundred years to get anything told about Montana's first hundred. Their weekly deadline was marching right at them and increasingly Riley was on the phone to the BB, assuring him that worldbeating words and pictures were just about on their way into the *Montanian,* you bet. Why, I more and more wondered, did Mariah want to put herself through this? Riley in and of himself was rough enough on the nerves. Add on the strain of both him and her breaking their fannies trying to find ultraperfect topics for the series, and this daughter of mine had let herself in for a whole hell of a lot.

It showed. We were down near Yellowstone Park at Quake Lake, where the earthquake in 1959 sloughed a mountainside down onto a campground of peaceful sleepers, when Riley prowled off by himself into the middle of a rockslide slope. I'd just caught up with Mariah after remembering to go back and lock up the rig as we all had to make a habit of because of her camera gear, and happened to comment that if Riley didn't muster what little sense he had and watch his footing up there, we'd be shipping him home to his momma in a matchbox. That was all it took for her to answer with considerable snap:

"Dad, I know your opinion of Riley by heart."

She hardly ever slipped and called me Dad. Mariah arrived home at Christmas from her first quarter away at college calling her mother and me by our given names. Maybe because she'd been somewhat similarly rejigged herself, back east in Illinois, where the nickname "Mariah Montana" was fastened onto her by her college classmates for her habit of always wearing blue jeans and a Blackfeet beaded belt and I suppose generally looking like what people back there figured a daughter of Montana must look like. Or maybe being on a first-name basis with her own parents had simply been Mariah's way of saying, I'm as grown as you are now. Even as a little girl she had seemed like a disguised adult, in possession of a disconcerting number of the facts of life. Our other daughter, Lexa, was a real ranch kid, always out with me among the sheep, forever atop a horse, so much like Marcella and I had been in our own growing up that it was as if we'd ordered Lexa from the catalogue. Mariah, though, ever seemed to be the only author of herself. Almost before we could catch our breath about having this self-guided child, she discovered the camera and was out in the arena dirt locally at Gros Ventre or down at Choteau or Augusta as a rodeo photographer, wearing hightop black basketball shoes for quick footing to dodge broncs. Tall colt of a girl she was by then, in one glance Mariah there in the arena would seem to be all legs. Then in some gesture of aiming the camera, she would seem entirely arms. Then she would turn toward you and the fine high breasts of the woman-to-be predominated. Next it would be her face, the narrow length of it as if even her smile had to be naturally lanky. And always, always, her mane of McCaskill red hair, flowing like the flag of our tribe. Even then guys were of course eyeing her madly, and by the time she was home from college for summers on the bucking circuit, the rodeo romeos nearly stared the ring finger off her left hand trying to see if she was carrying any gold. But a wedding band was not the circle that interested Mariah. Throughout high school and those college years of hers at the Illinois Institute of the Arts, a place her mother and I had never even heard of before she chose it for its photography courses, and on into her first job of taking pictures for the *Gros Ventre Weekly Gleaner,* only the camera lens cupped life for Mariah.

Until Riley.

That marriage and its breakup should have been sufficient cure of Riley for her, it seemed to me. Yet here she was, putting up with him for the sake of doing this centennial series. Here he was, as Riley as ever, like whatever king it was who never forgot anything but never learned anything either. And here I was, half the time aggravated by the two of them for letting themselves wallow around the countryside together this way and the other half provoked at myself for being ninny enough to be doing it along with them.

All in all, I was just this side of really peeved when we pulled into Virginia City, which Mariah and Riley had taken turns giving a tense pep talk about on our way up from Quake Lake, each needlessly reminding the other that this was it, this was the place, they had to do some fashion of story here or perish trying.

Not a town to improve my mood much, either, old Virginiapolis. Sloping down a brown gulch, one deliberately museumy street— sort of an outdoor western dollhouse, it struck me as—crammed with tourists like sheep in a shearing pen. But I determinedly kept my mouth shut, even about having to navigate the Bago in that millrace of people and rigs for half an hour before a parking spot emptied, and we set off on foot for whatever it was that these two figured they were going to immortalize here.

All the rest of the day, another scorching one, we touristed around like everybody else, in and out of shacky old buildings from the 1860s when Virginia City was both a feverish goldstrike town and the capital of brand-new Montana Territory and up onto Boot Hill where vigilantes did their uplifting ropework on a crooked sheriff's gang, and I myself utterly could not see the attraction of any of it. More than that, something about our tromping through town like a Cub Scout troop fresh off a yellow bus wore on my nerves more and more. Riley, you might know, seemed to be writing an encyclopedia about Virginia City in his notebook. And Mariah was in her surveying mood; today she was even lugging around a tripod, which made her look like a one-person surveyor crew, constantly setting up to sweep her camera with the long lens along the streetful of sightseers below us from where we stood hip-deep in sagebrush on Boot Hill, or aiming out across the dry hogback ridges all around. This was tumbled country. Maybe it took convulsed earth of this kind to produce gold, as had been the case in the Alder Gulch treasure rush here. Now that I think it over, I suppose some of what was grating on me is what a wreck the land is after mining. Miners never put the earth back. At the outskirts of Virginia City are miles of dishwater-colored gravel heaps, leavings of hydraulic and dredge mining like monstrous mole burrows. Or scratchings in the world's biggest cat box, whichever way you want to put it. If Mariah's camera or Riley's pen could testify to that ruination, well, okay, I had to figure that the day of lockstep sightseeing was maybe worth it. Maybe.

So I was somewhat mollified, the word might be, as the three of us at last retreated into a bar called The Goldpanner for a drink before supper, Riley rashly offering to buy.

Inside was not quite the oasis I expected, though. As we groped toward a table, our eyes still full of the long summer sunlight, Riley cracked in a falsetto tone, "Basic black, very becoming." Indeed the bar's interior was about as dark as a moviehouse, with flickery little bulbs in phony gas lamps on the walls, but a person probably couldn't do any better in a tourist town.

Out of the gloom emerged a strapping young bartender wearing a pasted-on handlebar mustache and a full-front white apron the way they used to.

"Gentlemen and lady," he orated to us. "How may I alter your consciousness?"

It took me aback, until I remembered where we were. The Virginia City Players do summer theater here, and this fellow must be either an actor or desperately wanting to be. He was going to need a more receptive audience than Mariah, who took no notice of either his spiel or his get-up while specifying a Lord ditch for herself. I told the young Hamlet, "You can bring me a scotch ditch, please." It occurred to me that I still had to get through supper with Riley, so I added: "Go light on the irrigating water, would you." Then I remembered he was buying and tacked on, "Make the scotch Johnny Red, how about."

Riley was regarding the pasted-together bartender as if he constituted the world's greatest entertainment. All the knothead said, though, in a movie cowboy voice, was, "Pilgrim, I'm gonna cut the dust of the day with a G-ball."

When the drinks came and Mariah and I began paying our respects to Lord Calvert and Johnny Walker—respect was right; Holy Jesus, in this joint the tab for drinks was $2.50 *apiece*; I could remember when it only took 25¢ to look into a glass—I glanced across and wondered disgustedly how we had ever, even temporarily, let into the family a guy who would sabotage his whiskey with ginger ale. But I suppose it couldn't really be said Riley was a G-ball drinker then. It was hard to know just what to call him. The very first night of this excursion of ours, in St. Ignatius after the buffalo range, he had studied the bottles behind the bar for about an eon and eventually asked the bartender there what he sold the most seldom of. "Water," the St. Ignatian cracked, but then pondered the inventory of bottles himself a while and nominated "Sloe gin, I guess it'd have to be." Whereupon Riley ordered one. Our night in Dillon, he'd taken another long gawk behind the bar and ordered an apricot brandy. In Monida, it'd been a Harvey Wallbanger. In Ennis, a benedictine. Evidently he was even going to drink goofy this whole damn trip.

But Riley's style of imbibing, or lack of one, was not what surprised me worst here. No, what got me was that I noticed he was holding his notebook up right in front of his eyes, trying to catch any glimmer of light from the sickly wall lamps, while he thumbed through page by page, shaking his head as he did and at last asking Mariah hopefully, "Got anything that works?"

She shook her head too, halfmoon earrings in and out of the red cloud of her hair as she did. "Still zippo."

This was just about it for me. An entire damn day of touristing this old rip-and-run gold town and not a particle of picture or print to show for it? After having chased all over this end of Montana? Little kids could produce more with fingerpaint than these two were.

I opened my mouth to deliver the message that the Bago and I had had enough of this centennial futility and in the morning would head ourselves home toward the Two Medicine country and sanity, thank you very goddamn much just the same, when instead an electronic chicklike *peep peep peep* issued from Riley's wrist.

"Shit oh dear," he uttered and shut off his wristwatch alarm. "I've got to call the BB about the teaser ad. He's going to be pissed when I tell him it'll just have to say 'Virginia City!' and then as vague as possible." As he groped off in search of a phone, Mariah too looked more than a little apprehensive.

Civilly as I could, I asked her: "Have you ever given any thought to some other line of work?"

"I know, the way Riley and I have been going about this must seem kind of strange to you." Kind of? "But," she hurried on, "we both just want this centennial series to be really good. Something different from the usual stuff we each end up doing. It's, well, it's taking a little time for the two of us to hit our stride, is all."

Despite her words her expression stayed worried. Tonight this was not at all the bossypants daughter who'd gotten me into this dud of a trip. This was a woman with something grinding on her.

"Maybe it's Riley," I diagnosed.

That got a rise out of her I hadn't expected. "Maybe what's Riley?" she demanded as if I'd accused her of orphanage arson.

"Well, Christ all get out, isn't it obvious? Riley goes through life like he's got a wild hair. Don't you figure that's going to affect how you're able to work, being around a walking aggravation like him?" What did it take to spell it out to Mariah? Riley flubbed the dub in that marriage to her, he turned down my ranch and as much as told me straight to my face that I was a dodo to try to keep the place going, not exactly the most relaxing soul to have around, now was he?

Speak of the devil. Riley returned out of the gloaming, appearing somewhat the worse for wear after the phone call.

"So how ticked off is he?" Mariah asked tautly as he plunked himself down.

"Considerably. This is about the time of day anyway he wakes up enough to get mean. The bewitching BB and his wee bitching hour. But he was shittier than average, I'd say." Riley fingered his mustache as if making sure it had survived the withering phone experience. "What he suggested was that instead of the teaser ad, he just leave a blank space in the paper all the time with a standing headline over it: WATCH THIS SPACE— MARIAH AND RILEY WILL EVENTUALLY THINK OF SOMETHING."

That plunged them both into a deep brood.

Oh, sure, Riley surfaced long enough to say as though it were a thought that was bothering him: "You know, every now and again that tightass SOB can be surprisingly subtul." But otherwise, these were two people as silent as salt.

The stumped look on the pair of them indicated they didn't need to hear trouble from me at that very moment. Besides, the Johnny Red was the pleasantest thing that had happened all day and it was soothing me sufficiently to begin what I thought amounted to a pretty slick observation. "I don't know all that much about newspapering, but—"

"—that's not going to keep you off the topic anyway, hmm?" Riley unnecessarily concluded for me. "What's up, Jick? You've had something caught crosswise in you all day here."

"Yeah, well, I'm just kind of concerned that you two didn't get anything today," I nicely didn't include *again, yet,* or *one more goddamn time,* "for your series."

By now Mariah seemed almost terminally lost in herself, tracing her camera trigger finger up and down the cold sweating glass in front of her. I could tell that she was seeing the day again shutter click by shutter click, sorting over and over for the fretful missing picture of the essence of Virginia City. For his part, Riley swirled his G-ball and took a major gulp as if it was soda pop, which it of course virtually was. Then he grinned at me in that foxy way, but he seemed interested, too. "And?"

"And so I just wondered if you'd maybe thought about some kind of story about the mining here. How it tore up the land like absolute hell and all."

Riley nodded acknowledgment, but said: "Mining has got to be Butte, Jick, when we get there in a couple of days. What the gold miners did here isn't a shovelful compared to Butte."

At least agreement could be reached about another round of drinks, and after those were deposited by the handlebar bartender I tackled Riley again. "Just tell me this then. What kind of stuff is it you're looking for to write about, exactly?"

In what seemed to be all seriousness, he replied:

"Life inside the turtle."

"Riley," I said, "how do you say that in American?"

"It takes a joke to explain it, Jick. So here you go, you lucky man." Riley was relishing this so much it all but puddled on the floor. "The world's greatest expert on the solar system was giving a talk, see. He tells his audience about the planets being in orbit around the sun, how the force of gravity works, and all of that. So then afterwards a little old lady comes up"—Riley caught a feminist glint from Mariah—"uhmm, a big young lady comes up to him and says, 'Professor, that was real interesting, but you're dead wrong. Your theory of gravity just doesn't make a lick of sense. The earth isn't a ball hanging out in thin air at all. What it is is a great big turtle and all of us live on top of its back, don't you see?'

"The scientist figures he's got her, right there. He says, 'Oh, really, madam? Then what holds the turtle up?'

"She tells him, 'It's standing on the back of a bigger turtle, what did you think?'

"He says, 'Very well, madam.' Now he knows he's got her nailed. He kind of rocks back on his heels and asks her: 'Then what can that second turtle possibly be standing on?'

"She gives him a look that tells him how pitiful he is. 'Another even bigger turtle, of course.'

"The scientist can't believe his ears. 'What!? *Another* turtle?'

" 'Naturally,' she tells him. 'It's turtles all the way down.' "

So, okay, I laughed in appreciation of Riley's rendition and

Mariah surfaced out of her deep think enough to chuckle at the back of her throat, too.

But Riley was just getting wound up. Now he crossed his arms on the table and leaned intently at me from that propped position, his shoulders square as the corners of a door, his voice suddenly impassioned.

"See, Jick, that's the way something like this centennial usually gets looked at. Turtles all the way down. Hell, it starts right here in Virginia City—the turtle of brave pioneers, like the vigilantes here making windchimes out of outlaws. And next the cattle kingdom turtle." Riley put his hands side by side on the table and pretended to type with his eyes shut: *"Montana as the last grass heaven, end of the longhorn trail.* It takes a little more effort with sheepherders than it does with cowboys, no offense intended, Jick, but there can be the sheep empire turtle too, woollies on every sidehill from hell to breakfast. And don't forget the Depression turtle, hard times on good people. Come all the way to today and there's the dying little town turtle. Or the suffering farmer turtle. Or the"—my distinct hunch is that he was about to say something like "the obsolete rancher turtle" but caught himself in time—"the scenic turtle, Montana all perfect sky and mountains and plains, still the best place to lay your eyes on even after a hundred years of hard use."

Riley finally seemed to be turtled out, and in fact declared: "I am just goddamn good and tired of stacking up turtles, in what I write. It's time, for me anyway," here he laid a gaze on Mariah, who received it with narrowed eyes but stayed silent, "to junk the old usual stuff I do. If my stories in this series are going to be anything, I want them to be about what goes on inside that usual stuff. Inside the goddamn turtle shell."

For me, this required some wrinkling inside the head. Granted that Riley's writing intentions were pure, which is a major grant from someone as skeptical toward him as I was, how the dickens was he going to go about this inside-the-turtle approach? Just for instance, I still was perturbed that the Big Hole haying, say, had been bypassed. To Riley and evidently Mariah as well, the Big Hole as an oldfangled hay kingdom qualified as usual stuff, known like a catechism from one end of Montana to the other. Yet not nearly a worn-out topic to me, who first heard of it before either of them was ever born. My first wages in life were earned as a scatter raker for my uncle Pete Reese, in the hayfields of the ranch I now owned. Those summers, when I was fourteen and fifteen and sixteen, daydreams rode the rake with me. The most persistent one was of traveling to the storied Big Hole, hiring on to a haying crew there, spending a bunkhouse summer in that temporary nation of hayhands and workhorses. Quite possibly take a summer name for myself; even there in Pete's little Noon Creek crew you might put up hay with a guy called Moxie or Raw Bacon Slim or Candy Sam all season, then when he was paid off find out that the name on his paycheck was Milton Huttleby or some such. Sure as hell take a different summer age for myself, older than my actual years—although it is hard now to remember that seething youngster urge for more age—and then do my utmost to live up to the job of Big Hole scatter raker there in the mighty fields ribbed to the horizon with windrows, hay the universe around me and even under me as the stuffing in the gunny sack cushion which throned my rake seat, the leather reins in my hands like great kite lines to the pair of rhythmically tugging horse outlines in front of me.

As I say, the Big Hole and its storied haying was a dream, in the sense that a world war and other matters claimed the summers when I might have gone and done. But that dream was a seed of who I am, too, for imagination does not sprout of nothing.

My haydream reverie was abruptly ended when I heard a bump behind me as someone stumbled into a chair and then a corresponding bump a little farther away, evidently a couple of customers finding their way to the table next to ours.

"It's even darker in here than it looks, Henry. How do they do that?" a female whisper inquired.

"They must use trick lighting somehow," came the male reply in an undervoice.

Meanwhile Mariah was staying cooped up with whatever was on her picture-taking mind while Riley was gandering off into the domain of the bartender behind her and me. Unusually thinkful, for a guy as wired up as him.

It didn't seem to me silence was normal for either of these two, so I was about to try and jog Mariah by asking if her notion about photographs was the same as Riley's about words, internal turtle work, when suddenly Riley's face announced inspiration. Quick as that, the sonofagun looked as if he had the world on a downhill pull.

"I see the piece!" he divulged.

Miriah sat up as if she'd just been shaken awake and peered at him through the bar gloom. "Where?"

"Here." He whomped his hand on the table. "This."

I squinted at the shellacked surface. "What, you're going to write about this table?"

"Gentleman and lady, you mistake me," Riley let us know in the bartender's Shakespeare tone of voice. "Not this table. This bar, and its innumerable ancestors the width and breadth, nay, the very depth, of our parched state. A piece about bars and bartenders! What do you say to that, Mariah Montana?"

Mariah took the last swig of her Calvert as if to strengthen herself, then studied Riley. What she said to it was, "This place? Get real."

He only mm-hmmed and rubbernecked past us to the bartender's domain as if trying to read the small print on the bottles. I could see Mariah gathering to jump him some more about this bar brainstorm of his, demand to know how the hell she was supposed to take a picture in here that wouldn't look like midnight in a coal bin. Myself, I thought Riley had finally hatched a halfway decent idea. There is just no denying that bars seem as natural to a lot of Montanans as caves to bears.

"Why don't we have another round," Riley was all sweet persuasion to Mariah now, "and talk it over," meaning his piece notion. Figuring that anything which might conceivably steer the two of them back on the track of their series was all to the good, I swung around in my chair to signal for the further round of drinks.

The bartender had changed sex.

That is to say, the handlebar specimen was gone and the 'tender now was a young woman—I say young; they all look young to me any more—in a low-cut red velvet outfit and brunette hair that lopped down on both sides long and crinkly like the ears of a spaniel and with a smile you could see from an airplane.

Need I say, it was a short hop to the conclusion that Riley's story idea about bars and their 'tenders had been fostered with the change of shifts which brought this female version onto the Goldpanner scene. Be that as it may, the velvet smiler was in charge of our liquid. I held up an indicative glass and called over, "We'll have another round of jelly sandwiches here, please, Miss," a word which brought Mariah's head sharply around.

I thought the new mode of bartender blinked at Riley a little quizzically when he beamed up at her and specified another G-ball, but maybe she was just that way, because when she brought the drinks her comment came out, "There you go?" and when she stated the damages, that too had a question curl on the end of it: "That'll be seven dollars and fifty cents?"

I don't know, is it possible that the more teeth there are in your smile, the less of anything you have higher up in your head? Watching Riley and this young lady exchange dental gleams, the theory did occur to me.

No sooner had Miss Bliss departed from us than Riley was onto his feet saying: "Actually, maybe I better go talk to her while she's not busy and find out how she goes about it." He gave Mariah a look of scrubbed innocence. "Bartending, that is."

"Riley," Mariah said too quietly, "you can go spread yourself on her like apple butter for all I care. I had my lifetime share of your behavior when we were married."

"Behavior?" Surprise and worse now furrowed the brow under his curly dance of hair. "What the hell is that supposed to mean, behavior? You never had any cause to complain about other women during our marriage."

"Oh, right," she said caustically. "What about that blond in Classified?"

"That doesn't count!" he answered, highly offended. "You and I were already separated then!"

With deadly evenness Mariah told him, "It all counts."

Riley seemed honestly baffled as he stared down at her. "What's got you on the prod? If it bothers you to see me have a"—he gave a quick glimpse in my direction—"social life, then look the other way."

"It wouldn't work," she levied on him next. "I'd just see you circling around to your next candidate to fuck."

Right there on the ef word my daughter's voice changed from anger to pain. And as if that kind of anguish is catching, Riley's tone sounded as afflicted as hers when he responded:

"Goddamn it, Mariah, you know I never played around while we were married. You know that." Silence was the best he could get from her on that. "What I do now is my own aff—business."

Mariah rattled the ice in her glass like a castanet. "Not if it interferes with the series. We were going to talk over your piece idea, you said."

"All right, let's talk and get it over with."

"Not with you standing there hot to trot."

Riley abruptly sat.

"You're rushing into this stupid bartender idea," Mariah began.

"My bartender idea is the best shot we've got," Riley began simultaneously.

"I think they're having a fight," the next-table woman whispered.

"I think you're right," the male undertone subscribed.

I would have refereed if I had known where to start. Riley, though, wasn't going to sit still for Mariah to pull his inspiration out from under him. "All righty right, you stay here and stew," he left her with as he scraped his chair back from the table. "I'll be over there doing the piece." With that he was away, taking up residence at the cash register end of the bar where the brunette item of contention had stationed herself. The solar increase of her smile showed that she didn't at all mind being Riley's topic.

I was beginning to see why Mariah had wanted me along as an ally against this guy. A paratroop battalion was about what it would take to jump on Riley adequately.

"Mariah, petunia," I tried to assuage, "that mophead is not worth—"

"It's okay, it's okay," she said in that too quiet way again. A sipping silence was all that followed that, from either of us. Spark patterns of light from the tiny bulbs trembled on the dim walls. Twinkle, twinkle, little bar. I watched Mariah watch Riley. He was right in one respect, she ought not to care how he conducted his life now that they were split. All too plainly, she cared with her every fiber. I don't know. Maybe a person simply cannot help getting the willies about what might have been.

Riley's sugared conversation with his story topic was going on and on and on. At last, though, here he came sashaying back to our table and in a not very good imitation of a matter of fact voice, wanted to know:

"What about a picture?"

Mariah eyed him as if he had slithered up through a crack in the floor.

"What about one, cradle robber?"

"Come on, Mariah, don't be that way. Honest to Christ, I was

going to do a bartender piece even before Kimi just happened to
come on shift."

"*Kimi!?* " Mariah voiced disbelievingly. "Riley, the only taste
you've got is in your mouth."

Riley rolled his eyes and stared at the barroom ceiling as if the
letters p-a-t-i-e-n-c-e were inscribed up there. "Just out of curiosity, Flash, what're you going to tell the BB when my written
part lands in there and no picture with it?"

Mariah gave him a world record glower. Then she all but leapt
out of the chair, tornadoed over to the end of the bar, began
exhuming electrical cords and lightstands out of her camera
baggage, and proceeded to aim into the targeted area of the
bartending brunette. Next she pulled out what looked alarmingly
like a quiver for arrows, but proved to be full of small white
reflecting umbrellas which she positioned various whichways to
throw more light on Kimi. *Prang prang prang*, Mariah yanked
the legs of her tripod into extension.

"Henry, look at those people now!" from the lead whisperer.

"Isn't this something?" murmured its chorister.

"Kimi, sweetie, give us your biggest smile, if you know which
one that is," Mariah directed in a kind of gritted tone as she
aimed her light meter pistola at the bar maiden. Riley was
hanging around right there handy, but she called out to me,
"Jick, could you come hold this?"

I gingerly went over to the action area. Mariah thrust me an
empty beer glass. "Hold it steady right there," she decreed,
positioning the glass about nose-high out in the air in front of me
and then stepping back behind the tripod and sighting her camera through the glass at Kimi.

Being in the shine of all the lights was making Kimi positively
incandescent. Through her smile she emitted, "This is totally,
like, exciting?"

Click, and some more quick triggerings of the shutter, and
Mariah was icily informing Riley the picture of the piece was
achieved and the rest was up to him, then unplugged and dis-
mantled the lights and the rest of the paraphernalia in about a
second and a half and rampaged back to our table and her
Calvert and water.

I joined her, but of course Riley stayed hovering at the bar. I
will say, he was laying it on thicker with his tongue than I could
have with a trowel. He would mouth something sparkling, Kimi

would mouth something, he would laugh, she would laugh—after a bit, Mariah declared: "If I have to watch any more of this I'll turn diabetic." Out she went to the Winnebago.

I am not naturally nocturnal. Not enough to sit around in a tourist bar into the whee hours while watching Riley lay siege to Kimi, at least. I drained the last of my drink and headed to the bar.

As I approached, Kimi was wanting to know where he got such a wild pair of contact lenses—"You can, like, color each eye different, I mean?"—and with a straight face Riley drawled that they were a hard-to-find kind called *aw, natural*. Then he was inquiring of her in a confidential way, "Okay now, Kimi, serious question. If I just came in here from Mars and asked for a drink, what would you give me?" Granted, he did have the notebook open in front of him. Maybe he was mixing business with pleasure, a little.

Kimi smiled a mile and said, "Oh, wow, I guess maybe a slow comfortable screw?"

Riley looked as if his ears could not believe their good fortune. My God, I thought to myself, does it just jump into his lap this way?

Kimi kept the smile beamed on him as she asked, "You know what that is, don't you?" Before Riley could muster an answer, which would have been highly interesting to hear, she was explaining: "It's sloe gin, Southern Comfort, and orange juice, like in a screwdriver? Get it? A Sloe Comfortable—"

"Got it," Riley vouched, trying not to look crestfallen. He downed a long restorative drag of his G-ball, evidently thinking furiously about how to get past that smile of Kimi's. Now he noticed me and frowned. "Something on your mind besides your hat, Jick?"

Something was, yes. A couple of somethings. How Riley and Mariah behaved toward each other wasn't any of my business, theoretically. Yet if you don't feel strongly enough about it to take sides with your own offspring, what in the hell did you spend the years raising the kid for? So on Mariah's behalf my intention had been to deliver some snappy comment to Riley that would let him know what a general louse he was being. But instead I seemed to be seeing myself, from the outside—I know that sounds freaky; it *was* freaky—standing there in a remembered way. As if I had stepped into a moment where I'd already been once: a waiting man beside me, his arm on the bar, a woman equally near: myself somehow suspended in the polar pull between them. Or was I imagining. Three scotch and waters will start the imagination going, I suppose. Whatever it swam in, the strange is-this-then-or-now remembering suddenly became not this bar but the Medicine Lodge, not this Riley-Kimi recipe but Stanley Meixell and Velma Simms. Velma in that long-ago time had been Gros Ventre's divorce champion, thrice married in an era that believed once ought to be plenty for anybody. That Fourth of July and others of the Depression years, she in her slacks of magical tightness served as timekeeper at the Gros Ventre rodeo, in charge of the whistle that signaled *time's up* during bronc rides; as one of the yearning hangers-on around the bucking chutes pointed out, "Think of all the pucker practice she's had." Stanley was . . . Stanley. The original forest ranger of the Two Medicine National Forest, who forfeited that million-acre job when his oldest friend, my father, turned him in for his hopeless drinking. Stanley who came back out of nowhere into our lives that summer of 1939 and freed our family of as much pain as he could. Who perched on that Medicine Lodge bar stool timelessly, the back of his neck lined and creased as if he'd been sleeping on chicken wire but the front of him durable enough to draw Velma Simms snuggling onto the bar stool close beside him. And there in the heat field between that woman and that man after I had popped in innocent as a day-old colt to discuss a matter with Stanley, I was the neutral element. The spectating zero rendered neutral by circumstances. Circumstantial youth, in that fifteenth summer of my life. Circumstantial widowerhood now.

"Jick?" Riley was asking. "Jick, are you okay?"

"Uh, you bet," I answered although I could feel that the backs of my hands were sweating as they do when my nerves are most upset. Spooky, how utter and complete, how faithful, that spasm of memory had seemed. As if there were furrows behind my brow, interior wrinkles to match the tracks of age across my forehead, and that memory out of nowhere clicked exactly into those grooves. I drew a breath and managed, "As good as a square guy can be in a round world, anyway. Just wanted to tell you, I'm calling it a night."

"Good idea," Riley said.

"Going on out to the Winnebago," I said.

"Yeah, fine," he said.

"Mariah's already out there," I said.

"Is she," he said.

"Morning will be here before we know it," I said.

Riley, still considerably furrowed up himself, studied me. Then he glanced at Kimi, who was giving us both a smile we could almost see our reflections in. When Riley turned back to me, his frown was severe. But to my surprise, he closed up his notebook, said a regretful thanks to Kimi for her inspiration, and accompanied me out into the night and the Winnebago.

Sure enough, readers of the *Montanian* were treated to Riley's dissertation about bartenders, that their wares were as integral to a citizenry such as ours as food and water, and that ever since the first saloons of Virginia City and the other goldstrike towns, a considerable portion of Montana's history could be measured the way irrigation is, by the liquid acre-foot. And of course: *These nights, if you hold your mouth right, the moisture of mercy may be dispensed to you by a Kimi Wyszynski . . .* At least a Sloe Comfortable You Know What was nowhere in it.

Mariah's picture had caught the smiling countenance of Kimi in the beer glass where the top portion begins to bulge out of the slender base. The woozy distortion puffed Kimi's cheeks out like a squirrel loaded for winter, made her teeth enormous, and squinched her eyes together. She resembled a nearsighted beaver looking at itself in a crazyhouse mirror.

We were camped that night on the Jefferson River just out of Silver Star, bracing for Butte the next day. Riley was in the shower at the back of the Bago, singing over and over: "*Oh, the moon still shines, on the moonshine stills, in the hills where the lupine twiiines!*" Conspicuously ignoring the melody of Riley, Mariah was across the dinette table from me fussing with one camera after another, whisking invisible dust off their lenses with the daintiest brush I'd ever seen.

I again studied the newsprint version of Kimi spread in front of me. I had to ask. "Mariah, is the newspaper really going to keep paying you and Riley for going around the state doing stuff like this?"

Without looking up she said, "We'll find out."

They named the place Butte, in the way that the night sky's

*button of light acquired the round sound of moon or the wind took
to itself its inner sigh of vowel. Butte was echoingly what it was:
an abrupt upshoot of earth, with the namesake city climbing out of
its slopes.*

Beneath Butte's rind of sagebrush and rock lay copper ore.

*That red earth of Butte held industrial magic: telephone lines,
radio innards, the wire ganglia of stoves and refrigerators, everything that made America electric began there in copper.*

*The red copper earth drew other red to it. Bloody Butte, with its
copper corpuscles. A dozen miners died underground in 1887, the
early days of more muscle than machinery. In 1916, as the
machine drill and the steam-hoisted shaft cage pressed the implaca-
ble power of technology against flesh and bone, Butte's underground toll for the year was 65 miners. The next year, a fire in the
Speculator Mine killed 164. All the while, the greater killer quietly
destroyed men's lungs: silicosis, 675 dead of it between 1907 and
1913.*

*On its earth and its people of the mines, then, Butte's history of
scars. Badges of honor, too, as scars sometimes are? It depends on
how much blood you mind having in your copper. Maybe less
arguable is Butte's history of chafe. "This beautiful copper collar,
that the Company gave to me" became Butte's—Montana's—wry
anthem of life under the Anaconda Copper Mining Company,
a.k.a. William Rockefeller and Henry Rogers and others of Wall
Street. The Butte miner was consistently the best paid workman in
Montana. The ACM Company also saw to it that he was the most
harnessed. Strikebreakers and Company police. The Company-
imposed "rustling card" you had to carry to rustle up a job in the
mines. The Montana National Guard stationed in the streets of
Butte after dynamite punctuated the labor struggle in 1914. In its
streets and its wallets and its caskets, Butte was its own kind of
example of how a copperwired society works.*

Enormous above Riley's words, Mariah's Butte photo was of
the Berkeley Pit, the almost unbelievable open-pit mine which
took the copper role from the played-out mineshafts everywhere
under the streets of the city: a bulldozed crater a mile wide and
deeper than the Empire State Building is tall. Ex-mine, it too
now was, having been abandoned in favor of cheaper digging in
South America.

*   *   *

"Quite the Butte story," I observed to the newspaper hotshots shortly after perusing it in that day's *Montanian*. "Who's going to deal?"

"I will," stated Mariah, plucking up the deck of cards and shuffling them with a fluent riffle which drew her a glance from Riley. We had pulled in at the Missouri Headwaters RV Park in Three Forks for the night. By now it had been most of a week since the Virginia City situation got so drastically Kimied, but conversation between Mariah and Riley still was only on the scale of "pass the ketchup, would you" and "here, take it." Thus an evening of playing pitch was my bright idea for cheering up Bago life. Of course I'd had to bribe Riley into it by letting him off the dishwashing for the next three nights, but well worth it.

"The Butte piece was just a thumbsucker," Riley took care to let me know as Mariah whizzed out six cards apiece to us.

I can put up with a lot while playing pitch, which to my way of thinking is the only card game worth sitting up to, and so I responded to Riley's latest codegram: "How do you mean? What's a thumbsucker?"

"A think piece. When a writer sticks a thumb in his mouth and thinks he's on the tit of wisdom," Riley said moodily.

"No way was that Butte story of his a thumbsucker," Mariah informed me past Riley as if he was not at the table with us. "He wrote what needed saying. Now he's just having one of those oh-my-God-I-shot-my-wad spasms writers get."

Damned with faint praise or praised with a faint damn or wherever it was Mariah's backhanded defense had left him, Riley only snorted and concentrated fiercely on the cards in his hand.

Mariah fanned her own cards out, gave them a quick pinched appraisal and asked, "Who dealt this mess?"

"You did, butterfly," I informed her.

"Oh. Then it's up to you to bid first."

"I know. I am. Give a person time." I mulled what I held, primarily the king and jack of diamonds and then a bunch of junk like the seven of hearts and three even littler clubs. "I'll say two."

"Three," Riley grandly upped.

Mariah passed, and Riley led out with the queen of hearts, which she unhappily had to top with her king, and now it was

my play. This is what's nice about pitch: the strategy needed
right from the first card. By making hearts trump, Riley transformed my jack of diamonds into the jick, which is to say, the off
card of the same color as the jack of trump. That, incidentally, is
where my nickname springs from, the pronouncement by a
family friend back when my folks were trying to fit the solemn
given name John and then the equally unright Jack onto the
child me that "He looks to me more like the jick of this family."
Nomenclature aside, though, the rule in pitch is that jack takes
jick but jick takes joker, and so here I could either mandatorily
follow suit, hearts, with my seven and hope to take some later
trick and maybe even somebody's joker or tenspot with my jick,
or, since Mariah's king was taking this trick, I could forthwith
sluff the jick to her so she would gain the point instead of the
bidder, Riley. See what I mean about what a strategic marvel
pitch is?

I sluffed my jick, drawing me a grin from Mariah and a dirty
look from Riley. Which got another load of topsoil added to it
after he trumped in on the next trick to regain the lead, led back
with his invincible ace of hearts and instead of capturing a jack
or joker or even a tenspot to count toward game, received an
out-of-trump spade from Mariah and my seven of hearts, equally
worthless to him.

Of his three bid, Riley so far only had one, that unlosable
trump ace he'd just played. He now was pondering so deep you
could almost hear his brain throb. His choices were perfectly
clear, really—lead with his next strongest card and try to clean
us out of any nontrump face cards or tens that would count
toward game, or lead something weak and keep back his strong
card to capture any of our face ones etcetera on the final trick—
and so I helped him employ his time by asking him, "Well,
then, Wordsworth, what kind of a Butte story would you rather
have done than the one you did?"

"You saw those faces in the M & M yesterday," Mariah
enlightened me as Riley tried to glower at each of us and study
his cards at the same time. "What the scribbler wants is for those
old Butte guys to read his stuff and fall off their barstools
backwards and kick their legs in the air while they shout, 'That's
me! Riley Wright told my whole life in that piece of his!' "

Riley clutched his cards rigidly and asked her with heat,
"What the fuck's wrong with that?"

"Not a thing," she told him as if surprised at his utter density. "Don't you know a fucking compliment when you get one?"

Yesterday's Butte faces, yes. We'd begun on Butte by stopping in the old uptown area for lunch at the M & M, an enterprise which is hard to pin down but basically includes a fry kitchen and counter on one side and a serious bar along the other and sporting paraphernalia such as electronic poker machines in the entire back half of the building, and within it all a grizzled clientele who appeared to be familiar with most of life's afflictions, plus a few younger people evidently in the process of undergoing that same set of travails. All my life until actually coming there with the newspaper pair I had been leery of Butte. Of its molelike livelihood, as mining seemed to us surface-of-the-earth types. Of THE COMPANY, as the Anaconda Copper Mining Company was known in big letters in the Montana of my younger days, because Butte and its ore wealth were why THE COMPANY took the trouble to run everything it could think of in the state. Of, yes, younger incarnations of the rugged clientele around the three of us at that moment, for in its heyday of nine thousand miners Butte was famously a drinking whoring fistfighting place; when you met up with someone apt to give you trouble from his knuckles, the automatic evaluation was "too much Butte in him." But now with the M & M as a kind of comfortable warehouse of so much that had been Butte, and replete with the highly delicious lunch—a pork chop sandwich and a side dish of boiled cabbage with apricot pie for dessert had done nicely for me—I'd been quite taken with the hard-used old city. Until I happened to glance at the latest case of thirst barging in the door of the M & M, and it was the ghost of Ed Heaney nodding hello to me.

Bald as glass, with middle age living up to its name by accumulating on his middle, Ed was owner of the lumber yard in Gros Ventre and the father of my best friend in my growing-up years. An untalkative man whose habits were grooves of behavior the town could have told time by, nonetheless he had pieces of life that spoke fascination to me; his own boyhood in unimaginable Butte, his medals from Belleau Wood and other battles of the First World War tucked away in a dresser drawer. As I stared across the M & M at Ed's reincarnation, there where I'd been sure that the past could find no reason to swoosh out all over me, my mind split again. The everyday part knowing full well that Ed Heaney was many years gone to the grave and that probably half of male Butte resembled Ed. The remembering remnant of me, though, abruptly seeing a front lawn at dusk, during a town trip when I had swung by to quick-visit my friend Ray, and as we gab there on the grass the front porch screen door swings open and Ed Heaney stands in its surprise frame of light, as his lookalike did now in this Butte doorway, the radio news a murmur steady as a rumor behind Ed. "Ray, Mary Ellen," Ed calling out into the yard to his son and small daughter that first evening of September of 1939, "you better come in the house now. They've started another war in Europe."

The *whap* of Riley's finally chosen card on the table brought me back from Butte and beyond. He'd decided to lead an inconsequential five of clubs, which Mariah nonchalantly stayed under with the trey, so I ended up taking the trick with my mere six of clubs. I at once led back with my king of diamonds, which sent Riley into ponder again.

Mariah decided to employ this waiting period by working on me. "You know, you'd have plenty of time to shave before Riverboat Wright here plays his next card."

Before I could come up with a dignified reply, Riley surprised me by rapping out to her on my behalf: "What the hell, the beard gives him a hobby where there's not much danger he'll saw his fingers off."

I knew, though, he wasn't so much sticking up for me and my whisker project as he was jabbing it to Mariah. He could have chosen a better time to do it; when he finally played he still didn't use his strong card, whatever it was, and merely followed suit on my king with a lowly diamond. Mariah immediately gave him a wicked grin and sluffed me the ten of spades. Hoo hoo. Riley was a screwed monkey, and by now even he knew it. Sure enough, for the final trick he'd been saving the jack of hearts, the highest trump card left, but all it earned him was my deuce of clubs and Mariah's eight of spades, neither worth anything.

I cheerfully scorekept. One wooden match to Mariah for the jick I'd sluffed her, two to myself—besides my having the highest count for game, courtesy of the tenspot she'd sluffed me, my seven of hearts proved to be the low of trump—and three broken-backed matches to Riley to indicate he'd gone set and now was three points in the hole.

"My God!" he uttered when the game concluded several

hands later with me at twenty-one, Mariah hot behind me at nineteen, and him still three in the hole. "Playing pitch with you two is like trying to eat a hamburger in the middle of a wolfpack."

Nor, despite being called a quitter every way Mariah and I could think of, and between us, that was quite a few, would Riley risk his neck any further in more pitch that evening. He took his mood off to bed at the back of the Bago, and while he got himself installed there I helped Mariah make up her couch bed per usual. Per usual she gave me a goodnight-in-spite-of-the-stickery-on-your-face kiss. Per usual I headed back to scrunch into bed beside Riley and speculate.

Nights with Riley were an ordeal. He dropped off to dreamville the moment he was horizontal, but before long the commotion would begin. There alongside of me he'd start to shimmy in his sleep, little jerky motions of his shoulders and arms and spasmy tiny kicks of his legs and ungodly noises from his throat. *Hnng. Nnhnng. Nnguhh!* Actually it was kind of fascinating in a way, like watching a spirited dog napping beside a stove, whimpering and twitching as he runs a dream rabbit. But as Riley's bed fuss went on and on I'd need eventually to whisper sharply, "hey, come out of it!" *Mmm*, he would acknowledge, almost agreeably, and I would try to rush to sleep before his next conniption.

I do my dreaming awake, and so the uproar going on in Riley in his zoo of sleep I could not really savvy. Was he writing, his mind restlessly sorting words there in the dark? Or yearning, his body at least, for the Kimies of the world . . . or remembering when Mariah's was the warm form beside him? Or was this merely something like an electrical storm in the night of the brain? Whatever was occurring, Riley Wright evidently paid for his days in the quivering of his nights.

Lewis and Clark had preceded Riley and Mariah a bit to this Three Forks area, discovering here in 1805 that a trio of rivers came together to make the source of the Missouri. Grandly christening every trickle of water they encountered all the way across the Dakotas and Montana, those original explorers nonetheless were smart enough to save up the names of their bosses, Jefferson, Madison and Gallatin, for these main tributaries, which I thought was more than passingly interesting. It didn't register so with the subsequent newspaper pair, however, and after a fruitless day of traipsing around the headwaters area they decided they wanted to go on to Helena for the night—but by backtracking through Butte instead of the only-half-as-long route through Townsend.

"Butte? Hold on a minute here. You did Butte."

"Our Lady of the Rockies," explained Mariah abstractedly.

"Who's she?"

"Jesus's mom," Riley put in with equal unhelpfulness.

"Riddle me no newspaper lingo riddles, you two. All I want to know is—"

"The Mary statue," Riley intoned with awful patience. "Up on the Divide, over Butte. Ninety feet tall, shiny white. Maybe you happened to notice it?"

"Oh. *That* Lady of the Rockies."

But even the Madonna, giant robed figure who seemed to have popped over the mountaintop and stopped short in surprise at the sight of Butte, didn't provide any miracle for these two. Or as they of course put it to one another: "Doesn't work."

Thus we were finally Helena-bound on the freeway, just getting rolling atop the rise north of Butte, when the steering wheel wobbled significantly in my hands. I gave the news, "We've got ourselves a flat," and pulled the Winnebago off onto the shoulder of the freeway.

"At least this goes real nice with the rest of the day," Riley groused as we all three climbed forth into the dusk and I went to get the spare tire out. "Stuff it, Riley," Mariah told him, and from her tone she quite possibly meant the entire spare tire.

"Do you suppose you two could manage to quit the bloodletting long enough to—" I began, but was interrupted by a car horn's merry *beep beepitybeepbeep beep beep!*

Shave and a haircut, six bits, my rosy rear end. I irritatedly waved the approaching car past us but no, here it gaily pulled off onto the side of the road in front of us, an '84 ketchup-red Corvette driven by an old guy wearing a ballcap. As I was about to shout to him that we had the situation under control, thanks anyway, there came the winding-down sound of another slowing car, and an '81 white Buick LeSabre, another ballcapped grayhead at the wheel, beeped past and ground to a stop on the shoulder gravel in front of the Corvette.

Riley and Mariah and I turned our heads to the highway behind us as if we were on one swivel.

A cavalcade of cars was approaching, every one of them

slowing. Already we were being given the beepitybeepbeep by the next about-to-pull-over vehicle, an elderly purple Cadillac.

Funeral procession, maybe? No, I'd never seen a funeral procession where everybody was wearing a ballcap. By now the first of what seemed to be geezerville on wheels, the Corvette pilot, was gimping his way along the barrow pit to us. "Got some trouble?" he called out cheerfully.

"We do now," muttered Riley. *Click*, I heard Mariah's camera capture our Corvette samaritan.

"Just a flat," I called back as the line of pulled-over vehicles built and built in front of us. "We appreciate your stopping and all. But honest, we can handle—"

"Aw hell, no problem," I was assured by Corvette, "we're plenty glad to help."

"Gives us somethin' to do," sang out LeSabre coming up at a stiff but hurried pace behind him.

"Yeah," I said slowly, looking at the long file of parked cars, each with its trouble blinkers winking on and off, like a line of Christmas lights. As if in rhythm with the trouble lights, Mariah's camera was clicking quick and often. Old men were hobbling out of the dusk toward us, two here, three there—they seemed to be a total of seven.

A long-haul truck thundered past, its transcontinental hurry accentuating the reposeful roadside caravan. "What are you guys," I felt the need to ask, "some kind of car club?"

"We're the Baloney Express riders," the Corvettier answered with a grin that transmitted wrinkles throughout his face.

"The who?"

"What happens, see, is that we ride around taking used cars where dealers need them," the explanation arrived. "Say for instance a used-car lot in Great Falls has got more vehicles than it wants, but a dealer down in Butte or over in Billings or somewhere ain't got enough. Well, see, the bunch of us drive a batch of cars down to the one who's short of them, and then go back home to the Falls in the van there." Sure enough, a windowed van such as is used for a small bus had ended up at the head of the parked procession. "Or like now," my tutor continued, "it's the other way around, the Butte guy got too many cars on hand and so he called up for us to come down and fetch these back to the Falls. The idea is, it's cheaper for the car dealers than hiring trucks to pack these cars around and besides it gives us," he jerked his head to indicate the further half dozen oldtimers now clustering around us like cattle at a salt lick, "a way to pass some time. Oh sure, we maybe like to gab a little, too, riding together in the van—one of our wives says the Pony Express had nothing on us, we're the Baloney Express. But see, we're all retired. If we wasn't doing this, we'd just be setting around being ornery."

Mariah was working her camera and Riley was staring at the ballcaps, all of which read *I ❤ bowling. Where else can you get a pair of shoes so cheap?* and so the conversational role seemed to be up to me. "Quite the deal," I more or less congratulated the assemblage on their roadlife-in-retirement. Now that I had a closer look at these geezers, most of them, although stove-up and workworn, didn't appear as ancient as I'd originally thought; somewhere into their seventies. Which meant that these retired specimens weren't that much older than me, I had to admit with a pang. The one exception was a stooped long-faced fellow, about half-familiar to me, who either was a lot farther along in years than the others or had led a more imaginative life. He in fact spoke up now.

"Only thing wrong with this car setup we got is that the speed limit needs an adjustment. What we figure, there ought to be a law that a person can't drive faster than what age he is. If you're nineteen, say, you could only go nineteen miles an hour. That'd give us a little leeway to try out our speedometers."

I chuckled and admitted the plan sounded highly logical. Meanwhile a subdelegation of Baloney Expressers was curiously inspecting the caved-in nose of the Bago where the Moiese buffalo had butted it. "What happened to your grill, you hit a helluva big deer?"

"Uh, not exactly."

"As much as I hate to break up this soiree," Riley announced in a contrary tone, "that tire still needs changing. Against my better judgment, I'll even pitch in. Jick, where's the jack?"

"Right there in the rear compartment. The lug wrench is there too," I tacked on as a hint.

Riley gave me a barbed look, then one at the motionless Baloney Express bunch, and off he stalked. The next sound out of him was as he began grunting away at loosening the lug nuts of the flat tire.

Throughout that effort and then as he undertook to jack up

the motorhome so the tire could come off, Riley's every move was watched by our clot of visitors, the whole bunch of them bent over intently with hands on knees like a superannuated football huddle. They in turn were watched by Mariah through her camera as she moved in behind them, sighted, frowned at the line of hunched-over backs, dropped to one knee, grinned and shot.

Evidently irked by his silent jury, none of whom yet had done a tap of work in the changing of the tire, Riley now indicated a nearby NO STOPPING roadsign and pointed out, "If a highway cop comes along and finds this congregation, he'll write tickets on you characters all night."

"No problem," Riley was assured by '83 Ford Fairlane, a scrawny guy about shoulder-high to the rest of us. "My nephew's the highway patrol along this stretch of road. If he comes along we'll just have him turn his siren on and make things official."

The Baloney Expressers all considered that a hilarious prospect, and a number of them gandered up and down the highway in hope of Fairlane's patrolman nephew.

I have to say, I was beginning to enjoy this myself, Riley doing all the work and these guys providing me sevenfold company. My original partner in conversation introduced himself, Jerome Walker, and cited among the spectators one who resembled him—"My brother Julius; he's older and smarter but I got the good looks"—and then the scrawny guy—"Another thing we call ourselves is The Magnificent Six And A Half, on account of Bill here"—and I handshook my way on down the line. The final guy Roger Tate, the stooped elderly-looking one, thought I looked as familiar as I thought he did. In Montana you only have to talk to a person for two minutes before you find you know them some way or another. But I wasn't able to place Roger, nor he me, until we both admitted lifetimes in the sheep business. Then he broke out with:

"By the God, now I know you! That herder I found up under Roman Reef that time, he was yours! What was his name again?"

Pat Hoy. Pat the pastor of pasture, Pat the supreme pilot of sheep, unfazed by mountain timber and bear and coyotes and July snowstorms, who in a dozen years of herding for me always grazed his band in the exact same slowgoing scatter-them-twice-as-wide-as-you-think-you-dare-to style which he enunciated as:

"Sheep don't eat with their feet, so running will never fatten them." I had inherited him, so to speak, from my father-in-law Dode Withrow when Dode at last declared himself too old for the sheepraising life. Thus I acquired not only a matchless herder but Pat's twice a year migrations into spree as well. How many times I made that journey to First Avenue South in Great Falls and fetched Pat out of one saloon or another, flat broke and shakily winding down from his two-week binge of at first whiskey and then beer and at last cheap wine. But for all the aggravation his semiannual thirsts provided, how much I would give to wipe out the day when I arrived to tend his camp and saw that Pat's sheepdog was there at the wagon but Pat and sheep were nowhere in sight. That sent an instant icicle through me, dog but no herder, and while I found the sheep scattered over half of Roman Reef, there still was no sign of Pat. The next day a Forest Service crew and ranchers from English Creek and Noon Creek and the Teton country helped me to search, and so it came to be Roger Tate of the Teton contingent who rode onto the scene of Pat's corpse near a big lone rock outcropping, the kind that draws down lightning. The lightning bolt had struck Pat in the head and followed the zipper of his coat down the body, searing as it went.

I remembered staring down at Pat before we loaded him onto the packhorse. Since the time of my boyhood, lightning has always been one of my dreads, and here was what it looked like.

"Right you are. Pat Boyd. That was the fellow," Roger Tate was saying over Riley's lug wrench grunts. "Sure was a terrible thing. But it happens."

What also happens, I realized, is a second obliteration, the slower kind that was occurring now. Pat Hoy had been as good at what he did as any of us ever can be. But Dode Withrow, who knew that and joyously testified to it at the drop of a hat in his countless yarns about Pat, Dode too was dead. Pat's favorite denizens of First Avenue South, Bouncing Betty and Million Volt Millie and other companions of his sprees and megaphones of his reputation betweentimes, were gone to time now too. Even Roger here, original witness of Pat passing into the past, by now was losing grasp of that struck-down sheepherder's name; and Roger's remaining years as a memory carrier of any sort could not be many. It hit me out of nowhere, that I very nearly was the last who knew anything of the wonders of Pat Hoy.

"How about yourself?" one of the group in the barrow pit asked me. I blinked at that until I managed to backtrack and savvy that he meant what was the purpose of my own travels in the motorhome here.

"Just, uh, out seeing the country." All I'd need would be to tell these guys what Riley and Mariah were up to, and there'd doubtless be a long choirsing from them about what was wrong with newspapers these days. Mariah by now had moved off into the sagebrush and was shooting shots of the whole blinking fleet of vehicles. "My daughter there kind of likes to take pictures. And the other one"—how was I going to put this? that Riley was her ex-husband but still tagging around with her?—"is a guy in the paper business we been letting ride with us. Kind of a glorified hitchhiker."

Riley by now had the spare tire on and the Bago jacked back down. All that remained was for him to take the lug wrench and reef down hard in a final tighten of the lug nuts, but his audience showed no sign of dispersing until the performance was utterly over. Mariah materialized at my side, camera still busy, just as the voice of Roger the van driver resumed what must have been a perpetual conversation among the Baloney Express riders.

"By the God, you just never know about these cars. Back in 1958 I paid a guy to haul away five Model T's just to get them off the place, *paid the guy!* And now what the hell wouldn't they be worth, the way people are fixing old cars up and using them in these centennial parades and all."

Riley did a final contortion over a lug nut, then headed stormily over to Mariah and me. "Okay, the goddamn tire's changed," he muttered, "let's abandon the Grandpa Club and—" then he went *oomp* as Mariah nudged him ungently in the ribs with her elbow. "Mariah, what the f—"

"Riley," she half-whispered, "will you shut your face long enough to look at what we've got here?"

"So you figure we just better hang onto these clunkers instead of turning them over to the dealer, do you, Rog?" one of the others was responding to the saga of the lost treasure of Model T's. "Make rich guys out of ourselves at the next centennial, huh?"

"Sounds good to me," chimed in another voice. "A hundred years from now, I'll still only be thirty-nine by then."

A round of laughter, which multiplied when somebody else put in on him, "Nick, we're talking age here, not IQ."

By now Riley had his notebook out. "Five hundred years' worth of geezers in one bunch," his mutter changed to murmur. "Could work," he acknowledged, almost as much to himself as to Mariah. He turned to her, doubtless to ask if she had a decent picture for the piece, thought better of it from the expression on her face, and headed over to talk the Baloney Expressers into more talking.

They listened silent as fenceposts as Riley told them who he and Mariah were and what they were up to, Mariah backing him with an encouraging encompassing grin. Then the seven oldsters cast glances at each other without a word. Incipient fame seemed to have taken their tongues.

Finally one of them broached: "You gonna put all of us in the paper? It wouldn't be too good if just some of us was in and not others, if you see what we mean."

"Every mother's child," Riley grandly assured them of inclusion. "Now here's how we're going to have to do this." He scooted off into the Bago and was back immediately with his mini tape recorder. I was wondering myself how Riley was going to conduct a sevenway interview. We couldn't stay camped on the shoulder of the highway forever; every couple of minutes now a pickup or car was pulling in at the head of the line of ferried cars and a voice calling down the barrow pit in the dusk, "Everything okay there?" and one or the other of the Baloney Expressers would cup his hands to his mouth and cheerfully shout back, "No problem."

Riley's program turned out to be as simple as leapfrog. He would ride with the first driver at the head of the cavalcade for ten minutes, then that car would pull over and he would hop back to the second car, which in turn would become the lead car and interviewee for ten minutes, and on back through the seven drivers that way by the time we all reached Helena. "You guys are going to have to tell fast," Riley warned as he set the beeper on his wristwatch. "No room for hooey." The Baloney Expressers looked collectively offended at that word, but tagteam storytelling plainly appealed to them. They didn't budge yet, though, all standing trying to look innocently hopeful in regard to a certain red-headed young woman.

"Ride with me, Mariah, would you?" I asked, breaking seven geezer hearts simultaneously. Away the Expressers gimped to their vehicles, Riley heading for the lead van with its driver.

*They have seen the majority of Montana's century, each of these
seven men old in everything but their restlessness, and as their
carefully strewn line of taillights burns a route into the night their
stories ember through the decades.*

*"I'm Roger Tate. I seem to be the oldest of this gang, if the truth
be told. Maybe that's why they let me drive the van. Or maybe it's
the fact that it's my van. Anyway, what I'd tell you about is my
dad and those Model T's. Back in the twenties we raised sheep out
a hell of a ways from town, west from Choteau there, and when my
dad bought his first Model T he figured it was a wonderful
advance, you know. Any time he wanted now he could scoot into
town and get lit up. Only thing was, every time he came home from
a spree like that he'd never bother to open a gate. Drive right
through all the barbwire gates between town and our place, four of
them. I was misfortunate enough to be the only boy in the family,
so the next day he'd send me out to fix those doggone gates. I must
have mended those four gates forty times apiece. That habit of his
was kind of hard on cars, too, which was how we ended up with
five Model T's. Eventually my dad gave out before the world
supply of whiskey did, and it fell to me to build the ranch back up.
But I've often thought, you know, thank the Lord that the old boy
had gone into sheep instead of anything else. Not even he could
entirely drink up the wool money each year before the lamb money
came."*

This spell of driving time alone with Mariah I figured I had
better make use of. I started off conversationally, "These pictures you're breaking your fanny on, petunia. What is it you're
trying to do in them, that inside-the-turtle kind of stuff Riley
was talking about?"

From the corner of my eye I saw her give that little toss of
head, her hair surging back over her shoulder. "Something like,
I suppose. But the way I think of it is that I'm trying to do cave
paintings."

I nodded and mmhmmed. She'd taken the next summer after
she and Riley split up, and gone to Europe to get over
him. When her mother and I asked what she'd seen, her answer
was caves. In France and Spain she had crouched and crawled
through tunnel after tunnel into the past to see those deep
walls with their paintings of bison and horses and so on from
Stone Age times. Maybe ten thousand years, she said, those

bison had been grazing and those horses running there in the stone dark.

> *The warning wink of brake lights. Like a flexible creature of the night, the chain of cars compresses itself to a halt on the shoulder of the freeway, then moves on.*
>
> *"Bill Bradley, I am. Not the long tall basketball senator, as you maybe already noticed. I guess I would want to tell about the grasshoppers. My folks and I was farming over towards Malta there in the Depression and just when we figured things couldn't get any worse, here came those 'hoppers and cleaned us out of our crop worse than any hailstorm ever could of. An absolute cloud of grasshoppers. You just can't believe how those buggers were. They sounded bad enough in the air, that sort of whirring noise the way sage chickens make when they take off, only a thousand times louder. But on the ground was worse. You could actually hear those things eating. Millions of grasshoppers and every last one of them chewing through a stem of wheat. I left my coat hanging on the door handle of the pickup and they even ate that to shreds. It still makes me about half sick to remember the sound of those grasshoppers eating, eating, eating."*

"Lascaux and Altamira," Mariah spoke the cave names as if talking of friends we both knew. "That's what I want my work to be like." Her voice came low and lovely, remembered tone of another woman I had loved, her mother.

"Do you see what I mean, Jick?" This next part she seemed to want me to particularly understand. "Something people can look back at, whenever, and get a grasp of our time. Another hundred years from now, or a hundred thousand—the amount of time between shouldn't make any difference. If my pictures are done right, people whenever ought to be able to say, 'oh, that's what was on their minds then.' "

And I think I did savvy what Mariah was getting at, that in a way—the waiting, the watching, the arrowing moment—she with her camera was in that cavewall lineage of portrait-painting hunters as patient as stone.

Down the long slope ahead of us, the car at the front of the cavalcade delivered its brakelight signal of stopping, *blink blinketyblinkblink blink blink.*

"*My name is Nick Russo. I came into this country after the Second World War. Oh, I'd been west before, kind of. See, when I went into the Civilian Conservation Corps in '34, just a punk kid from an alley in Philadelphia, the next thing I knew I was on a fireline in that big Selway forest fire in Idaho. Then I went from the CCC straight into the Army, so I was already a sergeant when the war hit. I saw Montana from a troop train and that was it for me. Little towns with all that land and sky around them. Right there I told myself that when my military time was in, if I lived to get my time in, I'd come out here and see if I could make something of myself.*"

On our minds. I could agree with Mariah there. We wear what has happened to us like a helmet soldered on.

Off the freeway to our right, the lights of the town of Boulder, which signaled the caravan's next stop and swap of Riley.

The used cars, a used man in each, move on.
"*My name is Bud Aronson and I was a packer until I got too stove up to do it any more. What you maybe want to hear from me happened when I was pretty much in the prime of life, back about 1955, and figured I could handle just about anything that came along, until this did. That hunting season I was running a pack string into the Bob Marshall Wilderness, so when there was a plane crash way back in there, I was the guy the search party sent for to bring the two bodies out. The plane had slammed into a mountain, pretty high up, and so the first thing I did was wrap the bodies in a tarp apiece just as they were and then we slid them on the snow down the mountain to the trailhead where we had to camp that night. See, my intention was to fold each body facedown across a packsaddle the next morning. But that night turned clear and cold, and in the morning we could not get those bodies to bend. Of all the packing I had ever done, this was a new one on me, how to fit those stiff bodies onto packhorses. What I finally did was take the biggest packhorse I had and sling both bodies onto it in a barrel-hitch tie, one lengthwise along each side for balance like you would with sides of meat. But that was the worst I ever handled, balancing that cargo of what had been men.*"

On a straight stretch where the Bago's headlights steadily fed the freeway into our wheels, I cast another quick glance over at

Mariah. The interiors of the two of us inside this chamber of vehicle; caves within the cave of night. What does it take to see the right colors of life? Whether or not that was on her mind as on mine, Mariah too was intent. She sat staring straight ahead through the windshield as though she could pierce the night to that frontmost car where Riley was listening and recording.

The night flew by the motorhome's windows as I thought over whether to say the turbulence in me or to keep on trying not to.

"I'm Julius Walker. This is tough to tell. But if you want to know the big things about each of our lives, this has got to be mine. Quite a number of people lost a son over there in Vietnam. But my wife and I lost our daughter Sharon. All through high school in Dutton, what she wanted most was to be a nurse. She went on and took the nursing course at Columbus Hospital there in Great Falls and then figured she'd get to see some of the world by going into the Army. I kick myself every day of my life since, that I didn't try to talk her out of that. She ended up at the evacuation hospital at a place called Cu Chi. Sharon was killed right there on the base, in a mortar attack. They eventually found out there were tunnels everywhere under Cu Chi. The Americans were right on top of a whole nest of Viet Cong. Good God Almighty, what were those sonsabitches Johnson and Nixon thinking about, getting us into something like that?"

"Mariah," it broke out of me, "I don't think I can go on with this."

In the dimness of the Bago's cab her face whitely swung around to me, surprise there I more could feel than see.

A minute of nothing said. The pale glow of the dashlights seemed a kind of visible silence between us.

Then she asked, her eyes still steady on me: "What brought this on?"

Here was opportunity served up under parsley, wasn't it. Why, then, didn't I speak the answer that would have included her situation with Riley and my own with the memory flood unloosed by the sight of Shirley in Missoula, the sound of Toussaint's voice ventriloquizing in me at the buffalo range, the war report of bald ghost warrior Ed Heaney, the return of Big Hole longings across fifty years, the ambush of Pat Hoy's lonesome death, the poised-beside-the-bar sensation again of Stanley

RIDE WITH ME, MARIAH MONTANA

Meixell and Velma Simms and the mystery of man and woman; the answer, simply but totally, "All this monkeying around with the past."

Instead I said, "I'm not sure I'm cut out for this rambling life, is all. With you newspaper people, it's long days and short nights."

"There's more to it than that, though, isn't there," Mariah stated.

"Okay, so there is," I admitted, wondering how to go on with the confession that I was being spooked silly by things out of the past. "It's—"

"—the ranch, isn't it," she helpfully spliced on for me. "You worry about the place like you were a mother cat and it was your only kitten."

"Well, yeah, sure," I acknowledged. "I can't help but have the place on my mind some."

The caravan resumes speed, into a curve of the highway, another bend toward the past.

"And I'm Jerome Walker. If there's one thing in my life that surprises me, it's that I've ended up in a city. Yeah, yeah, I know Great Falls isn't Los Angeles or New York. But pretty damn near, compared to how Julius and me grew up out in the hills between Cascade and Augusta on our folks' cow outfit. The home place there had been our granddad's homestead, and I suppose I grew up thinking the Walkers were as natural to that country as the jackrabbits. But I turned out to be the one who cashed it all in, back in 1976, when the wife and I moved in to the Falls to live on our rocking chair money. I suppose in earlier times we'd have just moved to town, Cascade or Augusta either one. A lot of towns in those days had streets of retired ranchers they'd call something like Horse Thief Row, you know. But our kids were already in the Falls, in their jobs there, and naturally the grandkids were an attraction. So we went in, too. It's still kind of like being in another country. I about fell over, the first time I went downtown in the Falls and heard a grown man in a suit and tie say, 'Bye bye.'"

"I'll make you a deal," this Mariah Montana daughter of mine resorted to. "If you want to check on the place so bad, we'll all three go on up to the ranch just as soon as we're done in Helena, how about. Riley and I have got to do some pieces along the High Line anyway, and there's no real reason why we can't swing through the Two country getting there. How's that sound?"

Sweet enough to whistle to. I kept my eyes on the dark unfolding road while I asked: "And then?"

"Then you decide. After you've looked things over at the ranch, if you still think you'd rather be on your lonesome than . . ." she let the rest drift.

I sat up straighter behind the steering wheel. Maybe I was going to be able to disengage from this traveling ruckus fairly simply after all. "You got yourself a deal," I told Mariah with fresh heartiness.

Ahead of us the signal of blinks danced out of the night one more time. As the entire series of cars pulled over to stop again, Roger Tate's van now had become the last in line in front of us. In our headlights the sticker on Roger's rear bumper declared: DIRTY OLD MAN, HELL—I'M A SEXY SENIOR CITIZEN.

Mariah mused, "We ought to get a bumper sticker of some kind for the Bago."

> *Driver seven, the last who has become first.*
> *"My name is Dale Starr. What I want to talk about is, am I losing my g.d. mind or are things repeating theirselves? I've tried to do a little thinking about it. The way all the bad I've seen in my lifetime and figured we'd put behind us seems to be coming around again now. People losing their farms and ranches. Stores out of business. All the country's money being thrown around like crazy on Wall Street. How come we can't ever learn to do better than that? Of course we know the weather has got some kind of a more or less basis of repeating itself. Nature does have its son-of-a-bitch side too, doesn't it. Like the big thirty-year winters, 1886 and 1919 and 1948 and 1978. And the drought just after the First World War and again in the thirties and again these past years now. But I guess what I keep wondering is, shouldn't human beings have a little more control over theirselves than the weather does over itself?"*
> *As he finishes, into view glow the lights of Helena, thousands of gemmed fires, each a beacon of some life young or old.*

Dawn is when I have always liked life most, the forming hour or so before true day, and that next morning at the Prickly Pear

RV Park, with Mariah up extra early to develop her shots of the Baloney Express contingent, I went out to sit on a picnic table and watch Helena show off its civic ornaments in the daybreak light. The dark copper dome of the state capitol. The Catholic Cathedral's set of identical twin steeples. The pale Arabianlike spire of the Civic Center. My favorite, though, stood perched on the high side of Last Chance Gulch, above the historic buildings downtown; the old fire watchtower up on four long legs of strutwork. Like a belltower carefully brought to where it could sound alarm into every street when needed. What a daystarting view it must be from there, out over the spread city and this broad shallow bowl of cultivated valley and the clasping ring of mountains all around.

In what seemed just another minute, the sun was up. That's the trouble with dawn, it doesn't last.

A joggedy-joggedy sound interrupted the quiet morning. Riley was out for his run. Mariah had already done her Jane exercises on the floor of the Bago. These two kept everything about themselves toned up except their heads. I watched as Riley rounded the endmost motorhome and cantered along the loop road toward the Bago and myself. He ran in a quick pussyfoot style, up on his toes as if dancing across hot coals.

"Feel better?" I greeted him as he trudged into our site, gulping air into his heaving chest.

"There's nothing like it," he panted, "except maybe chasing cars."

For a change, I didn't feel on the outright warpath against the guy, pacified as I was with the prospect of getting home to Noon Creek later today and not budging from there when Mariah and him set out to invade the rest of Montana. Let history whistle through their ears all it wanted. Mine were ready for a rest. So it was without actual malice, just kind of clinically, that I pointed out the bare wheelhub where the hubcap had flown off after Riley's tire-changing job of last night, and he gave a wheezing sigh and a promise to add a new hubcap onto the expense account along with the buffalohead dent in the hood. He'd regained some oxygen by now and started to take himself into the Bago for a shower.

"Whup, off limits yet," I warned. "Mariah's souping film."

Riley nodded to save precious breath. As he dragged over and draped onto the picnic table beside me to wait, I couldn't help but notice his running costume. Skintight and shiny, it made him look like he'd had a coat of black paint applied from the waist down to just above his knees. I let my curiosity ask: "What's that Spandex stuff made of?"

"Melted money," Riley formulated. "It'd be a whole lot cheaper to just do a Colter, I do admit."

As John Colter was the mountain man who was stripped naked and barefoot by the Blackfeet and given a few hundred yards headstart before they began chasing him over the prairie with murderous intent—talk about a marathon—I pleasantly enough passed the time imagining Riley in nude version hotfooting it across this valley going *oo! ow!* on the prickly pear cactuses.

But shortly the side door of the Bago opened and Mariah poked her head out and gave the all clear. She studied Riley in his running getup. "Good morning, Thunder Thighs."

In actual fairness, Riley's legs were not truly scrawny; but sectioned as they were into the top portion of pore-hugging black fabric and the elongation of contrasting skinwhite below, they did kind of remind a person of the telescoped-out legs on Mariah's tripod. But she'd said what she said with a grin, and although Riley gave her a considerable look, he decided not to go into combat over his lower extremities and instead asked, "How'd your geezer shots come out?"

"Show you after breakfast," she said, and somewhat to my surprise they both kept to their best behavior through that meal. Oh, still several tastes short of being sweet to each other, but civil, ever so carefully civil. Who knows, maybe it was only the temporary influence of my cheffing of venison sausage patties and baking powder biscuits swimming in milk gravy, or that Riley still was feeling sunny due to his epic of the Baloney Expressers, but in any event he perused Mariah's exactly apt photographic rendition of those seven bent-over elderly behinds judiciously clustered around the flat tire, seats of wisdom if there ever were, then he actually said: "Helluva picture, shooter. How good are you going to get?"

The little toss of her head, which stayed cocked slightly sideways as she eyed back at him. "How good is there?"

I honestly figured I was contributing to the general civility with my question. True, there was the consideration that the sooner I could get these two budged from Helena, the quicker we could motate to the ranch and I could see what that situation was. In any case, I asked: "So what kind of piece are you two going to do here today?"

Mariah looked brightly across at Riley. "We were just about to talk that over, weren't we."

"Ready when you are," Mister Geniality confirmed.

Her gaze at him stayed determinedly unclouded. "Mmm hmm. Well, I wondered if you had anything for here squirreled away in your notes."

"Actually, I did jot down one idea," he granted, spearing another biscuit.

"Trot it on out."

"I just absolutely think it captures the essence of early Helena."

"Sounds good. What is it?"

"You maybe won't be real keen on it."

"Why won't I? Come on, let's hear it."

"Promise not to get sore?"

"Riley, will you quit dinking around and just tell me what the fuck it is? I promise I'm not going to get sore, cross-my-heart-and-hope-to-die, will that do? Now then. What's this great Helena idea of yours?"

"Whores."

"*What?*"

"See, you're sore. I knew you would be."

Mariah expended a breath that should have swayed the trees outside. "I. Am. Not. Sore. But here we need some humongous idea for Helena and you come up with—"

"Pioneer businesswomen. Is that better?"

"Not hardly," she spoke the words like two cubes of ice. "Riley, take a reality check on yourself, will you? I am not going to burn film for that old half-assed male fantasy of prostitutes who just happen to be selling their bodies so they can save up to go to ballet school."

"That's just it. The wh—prostitutes here in Helena weren't. They were hard-headed real estate investors."

Mariah eyed Riley without mercy, trying to see if he was on the level. I have got to say, from the expression on his face his motive seemed purely horizontal. After a long moment she told him: "Say more."

Boiled down, Riley's discourse was about how, for a while back in the last century, the really quite extensive red-light district of Helena generated the funds for some of its, uhmm, practitioners to buy their own places of enterprise and that, whether you approved of their profession or not, their sense of local investment made them civic mothers just as much as any downtown mercantilist was a civic father. It of course didn't last, he said; that self-owned tenderloin trade went the way of other small frontier capitalists, done in by bigger market forces. But why shouldn't he and Mariah tell the story of those women, who'd tried to hold onto some financial independence in their desperate lives, just as readily as they would the one of some pioneer conniver who'd made his pile selling dry goods? I had to admit, it was something to think about. Who qualifies when it comes to history. Mariah too seemed to be mulling pretty hard by the time Riley got done dissertating.

From some distance off came the sound of someone opening the side door of a rig and announcing, "Going to be another hot one today, Hazel."

Mariah at last granted that Riley's idea was maybe worth a try but-he'd-better-know-what-he-was-talking-about-and-not-make-this-just-some-dippy-piece-about-whores-with-hearts-of-gold etcetera and when the newspaper aces went up to the state historical society to search out old photos of that domestically owned red-light district, I decided to tag along.

I ought to have known better than to hope that the two of them would get their photographic digging over with in a hurry and we could head to the Two country while the day was yet young, though. After some hours of killing time in the historical society I had all but memorized the countless exhibits about Montana's past. I had squinted at every everloving piece of the cowboy art of Charley Russell, reminded all the while of what Riley had said in one of his most notorious columns, that Montanans were as proud of the guy as if he had been Bertrand or Jane. By then my feet were like walking on a pair of toothaches and so I trudged upstairs one more time to check the place's library, where Mariah and Riley had said they'd meet me as soon as they surfaced from the photograph archives. Naturally, no trace of either of them. But this time I decided I would just find a place to sit until they eventually presented themselves.

Yet sitting doing nothing is not my best pastime either. Particularly not in a library, for it brought to mind Marcella, the

winter we started going together when she was the librarian in
Gros Ventre and I was conspicuously her most frequent patron.

No, I told myself, don't let it happen, don't get yourself swept
up in one of those memory storms. My mind determinedly in
neutral, I watched the library traffic. Over behind the librarian's
desk was a distinguished guy wearing a tie and a mustache both,
and though he was no Marcella he looked more or less civil.
People came up to ask him various things, but I could hear that
about every second one of them was pursuing genealogy.

Which set me to thinking. Family tree is nothing it ever
occurred to me to shinny up very far, but with time to spend
anyhow, why shouldn't I? Maybe that was the way: see what our
past looked like in an official place such as this, instead of letting
it ambush me barehanded as it kept doing. Of course, not even
try to trace back more than the couple of generations to the
other side of the Atlantic, that risky hidden territory of distant
ancestors; just see what I could find of the Montana McCaskills
and my mother's side of the family, the Reeses, by the time
Mariah and Riley ever decided to show up.

I stepped over to the librarian, and in gentlemanly fashion he
gave me what must have been his patented short course in
ancestor-seeking, which card catalogue to use when looking for
what, and so on.

"Any luck?" the library man asked on his next errand past
me.

None. I told him I guessed I wasn't really surprised, as we're
not particularly a famous family. Actually it is somewhat spooky
to learn that so far as the world at large knows, your people are
nonexistent.

"You might try over here." He ushered me to what he called
the Small Collections shelf. "To be honest with you, this cate-
gory is holdings we don't quite know what else to do with.
Reminiscences people have written for their grandkids, and short
batches of letters, and so on."

It makes you wonder, whether you really want to find anything about your family in the stray stuff. But I plucked out the
thick name index binder labeled *Ma* through *Me* and took a look.
The volume listed a world of *Mc*'s, but no McCaskills. Which
again didn't overly surprise me. As far as I knew, the only real
skein of writing either of my parents did was my father's forest
ranger diary, and a lot of that I did for him, when I rode with

him as a boy on our sheep-counting trips into the mountains of his Two Medicine National Forest. Now that would have been something: nose around here in search of the past and find my own words coming out at me.

R had a binder all its own and half a dozen *Reeses* had pages in it, all right, but none of them my mother's parents Isaac and Anna. So much for—

Then it came to me. The old family story of the immigration officer who decided to do some instant Americanizing on my Danish grandfather when he stepped off the boat.

I thumbed a little deeper into the *R*s and just past *Rigsby*, would you believe, there was my mother's father in his original form, *Riis, Isak*.

"*Noon Creek, Montana, rancher and horse dealer,*" the entry stated. "*Letters to his sister in Denmark, Karen Riis Jorgensen, 1886–1930. Originals at the Danish Folklore Archives, Copenhagen; translation by Centennial Ethnicity Study Project, with funding from Montana Committee for the Humanities. 27 items.*"

And so. When the library man brought out the long thin box of them to me, the letters were the farthest thing from what I had expected.

Kæreste Søster Karen—

Amerika og Montana er altid en spændende Oplevelse . . . The handwriting on the photocopied pages was slanting but smooth, no hesitation to it. Isaac's penmanship in Danish, though, was not the real surprise. The typed translation. The man of these words was the only one of my grandparents I held any memory of, him sitting gray-mustached and bent but still looking thoroughly entertained by life, there at the head of our table some long ago Sunday dinner when I could barely peek over that table. Old Isaac's family fame was for chewing his way through English as if it was gristle. My father always told of the time Isaac was asked which of his roan saddle horses was for sale, the one out in the pasture with a herd of other ponies or the one alone in the corral, and the old boy answered, "De vun in a bunch by hisself."

But the Isaac of these letters my eyes listened to in amazement, if it can be said that way.

8 November 1889

Dearest sister Karen—
America and Montana are ever an adventure. Today I journeyed

into the community of Gros Ventre for provisions and found there a proud new municipal adornment; beside the dirt of the village's main and only street, a flagpole of peeled pine with a fresh American flag bucking in the wind. Pole and flag were but hours old, as was the news that Montana has advanced from a type of colonial governance to become a fully equal state of the United States. In all truth, the celebratory merriment of Gros Ventre this day was so infectious it could not be resisted; but your Montanian brother nonetheless was truly moved by this fledging of his adopted land. DV, Montana and we in it shall ride the future as staunchly as that flag in the wind. . . .

12 June 1892
. . . The time is not far, my Karen, when I will have crews of teamsters at earnful labor throughout this Two Medicine country, and DV, I shall be able to stand about with my hands on my back, looking on like a baron. Streets, roads, reservoirs, all are to be built here in young Montana and the demand for my workhorses is constant. . . .

I carried these first few of the translated letters over to show the librarian. "This DV he sticks in every so often—do you happen to know where that comes from?"

"Deo volente, that'd be," he provided at once.

My high school Latin was quite a ways behind me. Oh, sure, like anybody I could dope out Deo as meaning God, deity, all that. But the other word . . .

" 'God willing,' it means," the librarian rescued me. "You find it a lot in letters of people who had some education back then."

Huh. Another surprise out of my horsetrading grandfather: I hadn't known there was an ounce of religion anywhere in our family line.

I went back to the table and resumed reading.

30 September 1897
. . . No doubt, dearest sister, you will notice a shine in the ink of these words, for I write to you as a freshly married man. Before she took mine, her name was Anna Ramsay—a lovely, lively woman,

Scotland-born, who arrived here last spring as the new teacher at our Noon Creek school. . . .

After that sunburst of marriage Isaac's pages breathed to life *our much wished for child, Lisabeth*—my mother, born in 1900 on the first of April, and although we kidded her about it nobody was ever less of an April fool—and a few years later her brother *Peter, a fine squalling boy who seems determined to visit the neighbors all along Noon Creek with his voice.* The early ups and downs of the ranch I now owned were traced here. The doings of neighbors were everlastingly colored in ink. The steady pen brought the familiar snow of Two Medicine winter, and transformed it into the green of spring. Letter after letter I read as if old Isaac, strangulated by spoken language but soliloquizing with the best of them here on paper, somehow had singled me out for these relived times.

25 June 1914

. . . I write you this from amid scenery that would put Switzerland in the shade. Our work camp this summer is at St. Mary Lake while my teamsters are building roads of the new Glacier National Park. Towering over us are mountains like castles of gray and blue, as if kings had come down from the sky to live even more royally at the top of the earth. Quite to my surprise, I was visited here this past week by Anna and the children; she took the impulse to come by wagon even though it is a tedious three-day journey from Noon Creek. Ever her own pilot through life, is my Anna. . . .

You want not to count on history staying pleasant or even civil, though.

I have been so numb with grief, dearest Karen, that not until now have I had the heart to write about . . . Anna. About her death, ten days before, in the influenza epidemic of 1918.

I pinched the bridge of my nose and swallowed hard to go on from that aching message of the loss of a wife. Isaac's Anna. My Marcella. The longest epidemic of all, loss.

Isaac too now seemed to falter, the letters foreshortened after that, even the one the next year telling of the wedding of my mother and father there at the Noon Creek ranch. Nor were there any more invocations of DV.

I was thumbing through the final little batch of translated

pages, about to admit that Isaac and I both seemed to be out of
steam for this correspondence, when my eye caught on the *McC*
at the start of a name.

*In the valley next over from this one, Lisabeth's father-in-law
Angus McCaskill has died. The report is that he was fixing a fence
after supper when his heart gave out. Such a passing I find less than
surprising, for Angus was a man whose hands were full of work from
daylight to last light. Still, although we know that all things find
their end, it is sobering to me that he has gone from life at an age
very like my own, neither a young man nor an old.*

*His leaving of life has brought various matters to the front of my
mind. At the funeral of Angus, when I went to speak consolation to
his wife and now widow Adair, I was much startled to learn that she
is removing herself to Scotland. "To visit, you surely mean." "No, to
stay," she had me know. She will wait to see Varick and Lisabeth's
child, soon due, into the world. But after greeting that grandchild
with her eyes, then she will go. I was, and am, deeply baffled that a
person would take such a step. You know that Denmark will never
leave my tongue, but this has become the land of my heart. Not so,
however, for Adair McCaskill. She has a singular fashion of referring to herself by name, and thus her requiem for the life she is
choosing to depart from was spoken as: "Adair and Montana have
never fitted together."*

Those two paragraphs held me. I reread and re-reread. My
rightful name is John Angus McCaskill. Christened so for this
other grandfather who abruptly was appearing out of the pen of
my grandfather Isaac. My father's father, so long gone, I had
never really given any thought to. A shadow in other time. My
main information on him was the remark one or the other of
my parents made every so often when Mariah was growing
up, that her rich head of hair came from her great-grandfather
Angus, of the deep shade the Scotch claim is the color of
their fighting blood. Yet here in ink Angus McCaskill suddenly
was, right out of nowhere, or at least the portion of him that
echoes in my own birth certificate. And with him, but evidently
on her own terms, was my grandmother I knew even less of.
So scant was any mention of Adair McCaskill by my parents
that I sensed she and my mother had been in-laws at odds,
but that was all. I'd always assumed the North Fork home-

stead claimed her as it did Angus. Willing reversal to Scotland
was new lore to me.

I read on.

*Until now I have forborne from any mention of Angus McCaskill
to you in my letters, dearest sister, because I believed the time would
come when I would need to tell you the all. You will see that while my
pen was quiet about Angus my mind rarely was, for his life made a
crossroad with my own almost from the first of our days here in the
Two Medicine country, some 35 years ago. He too was but young,
new and green to this America, this Montana, when I sold him the
first substantial horse he ever owned, a fine tall gelding of dark
brown with the lively name of Scorpion. In the years that came,
Angus cut an admired figure in the community, not only as an
industrious homesteader and sheepman but also as teacher at the
South Fork school. A man with poetry on his tongue and decent
intentions in his heart, was Angus. The word "neighbor" has no
better definition than the life he led. To me, however, Angus was
more than simply a neighbor, more than a familiar face atop a strong
horse which I had provided him. Greatly more, for the matter is,
Angus was in love with my Anna all the years of our marriage.*

*He manfully tried not to show his ardor for my wife, and never did
I have cause to believe anything improper took place between the two
of them. But his glances from across the room at her during our
schoolhouse dances and other gatherings (how many glances that adds
up to in 21 years!) told me louder than words that he loved her
from afar in a helpless way. What must have been even worse a
burden on the heart of Angus was that he won Anna's affections
before I did, or so he had every cause to believe. He was the first to
ask her to marry; Anna being Anna, she delayed answer until after
the ensuing summer; and that was the summer of 1897 when I hired
her to cook for my crew during the plowing of fireguards along the
Great Northern railway and her life and mine were joined. After we
were married that autumn, I tried never to show Angus that I knew of
Anna's spurning of him, believing that when she chose me over him
the bargain was struck and we all three could but live by it. Yet, even
after his own marriage, I could not help but feel pity for Angus,
unable to have Anna in his life.*

*Yet again—only now, dearest sister, and only to you on this
unjudging paper, can I bring myself to say this—I know with all
that is in me that if Anna had lived, she would have left me for*

Angus McCaskill. I could see it coming in her. She had a nature all her own, did my Anna; as measured as a judge in making her mind up, but passionate in her decision once she had done so. And so the moment merely waited, somewhere ahead in time, when Anna would have decided that she and I had had all of life together we could, and then she would have turned to Angus. I believe she was nearing that moment just before she died. Lisabeth was grown by then, Peter nearly so; consequences of ending our marriage no longer would fall directly on our children. I have spent endless nights wondering what would have ensued. Surely, if her mother had gone with Angus, Lisabeth would not then have married a McCaskill; strong-minded as she is, she would have spoken her vow to the Devil first. From that it follows that Lisabeth and Varick's little boy Alec, and the other child on the way, those existences come undone, do they not? As the saying is, all the wool in the world can be raveled sooner than the skein of a single life.

As for myself, my debate in the hours of night is whether it is more bearable to have become a widower than a rejected husband. It is a question, I am discovering, that does not want to answer itself.

By the time I was done reading this the first time, the backs of my hands were pouring sweat. Jesus H. Christ, what we don't know about how things were before they got to us.

Over and over I read that letter, but the meaning did not change in any way, the words would not budge from Isaac Reese's unsparing rendering of them. My father's father had been in love with my mother's mother. And she more or less with him. In love but married to others.

And not just that. August 12, 1924, the date on this letter in which Isaac told all; the other child on the way, less than a month from being born, the one whose existence would have been erased if Anna Reese had not died before she could take her future to waiting Angus McCaskill. That child was precisely me.

As if that child was suddenly six years old and yearning for the teacher to call rest period so that he could put his head down on his school desk into the privacy of closed eyes, I right then laid forward into my arms on the library table and cradled my head. I did not know the tears were coming until I felt the seep of them at my eyelids, the wet paths being traced over my cheekbones.

That quiet crying: who did I weep for? For Anna Reese? Did that woman have to die for me to happen? Become in death my grandmother, as she never would have in life? Alec and I, and by way of me, Mariah and Lexa; we were freed into life when the epidemic took her, were we? Or were my tears Isaac's, for his having lost a wife? Or for Angus McCaskill for twice having lost love, once at the altar and once at the grave? Or for Adair McCaskill, second-choice wife in a land, too, that was never her own? Or was this again my grief for Marcella, my tears the tide of her passing into the past with the rest of these?

I wept for them all, us all.

A hand cupped my shoulder. "Sir? Are you all right?" The library man was squatting down beside me, trying to peer in through my pillow of arms.

I lifted my head and wiped my eyes with both hands. Gaggles of genealogists around the room had put aside their volumes to watch me. "Uhm. I forgot . . . forgot where I was." Blew my nose. Tried to clear my throat. "Some things kind of got pent up in me. The stuff in these . . ." I indicated Isaac's letters.

"At least they mean something to you," the librarian said gently.

"Yeah. Yeah, they do."

The librarian having assured me he'd tell my daughter and any tall yayhoo with her that I'd meet them outside, I snuffled my way out into the sunshine. Into noon hour for the state workers, for across the street from the Historical Society the capitol's copper dome was like a hive for busy humanity below, men and women in groups and pairs as they hurried off to restaurants or chose shaded spots on the capitol lawn for bag lunch on the ground.

I plugged along slowly through the blanketing heat toward the Bago, trying not to look like a guy who had just made a public spectacle of himself. Talk about self-pandemonium. This trip was doing it to me something fierce. How the hell to ward it off, though? The past has a mind of its own, I was finding out. Maybe my weepy spell was over but I still felt flooded with those torrents of Isaac's ink.

"Hi, did you manage to keep yourself entertained this morning?" Mariah's voice caught up with me from behind. Before I could manage a response to that, she was alongside me with her arm hooked with mine and already was skipping on to "Ready for lunch, do I even need to ask?"

"Where's your partner in crime?" I inquired, glancing around for Riley.

"He's calling the BB to make sure our geezer piece got there okay. I missed a bet when we divorced. I should have sued the telephone for alienation of affection."

She, at least, seemed in an improved mood, which I verified by asking her how the red-light real estate piece was coming. "I think it's going to work," she conceded. "You never quite know with Riley when he reaches into that pantry of a brain of his. But his idea this time looks real zammo." Nor could you predict this newspaper pair. Less than twenty-four hours ago they could barely tolerate each other and here all of a sudden they were on their best productive behavior.

At the motorhome Mariah and I flung open all the doors and windows to let the heat out, but sultry as the weather was maybe a hotter amount flowed in. We moved off into the shade of a tree on the capitol lawn while waiting for Riley. Right next to us was a big oblong flowerbed in a blossom pattern forming the word CENTENNIAL; my God, they were even spelling it out in marigolds now.

The sky, though, had turned milky, soiled-looking. "What the hell's happened to our day?" I asked Mariah.

"Smog," she said, squinting critically at the murk; only the very nearest mountains around the city could be seen through the damn stuff. "Smoke from the forest fires in Idaho, I guess, and when it's this humid . . ."

Smog? Shit, what next. Even the air was getting me down now. I wished to Christ the scribbler would haul his butt out here and we could head for—

"Here you go," I heard next out of Mariah. The camera lifted to her eye and pointed at me. "A chance to pose with a general." Behind me stood the statue of General Meagher on horseback with sword uplifted like he was having it out with the pigeons. After the Civil War he'd been made territorial governor of Montana, but disappeared off a Missouri River steamboat during a night of drinking blackberry wine. I suppose they couldn't show that in a statue so they put him on horseback.

"Speaking of general," I tried on this daughter of mine without real hope, "these pictures you perpetually want to take of me are a general nuisance, do you know that?"

"Thaaat's my guy, just be your natural self if you can stand to," she launched into her picture-taking spiel behind that damn camera, "and you—"

For once she brought the camera down without a click. "You look kind of under the weather, Jick." Mariah's gray eyes took stock of me. "Are you okay?"

"I been better," I admitted. The morning in the unexpected company of our own sources was more major than I could put into words for her right then. Nor were the tears very far behind my eyes. "Must be the smog, is all." I tried to move my mind from the past toward some speck of the future. "So. We can hit on toward the ranch this afternoon, huh? Leave right after lunch and we ought to be able to get there by about—"

"Mmm, not quite," Mariah disposed of that hope in nothing flat. "We're going to have to hang on here until tomorrow. Riley and I still have a load of old pictures to go through in there. This has got to be the most photographed red-light district anywhere, you wonder if they were putting it on postcards."

Right then Riley emerged from the Historical Society building, a frown on him you could have plowed a field with.

"The BB wants to see us," he told Mariah of the phone call without any fooling around at all. "Right now. If not sooner."

What, a detour all the hell way back west to Missoula? At this rate the only chance I had of making a trip home to the ranch was to keep going in the opposite direction until I circled the globe to it.

"Why's he want to see us?" Mariah was asking warily.

"He wouldn't say," Riley reported. "He sounded like he was too busy concentrating on being mad."

"Oh, horse pucky," Mariah let out in a betrayed tone. She drew herself up even more erect than usual, as if having put on an armor breastplate to do battle. "Riley, you swore to me, you absofuckinglutely *swore* to me you weren't going to diddle around with the expense account this time! You know how pissed off—"

"Goddamn it, I haven't been!" Riley defended.

"—the BB gets when—" She halted and looked at him differently. "You haven't been?"

"No, I have not," he maintained, pawing furiously at his cookie duster. "This whole frigging trip, the only invented arith-

metic is going to be for those goddamn Bago repairs eventually.
If the BB has been sniffing around in our expense account so far,
all it'll tell him is that it's cheaper keeping us on the road than it
is having us cause trouble around the office. Huh uh. It's got to
be something else on his tiny mind."

The office of Baxter Beebe was in that turret of the *Montanian*
building, with a spiffy outlook across the Clark Fork River to
pleasant tree-lined Missoula streets.

The decoration of that round room, though, I would have
done something drastic about. Currently the motif consisted of
stuffed animal heads. They formed a staring circle around the
room, their taxidermed eyes aimed inward at Mariah and Riley
and me as we entered; an eight-point buck deer and an elk with
antlers like tree limbs and a surprised-looking antelope and a
moose and a bear and a bobcat and a number of African creatures I couldn't begin to name and, my God, even a buffalo.
Many bars used to have head collections on their walls and at
first I figured the BB simply had bought one of those zoos of the
dead when a bar was turned into a fern cafe. But then I noticed
there was a gold nameplate under each head, such as:

Bull Elk
shot by Baxter Beebe
in the Castle Mountains
October 25, 1986

He was a pale ordinary enough guy sitting there behind a
broad desk, but evidently he did his own killing.

As the three of us walked in, Beebe plainly wondered who
the dickens I was. Riley had just made that same point as we
parked the Winnebago in the *Montanian* lot and I remarked that
I'd be kind of interested to meet this famous boss of theirs. "Oh,
just great," he'd grumbled, "your general enthusiasm will help
us a whole fucking lot in handling the BB." But when Mariah
introduced me, the editor automatically hopped up, gave me a
pump-handle handshake—I suppose a person in his position gets
paid by the handshake—and instructed, "Call me Bax."

Riley and Mariah both sat down looking exceedingly leery, as
if the seats might be those joke cushions that go *pththbfft!* when
sat on. I found a chair too and did what I could to make myself
less than conspicuous.

The BB—Bax—sat with his hands folded atop a stack of

letters on the desk in front of him and stared expressionlessly at Mariah and Riley for what he must have thought was the prescribed amount of bossly time. Then he intoned in a voice so deep it was almost subterranean:

"Let me put it this way. There has been a very interesting response to your centennial series. A record number of letters to the editor. For instance." He plucked the top letter off the stack and held it straight out to Mariah and Riley as if toasting a marshmallow on the end of a stick. The two of them reached for the sheet of paper simultaneously and ended up each holding a corner. I leaned over to peek along as they silently read:

> *Your so-called series on the centennial is downright disgusting. If Riley Wright, whose name by rights ought to be Riley Wrong, can't find anything better about Montana than the guff he has been handing us, he should be put to writing about softball instead.*
>
> *Also, the pictures in your paper are getting weird. Since when is the Berkeley Pit art? I can go out to the nearest gravel pit with my Instamatic and do just as good.*
>
> *PO'd on Mullan Road*

Mariah started to say something, which I knew would be relevant to the letter writer's photographic judgment and general ancestry, but then caught herself and just gritted. For his part, Riley was grinning down at the letter as if he'd just been awarded the world prize for smart aleckry. Eventually, though, he became aware of the BB's solid stare.

"Yeah, I see your point here, Bax," Riley announced thoughtfully, too thoughtfully it seemed to me. "Before you can print this one," he flapped the letter in a fond way, "we've got to solve the PO'd style question, don't we. Grammatically speaking, PO'd has to stand for Piss Offed. So you'd think Pissed Off ought to be P'd O, now wouldn't you? But nobody ever says it that way, so do we go with PO'd as common usage? Shame to lose that nice rhyme, too, 'PO'd on Mullan Road.' " Riley brightened like a kid remembering what nine times eight equals. "Here we go. If the guy would move across town to Idaho Street, we'd have it made—'P'd O on Idaho!' What do you think, Bax? You figure we can get him to agree to move if we promise to publish his dumbfuck letter?"

"Riley," Beebe uttered in his deepest voice yet, "what are you talking about?"

Riley never got the chance to retort anything further smart, because the editor now started giving him and Mariah undiluted hell. How come Riley's pieces were all about slaughtered buffalo and coppered-out miners and, it was incredible but the fact of the matter was inescapable, the angelic qualities of bartenders? And where was Mariah getting picture ideas like the fannies of geezers and, it was incredible but the fact of the matter was inescapable again, Kimi the bartender seen woozily through the beer glass?

Wow, I thought to myself, and he doesn't even know yet about the hardheaded whores of Helena.

Beebe paused long enough in his bill of particulars to slap a hand down onto the stack of letters, *thwap*. Then he announced: "In other words, the two of you are outraging our readers."

Mariah tried to point out, "Bax, in Missoula people will write a sackful of letters to the editor if they think a stoplight is a couple of seconds slow."

The BB was less than persuaded. "This is very serious," he stated in a funeral tone and proceeded to elaborate all over again on how the expectations of the *Montanian*'s readers, not to mention his own extreme forbearance, were being very abused by the way the pair of them were going about the centennial series.

I do have to admit, my feelings were radically more mixed than I expected, sitting there listening to their boss ream out Riley and Mariah. Oh sure, I was as gratified as I ought to have been by the perfectly evident oncoming fact that he was working around to the extermination of the centennial series and our Bago sojourn. And any time Riley got a tromping, it suited me fine. But I hated to see Mariah catch hell along with him. Then there was the, well, what might be called this matter of office justice. Put it this way: it really kind of peed me off, too, that this yoyo of a BB could sit here in his round office and prescribe to Mariah, or for that matter even Riley, what they were supposed to be seeing, when they were the ones out there in the daylong world trying to do the actual work.

The beleaguered pair of them now were attempting to stick up for their series while Beebe went on lambasting it and them. So while the three of them squawked at each other, I gandered around at the BB's stuffed trophies. Massive moose. Small bobcat. African something or other. That big elk. *Dead heads*, I could just hear Mariah steaming to herself, *symbolic*.

"Excuse my asking, Bax," I broke in on the general ruckus, "but where's your mountain goat?"

Everything stopped.

Then Beebe eyeballed me as steadily as if a taxidermist had worked on him too, while Riley, damn his hide, started gawking ostentatiously around the room as if the mentioned goat might be hiding behind a chair. For her part, Mariah was shaking her head a millimeter back and forth and imperatively mouthing *No, not now!* at me.

Beebe set to answering me in a frosty way, "If you do any hunting yourself, Jack—"

"Jick," I corrected generously.

"Whatever. If you do any hunting yourself—"

I shrugged and put in, "Not quite fifty years' worth yet."

The BB blinked a number of times, then amended his tone considerably. "Then you will know it is very hard to achieve a mountain goat. I have never been privileged to shoot one."

"The hell!" I exclaimed as if he'd confessed he'd never tasted chocolate ice cream. "Christamighty, I got them hanging like flies on the mountains up behind my place."

"Your place?"

"My ranch, up along the Rocky Mountain Front. Yeah, I can sit in my living room with a half-decent pair of binoculars and watch goats till I get sick of them."

He steepled his fingers and peered at me over his half-prayerfulness. "That is very interesting, ah, Jick. But I would imagine that getting within range of them is another matter."

"No problem. Anybody who's serious about his hunting," I nodded to the dead heads along the walls, "and I can see you definitely are, I usually let them onto the place, maybe even take them up one of the trails to those goats myself. Tell you what, whyn't you put in to draw for a permit, then come on up this fall and we'll find you a goat?" I gave the BB a look overflowing with nimrod enthusiasm. What fault was it of mine if the mountain goats in west of my ranch actually were unreachable on the other side of the sheer walls of Gut Plunge Canyon? The BB had only asked me whether it was possible to get within range of them, not whether it was feasible to fire off a shot.

I figured I'd better land him before my enthusiasm played out. "In fact, Bax, how about you coming on up to go goating right after these two," I indicated Riley and Mariah with the same kind of nod I'd given the stuffed trophies, "get done with this centennial stuff of theirs in November?"

He kept gazing at me from behind his finger steeple for a while. Then he gazed a further while at Mariah and Riley. All three of us could see him working on the choice. Sacrificial sheep or mountain goat.

At last Baxter Beebe announced, "That is a very, very interesting offer, Jick. I am going to take you up on that." He turned toward the other two. "Riley, as I was getting to, there has been some marked reaction among our readers to your centennial pieces. Of course, one way of viewing it is that you are provoking people's attention. The exact same can be said of your photos, Mariah. So, speaking as your editor, I will tell you what." We waited for what. "As you continue the centennial series, I would expect that your topics will become somewhat more, shall we say, traditional. Perhaps I should phrase it this way: tone things down." The BB sent a final gaze around to Mariah, then to Riley, and even to me. He concluded: "Anyway, I thought you would want to know you are being read, out there in readerland."

I give Mariah and Riley due credit, they both managed not to look mock astonished that newspaper readers were reading newspapers.

No, instead Riley said in a hurry "You can't know what an inspiration that is to us, Bax," and stood, and Mariah was already up and saying brightly "Well, we'll go hit the road again then, Bax," and even I found my feet and joined the exodus while the BB shuffled the letters to the editor together, squaring them into a neat pile which he put in his OUT basket.

MOTATING THE HIGH LINE

Centennialitis will break out in Gros Ventre again on Thursday night. A combined work party and meeting of the Dawn of Montana steering committee will be held at the Medicine Lodge, beginning at 8:30 p.m. "Everybody better come or they're going onto my list to sweep up the parade route after the horses," stated committee chairperson Althea Frew. Other members of the steering committee are Amber Finletter, J. A. "Jick" McCaskill, Howard Stonesifer, and Arlee Zane.

—GROS VENTRE WEEKLY GLEANER,
AUGUST 1, 1989

BRRK BRRK.

My waking thought was that the guy who invented the telephone ought to have been publicly boiled in his own brainwater. Outside the bedroom window, dawn was just barely making headway against dark. If manufactured noise at such an hour isn't an offense against human nature, I don't know what is.

BRRK BRRK.

Christamighty, Mariah already, was my next realization. When I'd deposited her and Riley back in Helena the afternoon before to put the finishing touches on their masterpiece of mattress capitalism, that daughter of mine had told me she'd call me at the ranch today and let me know what time to come back and get her and her haywire companion. But *this* time of day, before there even properly was a day yet?

BRRK BRRK.

Maybe I would do that getting and maybe I just wouldn't. Late as I'd gotten in after the drive from Helena to Noon Creek, I hadn't even had a chance yet to see Kenny and Darleen and gather any report on the ranch. And even in so milky a start of the day, I couldn't help but wonder what order of fool I was for turning the BB around with goat bait the way I had. What got into me, there in Missoula, not to let His Exterminatorship go ahead and kill off the centennial series and my unwanted part in it?

BRRK BR—

I *hello*ed and braced.

"Oh, Jick, I'm so glad I caught you before you got out and around, I know what an early bird you are," a woman's voice arrived at full gallop. Never Mariah, expending words wholesale like that.

I elbow-propped myself a little higher in bed. "Uh, who—"

"Oh, you're funning me, aren't you, pretending not to know this is Althea. Next thing, you'll be claiming you forgot all about tonight."

"Forgot what?"

"Jick, our centennial committee meets tonight," the phone voice perceptibly stiffened into that of Althea Frew, chairperson. "We've missed you at the meetings lately."

"Yeah, well, I been away. Unavoidably so." And it mystified me as much as ever, how she and undoubtedly the whole Two Medicine country knew that in the dark of last night I had come back. Did bunny-slipper telegraph even need the existence of the telephone or did they simply emanate bulletins out through the connecting air?

"All the nicer to have you home with us again, just in time for tonight," she informed me with conspicuous enthusiasm. "We have an agenda that I know you'll be interest—"

"Althea, I'm not real sure I'm going to be able to stick around until tonight. I—"

"You're turning into quite a gadabout, Jick. But I'm sure you can make time for one eensy committee meeting. Oh, and would you ask Mariah if she can come take pictures for our centennial album sometime? See you tonight," and Althea toodled off the line.

The burden of conversation with Althea thus lifted, I sat up in the big double bed and by habit took a meteorological look out the window to the west. A moon new as an egg rested in the weatherless sky above the mountains. So far so good on that front, anyway.

I was at least out of bed and had my pants halfway on before the phone rang again. Typical Mariah. I grabbed the instrument

up, doubly PO'd at her for calling before I even had any breakfast in me and for not calling before Althea did her crowbar work
on me.

"Damn it, petunia, do you have some kind of sixth sense
about doing things at exactly the wrong time?"

Silence, until eventually:

"Uhmm, Jick, was you going to line us out on haying the
Ramsay place, before Darleen and me head up there?"

Kenny's voice, across the hundred feet between the old house
and my and Marce's. Jesus, the day was getting away from me.
Ordinarily I'd be over there by the time my hired couple finished up breakfast. Hurriedly I told Kenny, "Must've looked at
the wrong side of the clock this morning. I'll be right over."

"Darleen's got the coffeepot on," he assured me as if that was
foremost in my mind as well as his, and hung up.

> *"Sometimes you eat the bear,*
> *sometimes the bear eats you.*
> *Sometimes you drink the flood,*
> *sometimes you sip the dew.*
> *Sometimes you both are one,*
> *sometimes you break in two."*

When I got there, Kenny was walking jerky little circles
behind Darleen while she did the dishes, neither of them looking anywhere near at the other and the radio Roadkill bunch
yowling right along with them. I know there is no one style
for mating, but the fact that these two ended up with each
other still confounded me. While Kenny was forever performing his conversational perambulation or bringing a hand up
to rub the back of his neck or swinging his arms or craning
a look out the nearest window to get his eyes fidgeting along
with the rest of him, Darleen sloped along with no excess
motion, and often no motion at all. Or was theirs what was
meant by an average marriage, the way they so radically
averaged each other out.

Right off I noticed that Kenny now sported muttonchop
sideburns—they made him look like a shampooed lynx—for
Gros Ventre's centennial beard contest. But the moment I stepped
in the kitchen, it was my countenance that received a startled
going-over from Kenny and Darleen both. I wondered what

secret from myself was showing there, until I remembered my own accumulating snowy whiskers.

The two of them gave each other a side glance. Then Kenny felt the abrupt need to know, "Jick, how you doing this morning?" while Darleen matter of factly chipped in, "You must've seen a helluva swath of Montana by now."

"Okay" and "yeah" I recited to those and while we were getting coffeed up for the day, Kenny filled me in on ranch matters. Rather, he told me as much as he could think of and Darleen filled him in on all he forgot to tell. Haying was about a week behind because of breakdowns, but on the other hand Kenny did the repairing himself and avoided mechanics at multiple dollars per hour. For the first time in several summers Noon Creek was flowing a good head of water, but on the other hand the beavers were gaily working overtime on damming. A considerable stretch of fenceline had been mended, but on one more hand, the roof portions that blew off the lambing shed in the Alaskan Express storm of February hadn't been. A last prodding glance from Darleen further reminded Kenny that, uhmm, well, actually he hadn't got around to tending the sheepherder yet this week, either. All in all, things were not really any worse than I expected, nor a damn bit better.

Now came Darleen's turn, to give a cook's-eye view of how grocery prices were rocketing. As she recited a blow-by-blow of her latest bout with Joe Prentiss at his cash register in the Gros Ventre Mercantile, I nursed away at a second cup of Darleen's muscular coffee and tried to ponder how long I could operate this ranch by remote control through Kenny and her. How long did I want to keep trying? *You can't get decent help any more,* ran any rancher's chronic plaint; probably it went back to Abel's last recorded remark about Cain. But actually the pair here in this kitchen were as decent as I had any right to expect. Take Darleen, yakking away at a rate that had me thankful I wasn't paying her by the word. She was made of tough stuff, I always had to grant her that. When a foot of heavy wet snow hit on Memorial Day of this year, wonderful moisture for the grass but hell on young lambs and spring-shorn ewes, Darleen slaved side by side with Kenny and me through all that terrible day of fighting weakening sheep to shelter. And Kenny, although he couldn't manage his time even if you hung a clock on his nose, would whale away at any given task until he eventually subdued it; all you could ask of a person on the wages a rancher can pay, really. No, another Kenny, a different Darleen, would not inch my ranch situation toward solution.

". . . Joe Prentiss goes, 'What do you want me to do, give this stuff away?' " Darleen at last was wrapping up her grocery tale, "and I go, 'You bet that's what I *want,* but I sure don't see any sign of it *happening.*' "

I did what I could to grin approval of Darleen's defense of our kitchen budget, but my result was probably thin. All at once, the three of us seemed to be out of conversation. Kenny squirmed into a new configuration in his chair. Darleen appeared to have plenty more to say but instead was silently watching Kenny contort. I took sipping refuge behind my coffee cup and watched them both. What the hell now? Something was missing from this morning's session about the ranchwork, something that wanted saying but was being held back, and the other two knew it just as well as I did. Whatever it was I was about to cover it over by supposing out loud that we had better get to getting toward the day's labor—by now I had it worked out in my head that I'd camptend the sheepherder, fix any downed fence while I was up there, then swing home by way of upper Noon Creek to attack the beaver dam problem; I knew it would take Kenny three separate trips to achieve the same—when Kenny crossed his arms and put his hands on his shoulders as if hugging himself and brought out:

"Uhhmm, Jick, I met up with Shaun Finletter along the east fence there a couple days ago and he said to tell you he'd like to talk to you about the place."

And here it was, yet and again. The missing. The first peep of it, anyway. Because, the fact was that though Shaun Finletter's tongue would do that talking, the throat under the words was WW, Incorporated. The everloving goddamn corporaiders. Not twenty minutes after that conglomerated outfit bought the big Double W ranch from Wendell Williamson's heirs—as a tax write-off, naturally—some guy in a tie was here to make me an offer for this ranch. Other Double Dubsters had tried me regularly the past half dozen years, and now that Shaun was their manager of the Double W, I evidently was in his job description too: buy out the old pooter at the head of the creek. I have to say, in a way I missed Wendell Williamson, whom I despised heartily when he was alive. At least with Wendell you knew directly who was trying to gobble you; not some distant multibunch who saw you as a scrap of acreage they could make tax arithmetic out of.

"Did he," I at last remarked as neutrally as possible about Kenny's relay from Shaun and brought my coffee cup to the ready position for one more refill that I did not want. But at the stove Darleen was waiting for my real answer before she would lift the coffeepot, as if my words might make the load too much to handle; and Kenny still was in his self-hug. Both of them watching me so closely it was as bad as being in Mariah's strongest lens. They had reason. For if I sold, this ranch would be folded into the Double W holdings as one more cow pasture, the way every other ranch along Noon Creek had been. WW, Inc. saw no need for the Kennys and Darleens of this world.

BRRK BRRK.

Kenny sprang to the phone on the wall. "Hullo? You bet, he's right here." Before I could gather myself, Mariah's voice was in my ear:

"Hi. You know what? You don't have to come back to Helena for us."

"I don't?"

"See what a terrific daughter I can be when I half try? Riley and I can't tell yet when we'll be done here today, so we'll rent a car and come up to the Two whenever we are. We need to get going on that part of the state next anyway. Think you can keep yourself occupied without us a little while? Gas up the Bago. Bye."

It was midmorning by the time the grocery boxes and I made our escape from the Gros Ventre Mercantile and Joe Prentiss's opinion of Darleen, and headed west out of town toward the sheep camp.

Remarkable how quiet and thought-bringing a pastime it is to drive along without a photographer blazing away beside you and a wordwright whanging his laptop behind you. This road I knew like the back of my hand and so I simply had to hold the motorhome away from the slidey gravel edges of the roadbank and let my mind do whatever solo it wanted, this cream-of-summer morning. Everywhere ahead the mountains, the jagged rim where the Two Medicine country joins onto the sky, today were clear and near. A last few desperate patches of snow still showed bright among the topmost clefts of Roman Reef's wall of rock, but their destiny was evaporation in another week or so. The benchlands on either side of the valley road already were beveled pastures of crisp grass; summer in the Two country always takes on a tan by August. Against the slope of the high ridge south of town, the big GV outline in rocks painted white by the Gros Ventre high school freshmen each fall was by now like a fading set of initials chalked onto leather.

Yet the land still was green where it counted: beside me as I drove, the column of tall old cottonwood trees extending west alongside the county road, through hay meadow after hay meadow until at last thinning into a pair of willow lines that curved down out of the mountains—English Creek, its main channel and north and south forks like a handle and tines uncovering my beginnings to me.

There is nothing left standing of my father's English Creek ranger station. I inescapably know that, and could not help but see so, yet again, as the Bago topped the rise of the county road and started down the long slow slant of grade to the forks of the creek. But the absence always registers hard on me. The station. The house behind it where we lived from my fourth year of life through my fifteenth. Barn, corral, sheds, flagpole. Not a stick of any of those is left. In one way of looking at things this is appropriate, really. The U.S. Forest Service extinguished that site from our lives in the winter of 1939 when it directed my father, over his loudest kicks against the policy, to move his district office of the Two Medicine National Forest into town in Gros Ventre, and so the facade of that earlier English Creek time may as well have taken its leave.

Its thoughts, though, do not go.

"Mac, if headquarters doesn't send us out some new oilcloth one of these years, they are going to get A Piece Of My Mind." My mother, Lisabeth Reese when she began life and Beth McCaskill from her nineteenth year to her eighty-fourth and final one, had a certain tone of voice that signaled in high letters Watch Out. My father, officially Varick McCaskill but Mac to all who knew him in his lifetime of rangering, listened when he had to and otherwise went his way of simply loving her beyond all the limits. They stand in my memory at English Creek as if they were the highest two of those sky-supporting mountains. Her reminding him for the fourth time in as many days that his ranger diary for the week thus far was a perfect blank, lifting her black eyebrows significantly as she half-turned from the cookstove and supper-in-the-making to inquire, "Are you trying for a new record, Mac?" Him angling forward in his long-boned way as he peered out the west window, restless under any roof, declaring of the perpetual paperwork, "I tell you, Bet, USFS stands for just what it sounds like, Us Fuss. If there's an outfit with more fussing around to it than the Forest Service, I'd like to know where."

And the other echo. The one that clangs like iron against iron in my remembering. That never-ended argument from an English Creek suppertime.

"You're done running my life," my brother flinging behind him as he stomped from that vanished house.

"Nobody's running it, including you," my father hurling after him.

The issue was warm and blond, her name Leona Tracy. A blouseful of blossom, seventeen years old and already eternal. She and Alec vowed they were going to get married, they would find a way of existence different from the college and career that my Depression-haunted parents were urging onto Alec, they would show the world what fireproof love was like. None of it turned out that way. By that autumn of 1939 Alec and Leona were split. Her life found its course away from the Two Medicine country. And Alec's—

"Goddamn Riley anyhow," I heard declared in an angry voice. Mine. A lot was working on me. It always did, here along English Creek. But right now Riley somehow represented the whole business, Alec and Leona and my amazed grief as a not-quite-fifteen-year-old watching them cut themselves off from my parents and me, every nick of that past like scars across my own skin. Why is a centennial supposed to be such potent arithmetic, will somebody just tell me that? I mean, you think about it, it always is a hundred years since one damn thing or another happened; the invention of the dental drill or the founding of junk mail or some such. But the *half* centuries, the fifty-year wedges that take most of our own lifetimes, those are the truly lethal pieces of calendar. Instead of chasing off after olden topics, what about those closer truths? Maybe I was not such a hotshot at history as Riley Wright was, but this I knew deep as the springs of my blood: in spite of ourselves, or because of ourselves—I still cannot judge which—the family we McCaskills had been here at the English Creek ranger station never truly recovered from the ruction between my parents and my brother when Alec declared himself against the future they hoped for him, and in favor of linkage with Leona, that summer of fifty years ago.

Yet—there always seemed to be a yet where the goddamn guy was involved—the one person on this green earth to whom I'd shown my feelings about our McCaskill family fracture was Riley.

He did not know the entirety, of course. Not nearly. But its topmost raw residue in me, he knew. Four, five years ago, that English Creek evening of Riley and myself? Whenever, it was back before his and Mariah's marriage went off the rails, when during one of their weekend visits to the ranch at Noon Creek he mentioned that he'd been going around to cemeteries, seeing what he could gather for a column on tombstone inscriptions sometime, and did I suppose the Gros Ventre cemetery would have anything worthwhile? "Oh hell yeah," I assured him, ever helpful me, and so before sundown I found myself there amid the graves with Riley. Just we two, as Marcella and Mariah had let us know a cemetery visit was not their idea of entertainment.

The lawned mound of the Gros Ventre cemetery stands above the edge of town and the treeline of English Creek as if the land has bubbled green there; one single tinged knoll against the eastward grainfield plains and the tan benchlands stretching west like platforms to the mountains. I am never there without thinking of the care that the first people of Gros Ventre put into choosing this endsite.

Riley took to the headstones in the old part of the cemetery like a bee to red clover. He immediately was down on one knee, dabbing inscriptions into his notebook, looking close, looking around. I could tell when a person was involved with his job, so I told him I'd wait for him up in the area where people were being buried currently. The active part of the cemetery, so to say.

There I knelt and did a little maintenance against weeds on my father's grave. Beside him the earth on my mother's was still fresh and distinct. While I weeded, other more desperate upkeep was occurring nearby where a sprinkler went *whisha whisha* as it tried to give the ground enough of a drink after the summer day's hours and hours of sun.

Riley read his way along the headstones toward me, every now and then stopping to jot furiously. I noticed him pausing to copy the old-country commemoration off one particular lichen-darkened tombstone:

LUCAS BARCLAY
born August 16, 1852
Nethermuir, Scotland
died June 3, 1917
Gros Ventre, Montana
IN THE GREEN BED 'TIS A LONG SLEEP
ALONE WITH YOUR PAST, MOUNDED DEEP.

Then I was back into my own thoughts and lost track of Riley until he was almost to me, lingering at the grave just the other side of my parents'.

"Who's this one, Jick, an uncle of yours?"

"No." I got up and went slowly over to where Riley was, in front of the stone that read simply:

ALEXANDER STANLEY McCASKILL

"Mariah's uncle. My brother."

Riley gave me a sharp glance of surprise. "I never knew you even had one."

There's just a whole hell of a lot you don't know, I had the surging urge to cry out to him, but that was the pain of this place, these gone people, wanting to find a target.

I hunkered down to work on the chickweed on Alec's grave and managed to answer Riley only: "No, I don't guess you had any way of knowing. Alec was killed in the war. Although by now I suppose a person has to specify which one. The Second World War." The desert in Tunisia in 1943, the German plane slipping out of the low suppertime sun on its strafing run. The bodies, this one among them, in the darkening sand.

Whisha, the lawn sprinkler slung its arc of water down the cemetery knoll below us, then an arc back up the slope, *whisha.* After a minute I glanced at Riley; rare for him to be wordless that long. He was looking at me like a cat who'd just been given a bath. Which surprised me until I remembered: Riley had his own turn at war. Not that he ever would say much about it, but the once I had outright asked him what it had been like in Vietnam he answered almost conversationally: "Nam was a fucking mess. But what else would anybody expect it to be?" So it must have been the cumulative total of war, wars, that had him gazing into me and beyond to my destroyed brother.

"How old was he when—" Riley indicated with a nod of his head at Alec's grave.

"Twenty-two, a little short of twenty-three." Riley himself I knew was born in 1950; how distant must seem a life that ended seven years before his began, yet even now I thought of Alec as only newly dead.

Riley faintly tapped his notebook with his pen. He appeared to be thinking it over, whether to go on with the topic of Alec. Being Riley, he of course did. "You named Lexa after him."

"Kind of, yeah. That 'Alexander' has been in the family ever since they crossed the water from Scotland, and I guess maybe before. So Marce and I figured we'd pass it on through one of the girls. You got it right, though—Lexa's full name is Alexandra."

Riley was listening in that sponge way he had, as if every word was a droplet he wanted to sop up. His eyes, though, never left Alec's headstone.

"His stone," he said after a little. "It's—different."

By that he meant what was missing. No epitaph, no pair of years summing the sudden span of life. As though even the tombstone carver wasn't sure Alec's story was over with.

"Yeah, well, I guess maybe the folks"—I indicated the side by side graves of my mother and father—"didn't feel they were entitled to any particular last word on Alec. What happened was, there was a family ruckus between them and him. Alec, see, was brighter than he knew what to do with. My folks figured he had a real career ahead of him, maybe as an engineer, once he got out of his cowboy mode. But then he came down with a bad case of what he thought was love and they considered infatuation. In any event, Alec was determined to give up his chance at college and whatever else for it." (My mother bursting out at his news of impending marriage and staying on as a rider for the Double W: *Alec, you will End Up as Nothing More Than a Gimped-Up Saddle Stiff, and I for one Will Not*—) "The girl"—I swallowed hard, thinking of smiling lovely Leona and grinning breakneck Alec, the couple too pretty to last in a hard-edged world—"the girl changed her mind, so all the commotion was over nothing, really. But by then it was too late, too much had been said." (Alec at the other end of the phone line when I tried, beseeched, a summer-end mending between him and our parents: *Jicker, it's—it's all complicated. But I got to go on with what I'm doing. I can't*—Alec's voice there veering from what he was really saying, *I can't give in.*) Riley was watching me a lot more intently than I was comfortable with as I concluded both the weeding of the grave and the remembrance of Alec. "It was just one of those situations that turned out bad for everybody concerned, is all."

"Including you, from the sound of it."

"That is true." Unexpectedly the poisoned truth was rising out of me in flood, to Riley of all people. "I was only a shavetail kid at the time, trying to be on everybody's side and nobody's. But Alec and I somehow got crosswise with each other before that summer was over. It sure as hell wasn't anything I intended, and I think him neither. But it happened. So our last words ever to each other were an argument. By goddamn telephone, no less. The war came, off Alec went, then I did too. And then—" I indicated the tombstone and had to swallow hard to finish. "I have always hated how this turned out. Us ending as brothers with bad feelings between. Over somebody . . . something that didn't amount to all that much."

I could still feel Riley silently watching me. I cleared my throat and looked off to the sharp outline of the mountains against the dusk sky. "Getting dark. You got the epitaphs you wanted?"

Riley glanced at the remainder of unread headstones, then at me. "Enough," he said.

The Bago rumbled across the plank bridge of English Creek and I steered off the county road to head up the North Fork, past the distinctive knob overlooking that smaller valley.

In front of me now stood Breed Butte, whose slow arc of rise divides the watersheds of English Creek and Noon Creek beyond. I concentrated on creeping the motorhome along the rough road track, all the while watching and watching the grassy shoulders of Breed Butte and other hillsides for any sign of the North Fork's current residents, my sheep. I can probably never justify it in dollars, but midway through the ungodly dry summer of '85 I bought this North Fork land so as not to overgraze the short grass crop of my Noon Creek pastureland. As the drought hung on, every year perilous until finally this good green one, the North Fork became my ranch's summer salvation. This handful of valley with its twining line of creek had its moment during the homesteading era, when the North Fork was known as Scotch Heaven because of all the families—McCaskills, Barclays, Duffs, Frews, Findlaters, others—who alit in here like thistledrift from the old country, but the land had lain all but empty since. Empty but echoing. As I knew now from those letters in Helena, one of these Scotch Heaven homesteads harbored a silent struggle within it—*the matter is, Angus was in love with my Anna all the years of our marriage.* My grandfather Angus and the loved Anna he never attained. My grandmother Adair, in exile from Scotland and her own marriage as well. The first McCaskill battleground of the heart.

No sheep either. The only telltale splotch of light color was the herder's canvas-roofed sheepwagon high on the nearest shoulder of Breed Butte and so I veered the Bago from the creekside route to the sidetrack leading up to there, really no more than twin lines of ruts made long ago. Geared down, the Bago steadily growled its way up the slope, the dark timbered summit of the butte above to the west. The sheepwagon stood amid the buildings, what was left of them now that roofs had caved in and century-old corners were rotting out, of Walter Kyle's old place. I guess more truly the Rob Barclay place, as my father had always called it, for the original homesteader here—a nephew or some such of the Lucas Barclay with the grandly proclaiming tombstone. This Barclay must have been a stubborn cuss, to cocklebur himself so high and alone on Breed Butte for the sake of its lordly view. Like him, though, my current herder preferred to have the wagon up here even though it meant hauling water from the North Fork; a dusty reservoir about a quarter of a mile west of the falling-down buildings testified that there'd once been a spring there but it long since had dried up. I unloaded the groceries in the wagon and climbed back into the Winnebago to resume the search for the sheep and their keeper.

On impulse I drove to the brow of the slope above the buildings instead of back down to the creek road immediately. As a rancher trying to make a living from this country I subscribe to the reminder that view is particularly hard to get a fork into. Yet I somehow didn't want to pass up this divideline chance to sightsee. Onward east from where I was parked on Breed Butte now, a kind of veranda of land runs parallel between English Creek and Noon Creek, a low square-edged plateau keeping their valleys apart until they at last flow into the Two Medicine River. In boyhood Julys, I rode horseback across that benchland at dawn to help with the haying on Noon Creek. When the sun rose out of the Sweetgrass Hills and caught my horse and me, our combined shadow shot a couple of hundred feet across the grassland, a stretched version of us as if the earth and life had instantly wildly expanded.

But for once my main attention was ahead instead of back. Between the benchlands of the Blackfeet Reservation in the distance and my vantage point there on Breed Butte the broad valley of Noon Creek could be seen, the willowed stream winding through hay meadows and past swales of pasture, a majority of it the Double W's holdings. Of that entire north face of the Two Medicine country I was zeroed in on the corner of land directly below toward the mountains, my ranch. The old Reese house that was now the cookhouse. The new house, all possible windows to the west and the mountains, that Marcella and I had built. The line of Lombardy poplars marking our driveway in from the Noon Creek road. The lambing shed. Even the upstream bend of hayfield where Kenny and Darleen were baling. Every bit of it could be enumerated from here.

Enumerating is one thing and making it all add up is a hell of another. Oh, I had tried. I'd even had the ranch put through a computer earlier this year. A Bozeman outfit in the land analysis business programmed it all for me and what printed out was that, no, the place couldn't be converted into a dude ranch because with the existing Choteau dudity colonies in one direction and Glacier National Park in the other, Noon Creek was not "destination-specific" enough to compete; that maybe a little money could be made by selling hay from the ranch's irrigated meadows, if the drought cycle continued and if I wanted to try to live on other people's misfortune; that, yes, when you came right down to it, this land and locale were best fitted to support Animal Units, economic lingo for cattle or the band of sheep I already had on the place (wherever the hell they were at the moment). In short, the wisdom of the microchips amounted to pretty much the local knowledge I already possessed. That to make a go of the ranch, you had to hard-learn its daily elements. Pace your body through one piece of work after another, paying heed always to the living components—the sheep, the grass, the hay—but the gravitational wear and tear on fences and sheds and roads and equipment also somehow attended to, so that you are able to reliably tell yourself at nightfall, that was as much of a day as I can do. Then get up and do it again 364 tomorrows in a row. Sitting there seeing the ranch in its every detail, knowing every ounce of work it required, Jesus but how I right then wished for fifteen years off my age. I'd have settled for five. Yet truth knows every way to nag. Even if I had seen that many fewer calendars, would it do any good in terms of the ranch ultimately? Maybe people from now on are going to exist on bean sprouts and wear polyester all over themselves, and lamb and wool belong behind glass in a museum. Maybe what I have known how to do in life, which is ranching, simply does not register any more.

It took considerable driving and squinting, back down to the creek road and on up the North Fork toward the opposite shoulder of Breed Butte, before I spotted the sheep fluffed out across a slope. Against the skyline on the ridge above them was the thin, almost gaunt figure of my herder, patchwork black and white dog alongside.

The sight of the sheep sent my spirits up and up as I drove nearer. In a nice scatter along the saddleback ridge between Breed Butte and the foothills, their noses down in the business of grazing, the ewes were a thousand daubs of soft gray against the tan grass and beside them their lambs were their smaller disorderly shadows. As much as ever I looked forward to moseying over and slowly sifting through the band, estimating the lambs' gain and listening to the clonking sound of the bellwether's bell, always pleasure. But the iron etiquette between camptender and sheepherder dictated that I must go visit with the herder first. I climbed out of the Bago and started up the slope to her.

Helen Ramplinger was my herder this summer and the past two. Tall for a woman, gawky really; somewhere well into her thirties, with not a bad face but strands of her long hair constantly blowing across it like random lines of a web. I was somewhat bothered about having so skinny a sheepherder, for fear people would blame it on the way I fed. But I honestly did provide Helen whatever groceries she ordered—it was just that she was a strict vegetarian. She had come into the Two country to join up with some back-to-the-earth health-foody types, granolas as they were locally known, out of a background of drugs and who knew what else. I admit, it stopped me in my tracks when Helen learned I needed a herder and came and asked for the job. Marcella, too; as she said, she figured that as Dode Withrow's daughter she'd listened to every issue involving sheepherders that was possible but now here was gender. It ended up that Marce and I agreed that although Helen's past of drugs had turned her into a bit of a space case, she seemed an earnest soul and maybe was only just drifty enough to be in tune with the sheep. So it had proved out, and I was feeling retroactively clever now as I drew near enough to begin conversation with her.

"Jick, I'm quitting," Helen greeted me.

I blanched, inside as well as out. Across the years I had been met with that pronouncement from sheepherders frequently and a significant proportion of the time they meant it. If they burned supper or got a pebble in their shoe or the sky wasn't blue enough to suit them, by sheepherder logic it was automatically the boss's fault, and I as boss had tried to talk sweetness to sour herders on more occasions than I cared to count. Here and now, I most definitely did not want to lose this one. With herders scarcer than hen's teeth these days and Kenny and Darleen tied up in haying and me kiting around the state with Mariah and Riley, what in the name of Christ was I going to do with this band of sheep if Helen walked off the job?

"Aw, hell, Helen. You don't want to do that. Let's talk this over, what do you say." I made myself swallow away the usual alphabet of sheepherder negotiation—fancier food, a pair of binoculars, a new dog—and go directly to Z: "If it's a matter of wages, times are awful tough right now, but I guess maybe I could—"

"Hey, I didn't mean now." Helen gave me an offended look. "I mean next summer. I've had some time"—she gestured vaguely around us, as if the minutes and hours of her thinking season were here in a herd like the sheep—"to get my head straight, and I've decided I'm not going to be a herder any more. I'll miss it, though," she assured me.

Momentarily relieved but still apprehensive, I asked: "What is it you're going to do, then?"

"Work with rocks."

"Huh?"

"Sure, you know. Rocks. These." She reached down between

the bunchgrass and picked up a speckled specimen the size of a grapefruit. The dog looked on with interest. "Don't you ever wonder what's in them, Jick? Their colors and stuff? You can polish them up and really have something, you know." Helen peered at me through flying threads of her hair. "Gemology," she stated. "That's what I want to do. Get a job as a rock person, polishing them up and fitting them into rings and belt buckles and bolo ties. I heard about a business out in Oregon where they do that. So I'm gonna go there. Not until after we ship the lambs this fall, though."

Helen gently put the young boulder down on the ground between the inquisitive dog and me, straightened to her full height, then gazed around in wistful fashion, down into the valley of the North Fork, and north toward Noon Creek, and up toward the dark-timbered climb of Breed Butte between the two drainages, and at last around to me again. "This is real good country for rocks, Jick," she said hopefully.

It was my turn to gesture grandly. "Helen, any rocks in my possession"—and on the land we stood on I had millions of them—"you are absolutely welcome to."

My sheepherder's change of career to rocks had not left my mind by that evening, but it did have to stand in line with everything else.

Kenny and Darleen and I were just done with supper when something about the size of a red breadbox buzzed into the yard and parked in the shadow of the Bago. Some dry-fly fisherman wanting to see how Noon Creek trout react to pieces of fuzz on the end of a line, was our unanimous guess, but huh uh. Doors of the squarish little red toy opened and out of it unfolded Mariah and Riley.

"It's a Yugo," Mariah informed us before I could even open my trap to ask, once she'd pecked me a kiss and said hi to Kenny and Darleen and they'd had the dubious pleasure of meeting Riley. "As close as the *Montanian*'s budget will ever come to Riley's dream of renting a Buick convertible."

"She just has no concept of what an expense account is for," Riley confided to Kenny and Darleen as if they were his lifelong co-conspirators. "I could have done arithmetic camouflage on that Buick so easy."

"Oh, sure, I can see it now—*'pencils and paper, $97.50 a*

day,' " Mariah mocked him right back but with most of a grin. "Send the BB a signed confession while you're at it, why don't you."

Well, well, well. Positively sunny, were they both, after their Helena delving. That was one thing about Mariah—putting herself to work always improved her mood. Apparently the same was true of goddamn Riley. They seemed to have found their writing and picture-taking legs. Until one of them next delivered the other a kick with a frozen overshoe again, anyway.

"Darleen, don't you think travel agrees with him?" my newly zippy daughter turned her commentary onto me. "Except for his facial grooming." It was something, how Mariah could be bossy and persuasive at the same time. Yet I didn't even bristle at that, appreciably, because I was too busy noticing how much she looked in her element here. In this kitchen, this house—this ranch—where she had grown up. She moved as if the air recognized her and sped her into grooves it had been saving for her, as she crossed the kitchen and planted her fanny against the sink counter in the perfect comfortable lean to be found there, reaching without needing to look into the silverware drawer for forks for Riley and her when Darleen tried to negotiate supper into them and they compromised with her on monstrous pieces of rhubarb pie. Every motion, as smooth as if she knew it blindfolded. Then it struck me. Mariah *was* the element here. The grin as she kept kidding with Darleen and Kenny and Riley was her mother's grin, Marcella's quick wit glinting in this kitchen once again. The erectness, the well-defined collarbones that stated that life was about to be firmly breasted through—those were *my* mother's, definitive Beth McCaskill who had been born on this ranch as a Reese. Born of Anna Ramsay Reese, *ever her own pilot through life, is my Anna.* And on the Scotch Heaven side, the McCaskill side, Adair odd in her ways but persevering for as long as there was anything to persevere for. Mariah: as daughter, granddaughter, great-granddaughter, the time-spun sum of them all? Yet her own distinct version as well. The lanky grace that begins right there in her face and flows down the longish but accomplished geometries of her body, the turn of mind that takes her into the cave of her camera, those are her own, Mariah rara.

And couple Riley with her, the set of shoulders that had shrugged off my offer of this ranch. Right now he was as electric

as that commotion of hair of his, regaling Kenny and Darleen
with the time he'd written in his column that *some of the Governor's notions are vast and some are half-vast* and the BB didn't get
it until the Guv's press secretary angrily called and suggested he
try reading it out loud. I had to grant, there was a mind clicking
behind that wiseacre face. There were a lot of places in the
world where they would license Riley's head as a dangerous
weapon. I eyed him relentlessly while the general chitchat was
going on, wanting to see some sign of regret or other bother show
up in him here on the ranch he had rejected, here across the
kitchen from the woman he could have made that future with. I
might as well have wished for him to register earthquakes in
China.

"I gotta see what's under the hood of that Hugo," Kenny soon
exclaimed, squirming up out of his chair. "You want to come
take a look, Darleen?"

"Thanks just the same," demurred Darleen placidly. "Don't
look too long, hon. We've got to get to Choteau. My folks'
anniversary," she explained to the rest of us. "We hate like
anything to miss the centennial shindig in town tonight, but you
can tell us all about it in the morning, Jick."

This caused me to ponder Darleen and whether there was
some kind of secret sisterhood by which she had become an ally
of Althea Frew, but I ultimately dismissed the suspicion. Darleen
isn't your ally type. Anyway I now had to tell Mariah what my
centennial involvement was all about—Riley had his ears hanging out too—and transmit the request for her to take some
commemorative pictures for Gros Ventre posterity. She rolled
her eyes at the mention of Althea, but concluded as I did that we
might as well go in tonight and get it over with.

"Mind if I tag along?" Riley asked in a supersweet way.

"Yeah," I confirmed. "But I imagine you will anyway, huh?"

"No problem," he asserted, which had become a major part of
his vocabulary since we met up with the Baloney Expressers.
"I'll be next thing to invisible."

The sun was flattening down behind Roman Reef for the night
as the three of us left for town. Behind us the peaks and crags of
the Rocky Mountain Front were standing their tallest there at
the deepening of evening, while the Two Medicine country
around us rested in soft shadows unrolling under that sunset

outline of the mountains. This may be my own private theory
about such summer evenings but it has always seemed to me
that lulls of this sort are how a person heals from the other
weather of this land, for the light calmly going takes with it the
grievances that the Two is a country where the wind wears away
at you on a daily basis, where drought is never far from happening, where the valley bottoms now in the perfect shirtsleeve
climate of summer dusk were thirty-five degrees below zero in
the nights of February.

The Bago kept pace with that pretty time between day and
night as the road swung up onto the benchland between Noon
Creek and English Creek. Until, of course, Riley set things off.
Maybe a genealogist could trace whether his talent for aggravation ran in the family for hundreds of generations or whether the
knack was a spontaneous cosmic outbreak with him like, say,
sunspots. Either way, there on the road into town he apparently
did not even need to try, to succeed in ruffling my feathers.
Merely gawked ahead at the strategic moment and declared,
"I'll be damned. Ye Olde Wild West comes to Noon Creek,
hmm?"

"Aw, that bastardly thing," I murmured in disgust. "If they
want something weird hung, they ought to hang themselves up
by their—"

But he'd roused Mariah and her camera. In the passenger seat
she suddenly spoke up. "No, wait, Riley's right." Since when?
The next was inevitable. "Pull over," she directed, "and let me
get some shots of that against those clouds."

The summer sky, with a couple of hours of evening light yet to
be eked out, was streaked with high goldenish strands, the
decorative dehydrated kind called mare's tail. Clouds are one
matter and what's under them is another. Beside us where I had
reluctantly halted the motorhome stood the main gate into the
Double W. A high frame made of a crosspiece supported by
posts big as telephone poles and almost as tall, it had loomed in
the middle of that benchland for as long as I could remember.
Until not so many years ago the sign hanging from the crosspiece
had proclaimed the Williamsons as owners of everything that
was being looked at. Now it read:

WW RANCH
INCORPORATED

More than that, though. Just under the sign, a steer skull swung in the breeze where it was hung on a cable between the gateposts. Weather-bleached white as mica, short curved Hereford horns pointing, eye sockets endlessly staring.

That skull locket against the Double W sky was the idea of one of the managers who'd been sent out before Shaun Finletter was installed in the job a year or so ago. Goddamn such people. I drove past that dangling skull whenever I went to or from town and it got my goat every single time. That skull, I knew, was from a boneyard in a coulee near my east fenceline with the Double W, where there were the carcasses of hundreds of head of Double W cattle that piled up and died in the blizzard of 1979. Even the Williamsons, who always had more cattle than they had country for and took winter die-offs as part of their way of business, never used the skulls as trinkets.

"Guess what, I need somebody in the foreground for scale," Mariah called over from where she was absorbedly sighting through her camera. "Somebody real western. Jick, how about if you and your Stetson come stand there under the—"

"I will not."

The flat snap of refusal, in my tone of voice as much as my words—hell, in *me*—startled her. She whirled around to me, her hair swinging, with an odd guilty look.

"Sorry," Mariah offered, rare enough for her, too. "But it's a shot I ought to take. The way it looms there over everything, it makes a statement."

"I know what it makes."

In my mind's eye I saw how I would like to do the deed. Wait until dark. Nothing but blackness on either side of this benchland road until the Double W gateframe comes into the headlights. I flip onto bright, for all possible illumination for this, and stop the Bago about seventy-five feet from the gateway, its sign and the skull under swaying slightly in the night breeze that coasts down along Noon Creek. I reach to the passenger seat where the shotgun is riding, step out of the motorhome and go in front of the headlights to load both barrels of the weapon. Bringing the butt of the shotgun to my shoulder I sight upward. Do I imagine, or does the steer skull seem to sway less, quiet itself in the breeze, as I aim? I fire both barrels at once, shards and chunks of the skull spraying away into the night. One eye socket and horn dangle from the wire. Close enough. I climb back in the

Bago and head toward a particularly remote sinkhole I know of
to dispose of the shotgun.

I brought myself back from that wishdream, to Mariah, to
what we were saying to each other. "Take a picture of the
goddamn thing if you think you have to," I finished to her, "but
it's going to be without me in it."

All was as silent as the suspended clouds for a long moment.
Then Riley came climbing over the gearbox hump of the Bago
past me and out the passenger door. Without a word he strode
across the road and centered himself in the gateway for my
daughter.

One whole hell of a promising evening, then, by the time we
hit Gros Ventre and were heading into the Medicine Lodge Bar.
Bar and Cafe, I'd better get used to saying, for the enterprise
took on a split personality when Fred Musgreave bought it a few
years ago. The vital part, the bar, was pretty much the same as
ever, a dark oaken span polished to a sacred shine by generations of elbows, its long mirror and shelves of bottles and glasses
a reflective backdrop for contemplation. But the other half of the
wide old wooden building, where there likely were poker tables
in the early days and in more recent memory a lineup of maroon
booths which were rarely patronized, Fred had closed off with a
divider and turned that outlying portion into an eatery. ("Can't
hurt," his economic reasoning ran. "Could help.") By this time
of evening, though, tourists sped on through to Glacier Park for
the night and anybody local who was going to eat supper out
would have done so a couple of hours ago, and thus Fred didn't
mind providing the Medicine Lodge's dining side as the meeting
place on centennial committee nights.

He must have had his moments of wishing these were paying
customers, however. Through the cafe window we could see the
place was pretty well jammed. Ranchers and farmers in there
jawing at each other about crops and livestock prices, all trade-
marked with summer-tanned faces and pale foreheads as if bearing instructions *fit hat on at this line*. Of the women, a dressy few
were in oldfangled centennial raiment, but most had restrained
themselves. Beside me as we headed in I heard Mariah already
grappling camera gear out of her Appaloosa bag.

The three of us stopped instantly inside the cafe door.
We had to. Our feet were in a tangle of power cords, as if

we'd gotten ensnared in some kind of ankle-high electrification project.

"Aw, crud," Riley uttered, grimacing up from the mess we'd stepped in to its source just inside the entryway. "Tonsil Vapor Purvis."

"There goes the neighborhood," agreed Mariah grimly.

Actually the television camera and tripod and lights and other gear were being marshaled by a pair of guys, but I did not have to be much of a guesser to pick out the one Riley and Mariah were moaning about. An expensive head of hair that was trying to be brown and red at the same time—Riley ultimately identified the shade for me as Koppeltone—atop not nearly that boyish a face atop a robin's egg blue sport jacket; below the torso portion that fit on a television screen, bluejeans and jogging shoes.

"Well!" the figure let out in a whinnying way that turned the word into *weh-heh-heh-hell!* "Rileyboy!"

"And you managed to say that without a cue card," Riley answered in mock admiration. Tonsil Vapor Purvis didn't seem to know Mariah or even to care to, but his cameraman and her exchanged frosty nods.

"I haven't noticed you at any of the official centennial events," Tonsil Vapor informed Riley in a voice that rolled out on ball bearings. "Where are you keeping yourself?"

"Working," Riley stated as if that was a neighborhood the televisioneer naturally wouldn't be anywhere around.

"Isn't this centennial fantastic though?" declared Tonsil Vapor. "Have you had a chance to watch my Countdown 100 series?" When Riley shook his head, Tonsil Vapor rotated toward me. When I shook my head, he turned toward Mariah but she already had slid away and was taking pictures of people, cajoling and kidding with them as you can only when you've known them all your life.

"One hundred nightly segments on the centennial," Tonsil Vapor enunciated to the remaining captive pair of us to make sure we grasped the arithmetic.

"No kidding," Riley responded, gazing at Tonsil Vapor with extreme attention as if the centennial was the newest of news and then jotting something down. When he turned the notepad so I could see it, it read: *A $25 haircut on a 25¢ head.*

"Builders of Montana, this week," the TVster was spelling out for us next. "We"—the royal We from the sound of it; the cameraman was showing no proprietary interest whatsoever— "are interviewing people about their occupational contribution to our great state. It occurred to me that an occasion like this, with oldtimers on hand," he sent me a bright smile, damn his blow-dried soul, "would turn up a fascinating livelihood of some kind."

"I don't have a paying occupation," I hastened to head off any interest in me as a specimen, "I'm a rancher."

"What do these epics of yours run, a minute forty?" asked Riley drily.

"No, no, the station is going all out on this. I'm doing *two-and-a-half-minute* segments, would you believe."

Riley let out a little cluck as if that was pretty unbelievable, all right, then sardonically excused himself to go get to work lest television leave him even farther back in the dust. Still leery of being a candidate for oldtimer of the night, I closely tagged off after Riley. We left Tonsil Vapor Purvis fussing to his camera-man, "This doesn't make it for my opening stand-up. Let's set up over there instead."

"Fucking human gumball machine," Riley was muttering as we rounded the partition between the cafe counter and the dining area in back. "Fucking television has the attention span of a—"

He halted so abruptly I smacked into his back. Riley, though, never even seemed to notice, in the stock-still way he was staring toward the rear of the cafe.

"WHAT is *that?*" his eventual question piped out in a three-note tune.

Golden as the light of the dawn sun, the cloth creation embla-zoned the entire back wall of the cafe and then some. That is, the roomwide cascade of fabric flowed down from where it was tacked on lath along the top of the wall and surged up like a cresting molten wave at the worktables and quilting frames where stitchery was being performed on it, then spilled forward onto the floor in flaxen pools of yet to be sewn material.

Add in all the people bent over sewing machines or plucking away with needles or just hovering around admiring and gab-bing, and I suppose you could think, as Riley obviously did, that the town of Gros Ventre had gone on a binge and decided to tent itself over.

"Just what it looks like," I enlightened the scribbler. "Our centennial flag."

Mariah whizzed past us.

"Looks like they're getting ready to declare independence, doesn't it," she appraised the room-swallowing flag and kept right on going to zero in on the sewing battalion.

Riley still stood there gawking like a moron trying to read an eyechart, although the flag didn't seem to me all that tough to decipher. Plain as anything, the line of designs spaced across its top like a border pattern was livestock:

And down the sides the motifs were homestead cabins and ranch houses:

And although the sewing brigade had a way to go to get there, it only took the least imagination to see that the bottom border needed to be forest and stream:

In extenuation of Riley, it was true that the flag's full effect would not register until all the other elements were in place on it. The project the Heart Butte schoolkids were doing, for instance, of a Blackfeet chief's headdress in black and white cloth to resemble eagle feathers—rampant, as is said in flag lingo. And the combined contribution of the English Creek and Noon Creek ranch families, one entire cloth panel—the flag was so big it was

being done in lengthwise sections, which were then quilted
together—which was going to be a sawtooth pattern of purple-
blue embroidery all the way across, signifying the mountains
across the Two country's western skyline. Then at the hem of
the mountains would come a cluster of buildings, being sewn
away at by several townspeople even as Riley and I watched, to
represent Gros Ventre: the spiked helmet outline of the Sedgwick
House hotel, the sharp church steeples, the oldstyle square front
of the Medicine Lodge itself, and so on. Finally, to top it all off,
so to speak, for actually this constituted the very center of the
whole flag scheme: the sun. Atop a dark seam of horizon the
molten arc of it, spiffily done in reddish orange fabric that even
looked hot, just beginning to claim the sky for the day. And
over, under, and around the sun, in mighty letters of black, the
message:

THE TWO MEDICINE COUNTRY

1889   1989

GREETS THE DAWN OF MONTANA

Riley at last managed to show some vital signs. He wondered
out loud, plenty loud:

"Who thought up this sucker?"

That particular question I was not keen to deal with because,
when you traced right back to it, the party who brought up the
flag idea in the first place was more or less me. History's jukebox, John Angus McCaskill. It had been last fall when our
steering committee was flummoxing around for some event worthy of marking Montana's centennial with, when Althea Frew
pined what a shame it was that we didn't know what had gone on
in Gros Ventre that epic day of statehood a hundred years ago.
All the cue needed, of course, for me to spout off what I'd so
long ago heard from Toussaint Rennie, that the 1889 citizenry of
Gros Ventre, such as there was of it back then, took it into their
collective head to be the very first to fly the revised American
flag when Montana came onto it as the forty-first star and so got
up early enough to do that municipal flag-hoisting at the exact
crack of day. Which inspired some other member of our committee to suggest that we simply emulate our forebears by raising a
forty-one-starred flag at dawn on Centennial Day. But that was
objected to as a backward step, nine of them in fact, in stars-and-
stripes history. Okay, somebody else proposed, then let's put up
a present-day American flag but a monumentally big one. But

somebody yet again made the point that there were already in existence flags damn near as big as America itself—weren't we seeing Bush practically camped out in front of a whopper of a one during the presidential election campaign?—and we didn't have a prayer of competing in size. You might know it would be Althea who hatched the plan of making our own flag. Contrive our version as big as we could without smothering ourselves in it, sure, but most of all, design and fabricate the whole thing ourselves and hoist the Two Medicine country and Gros Ventre's own heralding banner at dawn on the centennial.

"It just kind of occurred," I summarized in answer to Riley and moved on into the needlery scene, tagged after by him. Primarily the women were getting things accomplished there at the sewing machines and worktables while the men mostly were standing around looking wise, both sets being duly chronicled by Mariah and her camera. Being greeted by the dozens and greeting back in equal number, I wound my way through the assemblage until I reached the quilting frame which held the panel our English Creek–Noon Creek mountain panorama was being embroidered on.

Lifelong familiar outlines met me there. Roman Reef's great bow of rimrock. The tall slopes of Phantom Woman Mountain. The Flume Gulch canyonline where Noon Creek has its source, and opposite that the comblike outcropping of Rooster Mountain. Really quite beautiful, how all the high skyline of the Two Medicine was transposed there onto the flag in heaviest darning yarn. All, that is, except the finale. The northmost mountain form, Jericho Reef's unmistakable wall-like silhouette, was sketched in pencil on the golden cloth for the next seamstress to follow.

Seamer, rather, for on the Jericho sketch was a pink paper stick-on with Althea's loopy but firm handwriting, which read:

Jick McCaskill—please stitch here!

So if Jericho was going to get sewn it was up to me, and there was no time like the present. "Got any socks you want darned, you should have brought them," I notified Riley and seated myself to perform fancywork.

"You know how to do that?" he asked skeptically as I plucked up the waiting needle and started trying to match the kind of stitches on the other thread mountains.

"Close enough," I said. "I've sewed shut more woolsacks than you can count."

Whether it was my example of industry or not, Riley suddenly snapped out of his tourist mode. "This night might actually turn into something. Hold the fort, Jick, I'm going out to the Bago for my listening gear."

Nature never likes a vacuum. No sooner was I shed of Riley than Howard Stonesifer happened by and stopped to spectate my labors. Which probably was good for my stitching because it lent a little feeling of scrutiny by posterity, Howard being the undertaker.

"Where you been keeping yourself?" Howard asked.

"Out and around," I summarized. "How's the burying business?"

"Mortally slow," he answered as he always did. "Isn't that Riley Wright I just bumped into?"

"I'm sorry to report, it is."

"Mariah and him are back together, eh?"

"They are not. They're just doing a bunch of these centennial stories togeth—with each other, is all. I'm traveling around with them while they do."

He studied down at me. "All three of you are together?"

"Well, yeah, together but not *together*. Thrown in with one another, more like. Howard, it's kind of complicated."

"I imagine it is," Howard said and departed.

My next visitor was none other than Mariah, who by now had cut her photographic swath across the room to those of us at the sewing frames and tables.

"I bet you never knew Betsy Ross had a beard," I addressed to her, jabbing my needle elegantly into the flagcloth as she neared.

It didn't even register on her. She wore a puzzled frown and even more uncharacteristically had dropped the camera from her eyes and was drilling a snake-killing gaze across the room.

I leaned out and saw for myself what was bugging her. Our centennial bunch was not exactly a youth group and wherever there was a Gros Ventrian wearing glasses, which was to say virtually everywhere, bright points of light glittered off both lenses. Or if a person happened to be anywhere near a wall, his or her skin was paled out and huge shadows were flung up behind the wan spectre. Any shot by Mariah was going to look like fireflies flitting through a convalescent ward.

Perfectly unconcerned about dazzling the populace, Tonsil Vapor had decided our centennial flag was a backdrop worthy of him and was having his cameraman move the lightstands here and there in front of the sewing tables. What astounded me was that everybody was pretending to be unaware they were being immersed in a pool of television light. Squint and bear it, was the code of the televised.

Not with Mariah. Under the pressure of her glower, the TV cameraman roused himself enough to shrug and indicate with a jerk of his head that Tonsil Vapor was the impresario here. Tonsil Vapor meanwhile was holding his sport-jacket sleeve against the wall of flag to make sure robin's egg blue went well with golden.

Mariah marched on him.

"Hey, I'm getting bounce from your lights in every shot I try. How about please holding off for a couple of minutes until I'm done back here?"

"We're setting up for my opening stand-up," Tonsil Vapor informed her.

"I can tell you are. How-about-turning-off-your-lights-for-two-minutes-while-I-finish-shooting-here."

"Television has every right to be here," Tonsil Vapor huffed. "This is a public event."

"That's the whole fucking point," Mariah elucidated. "It's not yours to hog."

"Let's do my stand-up," Tonsil Vapor directed past her to his cameraman and focused his concern on whether his tie was hanging straight.

"Whoa," Mariah told the TV pair. "If you're so determined to shoot, we'll all shoot."

She reached in her gear bag and pulled out a fresh camera, aiming it into the pleasantly surprised visage of Tonsil Vapor. I was more than surprised: it was the motorized one she'd used to take the rapid-fire photographs of the marauding buffalo bull at Moiese. Tonsil Vapor Purvis didn't look to me like he was that much of a mobile target.

With the bright wash of light on him, he fingered the knot of his tie. Brought his microphone up. Aimed his chin toward the lens of the TV camera. "Ready?" he asked his cameraman, although with a little peek out the corner of his eye at Mariah to make sure she was set to shoot, too. The TV cameraman echoed "Ready" flatly back.

"This is Paul *whingwhingwhing* Purvis, bringing you another Countdown 100 *whingwhingwhing* moment from here in *whing-whing—*"

"Cut!" yelped the cameraman, pulling the earphones out away from his ears. Mariah quit firing the motorized shutter and the ricochet sounds stopped.

Tonsil Vapor swiveled his head toward her. "Your camera. We're picking up the noise."

"That's okay, no charge," Mariah answered calmly, keeping the offending camera zeroed into Tonsil Vapor's face. "You've been donating all kinds of light into my photography."

"Seriously, here," Tonsil Vapor said, a bit pouty. "We have an opening stand-up to do."

"Up you and your stand-up both," Mariah told him. "This is a public event and my gear has every right to be here."

Tonsil Vapor stared at her. Uncertainly he edged the microphone up toward his mouth. Mariah triggered off a couple of *whings* and he jerked the mike back down.

With a scowl, Tonsil Vapor swiveled his head the other direction and addressed his cameraman. "Can we edit out her noise?" The cameraman gave him the French salute, shrugging his shoulders and raising the palms of his hands at the same time.

Tonsil Vapor visibly thought over the matter. Mariah did not bring the commotional camera down from her eye until he announced, "Actually, the bar is a more picturesque spot to do my opening stand-up."

Riley, prince of oblivion, sashayed back in from the Bago with his tape recorder as TVdom was withdrawing to the bar and Mariah was setting to work again on the sewing scene at the far end of the flag. He made a beeline to me.

"Quite a turnout, Jick," he observed brilliantly.

"Mmhmm," I replied and sewed onward.

"Lots of folks," he said as if having tabulated.

"Quite a bunch," I confirmed.

"I was wondering if you could kind of sort them out to me, so I can figure out good ones to talk to," he admitted, indicating to the tape recorder as if this was the machine's idea rather than his. "You know more about everybody here than they do about themselves."

"Gee, Riley, I wouldn't know where to start." I did a couple more stiches before adding: "Everybody in the Two country is equally unique."

Had I wanted, I indeed could have been Riley's accomplice on almost anyone in that filled room, for the Two Medicine country was out in force tonight. These are not the best of times for towns like Gros Ventre or the rural neighborhoods they are tied to. The young go away, the discount stores draw shopping dollars off to bigger places, the land that has always been the hope of such areas is thinner and thinner of people and promise. Yet, maybe because the human animal cannot think trouble all the time, anybody with a foot or wheel to get here had come tonight to advance the community's centennial rite. All the couples from the ranches along English Creek: Harold and Melody Busby, Bob and Janie Rozier, Olaf and Sonia Florin. From up the South Fork, Tricia and Gib Hahn, who ran the old Withrow and Hahn ranches combined. My longtime Noon Creek neighbor Tobe Egan, retired to town now. A number of the farm families from out east of town, Walsinghams and Priddys and Van Der Wendes, Tebbetses and Kerzes and Joneses. Townspeople by battalions: Joe and Myrna Prentiss from the Merc, the Muldauers who ran the Coast-to-Coast hardware store, Jo Ann and Vern Cooder from the Rexall drugstore. Riley's infinite faith in me to the contrary, one pair I didn't know the names of yet—the young couple who had opened a video parlor where The Toggery clothing store used to be. The bank manager Norman Peyser and his wife Barbara. Flo and Sam Vissert from the Pastime Bar three doors down the street. Others and others—not least, the new Gros Ventrian whom I addressed now as he bustled past Riley and me carrying a coffee urn as big as he was. "Nguyen, how you doing?"

"Doing just right!" Nguyen Trang Hoc and his wife Kieu and their three kids were being sponsored by a couple of the churches there in town. They were boat people, had come out of Vietnam in one of those hell voyages. Nguyen worked as a waiter here in the Medicine Lodge cafe, already speaking English sentences of utmost enthusiasm: "Here is your menu! I will let you look! Then we will talk some more!"

Naturally Riley was scanning the night's civic outpouring in

RIDE WITH ME, MARIAH MONTANA

his own cockeyed way. "Who's the resurrection of Buffalo Bill over there?" he asked, blinking inquisitively toward the figure hobbling ever so slowly through the front door.

"Aw," I began, "that's just—" and then the brainstorm caught up with me.

I identified the individual to Riley with conspicuous enthusiasm. "Been here in the Two country since its footings were poured. You might find him highly interesting to talk to. Garland's kind of a shy type, but I bet if you tell him you're from the newspaper that would encourage him a little."

"History on the hoof, hmm?" Riley perked right up and headed toward the front. "You're starting to show real talent for this centennial stuff, Jick."

While it is true I was the full length of the cafe away from Riley's introduction to the arrivee, there was no lack of volume to hearing what followed.

"NEWSPAPER! JUST THE GUY I WANT TO SEE! YOUNG FELLOW, WHAT YOU OUGHT TO BE WRITING A STORY ABOUT IS ME! YOU KNOW, I WAS BORN WITH THE GOSHDAMN CENTURY!"

Eyes rolled in all of us who were within earshot, which was to say everybody in the Medicine Lodge. Multiply the crowd of us by the total of times we had each heard the nativity scene of Good Help Hebner and you had a long number. Riley didn't seem grateful to be the first fresh listener of this eon, either. The look he sent me still had sting in it after traveling the length of the cafe. I concentrated on needlework and maintaining a straight face. "BY NOW HALF THIS COUNTRY IS HEBNERS, YOUNG FELLOW! AND I STARTED EVERY ONE OF THEM OUT OF THE CHUTE!"

Riley had no way of knowing it but that particular procreatorial brag was as close to the truth as Good Help was ever likely to come. Which made me shake my head all the more at the fact that it had taken the old so-and-so until his eighty-ninth year to start looking paternal, let alone patriarchal. For as long as I could remember, Good Help—need I say, that nickname implied the exact opposite—had lazed through life under about a week's grayish grizzle of whiskers; never enough to count as an intentional beard, never so little as to signify he had bothered to shave within recent memory. But now for the centennial he somehow had blossomed forth in creamy mustache and goatee. To me it still was a matter of close opinion whether Good Help

127

more resembled Buffalo Bill or a billy goat, but definitely his new facial adornment was eyecatching.

"YOU GOT TO GO DO WHAT, YOUNG FELLOW? SPEAK UP, I'M GETTING SO DEAF I CAN'T HEAR MYSELF FART!" I couldn't actually hear either the excuse Riley was employing to extricate himself, but Good Help provided everybody in town the gist of it: "GOT TO GO SEE A MAN ABOUT A DOG, HUH? YOU KNOW WHAT THEY SAY, STAND UP CLOSE TO THE TROUGH, THE NEXT FELLOW MIGHT BE BAREFOOT!"

While Riley now tried to make an invisible voyage to the men's room in the bar half of the Medicine Lodge, I chuckled and checked on Mariah's doings. Easily enough done. She was wearing the turquoise shirt she'd had on at the Fourth of July rodeo and you could see her from here to Sunday. As she gravitated through the crowd, ever scouting for the next camera moment, it struck me what a picture she made herself.

"Oh, Jick, I'm so relieved to see you here," Althea Frew pounced in on me out of nowhere. In her centennial getup of a floor-length gingham dress with a poke bonnet, she looked as if she'd just trundled in by prairie schooner. "We were afraid you'd given up on the committee."

"Would I do that?" I denied, right then wishing I had.

"It's nice to see you back in the swim of things," she assured me and patted my arm. Althea was the kind of person full of pats. "Can't I bring you a cup of coffee?" she offered avidly.

Only if it is big enough for me to torpedo you in, I thought to myself. Dave Frew had died of emphysema a year or so ago and all too evidently Althea had formed the notion that because she was a widow and I now was a widower, we were going to be an ordained pair at gatherings such as this. My own notion was, like hell we were. Already I had dodged her on card parties and square dancing at the Senior Citizens' Center. Althea seemed to regard me as an island just waiting to have her airdropped onto it. Let her land and there'd be an instant new civilization, activities for all my waking hours. Christamighty, I more than anybody knew that I needed refurbishing of some kind from my grief for Marcella. But to put myself up for adoption by Althea . . .

"You take it with just a dab of cream, don't you?" Uh oh. She'd already started to catalogue me. I knew where that would go. If she inkled out the dosage in my coffee, as the night follows the day it would lead to how crisp I like my fish fried and from there onward to my favorite piece of music, on and on until she would know my underwear size.

"Black," I lied. "Don't bother, I'll get myself a cup, I was about to head that direction anyhow."

As I recessed from my sewing and tried to tactically retreat to the coffee urn, Althea fell in step as if I'd invited her along. Wasn't this just ducky, now. She had us in motion in tandem in public, a hearts-and-flowers advertisement for the whole town to see. I craned around for Mariah's reaction to this. For once I was thankful to have her immersed in her picture-taking, across the room with her back to Althea and me as she immortalized Janie Rozier zinging a seam of the flag through her sewing machine.

I will swear on any Bible, I did not have anything major against Althea Frew. But I had nothing for her, either. True, Marcella and I had known her and Dave ever since we were young ranch couples starting out. Neighbors, friends, people who partnered each other a few times a night at dances, but not more than that. You cannot love everyone you know. Love isn't a game of tag, now you're it, now she's it.

I sipped at the plastic cup of coffee Althea bestowed on me and tried not to wince at its bitter taste. For that matter, I had no illusions that Althea was after me for my irresistible romantic allure. Simply put, pickings were slim in the Two Medicine country for women who outlived their husbands, as most of them showed every sign of doing. Here tonight for instance, Howard Stonesifer was one of those mother-smothered bachelors; Althea knew that even if old lady Stonesifer ever passed on, there was no denting Howard's set of habits. Tobe Egan over in the corner was a widower but his health was shot, and why should Althea take on another ill case after the years she had spent with Dave's emphysema? Go through this entire community and the actuarial tables were pretty damn bare for Althea's brand of husband-looking. Which was why yours truly was about to be the recipient of a whopping piece of the *Happy Birthday, Montana!* cake Althea was now adoringly cutting.

Right then Riley re-emerged from the direction of the men's room, cautiously checking around for the whereabouts of Good Help Hebner. I was not keen on fending with him just then, particularly if he was going to notice the close company Althea

was keeping me, but it turned out Riley was pointedly ignoring
my existence and instead migrated directly to Mariah.

Whatever he was saying to her, for once it seemed to be in
earnest. She listened to him warily, but listened. Then came her
speaking turn, and he nodded and nodded as if he couldn't agree
more. It dawned on me that they must be conferring about
whether to do a piece about tonight. I willed Mariah to tell him
to go straight to hell, that their mutual woe of ending up in
marriage had started here when she shot and he wrote that
earlier Gros Ventre centennial shindig. Instead she studied him
with care, then turned and pondered the cafeful of people as if
taking inventory. While Althea yattered at me and I took solace
in cake, Mariah led Riley over near us where Nan Hill, snow-
haired and tiny with age, was sitting sewing.

"Nan, this man would like to talk to you for a story in the
newspaper. How about telling him about doing the washing at
Fort Peck while I take a picture, would you mind?" As Riley
moved in with his tape recorder and a smile that would make
you want to take him home and give him a bed by the fire,
Mariah checked her light meter, then stood back, biting her
lower lip as she held the camera up under her neck, lens pointing up, waiting. Waiting. Then ahead of the moment but somehow having seen it on its way, she swiftly but unobtrusively
shifted the camera over to her eye as the old woman warmed
into the telling.

*Age is humped on her small back. It began to descend there in
1936 in daily hours over a washboard, scrubbing at the Missouri-
mudded clothing of the men at labor on the biggest earthen dam in
the world, Fort Peck. "We went there with just nothing and J. L.
got on as a roustabout. I wanted to find some way of earning, too,
so I put up a sign* Laundry Done Here. *I charged 15¢ for
shirts—and that was washed, ironed, mended and loose buttons
sewed on—and 10¢ for a pair of shorts, another 10¢ for an
undervest, 5¢ for a handkerchief, and 10¢ for a pair of socks.
Any kind of pants was 25¢ for washing and pressing. I had the
business, don't think I didn't. Those three years at Fort Peck, I
always had six lines of clothes hanging in the yard."*

The waltz of the camera, Riley following, led on from Nan to
the Hoc family, Mariah poising in that long-legged crouch of

hers while focusing on the little Hoc girl, her left hand under the camera cupping it upward in an offering way, right hand delicately fingering the lens setting, her shoulderlong flow of hair behind the camera like an extravagant version of the hood a photographer of old would hide his head under, and her voice going through a repertoire of coaxes until one brought out on the little Hoc girl what was not quite a smile but an expression more beautiful than that, Mariah telling her as if they had triumphed together, "Thaaat's what I want to see."

They are Asian delta people, newly come to American mountain headwaters. Their immense journey pivots on the children, especially on the lithe daughter made solemnly older by the presence of two cultures within her. Driver's license, income tax, television, food budget, rock music, all the reckless spill of America must come to her family through the careful funnel of this ten-year-old woman who is now the mother of words to her own parents.

Althea was saying in my ear now, "It's so nice to see Riley back in your family. He and Mariah make such a wonderful couple."

"They are not—"

"People their age, they should take happiness while they can, don't you think?"

What I thought was that people any age shouldn't be trying to fool one another. That I should be able to say flat out to Althea, "Look, terms have not changed between us even though our lives have. I am not second-husband material for you, so kindly just put the pattern away, please."

But that was blunter than can be spoken in a room crowded with everyone who knew us. Even so, Althea didn't take the chance that I might blurt the impolite truth. "Oh foo, look what time it's gotten to be already. I'd better go look over the agenda for our meeting. It'll seem so much more like a committee now that you're back, Jick," she left me with, but not before a last fond assault on my arm, pat pat.

My ears got the next unwelcome traffic, a mimicking voice approaching fast: "He's kind of a shy type, but I bet if you tell him you're from the newspaper . . ."

Innocence seemed the best tack to take with Riley right then. "Get a lot of fascinating stuff out of Good Help, did you?"

"Gobs and gobs," he replied sardonically. "I figured I'd write that he's as intrinsically American as the Mississippi River."

"Oh yeah?"

"Yeah. A mile wide at the mouth."

"Gee," I said, genuinely interested in the prospect, "if you say that in the newspaper about a guy, won't he sue your nuts off?"

"Put your mind at ease," Riley told me. "Jick, damn you, you know that old codger could talk for a week and only ever tell the truth by accident. Even the BB would recognize it as the rankest kind of bullshit." Riley's two-toned gaze left me and went to the wall of fabric behind me. "The real story here is that humongous flag. If you characters ever manage to get it in the air." Riley scanned the room as if in search of anyone capable of that feat. He got as far as Althea, busy in her bonnet, and inquired: "By the way, who's your ladyfriend?"

"She is not—"

"Bashful never won the bushelful," he trilled out, god damn him. "Don't worry, I won't snitch to Mariah that you're busy girling behind her back. So, what's next in this festive evening?"

Barbecuing a fatmouthed newspaper guy over a slow fire, was what I wished could be next on the agenda. But instead I told Riley I had my needlework to tend to, in a tone that let him know it was a pursuit preferable to conversation with him, and headed myself from the coffee urn toward the Two Medicine mountainline panel of the flag.

I wasn't much more than in motion before a voice called out:

"Talk to you a minute can I, Jick?"

I was beginning to wonder: was there a procession all the way out into the street of people lined up to take aim on me?

This voice was that of Shaun Finletter from the Double W and so I at least knew what the sought minute of talk was going to be about. I turned around to Shaun's faceful of blondish fuzz—some of these beardgrowers were maybe going to need a deadline extension to Montana's *bi*centennial—and responded as civilly as I could manage: "How's tricks?"

"Oh, not bad, Jick. Yourself?"

"Just trying to stay level."

Shaun then plunged right down to business, which was the way Finletters were.

"Jick, I been hearing from headquarters. They're still real interested in making you an offer on your place."

"Are they." I felt like adding, are you sure that was headquarters making itself heard instead of hindquarters? But Shaun was a neighbor, even if I did wish his bosses in big offices would take a long walk off a short balcony.

Shaun rattled it off to me. "It's nothing against you at all, Jick . . . just a matter of big-scale economics . . . better able to put maximum animal units on that land . . ." The Double Dub had a great history of that, all right. Running more cattle than it had country for. The original Williamson, Warren, had practically invented overgrazing, and his son Wendell got in on buying up bankrupt smaller ranches during the Depression and *really* sandwiched cattle along Noon Creek from hell to breakfast, and now the corporation computers doubtless were unitizing cows and calves onto every last spear of grass.

Yet it was their business and none of my own, how the Williamsons or the corporaiders comported themselves on WW land they had title to. The patch of earth *I* held title to was the matter here, and Shaun now stated the dollars per acre, a damn impressive sum of them, that WW, Inc. would pay to take the ranch off my hands. "You know that's top dollar, the way things are, Jick."

Shaun was a nice enough human being. Someone who would look you square in the eye, as he was now while I scanned back at him and noticed he was growing beefier, a little more face, a bit more belly, than since I'd last seen him. Actually just a year or so older than Mariah, he and she had gone together a while in high school. My God, the way things click or don't. If that had worked out into marriage instead of her going on to photography and him to an ag econ degree at Bozeman, Shaun might well have been the answer to run my ranch; might have become the one to perpetually tell the Williamsons and WW, Inc. of the world to go to hell, instead of being their errand boy to me.

If I had pounds more of brains I might be smarter, too. I struggled to get myself back on the necessary train of thought. How to reply to the dollar sign. It wasn't as if I hadn't had practice closing one or both eyes to money. The first corporate guy, who'd acted as if he already owned my ranch and me as well, I'd told to stick his offer where the sun doesn't shine. All the others since, one or two every year, I'd just told nothing doing. But now here I was being perfectly polite with Shaun because even though he was the current factotum, I had known his family and him from when he was a waggy pup. Even I had to admit I seemed to be trending away from that original stick-it stance.

Click.

Shaun gave a little jump as if he'd been goosed. For once I didn't even mind that Mariah included me in her picture ambush. It was worth it to see the caught-while-sucking-eggs expression on Shaun.

"Don't let me interrupt Noon Creek man talk," Mariah put forth coolly with the camera still up to her eye. This was a different one than I'd yet seen her use tonight. Did she possibly have a calibre for every occasion?

"It'll keep," said Shaun, wincing at the next *click*. Maybe it had been purely coincidental but after splitting up with Mariah he all but instantly married Amber, who notably stayed home and raised kids. "Think the proposition over and let me know, Jick. Mariah, it's always an event to see you," and he headed rapidly off out of pointblank range.

"He always was about halfway to being a dork," Mariah mentioned as we watched Shaun retreat. "He even necked like he was doing math."

"Yeah, well, he's maybe getting better at his calculations," I let her know. "You sure you don't want a ranch?"

"You saw how far I've gotten from the place," Mariah answered after a moment. "On the way into town."

It took me a moment, too, to discard that incident at the Double W gate. "I guess when you get to my age you're a little touchy about skulls."

"Quit that," she directed quickly. "You're much too young to be as old as you are."

Didn't I wish. But I let that pass and instead took Mariah by the elbow and turned her around to the golden flood of flag cloth. "Something I need you to do." I indicated to the panel where I'd sewn Jericho Reef halfway to completion; the panel for the McCaskills to have their stitches ride the wind on. "Sit down there and immortalize yourself."

"You promise I won't get a reputation for domesticity?" she kidded, but I could see she was tickled pink to be included in the centennial stitchwork.

"Probably not much danger," I said, and we laughed together as we hadn't for a long time.

So Mariah sat and had at it, the needle disappearing and then tugging through another dark dash of the mountainline above the ranch earth where we were both born. "It's like putting ourselves on a quilt, isn't it," her similar thought came out quietly.

"Kind of, yeah." I stood and watched her neat intense work with the needle. "But the next hundred years don't look that simple."

She knew I meant the ranch and whether to sell now or stagger on. "How are you leaning?"

"Both directions. Any advice from somebody redheaded would be a whole lot welcome."

Mariah crinkled a little face and I thought she'd stuck herself. But it turned out to be the topic that was sharp.

"You know I couldn't wait to get off the place when I was growing up," she mused. "Away to college. Away to—where I've been. I got over that and before I knew it I was fond of the place again. The ranch meant, well, it meant you and Mother, in a way. As if it was part of you—some member of the family you and she made out of the land." Now Mariah addressed downward as if reasoning to the sliver of metal passing in and out of the cloth. "But it'll never be part of me in that same way. It hurts to say, but I'm just a visitor at the ranch any more. Lexa and I dealt ourselves out of it by going off to our own lives. That's what happens. You and Mother maybe didn't know you were raising an Alaskan and a Missoulian, but that's how we turned out, didn't we. So it has to be up to you what to do with the place, Dad. It's yours. Not ours in any way that we should have a say."

"You want me to walk over there and tell Shaun the Double Dub's got itself a deal, is that it?"

Mariah swallowed, but both the tug of her needle and the look she sent me stayed steady. "It's up to you," she stood by.

Maybe I would have made that journey across the room to Shaun, right then and there, if Mariah had not abruptly put down her needle in exchange for her camera, twirled a lens on, and aimed in sudden contemplation of something occurring behind me. In curiosity, not to mention self-defense, I shifted half-around to see.

Riley at work. He had sicced his tape recorder onto the lawyer Don Germain, who for once had the quite unlawyerly look that he wasn't sure how he got into this but didn't know how to get out either. Without being able to hear the words, I could tell by the carefully innocent way Riley asked his questions and Don's pursed lips as he cogitated his answers that the interview topic must be something fundamental.

How and when should we lift our own roots? Or as we more usually ask it in this spacious nation, how many times? His were temporarily shifted for him from Rhode Island after law school, when his military stint put him at Malmstrom Air Force Base in Great Falls. Malmstrom made him a galvanized westerner, the shirts with pearlescent snap buttons and the brass belt buckle proclaiming THE BUCKAROO STOPS HERE *on his outside but the original element underneath, so he chose a place (Gros Ventre, but it could have been any of a thousand others) to try this trafficless wide-sky life. He himself tells the joke that the town is too small for one lawyer but big enough for two. Readily enough, too, he reveals his snug fit into his generation's statistics: a second wife, two children, considerable tonnage of vehicles-TVs-VCR-snowmobile-gas barbecue-power tools-satellite dish. It is his wife, though, who teasingly tells that he has been struggling with the decision of whether to keep his centennial contest beard or not, because of the gray showing up in it.*

So, he meets middle age in the mirror these mornings and they debate. "I've really liked living here, don't get me wrong. Cathy and I both would hate to leave Montana. But the money is better almost anywhere else you can name. Sure, this has been a good place to raise the kids. But whether to spend the rest of my life here . . ."

Ever so casually I said to Mariah, "I see you and Riley are piecing up a storm."

"We're managing to," she said, and picked up where she had left off in her stitching.

While Mariah completed Jericho Reef, I decided I had better seize that opportunity to heed a certain call of nature—damn Althea and her loveydovey cups of coffee anyway—and headed myself into the bar toward the men's room.

And popped around the corner into light so extreme it set me back on my heels. Tonsil Vapor and accomplice had Good Help Hebner sitting there posed against the dark oaken bar.

Not even a TV guy would voluntarily go near Good Help if he knew what he was getting himself into, would he? During my business in the men's room I worked out what must have taken place: after his opening stand-up Tonsil Vapor had poked his head back into the supper club, discerned Riley getting both ears loaded by Good Help, and figured there was his ripe interview subject.

When I emerged, Fred Musgreave was behind the near end of the bar, ever so slowly wiping the wood with a dish towel as he eyed the million-watt spectacle. Fred by nature was so untalkative it was said of him that he was an absentee owner even when he was here on the premises of the Medicine Lodge, so I merely walked my fingers along the bar top to indicate to him that this was a night that needed some Johnny and propped myself there to spectate, on the chance that television might be more interesting outside the box than in.

Poised beside Good Help, Tonsil Vapor gave a royal nod, the camera's red light lit up, and he intoned into his microphone: "Here with us now is tonight's builder of Montana, Gros Ventre's own Garland Hebner—born, as he likes to say, with the century. Mr. Hebner, first off let me ask you, what was your line of work?"

"I have did it all," our new TV star airily assured his interlocutor.

"I'm sure you have," emitted Tonsil Vapor with a chuckle that sounded a trifle forced. "But what I meant was, what did you do for a living?"

"I was what you call self-employed."

Self-unemployed was more like it. Garland Hebner's only known activity had been that one that produces children, and as soon as they were big enough to be sent out to herd lamb bunches in the spring or drive a stacker team in haying, Hebner child after Hebner child brought home the only wages that tatterdemalion household ever saw.

"Cut," called out Tonsil Vapor, looking nonplussed. "But Mr. Hebner, this is an interview about how you helped to build Montana. Isn't there *some* interesting job you held, sometime or another?"

This did stump Good Help. He sat there blinking as if each of his eighty-nine years was being projected one after another onto the inside of his eyelids. Until:

"By the Jesus, I remember now! Sure, I had a job! Goshdamn interesting one, too! What it was, I—"

"No, no, wait until we roll and tell me then. Spontaneity is the lifeblood of television, Mr. Hebner. Now, then. Ready?" The cameraman minimally indicated he was, and Good Help appeared to be absolutely primed and cocked. The instant the line-of-work question had been recited again, Good Help got hold of Tonsil Vapor's mike hand, drew the instrument almost into his mouth and pronounced in a kind of quavery roar:

"I was the pigfucker! One entire summer! Ought to been the summer of 19-and-18, no, was it 19-and—"

"Cut!" squawked Tonsil Vapor as if he just had been.

The TV maestro stepped back a large pace, his mouth twice as far open as it had been yet tonight. Holding the microphone protectively against his sport jacket, he took stock of Good Help.

Eventually he managed, "Mr. Hebner, I'm afraid you misheard my question. What I asked you was what you did for a *living*, not—"

"I just was telling you! Don't you hear good? I was the pigfucker! Over across the mountains in that white pine country, in them big woods! Best goshdamn job I ever—"

While Tonsil Vapor expelled in a rapidly rising voice, "But we can't let you say that *on the AIR*!" I took a contemplative sip of my scotch ditch. Riley and Mariah's story on the red-light duchesses of Helena and now Good Help's unexpected occupation; kind of a rough day for history.

"He's trying to tell you the truth for once," I called down the bar.

Good Help squintily glared my way while Tonsil Vapor's coiffure rotated toward me. My own startlement had not been at the nature of Good Help's job but that he'd ever held one at all. 1918, though, explained it: enlistment into employment rather than the war in Europe.

Tonsil Vapor approached me, trailed by his electronic Siamese twin. He wore an expression as concerned as his cameraman's was languid. Leaning close, Tonsil Vapor asked me in a hushed tone:

"You mean to tell me that your town's historic citizen had

sexual congress with—" and twirled his index finger in the
corkscrew pattern of a pig's tail.

"Well, I can't testify one way or the other on that," I hedged.
"But what he's trying to tell you about here is something else.
One of the jobs on those logging crews over west of the moun-
tains was, uh, like he says."

Tonsil Vapor peered at me in even more perplexity.

"Pigfucker," I clarified. "See, in those days when they'd go to
skid logs out of the woods they'd string them together end to end
with eyebolt hitches, sort of like links of sausage. And the last
log they'd hitch on was a hollowed-out one called the pig. After
all the other logs were snaked out of the woods, then the eye-
bolts and tools and anything else got thrown in the pig—I guess
that's maybe why they called it that, you could toss anything
into it—and it'd be skidded back into the timber for the next
string of logs, same again. Anyway, the guy, usually he was just
a punk of a kid," although it was at least as hard to think of
Good Help Hebner young as it was to imagine him employed,
"who threw the stuff into the pig was called the—"

"Pigfucker," intoned Tonsil Vapor, gazing down the bar to
where Good Help was passing the time by grooming his goatee
with his fingers. "But wasn't that job ever called anything *nicer?*"

I shrugged. "Not that I ever heard of. Lumberjacks tend not
to be dainty talkers."

The bored cameraman shifted his feet as if settling down for
another wait, and he and Fred and I watched Tonsil Vapor chew
the inside of his mouth as he continued staring down the bar at
Good Help.

At length the cameraman suggested, "Let's just bleep out the
mothering word."

"Shit, that just *emphasizes* it," Tonsil Vapor let out peevishly.
"No, we've got to get our historic citizen to talk about the job
without . . . Wait, I know!" His face lit up as if the camera and
lights were on him. "I'll just say, 'Mr. Pigner, I—' "

"Hebner," I prompted.

" 'Mr. Hebner, I understand you once worked in a logging
crew, quite a number of years ago in this Montana of ours.
Would you please share with our viewing audience what you did
in that job?' That way, he won't need to say—"

"Pigfucker," Good Help recited before the TVing was to
commence again, "is what I ain't supposed to say on the televi-

sion but just tell what that job with the pig was?" He squinted anxiously up at Tonsil Vapor, wanting to make sure he had the new ground rules straight.

"Perfect!" Tonsil Vapor pronounced. He turned to the cameraman one more time, got one more bored nod, aimed his chin into the lens and the bright lights came on again.

The Here-with-us-now part and so on went along fine, and I had to admit, Good Help Hebner ensconced there with the carved dark oak of the Medicine Lodge's ancient bar behind him looked amply historical. And I could tell by his squint of concentration that he had Tonsil Vapor's cue about his logging job clamped in mind.

"—share with our viewing audience that experience in the woods?" Tonsil Vapor got there as smooth as salve from a new tube and held the microphone in front of Good Help's venerable lips.

Good Help craned forward and carefully brayed:

"What I done was, I fucked the pig! One whole summer! Best goshdamn job—"

I left the TV perpetrator staring in despair at Good Help and took my restored good humor back into the cafe. Only to be met by Althea shooing the crowd into chairs. "Oh, Jick, you're just in time, we're about to have the committee meeting."

Riley already had gone over and propped himself along the wall where he could study sideways into either the audience or our committee, dutiful nuisance that he was. Mariah meanwhile was signifying by pointing urgently to my chair at the pushed-together cafe tables where the committee members were supposed to sit that she wanted me up there for a group picture. No rest for the civic.

On my way to my seat, though, I paused at the end of the committee table to say brightly to Amber Finletter, who had been a wonderful neighbor to us when Marcella fell sick, "How you doing, Amber?" And wordlessly got back the merest little picklepuss acknowledgment.

Oh, horse pucky. Amber had her nose out of joint, McCaskillwise, because she figured Mariah was making a play for Shaun during that picture-taking of him and me. Jealousy has more lives than Methuselah's cat.

Then no sooner was I sat than I was afflicted with Arlee Zane.

Arlee and I have known each other our entire lives and disliked each other that same amount of time.

Leaning over from his chair next to mine, Arlee now hung his fat face almost into mine and slanted his eyes in the direction of Althea at her speaking stand. Grinning like a jackass eating thistles he semiwhispered, "Jick, old son, are you getting any?"

I cast a glance of my own across the room toward Arlee's wife Phoebe and asked in turn, "Why? Have you noticed some missing?"

That settled the Arlee situation for a while, and I was able to direct my attention to Howard Stonesifer seated on the other side of me. "Catch me up on what's been happening here, Howard."

"Shaun Finletter and Mike Sisti rounded up a flagpole," he reported. "They went all the way across the mountains to Coram for the tree, to get one big enough to take this flag. Other than that, everybody's just sewing"—he cast a look at my chin shrubbery—"or growing."

With a soft *raprap raprap raprap* of her gavel—would you believe, even her hammering sounded like pats—Althea was commencing to officiate.

"The meeting will please come to order, everybody, including you, Garland Hebner." Good Help had spied Riley at his listening post there along the wall and doubtless was creaking his way over to deliver an hour or two of autobiographical afterthought, but Althea's injunction halted the old boy as if he'd been caught slinking into the henhouse.

"It's so wonderful to see so many of you being so public spirited here tonight," Althea proceeded on. "I won't have to go door to door around town handing out pushbrooms after all." She smiled sweetly in saying that, but testimony could have been elicited in that audience from any number of persons who were choosing to put up with an evening of committee crap rather than risk Althea putting them in the wake of our centennial parade's horse version.

Under Althea's generalship we whipped right through Howard's minutes of the last meeting and Amber's treasurer's report, and when we got to the first order of business, guess whose it was.

"We need to give some thought to our flag-raising ceremony," Althea informed all and sundry. "It would be nicest, wouldn't it, if we could re-enact that dawn just the way it happened a hundred years ago, when our Gros Ventre forebears flew Montana's very first flag of statehood. But of course we don't know what was said on that wonderful occasion."

The funny thing was, I did know. To the very word, I possessed the scene that ensued that exact morning of a century ago. I had heard it from Toussaint Rennie, who inevitably was on hand at the occasion. The gospel according to Toussaint was that Lila Sedgwick had officiated. Strange to think of her, a mind-clouded old woman wandering the streets of Gros Ventre conversing with the cottonwood trees when I was a youngster, as ever having been vital and civic. But there in her young years Lila and the handful of others this community was composed of in 1889 had mustered themselves and made what ceremony they could. "Way before dawn," Toussaint's purling voice began to recite in me again now, there, at that committee table. "Out to the flagpole, everybody. It was still dark as cats, but—"

I had an awful moment before I could be sure Toussaint's words weren't streaming out through my mouth. Another spasm of the past, and this one as public as hell. It was one thing to have my memory broadcast out loud around Mariah and Riley and totally another to blab out here in front of everybody who knew me. I tried to fix an ever so interested stare on Althea as she continued to preside out loud and meanwhile clenched my own lips together so tightly I must have looked like a shut purse. But these cyclones out of yestertime into me: what was I going to do about them? I mean, when you come right down to it, just where is the dividing line between reciting what the past wants you to and speaking gibberish? Was I going to be traipsing around blabbering to the cottonwoods next?

"A ceremony isn't really a ceremony unless it has a speech, now is it?" Althea asked and answered simultaneously. "So, before our wonderful flag is hoisted Centennial morning, we really should have someone say a few words, don't you all agree?"

I wholly expected her to go into full spiel about what the speech ought to be about, and then somebody, quite possibly even me, could stick a hand up and suggest that she spout all of it again on Centennial morning and that would constitute the speech, but no, oh hell no. All Althea trilled forth next was:

"I nominate Jick McCaskill as our speaker."

From the various compass points of the committee table, Howard's hearty voice and Arlee's malicious voice and Amber's vindictive voice chorused: "I second the motion."

"Whoa, hold on a minute here," I tried to get in, "I'm not your guy to—" but do you think Althea would hear of it?

"Oh foo, Jick, you're entirely too modest. If you're stuck for what to say I'll be more than glad to help out, you always know where to find me. Now then, all in favor of Jick McCaskill . . ."

"Tell me, Mariah Montana," goddamn Riley started in, doing a syrup voice like that of TV Purvis, on our way home to the ranch. "When did you first realize your father is in the same oratorical league with Lincoln, Churchill, and Phil Donahue?"

"Oh, I always knew he was destined for public speaking because of how he practiced on the sheep," Mariah ever so merrily got into the spirit with a Baby Snooksy tone of her own. "He just has this wonderful talent for talking to sheep"—here she expertly made with her tongue the *prrrrr prrrrr prrrrr* call half-purr, half-coo, that I had taught her to coax sheep with almost as soon as she could toddle—"and so people are probably easy for him."

"Up yours, both of you," I stated wearily.

Maybe it was the prospect of chronic aid from Althea, from then until I had to get up in front of everyone on Centennial dawn and insert my foot into my mouth. Maybe it was that I did not see my presence could cure the ranch situation any, just then; Kenny and Darleen and Helen were going to keep on being Kenny and Darleen and Helen, whether or not I hovered over them, and so I might as well wait until they had the hay up and the lambs fattened for shipping before I faced what to do with the place. Maybe it was hunch. Or its cousin curiosity, after Mariah and I emerged from the house the next morning and encountered Riley, daisyfresh from solitary sleep in the motorhome, who told her he'd already been to the cookhouse and made the phone call and it was all set, and she in turn gazed at him and then for some reason at me, before saying solemnly, "Heavy piece, Riley."

So, yes, the three of us applied ourselves to the road again. Mariah and I in the Bago trailed Riley and the rental Yugo to town to turn the thing in at Tilton's garage, then I pointed the motorhome toward Choteau, as the *Montanian* pair had informed me that this next piece of work of theirs awaited there in the Teton River country.

"Has this got to do with dinosaur eggs, I hope?" In that vicinity, out west of Choteau, lay Egg Mountain—no more than a bit of a bump in the prairie, really, but where whole nests laid by dinosaurs had been found, and while I can't claim to know much more about paleontology than how to spell it, any scene where creatures of eighty million years ago hatched out their young like mammoth baby chicks sounded to me highly interesting.

"Umm, not exactly. Here's your turn coming up," Mariah busily pointed out, "that sign, there where it says—"

"Yeah, I can see that far," I said and gave her a look. What, did she figure I'm getting so decrepit I couldn't read the obvious roadside sign, which directed in perfectly clear lettering:

PINE BUTTE SWAMP PRESERVE
established 1978
protected and maintained by
The Nature Conservancy
14mi.————————➤

The Teton country is quite the geography. Gravelroading straight west as the Bago now was, we had in front of us the rough great wall of the Rockies where gatelike canyons on either side of Indian Head Rock let forth the twin forks of the Teton River. The floorlike plain that leads to the foot of the mountains is wet and spongy in some places, in others bone-dry, in still others common prairie. And even though I usually only remark it from a distance when I'm driving past on a Great Falls trip, Pine Butte itself seems like a neighbor to me. It and its kindred promontories make a line of landmarks between the mountains and the eastward horizon of plains—Heart Butte north near the Two Medicine River, Breed Butte of course between Noon Creek and English Creek, Pine Butte presiding here over the Teton country like a surprising pine-topped mesa, Haystack Butte south near Augusta. Somehow they remind me of lighthouses, spaced as they are along the edge of that tumult of rock that builds into the Continental Divide. Lone sentinel forms the eye seeks.

We drove in sunny silence until I said something about how surprising it was to have a swamp out on a prairie, causing Riley to get learned and inform me that the Pine Butte swamp actually was underlain with so much bog it qualified as a fen.

"That what you're going to do here, some kind of an ecology piece?" I asked.

"Sort of," Mariah said.

"Sounds real good to me," I endorsed, gandering out at the companionable outline of Pine Butte drawing ever nearer and the boggy bottomland—in Montana you don't see a fen just every day—and the summits of the Rockies gray as eternity meeting the blue August sky. This area a little bit reminded me of the Moiese buffalo range where we'd started out, nice natural country set aside, even though I knew the Pine Butte preserve wasn't that elaborate kind of government refuge but simply a ranch before the land was passed on to the Conservancy outfit, which must have decided to be defender of the fen. I couldn't help but be heartened, too, that the news duo at least had progressed from getting us butted by buffalo to moseying through a sweet forenoon such as this. "Great day for the race," I chirped, even. Oh, I knew full well Mariah had heard that one a jillion times from me, but I figured maybe Riley would fall for it by asking "What race?" and then I'd get him by saying "The human race"—but huh uh, no such luck. Instead Riley busied up behind me and announced, "Okay, gang, we've got to start watching along the brush for the state outfit. Should be easy enough to see, there's a crane on the truck they use to hoist the—"

"I'll watch out this side," Mariah broke in on him and proceeded to peer out her window as if she'd just discovered glass is transparent.

Dumb me. Even then I didn't catch on until another mile or so down the road when I happened to think out loud that even though we were going to be with ecology guys we'd all need to watch a little bit out in country like this, because the Pine Butte area is the last prairie habitat of—

The stiffening back of that daughter of mine abruptly told it.

"*Grizzlies?*" I concluded in a bleat. "Has this got to do with *grizzlies?*"

"Just one," said Mariah, superearnestly gazing off across the countryside away from my stare.

"That's way too damn many! This isn't going to be what I'm afraid it is, is it? Tell me it isn't."

Of course neither of this pair of story-chasing maniacs would tell me any such thing and so the nasty hunch that had been crawling up the back of my neck pounced.

"Bear moving!" I slammed on the brakes and right there in the middle of the county road swung around in my seat, as mad as I was scared—which is saying a lot—to goggle first at Mariah who ought to have known better than this and then at Riley whose goddamn phone call this morning all too clearly led into this. "Jesus H. Christ, you two! Anybody with a lick of sense doesn't want to be within fifty miles of moving a grizzly!"

"I reckon that's why the job falls to us," Riley couldn't resist rumbling in one of his mock hero voices. "What's got you in an uproar, Jick? The good news is you don't have to chauffeur the bear in the Bago. The state Fish and Game guys load him into a culvert trap."

I didn't give a hoot if they had portable San Quentin to haul a grizzly in, I wanted no part of it and I then and there let Mariah and Riley know exactly that. Didn't they even read their own newspaper, for Christ's sake? Only days ago a hiking couple in Glacier Park had encountered a sow grizzly and her two cubs, and survived the mauling only because they had the extreme guts and good sense to drop to the ground and play dead. And not all that far from where we right now sat, several—*several*—grizzlies lately kept getting into the geese and ducks at the Rockport Hutterite Colony until the Hutterites managed to run them off with a big tractor. The Bago, I emphasized, was no tractor.

Which did me about as much good with those two as if I'd said it all down a gopher hole.

Riley was mostly the one who worked on me—Mariah knew good and well how ticked off I was at her for this—and of course argument might as well have been his middle name. "The bear is already caught in a steel cable snare, the state guys will conk him out with a tranquilizer gun, and then they'll haul him in a chunk of culvert made of high tensile aluminum he'd have to go nuclear to get out of. Where's the problem?" he concluded, seeming genuinely puzzled.

The rancher portion of me almost said back to him, the problem is the grizzly, you Missoula ninny.

Instead, in spite of myself, my eyes took over from my tongue. They scrutinized the brush-lined creek as if counting up its willows like a tally with wooden matchsticks, they probed each shadowed dip of the Pine Butte fen, they leapt to every ruffle of breeze in the grass. Seeking and seeking the great furry form.

All the while, Riley's bewilderment was stacking up against the silent bounds of me and Mariah, who was keeping ostentatiously occupied with her camera gear. "Gang, I don't know what the deal is here," the scribbler owned, "but we can't just sit in the middle of this road watching the seasons change."

"Are you two going to this bear whether or not I'm along?" I managed to ask.

Say for Riley that he did have marginally enough sense to let Mariah do the answering on that one.

"Yes," she said, still without quite ever looking at me. "The Fish and Game guys are waiting for us."

I jammed the Bago into gear and we went on down the road for, oh, maybe as much as a quarter of a mile before Riley's bursting curiosity propelled out the remark, "Well, just speaking for myself, this is going to be something to remember, getting a free look at a grizzly, hmm?"

When neither of us in the cab of the motorhome responded, he resorted to: "You, ah, you ever seen one before, Jick?"

"Yeah."

"But up close?"

"Close enough." I glanced over at Mariah. Her face carefully showed nothing, but I knew she was replaying the memory, seeing it all again. Who could not? "I killed one once."

"The hell!" from Riley in his patented well-then-tell-me-all-about-it tone. "There on Noon Creek, you mean?"

"In the mountains back of the ranch, yeah." As sudden as that, the site near Flume Gulch was in my mind, as if the earth had jumped a click in its rotation and flung the fire-scarred slope, the survivor pine tree with its claw-torn bark, in through my eyes.

Greatly as I wished he would not, Riley naturally persisted with the topic. "You run across him by accident or track him down?"

"Neither."

"Then how'd you get together with Brother Griz?"

"I baited him."

Strong silence from behind me.

At last Riley said: "Did you. My dad did some of that, too, whenever he'd lose a calf. But black bear, those were. We didn't have grizzlies in the Crazy Mountains any more." Those last two words of his said the whole issue. Originally the West had been absolutely loaded with grizzly bears, but by now they were on the endangered species list.

"I'm not one of those Three S guys, if that's what you're thinking," I told Riley stonily. Law on the side of the grizzly notwithstanding, there still were some ranchers along these mountains who practiced the policy of shoot, shovel and shut up. Better a buried bear who'd be no threat to livestock or the leasing of oil rights than a living exemplification of wilderness, ran that reasoning.

"Riley never said you were," Mariah put in her two bits' worth.

Actually, except for her contribution being on his behalf it was just as well she did ante herself into this discussion, for my ultimate say on the grizzly issue needed to be to her rather than to some scribbler. I spoke it now, slowly and carefully:

"I don't believe in things going extinct. But that includes me, too."

I knew Riley was grinning his sly grin. "A grizzly couldn't have said it any better, Jick," issued from him. I didn't care. From the tight crinkle that had taken over her expression I could see that my words had hit home in Mariah, complicating what she had been remembering, what we both were remembering, of that time of the grizzly twenty-five years before.

It started with a paw mark in the pan of the slop milk Mariah had given the chickens.

Why that pan caught her eye so soon again after she'd done her morning chore of feeding the poultry flock, I do not know. Maybe even at ten years old as she was then, Mariah simply was determined to notice everything. When she came down to the lambing shed to find me I was surprised she and Lexa hadn't left yet for school, but nowhere near so surprised as when she told me, "You'd better come see the bear track."

I dropped to one knee there in the filth of the chicken yard, mindful only of that pale outline in the pan. My own hand was not as steady as I would have liked when I measured the bear's print with it. The width of the palmlike pad was well over six inches, half again wider than my hand. That and the five clawmarks noticeably off the toes distinguished what kind of bear this was. Not just a grizzly but a sizable one.

Considerations of all kinds swarmed in behind that pawprint. No sheep rancher has any reason to welcome a grizzly, that I know of. A grizzly bear in a band of sheep can be dynamite. So my mind flew automatically to the bunches of ewes and lambs scattered across the ranch—late April this was, the tail end of lambing season—like clusters of targets. But before that thought was fully done, the feel of invasion of our family was filling me. The creature that slurped the chickens' milk and tromped through the still-damp pan had been here astride the daily paths of our lives. Marcella merely on her way out to the clothesline, Mariah simply on her way to the chicken house, Lexa kiting all over the place in her afterschool scampers—their random goings surely crisscrossed whatever route brought the grizzly, coming out of hibernation hungry and irritable, in to the ranch buildings. Nor was I personally keen to be out on some chore and afterward all they'd ever find of me would be my belt buckle in a grizzly turd.

So when I phoned to the government trapper and his wife said he was covering a couple of other counties for the rest of the week, I did not feel I could wait.

It was the work of all that day to pick and prepare the trap site. Up toward Flume Gulch I was able to find the grizzly's tracks in the mud of the creek crossing, and on the trail along the old burn area of the 1939 forest fire I came across what in every likelihood was the same bear's fresh dropping, a black pile you'd step in to the top of your ankle. I chose the stoutest survivor pine there at the edge of the old burn and used the winch of the Dodge power wagon to snake a long heavy bullpine log in beside the base of the tree. Around the tree I built a rough pen of smaller logs to keep any stray livestock from blundering in, and even though the other blundersome species wasn't likely to come sashaying past I nonetheless nailed up a sign painted in red sheep paint to tell people: LOOK OUT—BEAR TRAP HERE. Then I bolted the chain of the trap to the bullpine log and set the trap, ever so carefully using screw-down clamps to cock its wicked steel jaws open, in the middle of the pen and covered it with pine swags. Finally, from the tree limb directly over the trap I hung the bait, a can of bacon grease.

One thing I had not calculated on. The next day was Saturday, and I got up that next morning to two schoolless daughters who overnight had caught the feverish delusion that they were going with me to check the bear trap.

They took my "No" to the court of appeal, but even after their mother had upped the verdict to "You are not going and let's not hear one more word about it," their little hearts continued to break loudly. All through breakfast there were outbreaks of eight-year-old pouts from Lexa and ten-year-old disputations from Mariah. As the *aws* and *why can't we*'s poured forth, I was more amused than anything else until the older of these caterwauling daughters cut out her commotion and said in a sudden new voice:

"You'd take us if we were boys."

Mariah should have grown up to be a neurosurgeon; she always could go straight to a nerve. Right then I wanted to swat her precocious butt until she took that back, and simultaneously I knew she had spoken a major truth.

"Mariah, that will do!" crackled instantly from her mother, but by Marcella's frozen position across the table from me I knew our daughter's words had hit her as they had me. Mariah still was meeting our parental storm and giving as good as she got, at risk but unafraid. Beside the tense triangle of the other three of us, Lexa's mouth made an exquisite little O in awe of her sister who scolded grownups.

That next moment of Marcella and I convening our eyes, voting to each other on Mariah's accusation, I can still feel the pierce of. At last I said to my fellow defendant, "I could stand some company up there. How would you feel about all of us going?"

"It's beginning to look like we'd better," Marcella agreed. "But you two"—she gave Lexa a warning look and doubled it for Mariah—"are staying in the power wagon with me, understand?"

When we got up to Flume Gulch, we had a bear waiting.

Its fur was a surprisingly light tan, and plenty of it loomed above the trap pen; this grizzly more than lived up to the size of his tracks. The impression the caught animal gave, which shocked me at first, was that it was pacing back and forth in the trap pen, peering over the stacked logs as if watching for our arrival. Then I realized that the bear was so angrily restless it only seemed he was moving freely; in actuality he was anchored to the bullpine log by the chain of the trap and could only maneuver as if on a short tether. I will tell you, though, that it dried my mouth a little to see how mobile a grizzly was even with a hind leg in a steel trap biting to its bone.

We must have made quite a family tableau framed in the windshield of the power wagon. Lexa so little she only showed from the eyes up as she craned to see over the dashboard. Mariah as intent as an astronomer in a new galaxy. Their mother and I bolt upright on either side trying not to look as agog as our daughters.

"I better get at it," I said as much to myself as to Marcella. Something bothered me about how rambunctious the bear was managing to be in the trap. Not that I was any expert on grizzly deportment nor wanted to be. Quickly I climbed out of the power wagon and reached behind the seat for the rifle while Marcella replaced me behind the wheel and kept watch on the grizzly, ready to gun the engine and make a run at the bear in event of trouble. Mariah craned her neck to catalogue my every move as I jacked a shell into the chamber of the rifle and slipped one into the magazine to replace it and for good measure dropped a handful of the .30–06 ammunition in my shirt pocket. "Daddy will show that bear!" Lexa piped fearlessly. Daddy hoped she was a wise child.

Armed and on the ground I felt somewhat more businesslike about the chore of disposing of the bear. Habits of hunting took over and as if I was skirting up the ridge to stay above a herd of deer below, in no time I had worked my way upslope from the trap tree and the griz, to where my shot would be at a safe angle away from the spectating trio in the power wagon. All the while watching the tan form of trapped anger and being watched by it. Great furry block of a thing, the grizzly was somehow wonderful and awful at the same time.

I drew a breath and made sure I had jacked that shell into the chamber of the .30–06. All in a day's work if this was the kind of work you were in, I kept telling myself, aim, fire, bingo, bruin goes to a honey cloud. Hell, other ranchers who had grazing allotments farther up in the Two Medicine National Forest, where there was almost regular traffic of grizzlies, probably had shot dozens of them over the years.

Abruptly and powerfully the bear surged upright and lurched toward the standing pine tree, as if to shelter behind it from me and my rifle. The chain on the trap was only long enough for the bear to get to the tree, not around it. But as the animal strained there I saw that only its toes of the left rear foot were clamped in the jaws of the trap, not the rear leg itself, which awfully suddenly explained why the bear seemed so maneuverable in the trap pen. *Next thing to not caught,* the trapper Isidor Pronovost used to say of a weasel or a bobcat toe-trapped that way, barely held but unable to escape, and such chanciness seemed all the mightier when the caught creature was as gargantuan as this grizzly.

I will swear on all the Bibles there are, I was not intentionally delaying the bear's execution. Rather, I was settling the barrel of the .30–06 across a silvered stump for a businesslike heart shot when instead the grizzly abruptly began climbing the tree. Attacking up the tree, erupting up the tree, whatever way it can strongest be said, branches as thick as my arm were cracking off and flying, widowmakers torn loose by the storm of fur. The dangling bait can sailed off and clanked against a snag not ten feet from me. The fantastic claws raking furrows into the wood, the massively exerting hulk of body launching and launching itself into that tree. The trap dangling from the bear's rear toes was coursing upward too, tautening the chain fastened into the bullpine log.

Awful turned even worse now. The log lifted at its chained end and began to be dragged to the tree, the bear bellowing out its pain and rage at the strain of that taut pull yet still mauling its way up the tree. I stood stunned at the excruciating tug of war; the arithmetic of hell that was happening, for the log's dead-weight on those toes could—

Then I at last realized. The grizzly was *trying* to tear its toes off to get free.

All prescribed notions of a sure heart shot flew out of me. I fired at the bear simply to hit it, then blazed away at the region of its shoulders again, again, as it slumped and began sliding down the tree trunk, claws slashing bark off as they dragged downward, the rifle in my arms speaking again, again, the last two shots into the animal's neck as it crumpled inside the trap pen.

All those years after, I could understand that Mariah was uneasy about that memory of the toe-caught but doomed grizzly. What the hell, I was not anywhere near easy about it myself, even though I yet believed with everything in me that that particular bear had to be gotten rid of. I mean, six-inch-wide pawprints when you go out to feed the chickens? But I knew that what was bugging Mariah was not just the fate that bear had roamed into on our ranch. No, her bothersome remembering was of us, the McCaskills as we were on that morning. Of the excitement that danced in all four of us after I had done the shooting—Marcella with her worldbeating grin, Lexa hopping up and down as she put out her small hand to touch the pale fur, Mariah stock-still but fever-eyed with the thrill of what she'd witnessed, myself breaking into a wild smile of having survived. Of our family pride, for in honesty it can be called no less, about the killing of the grizzly, with never a thought that its carcass was any kind of a lasting nick out of nature. Late now, though, to try to tack so sizable an afterthought into that Flume Gulch morning.

Clearly this day's grizzly already knew that matters had become more complicated. The snared bear stood quiet but watchful in a pen of crisscrossed logs—much like the one I built—under a big cottonwood, a respectful distance between it and the two state men beside their truck when the motorhome and the three of us entered the picture.

Riley forthwith introduced himself and then Mariah and me to the wildlife biologist, and the biologist in turn acquainted us with his bear-management assistant, a big calm sort who apparently had been hired for both his musclepower and disposition. After we'd all handshook and murmured our hellos, the immediate next sound was Mariah's camera catching the stare of the bear. Inevitably she asked, "How close can I go?"

No sooner was the utterance out of her mouth than the grizzly lunged through the side of the pen, lurching out to the absolute end of the cable it was snared by. That cable was of steel and anchored to the tree and holding the bear tethered a good fifty yards away from the five of us, but even so . . .

"Right where you are is close enough until we get the tranquilizer in him," the biologist advised. He gave a little cluck of his tongue. "I've been at this for years and my heart still jumps out my throat when the bear does that."

Mine was halfway to Canada by now. I got calmed a little by reminding myself that the assistant bear mover had in hand a .12–gauge semi-automatic shotgun with an extended magazine holding seven slugs, armament I was glad enough to see.

Riley went right on journalizing. With a nod toward the

bear he asked, "What have we got here?" I sent him a look.
We?

"A sub-adult, probably about a two-year-old," the biologist
provided and went on to explain that a young bear like this one
was a lot like a kid on the run, no slot in life yet and getting into
trouble while it poked around. More than probably it had been
one of the assailants on the Hutterites' fowl. Mischief this time
was spelled v-e-a-l, a white-faced calf killed in the fence corner
of the rancher's pasture we were now in.

> *This contest too is tribal. Ignore the incidental details that one*
> *community is four-footed and furred and the other consists of*
> *scantily haired bipeds, and see the question as two tribes in what*
> *is no longer enough space for two. Dominion, oldest of quarrels.*
> *The grizzly brings to the issue its formidable natural aptitude,*
> *imperial talent to live on anything from ants to, as it happens,*
> *livestock. But the furless tribe possesses the evolutionary equiva-*
> *lent of a nuclear event: the outsize brain that enables them to*
> *fashion weapons that strike beyond the reach of their own bodies.*

Riley did a bunch more interviewing of the biologist and the
biologist talked of the capture event and the relocation process
and other bear-management lingo, Mariah meanwhile swooping
around with her camera doing her own capturing of the bear-
moving team and Riley and for whatever damn reason, even
me. Even she couldn't help generally glancing at the snared
grizzly, as we all kept doing. Yet somehow the bear's single pair
of eyes watched us with greater total intensity than our five
human pair could manage in monitoring him. And a grizzly's
eyes are not nearly its best equipment, either. Into that black
beezer of a nose and those powerful rounded-off ears like tunnels
straight into the brain, our smells and sounds must have been
like stench and thunder to the animal.

The majority of my own staring went to the rounded crown of
fur atop the bear's front quarters, the trademark hump of the
grizzly. Not huge, just kind of like an extra bicep up there, an
overhead motor of muscle that enabled the grizzly to run bursts
of forty-five miles an hour or to break a smaller animal's neck
with one swipe. Or to rip off its own trapped toe.

My throat was oddly dry when the question came out of me.
"What do you bait with?"

The biologist turned his head enough to study me, then sent

Riley an inquiring look. Who, goddamn his knack for aggravation, gave a generous okaying nod. Just what my mood needed,
the Riley Wright seal of approval.

"Roadkills," the biologist told me. "I collect them. Heck of a
hobby, isn't it? This one's a deer, good bear menu."

Now that he'd obliged Riley's notebook and Mariah's camera,
the biologist said "We'd better get this bear underway. First we
dart him off."

With doctor gloves on, he used a syringe to put the tranquilizer dose into a metal dart and then inserted the dart
into what looked almost like a .22 rifle. The assistant hefted
the shotgun and with their respective armaments the two bear
men edged slowly out toward the grizzly, the biologist saying to us in reluctant tone of voice, "This is always a fun
part."

When the pair neared to about thirty yards from him the bear
really lunged now. At the end of the cable tether it stood and
strained. My God, even the fur on the thing looked dangerous;
this griz was browner than the tan one I'd shot, and the wind
rippled in that restless dark field of hair.

Clicking and more clicking issued from Mariah's camera while
the biologist and his guardian eased another ten yards closer to
the bear. Riley alternately jotted in his notebook and restlessly
tapped his pen on it. I wonder now how I was able to hear
anything over the beating of my heart.

When he was no more than twenty yards from the bear, the biologist raised his dart rifle, leveled it for what seemed a long time, then
fired, a compressed air *pfoop*. The dart hit the grizzly high in the
hind quarters. As the Fish and Game men rapidly walked backwards
to where we were, the bear reared up behind, thrashed briefly,
then went down, lying there like a breathing statue as the
paralyzing drug gripped it.

The bear men stood and waited, the shotgunner never taking
his eyes off the bear, the biologist steadily checking his watch
and the animal's vital signs. After about ten minutes the biologist
said, "Let's try him."

He reached in the back of the truck for a long-handled shovel. Going over beside the hairy bulk with a careful but steady stride while
the helper trailed him, shotgun at the ready, the biologist took a
stance and rapped the near shoulder with the end of the shovel
handle, not real hard but probably plenty to start a fight if
the other party is a grizzly.

When the bear just lay there and took that, the biologist announced: "Okay, he's under."

Christamighty, I hadn't known there was even going to be any doubt about it or I for sure would have watched this part of the procedure from inside the metal walls of the motorhome.

There was a surprising amount of business to be done to the sedated bear. Weighing it in a tarp sling and scale that the state pair rigged from the stoutest branch overhead. Checking its breathing rate every few minutes. Fastening a radio collar— surveillance to see whether this was going to be a repeat offender— around its astonishing circumference of neck. Putting salve into its eyes to keep them from drying out during this immobilization period. And of course as the biologist said, "the *really* fun part," loading the thing into the culvert cage. All of us got involved in that except Mariah. For once I was thankful for her cameramania as she dipped and dove around, snapping away at the two state guys and Riley and me huffing and puffing to insert the three-hundred-pound heap of limp grizzly into the tank-like silver trap. Every instant of that, remembering the fury exploding up that tree of twenty-five years ago, claws slashing bark into ribbons and broken branches flying, I was devoutly hoping this bear was going to stay tranquil. Sure, you bet, no question but that it was snoozing as thoroughly as drug science could make it do. Yet this creature in our hands felt hotblooded and ungodly strong, and all this time its eyes never closed.

Heaven's front gate could never sound more welcome than that clang of the door of the trap dropping shut when we at last had the bear bedded inside. "Nothing much to this job, hmm?" the panting Riley remarked to the biologist.

The state men then employed their crane to lift the cage onto the flatbed truck and soundly secured it with a trucker's large tie-down strap.

"Well, there," I declared, glad to be done with this bear business.

Almost as one, Mariah and Riley looked at me as if I was getting up from supper just as the meat and potatoes were put on the table.

Good God, how literal could they get, even if they were newspaper people. I mean, the movers had the bear all but underway. Did we need to watch every revolution of the truck's wheels, tag along like the Welcome Wagon to the grizzly's new home, to be able to say we'd seen bear moving?

By Mariah and Riley's lights, indubitably. Out our caravan proceeded to Highway 89 and then south and west down thinner and thinner roads, to a distant edge of the Bob Marshall Wilderness. As we went and went, maybe the bear was keeping his bearings but I sure as hell couldn't have automatically found my way back to the Pine Butte country.

> *Exile is the loser's land. Others set its borders, state its terms, enforce the diminishment as only the victors know how; the outcast sniffs the cell of wilderness.*

The motorhome had been growling in low gear for what seemed hours, up and up a mountain road which had never heard of a Bago before, until at last the truck ahead swung into a sizable clearing.

"Here's where we tell our passenger adios," the biologist came over to us to confirm that this at last was the release site, sounding several hundred percent more cheerful than he had all day. The idea now, he told Riley and Mariah, was to simply let the bear out of the culvert, watch it a little while to be sure the tranquilizer was wearing off okay, and allow it to go its wildwood way, up here far from tempting morsels of calf etcetera.

He could not have been any readier than I was to say goodbye to the grizzly. The back of my neck was prickling. And though I couldn't see into the culvert trap, I somehow utterly knew, maybe the memory of the bear I had killed superimposing itself here, that the ruff of hair on the young grizzly's hump was standing on end, too.

"You folks stay in your vehicle," the biologist added, somewhat needlessly I thought, before heading back to the truck. The state pair themselves were going to be within for this finale of bear moving, for they could operate the crane from inside the cab of the truck to lift the trap door. Except for rolling her window down farther than I liked, even Mariah showed no great desire to be out there to greet the bear and instead uncapped a long lens and fitted it onto her camera.

The remote control debarkation of the bear began, the state guys peering back through the rear window of the truck cab to start the crane hoisting the culvert door so the bear could vamoose. We waited. And waited.

It was Mariah, scoping over there with her lens, who said it aloud. "Something's fouled up."

The truck doors opened and the two bear movers stepped out, the helper carefully carrying the shotgun. Reluctantly but I suppose necessarily, I rolled my window down and craned my head out, Riley practically breathing down the back of my neck.

"Equipment," the biologist bitterly called over to us as if it was his personal malady. "Murphy's Law seems to have caught up with the crane—probably some six-bit part gave out. This won't be as pretty but we can do the release process manually."

The pair of men climbed onto the flatbed of the truck. The shotgun guard stationed himself back by the truck cab while the biologist carefully climbed atop the trap and began the gruntwork of lifting the aluminum door up out of the slotted sides.

From the trap there was the sound of great weight shifting as the grizzly adjusted to the fact of freedom out there beyond the mouth of daylight. The big broad head poked into sight, then the shoulders with the furred hump atop them. I breathed with relief that we were about to be through with that haunting passenger.

The bear gathered itself to jump down to the ground but at the same time aggressively bit at the edge of the trap door above it. By reflex the biologist's hand holding that edge of the door jerked away.

The grizzly was all but out of the trap when the heavy door slammed down on its tailbone.

As instantly as the grizzly hit the ground it whirled against what it took to be attack, snarling, searching. The men on the truck froze, not to give the bear any motion to lunge at.

With suddenness again, the bear reared up on its hind legs to sense the surroundings. It saw the man on top of the culvert trap.

The grizzly dropped and charged, trying to climb the side of the truck to the men.

"Don't, bear!" the biologist cried out.

BWOOMWOOM, the rapid-fire of the shotgun blasted, and within the ringing in my ears I could hear the deep peals of echo diminish out over the mountainside.

Both shotgun slugs hit the grizzly in the chest. Stopping-power, the human tribe calls such large calibre ballistics, and it stopped the life of the bear the instant the twin bolts of lead tore into his heart and lungs. The bear slumped sideways, crumpled, and lay there in the clearing. Above the sudden carcass the two bear men stood rooted for a long moment. For one or maybe both of them, the shotgun had bought life instead of death by mauling.

Of all of Mariah's pictures of that day, here was the one that joined into Riley's words.

But as the shotgunner still held the gun pointing toward the grizzly, these survivors, too, seemed as lifeless as the furred victim.

Normally I do not consider myself easy to spook. But that bear episode, close cousin to the outcome of my own grizzly encounter at Noon Creek, jittered me considerably. All this that was marching around in review in my head and then, kazingo, storming out in fresh form in the pieces Mariah and Riley found to do: I couldn't keep the thought from regularly crossing my mind—was I somehow an accomplice to occurrences? What was it that had hold of me, to make memory as intense as the experiences themselves? Maybe I was given somebody else's share of imagination on top of my own, yet tell me how to keep matters from entering my mind when they insist on coming in. Don't think I didn't try, day and night. But I could not get over wondering how contagious the past is.

Nor was I the only one with a mind too busy. The first several nights after the grizzly episode, Riley was as restless in bed beside me as if he was on a rotisserie. I laid there next to him as he sloshed around, wondering why I was such a glutton for punishment, until I just could not take it any longer and would give him a poke and call him a choice name, which might settle him down for maybe half a minute. Mariah was the opposite case on her couch at the other end of the Bago; too little movement could be heard from her, no regular breathing or other rhythms of sleep, and so I knew she was stark awake and seeing her photos of that Pine Butte day over and over. And if I was this well informed on the night patterns of those two I wasn't exactly peacefully slumbering myself, was I.

The day the *Montanian* duo decided to try their luck in the High Line country was one of those newmade ones after a night of rain. At the Hill 57 RV Park in Great Falls a lightning storm had crackled through about ten o'clock the night before, white sheets of light followed by a session of stiff windgusts that made me wonder why recreational vehicle parks are always in groves of big old brittle cottonwood trees, then the steady drum of rain on the motorhome roof which at last escorted me, and for all I knew Mariah and Riley as well, off to sleep. Out around us now as we drove north up Interstate 15 were wet grainfields and nervous farmers. After deathly drought the previous year, they finally had a decent crop and now August was turning so rainy they couldn't get machinery into those fields to do the round dance of harvest.

Maybe the rain-induced sleep was a tonic, maybe the road hymn of the tires was comfortably taking me over, but I felt a little bolstered this morning. Interested in the freeway community of traffic as cars and trucks and other rigs walloped along past the Bago. A venerable Chrysler LeBaron slid by with pots of little cactus in the hothouse sunshine of its rear window. A pickup pulling a horse trailer whipped past, bumper sticker saying CALF ROPERS DO IT IN FRONT OF THEIR HORSES.

Beyond the Valier turnoff the freeway traffic thinned away and I put our own pedal to the metal. I had the rig rolling right along at a generous sixty-five—which is the spot on the speedometer just beyond seventy—when I noticed a speck in the sideview mirror. Steadily and promptly it grew into a motorcycle, one of those sizable chromed-up ones with handlebars like longhorns. The rider rode leaning back, arms half-spread as if resting his elbows on the wind. That would be highly interesting, I thought, to cross the country that wide-open way, hurtling along directly on top of an engine, like saddling a peal of thunder and letting it whirl you over the land.

This skein of thought took my eyes off the sideview mirror longer than I realized, because when I glanced there again the motorcycle was gone. Vanishimo. Which puzzled me because I couldn't account for any exit where the thunder rider could have left the freeway.

Then there was a knocking on the Bago's door beside me.

I about rocketed up through the roof. In that erect new posture, though, I could see that the motorcyclist was right there alongside the front wheel of the Bago, directly under the side mirror. Kind of a windmussed guy, as I suppose was to be expected, he had an unlit cigarette in his mouth. Taking one hand off the handlebars he indicated toward the cig with a pointing forefinger.

Mariah had been catnapping in the passenger seat until the *knock knock knock* on my door brought her eyes open wide. Riley, dinking around on his laptop back at the nook table where he couldn't see what was happening, assumed the noise was the doing of one of us and figured he was being funny by asking, "Who wants in?"

"Guy on a motorcycle here," I reported, oh so carefully keeping the Bago at a constant speed and not letting it wander sideways into the visiting cyclist. One nudge from the motorhome and he'd be greasing a mile of Interastate 15 with his brains. "I guess maybe he wants a light for his cigarette."

Mariah scrambled out of the passenger seat, camera already up and aimed down across me at the motorcyclist while Riley yelped out, "Holy Christ, Mariah, the photo chance of a lifetime! A guy lighting a match in a seventy-mile-an-hour wind! The BB'll be so fucking proud of us he'll put us up for a Pulitzer! Get ready to shoot when I hand this nut a matchbook, okay?!"

"Riley, get stuffed," Mariah told him but only in an automatic way. She took time out from her clicking—the motorcyclist with his cigarette cocked expectantly was frowning in at us like he wondered what was taking so long—to reach down to the dashboard and shove in the cigarette lighter. "But Jick," Mariah went on as she clapped the camera back up to her eye, "you really ought to tell him it's a bad habit."

Whether she meant the smoking or pulling up companionably alongside rapidly moving large vehicles I am still not clear. Anyway, I rolled down the window and when the lighter popped out ready, I gingerly reached across and then handed it down into the windstream in the direction of the motorcyclist. His fingers clasped it from mine, then in a moment returned it. Satisfactorily lit, he veered away from the side of the Bago, waved thanks, and drew rapidly away down the gray thread of the freeway. As we watched him zoom toward the horizon, Riley said: "Is this a great country, or what."

Soon we were crossing the clear water of the Marias, literally Mariah's river. Oh, the name *Maria's* applied by Meriwether Lewis in 1805 to honor a lady of his acquaintance did not have the *h* on the end but it's said the same, the lovely lilting *rye* rising there in the middle. Midbridge of this lanky river that gathered water from the snows of the Continental Divide and looped it across the plains into the Missouri, I sneaked a quick look to the passenger seat and the firehaired daughter there. Whatever Marcella and I expected, our Mariah definitely had a hue all her own.

A quick handful of miles beyond the Marias put us at our

noontime destination. To me the town of Shelby is the start of the High Line country, the land by now leveling eastward after all its geographical stairsteps down from the Divide seventy miles to the west. To look at, Shelby isn't particularly surprising, yet I always think of it as a place with more ambition than its situation warrants. Even now the town is best known for having put up a fat guarantee to lure the heavyweight championship fight between Jack Dempsey and Tommy Gibbons in 1923. Shelby took a bath in red ink but the fight gave it something to talk about ever since. Indeed, when Mariah and Riley and I stashed the Bago and went in the Sweetgrass Cafe for lunch, a lifesize blowup of Dempsey with his mitts up, maybe demanding his money, challenged us from the wall.

"There you go," I found myself saying as we awaited our grilled cheese sandwiches. "How about a piece on that fight?"

"Mmm," was all that drew from Mariah.

"Naw," came the instant verdict from Riley, although he did turn and contemplate the businesslike scowl of the pugilist. "The Manassas Mauler or the Molasses Wallower or whatever he was, Dempsey's been written about by the ton."

Mariah and I had the thought at the same instant. Riley must have wondered what sudden phase of the moon had the two of us grinning sappily at each other.

Heritage demanded that the family bywords be said in a woman's voice, and so Mariah tossed the hair out of her eyes and cocked her head around to deliver to Riley: "What about The Other Man."

"The other man?" Riley blinked back and forth between Mariah and me. "Who, Gibbons?" He quit blinking as the idea began to sink in. "Gibbons. What about him?"

Over lunch Mariah told him the tale just as I had told it to her, just as I had heard it from my mother.

When she'd finished, Riley expelled:

"Jesus H. Christ, that's a better idea for a piece than we've been able to think up all week! Maybe we ought to buy a Ouija board and let your grandmother do this whole series."

He glanced from one to the other of us as though deciding whether to say something more. And at last said it, quite quietly. "I wish Granda would have ever let me interview her."

Surprising to hear him speak her nickname within our family, as if he and Mariah still were married. As if Beth McCaskill still were alive.

Then the two of them headed off to the Marias Museum to get going on Gibbons.

The morning of the day he had spent his life fighting to get to, Tommy Gibbons disappeared.

He slipped out of the hotel at dawn while his wife and children still slept and walked up onto the treeless benchland above Shelby. The town was encased by its land, the rimming benchlands as straight and parallel as the railroad steel below. But here above the boomtown splatter of hasty buildings and tents and Pullman cars, another view awaited: the Sweetgrass Hills, five magical dunes of earth swooping up out of that ledger-straight northern horizon.

Equally unlikely, the forty-thousand-seat arena of fresh lumber sprawled below Gibbons as he roamed the ridgeline, trudging and pausing, trudging and pausing. Shelby was losing its shirt on promotion of the fight, yet its dreamday of making this oil-sopped little town known to the world was about to actually happen. A matter of hours from now Jack Dempsey would arrive on his royal train from Great Falls. Dempsey had taken the heavyweight championship of the world four years ago to the day, on another July Fourth, by pounding Willard senseless in three rounds. Two Julys ago, Dempsey the champion had demolished Carpentier in four rounds the way a butcher uses a cleaver on a side of beef.

Tommy Gibbons was a thirty-two-year-old journeyman boxer. It had taken him eighty-eight fights to reach today. His distinction was that he had never been knocked out, never even knocked down. This afternoon he faced fifteen rounds in that prairie arena against the hugely favored Dempsey.

Gibbons went back down the slope into Shelby. He said something to his alarmed family and entourage about not being able to sleep and having just wanted a walk. Then he sat down to breakfast.

She'd have eaten willows, my mother, in preference to being interviewed by Riley Wright. I'd had to talk like a good fellow even to get her to let the young new *Gros Ventre Gleaner* editor do his piece on her eighty-fourth birthday—the last of her life, it proved to be—about the fact that she was born, with utmost inappropriateness, on April Fool's Day of 1900. No sooner had the *Gleaner* man gone out the door than she let me know she was chalking him onto the roster of the world's fools. She said severely, "I wonder why that young man didn't ask me about The Shelby Fight."

"How was he supposed to know to?"

"Jick, anybody with a Lick Of Sense At All knows that fight was a big doings. That's why your father and I and Stanley were there."

"*You* were there?" I let out before I thought.

She gave me that look of hers labeled Of Course, You Ninny. "Your father or Stanley neither one told you about The Bet?"

My sixty years of close acquaintanceship with my mother still had given no guide as to whether silence or daylong interrogation was the wiser lubricant to get her to talking. This time I tried a dumb shake of my head.

"Well, I'm not surprised. It certainly wasn't anything for the two of them to brag about." She unfastened her gaze from me and seemed to be focusing off into a distance. "We saw the other man that morning just after dawn, you know."

No, I didn't. "Saw who?"

"The man Jack Dempsey was going to fight, of course. He came walking up over the brow of the hill ordinary as anything, right past our tent." I must have looked as though I'd missed the conversational train by some miles, because she deigned to circle back and explain. "We camped that night, your father and Stanley and I, up on the bench there above Shelby. With everybody who'd come to see the fight, you couldn't get a room in town for love nor money." She paused ever so briefly, then gave a glint of smile: "Well, for love, maybe. Anyway, we'd simply brought a ridgepole tent—a lot of others did the same, it was a regular tent town there the night before the fight. Your father and I woke up at dawn, out of habit. Stanley was still fast asleep out under our Model T—there'd been a dance the night before and he'd gotten pretty well oiled—and so maybe there was some excuse for him. But your father saw the man as plain as I did. We both knew him right away, his picture and Dempsey's had been in every newspaper for months. He went right past our open tent flap and said, 'Good morning, quite a morning.' We watched him for, oh, most of an hour after that, walking around here and there on top of the bench. Your father figured the man must be worried half to death, to be out wandering around that early on the morning of a fight. I pointed out to him how silly an idea that was. We were up that early every blessed morning of our lives, weren't we?

"Your father and Stanley," my mother stated conclusively as if citing the last two mysteries of the universe. "How they ever thought Jack Dempsey would knock the other man out, I will never understand."

"Maybe because Dempsey knocked out almost everybody he fought?"

"All your father and Stanley had to do was use their eyes," she went right on. "Jack Dempsey was like somebody trying to hit a bee with a sledgehammer." To my startlement, she balled up her hands and swung a roundhouse right and then a matching orbit of left haymaker in the air between us. Even at age eighty-four, Beth McCaskill in fists was something to pay notice to.

"Just like that," she emphasized. "Sometimes he missed by only a little, other times by a lot. But he kept missing. Jick, anyone with a brain bigger than a cherry pit could savvy that there were only two possible reasons. Either Jack Dempsey was missing the other man on purpose, or he just could not manage to hit him squarely. Either way, it came to the same."

"But as I heard it, Gibbons was getting the cr—pudding beat out of him all through the whole fight."

"Oh, he was. Especially in the third round. That's when we started The Bet."

Dempsey pounded at Gibbons' body, trying to make him lower his jaw-guarding gloves. With a dozen rounds to go, Gibbons already was breathing heavily. Dempsey missed with a whistling uppercut. He resumed on the body, hitting Gibbons harder and harder until the bell.

"Your father of course set it all off," my mother declared. "Can't you just hear him—'Jack Dempsey is eventually going to connect with one of those and knock that guy into the middle of next week, I'd bet anybody.' "

I could hear that, yes, and also the ominous ruffle of what was on its way to my father.

"Naturally," my mother said imperially, "I told him I would bet him a month of my filling the woodbox against a month of his doing the supper dishes, that the other man wouldn't be knocked out." My mother's turn to shake her head, but with incredulity. "Then Stanley had to get into it."

I believe it is not too strong to say that my family loved Stanley Meixell, almost as you are meant to love the person beside you at the altar when the bands of gold fasten your lives together. My father was but a redtopped sprig of a homestead boy the day he saw Stanley arrive, a ranger atop a tall horse, sent to create the Two Medicine National Forest. That day set the course of my father's life. Just as soon as he was big enough he was at the English Creek ranger station in the job of flunky that Stanley contrived for him, and as soon as he entered manhood he emulated Stanley by joining the U.S. Forest Service. By then my mother had come into the picture, and brisk as she was about the shortcomings of the world and particularly its male half, Beth McCaskill adopted that bachelor ranger Stanley Meixell, fussing over him when he shared our supper table as though he were her third small son beside Alec and me. Stanley eventually drank himself into blue ruin, a crash of career and friendship that was to haunt my parents until he righted himself, in their eyes and his own, a full ten years after. But at that earlier point he still had the bottle more or less under control and so the fondness was as thick as the exasperation in my mother's voice as she told me of Stanley's Shelby role.

" 'Aw, Beth, you're letting this sharpster husband take advantage of you,' " she quoted Stanley's Missouri drawl with deadly precision. "So of course I bet him too, that I would cook whatever he wanted for Sunday dinners for a month, against his bringing me a batch of fish every week for a month." She scanned me as if there must somewhere be an explanation of male gullibility. "They were so sure of that Jack Dempsey."

They sure must have been sure. I recalled that Stanley Meixell actively despised fishing, and dishwater was not my father's natural element.

The seventh round ended with Gibbons bleeding from nose and mouth and over an eye. In the eighth, Dempsey staggered him with a punch that found the jaw. The fighters traded jabs and hooks, clinched, sparred again. Dempsey swung again for the jaw but missed, swung with his other hand and missed again, then methodically hit Gibbons over the heart. They clinched until the bell.

"The other man was not a pretty sight, I do have to say," my mother acknowledged. "With the fight only half over, your father was grinning like a kitten in cream. Which must have been what inspired me to up our bet, don't you think?" I nodded instantly. "A month of my taking out the stove ashes," she proclaimed as if the upping was occurring again, "against a month of his washing the parts of the cream separator."

I flinched for my father. Washing the many discs and fittings of a cream separator was one of the snottiest jobs ever.

"Stanley of course couldn't stand prosperity either," my mother continued, "so I bet him a gallon of chokecherries every week—I pointed out that he could pick them while he was doing all that fishing—against my keeping him in pie and cake for a month."

> *Gibbons looked like a drowning man clinging to a rock as he clinched with Dempsey in the twelfth round, taking repeated punishment in the body. In the thirteenth, Dempsey almost wrestled him off his feet in a clinch, then threw a hook which Gibbons blocked with an elbow. At close quarters, Gibbons hit Dempsey twice, then a swing from Dempsey grazed his chin. Dempsey aimed for the jaw again, and missed. Gibbons struck him with one hand and then the other. They backed off and sparred until the bell.*

Did she have it in mind from the start, hidden and explosive there in the ante? Or did it arrive to her as pure inspiration, Madame Einstein suddenly divining the square root of the universe? There between rounds thirteen and fourteen, my mother coolly bet those two rubes of hers the task of plucking her fifty spring chickens for canning, against a pair of handstitched deerhide dress-up gloves she would make for each of them if she lost.

And there my father and Stanley dangled in the noose of their own logic. Dempsey was whaling the ribcage off Gibbons with those body blows. Surely Gibbons' mitts had to drop, inevitably one of Dempsey's smashing tries had to find an open jaw. Not to mention the mutual vision of two forest rangers arriving at community dances with their workday hands princely in soft yellow deerskin, handstitched. But the plucking of fifty chickens . . . .

By then the heat in the Shelby arena was tropical. People had draped handkerchiefs under their hats down the back of their sun-hit heads and necks so that the scene resembled Arabia, remembered my mother. Probably not all the sweat on my father and Stanley Meixell was solar, for now my mother was making philosophical remarks to Shelby at large about the surprising number of pikers in the ranks of the U.S. Forest Service.

Stanley and my father turned to each other.

One gritted out, "In for an inch, in for a mile, I guess, huh?" The other nodded painfully.

When Gibbons survived the fourteenth round, the crowd threw seat cushions into the ring in exultation. The boxers shook hands as the final round began.

Dempsey crowded Gibbons, Gibbons held onto Dempsey. Dempsey hit Gibbons in the body with each hand, then missed with a punch at the jaw. Gibbons reeled out of range, accepted two blows, and held onto Dempsey. Dempsey pulled back and fired a fist at Gibbons' jaw. It sailed over Gibbons' neck as the final bell rang.

The referee, who was also the only fight judge, raised Dempsey's hand to signal that he was winner and still champion.

Gibbons had the victory of the solitary, of the journeyer alone beyond what we had been—he was not destroyed.

Thus the stew of dishwater and fishline and chokecherries and chicken feathers that my father and Stanley Meixell existed in for the rest of the summer of 1923.

"The melodius thunk of Thelonius Monk, the razzmatazz of the snazziest jazz, is the tuuune my heart beattts for youuu . . ."

From Riley's merry uproar in the shower that evening, you'd have thought he had just gone fifteen rounds in the ring himself cleaning Jack Dempsey's clock. Mariah too looked almost ready to purr, and for my part I was glad enough to have been the inspiration, by proxy of Beth McCaskill, for their "other man" tale. Yet something uneasy kept tickling at me after supper there in the Bago as Mariah and I waited for Sinatra to finish his shower so that the three of us could head uptown and see what was what in Shelby after they turned the night on. Was I imagining, or did it seem that day by day where she and Riley were concerned, corners came off a little more? That the way they were managing to merge in their work was maybe causing them to creep beyond that? That the two of them had begun showing such civil tendencies toward each other that if you didn't know there had been a bloodthirsty divorce between them you would think they were companionably, uhm, merged?

Yet again, Mariah on the other side of the table nook from me did not appear particularly smitten with anybody except possibly the inventor of the camera. She was intent at marking up contact sheets of her day's Shelby photos with a grease pencil, and simultaneously eating a microwarmed apple turnover for dessert. With the same hand. Employing the utensil while holding the grease pencil tucked at a writing angle between her index and second fingers looked like there was every risk of forking her contact sheets or crayoning her pastry, but that was Mariah for you.

Conversational me, I waxed: "So, did you get the picture you wanted today?"

"I never do quite get that one," she responded between some slashes of cropping marks and a bite of turnover. "But maybe today's is a little closer to it." That chosen picture when it appeared with Riley's story extended all the way across the newspaper page: the wide, wide tan northern horizon as Gibbons would have seen it on his fight day dawn, absolute rim of the world blade-straight across human eyespan, but on that line of earth the bits of promontory that are the Sweetgrass Hills—a cone of dune, space, a blunter humped swell, space, another dune. As if saying no brink, even the planet's, stays so severe if taken one strip at a time.

By now Riley was trying the monkey-thunky stanza about the seventeenth different way and still didn't sound to me within hailing distance of any tune. Meanwhile Mariah had polished off both dessert and contact sheets and gone to putting on earrings for the evening, dangly hoops festooned with tiny pewter roses. Doing so, she remarked: "I always have wondered why he never goes on to the rest of a song."

"Yeah, well, this rig doesn't hold enough hot water for him to think his way past the first verse, is my guess." Her raised arms as she fastened the earrings brought up a point I would rather not have noticed. Two points, actually, making themselves known where the tips of her breasts tested the fabric of her green blouse. Mariah had showered before supper and pretty plainly her bra went missing in the aftermath. Be damned, though, if I was going to tell a thirty-five-year-old daughter how to dress herself.

The laundered Riley at last appeared, declaring Mariah and I had kept him waiting long enough. Any social suspicion I had was not borne out by him either, for although he gave Mariah a commendatory glance he passed up the chance to say anything flirty and just ushered us out into the night by yapping out a ring announcer's announcement of round sixteen.

We went north of the railroad tracks to a bar called the Whoop-Up, on Riley's insistent theory that the places across the tracks are always more interesting.

More interesting than what, I should have asked him the instant we set foot inside the sorry-looking enterprise.

Floor that must have been mopped annually whether it needed it or not. Orangish walls. Pool table, its green felt standing out like a desperate sample patch of lawn. Total crowd of three, one of them the bartender pensively hunched over a chess board at the near end of the bar. Nobody was smoking at the moment, but the barroom had enough accumulated tobacco smell to snort directly.

Perhaps symptomatically, bar stools were few and we ended up perched right next to the extant two customers, beer drinkers both, the beef-faced variety who still look like big kids even though they're thirty-some. Riley and me they gave minimum nods, Mariah and her blouse they gave maximum eyeballing. With distinct reluctance the bartender left his chess cogitation long enough to produce my scotch ditch and Mariah's Lord ditch, Riley meantime whistling tunelessly as he did his habitual shopping of the bottles behind the bar. "Lewis and Clark blackberry brandy," he eventually specified. "Always a good year."

The bartender went back to staring at his chess board. The two beer consumers resumed muttering to each other about how life was treating them. The three of us sipped. The most activity was generated by the clock above the cash register, one of those just barely churning ones that flops a new advertising placard at you about every half minute. Before long I was forcing myself not to count the number of times the ad for DEAD STOCK RE-MOVAL, with a cartoon drawing of a cow with a halo, 24-HOUR SERVICE, flopped into view.

"I'm trying to remember," Riley murmured to Mariah after a spell of this whoopee in the Whoop-Up. "Did we live this nerve-tingling kind of life before we were divorced?"

"Every night was an extravaganza," she assured him with almost a straight face.

Any fitting response to that seemed to elude Riley, and he focused off toward the bartender who was staying as motionless as his chess pieces. Riley of course grew curious. The two at the end of the bar near us did not look like chess types. Ever interrogative, Riley put forth to the bartender: "Where's your other player?"

"Sun City, Arizona. Take turns calling each other every fifteen minutes with a move."

That floored even Riley, at least briefly. But sure enough, on the dot when a quarter past came the bartender reached to the phone, punched a bunch of digits, rattled off what sounded like pawn to queen four, and hung up.

Activity picked up too at my ear nearest the beer pair. "Tell you, Ron, I don't know what you got going with Barbara Jo, but don't let her get you in front of no minister. This marriage stuff is really crappy. You take, Jeannie's mom is always on my back about why don't we come over more. But we go over there and the stuff she cooks, she never salts anything or anything, and I don't eat that crap without no salt on it. Last time she called up and asked Jeannie why we weren't coming over, I told Jeannie to tell her I had to lay down and rest. Then there's Jeannie's dad, he just got dried out down at Great Falls. Cranky old sonofabitch, I think they ought to let him have a few beers so he wouldn't be so much of a craphead, is what I think. And you know what else, Jeannie's brother and sister-in-law had a Fourth of July picnic and didn't even invite us. That's the kind of people they are. Jeannie and I been talking a lot lately. I told her, I about had it with her crappy family. Soon as the first of the year and I get enough money ahead to buy my big bike, I'm heading out to the coast and go to school somewhere."

"Yeah?" Ron responded. "What in?"

"Social work."

Our sipping went on as if we had glassfuls of molasses, so I admit it was an event out of the contagiously drowsy ordinary when Mariah took herself off to the ladies' room. She didn't realize it but she had company all the way, the double sets of bozo eyeballs from beside me. "Divorced, did I hear them say?" the nearer of the two, the Ron one, checked with the other in a muffled tone.

"Yeah, I heard the word," confirmed the other bar stool resident. "A free woman. Always the best price."

"She looks sweet enough to melt in your mouth, don't she," said the first.

"I'd sure like to give that a try," pined the other.

"Like to, hell. I'm gonna. You just watch."

I had turned and was sending them a glower which should have melted their vocal cords shut, but it is difficult to penetrate that much haze of beer and intrinsic lard. Nor was goddamn Riley any help. "Don't look at me," he murmured. "She was only ever my wife. You're stuck with her as a daughter permanently."

All too soon Mariah was emerging from the ladies' room, to the tune of the under-the-breath emission beside me, "Look at the local motion in that blouse." Ron the Romancer was applying a companionable leer all over her as she came back to the bar. If called into court, his defense could only have been that at no time did his eyeballs actually leave his body.

"Hey you, yayhoo," I began to call him down on his behavior just as Mariah gave him a look, then a couple of sharper glances as it dawned on her where his interest lay. But her admirer continued to spoon her up with his gaze even after she reached the bar and us again. Then, as if in a staring contest with what were standing sentinel in Mariah's blouse, the would-be swain swanked out to her: "That green sure brings out your best points."

I brightly suggested we call it a night.

"Ohhh, not till I finish this," Mariah said, and picked up her drink but didn't sit down with it. Instead she delivered me a little tickle in the ribs and said, "Trade places with me, how about."

That would put her directly next to the pair of shagnasties, removing me as a barrier of at least age if not dignity. "Uh, actually I'm just real comfortable where I am."

The tickle turned into an informative pincer on my rib. "Riley needs the company," she let me know. I flinched and made the trade.

Sidling onto the stool where I'd been, Mariah remarked to the staring bozo, "You seem pretty interested in what I'm wearing."

He looked like he'd been handed candy. "Yeah, I like what you haven't got on."

"Aw, crud," Riley uttered wearily and began to get off his stool in the direction of combat.

Mariah halted him with a stonewall look and a half-inch of headshake. Riley considered, shrugged, sat back down.

Turning around to her unremitting spectator again, who now seemed hypnotized by her earring dealybobs, she said in a way that left spaces in the air where her words had been: "Well then now—what's on your mind besides what's on my chest?"

He blinked quite a number of times. Then: "I was wondering if you'd, er, want to go out."

Mariah presented him what I recognized as her most dangerous grin. "Now doesn't that sound interesting," she assessed. "I'll bet you're the kind of guy who shows up for a date in your ready-to-go tuxedo."

"Er, I'm not sure I've got—what's a ready-to-go tuxedo?"

Mariah swirled her Calvert and water, took a substantial swig, then delivered in a tone icier than the cubes in her glass:

"A ten-gallon hat and a hard-on."

Into our drinks Riley and I simultaneously snorted aquatic laughs, which doubtless would have drawn one or the other of us the wrath of the red-faced bozo, except that his buddy on the other side of him gave out a guffaw that must have been heard in northernmost Canada and then crowed, "He can at least borrow the hat someplace, lady!"

"Screw you, Terry," the still-red shagnasty gritted out, in a 180–degree turn of his attentions. Then he swung around on his stool with his right fist in business, socking Terry in the middle of his hilarity and sending him sailing off backwards.

Terry rebounded off the pool table and with a roar tackled Mariah's suitor off his stool. The locked pair of them swooshed past us in midair, landed colossally and then rolled thumpedy-thump-thump across the floor in a clinch, cussing and grunting.

"Maybe I missed a chance there," Mariah reflected as the bartender whipped out a Little League baseball bat and kept it within quick reach while phoning the town marshal. She cast a last glance at the tornado of elbows and boots and *oof*s and *oogh*s as it thrashed across the floorboards. "He does seem to be a person who cares a lot."

Leaving the second battle of Shelby behind, we truly began

tooling along the High Line, eastward on Highway 2 across that broad brow of Montana.

The Bago purred right along but the other three of us seemed to have caught our mood from the weather, which had turned hazy and dull. No trace whatsoever of the hundred-mile face of the Rockies behind us to the west, and on the northern horizon the Sweetgrass Hills were blue ghosts of themselves. With only the plains everywhere around I began to feel adrift, and Mariah and Riley too seemed logy and out of their element. As far as we were concerned this highway had been squeezed out of a tube of monotony. I wished the day could be rinsed, to give the High Line country a fairer chance with us.

Soon we were in the wheat sea. Out among the straw-toned fields occasional round metal bins and tall elevators bobbed up, but otherwise the only color other than basic farming was the Burlington Northern's roadbed of lavender gravel, brought in from somewhere far. That railroad built by Jim Hill as the transcontinental Great Northern route—farthest up on the American map and hence its Montanized designation "the high line" —cleaved open this land to settlement in the first years of this century and even yet the trackside towns are the only communities in sight. One after another as you drive Highway 2 they come peeping over the lonely horizon, Dunkirk, Devon, Inverness, Kremlin . . . a person would think he really was somewhere. Which can only have been the railroad's idea in naming these little spots big.

Our destination today was Havre, which didn't reassure me either. I'd been there a number of times before when livestock business compelled me to and knew it wasn't the kind of place I am geared for, out as the town is like a butter pat in the middle of a gigantic hotcake. So any conversation was something of a relief, even when Mariah caught sight of a jet laying its cloud road, the contrail stitching across a break in the sky's thin murk ahead of us, and said in disgruntled photographer fashion, "The Malmstrom flyboys have got the weather I want, up there."

That roused Riley to poke his head between us and peer through the windshield at the white route of the bomber or fighter or whatever the plane from the Great Falls air base was. "Another billion-dollar silver bullet from Uncle Sam," he preached in a gold-braid voice. "Take that, you enemy, whoever the hell you are any more."

"Reminds me of your ack-ack career, petunia," I contributed to the aerial motif.

"Mmm, that time." The start of a little grin crept into Mariah's tone.

"Old Earlene." I couldn't help but follow the words with a chuckle.

"Brainpain Zane." Mariah escalated both of us into laughter with that.

Riley had sat back into his dinette seat. "I knew I should have brought a translator along when I hooked up with you two."

"This goes back to when I was a freshman in high school," Mariah took over the telling of it to him. "Initiation Day—you remember how dumb-ass those were anyway. This one, the seniors had us all carry brooms and whenever one of them would catch us in the hallway between classes and yell 'Air raid!' we were supposed to flop on our back and aim the broom up like an antiaircraft gun and go '*ack-ack-ack-ack*.' Cute, huh? Somehow I went along with the program until Earlene Zane, the original brainpain as we called her, caught me walking across the muddy parking lot to the schoolbus and yelled out, 'Air raid, McCaskill! Dump your butt in that mud, freshie!' I looked down at that mud and then I looked at Earlene, and the next thing I knew I'd swept the broom through the gloppiest mudhole, right at her. Big globs flew onto the front of her dress, up into her face, all over her. So I did it a bunch more times."

"Hey, don't leave out the best part," I paternally reminded her as Riley chimed in with our chortling.

"Oh, right," Mariah went on in highest spirit. "Every time I swatted a glob onto old Earlene, I'd go: *ack-ack-ack-ack*."

By the time we'd laughed ourselves out at that, we were beyond Kremlin, with only another ten minutes or so of hypnotic highway to put us into Havre. I figured we had this High Line day made, whatever the rest of them were going to be like, when abruptly a spot of colors erupted at the far edge of the road.

Like a hurled mass the flying form catapulted up across the highway on collision course with the windshield in front of my face. Before it could register on me that I'd done any of it, I yelled "Hang on!" and braked the motorhome and swerved it instinctively toward where the large ringneck had flown up from, trying to veer over just behind the arc of its flight. The body with its whirring wings, exquisitely long feathered tail, even the red wattle mask of its head and the white circle around the bird's neck, all flashed past me, then sickly thudded against the last of the uppermost corner of the windshield where the glass meets the chrome fitting, on Mariah's side of the Bago. She ducked and flung up both arms in a horizontal fence to protect her face, the way a person automatically desperately will, as the web of cracks crinkled down from the shatterpoint.

By the time any of this was clear to me, the pheasant was a wad of feathers in the barrow pit a hundred yards behind us.

"You all right?" I demanded of Mariah as I got the Bago and myself settled back down into more regular road behavior. "Any glass get you?"

"Huh uh." She was avidly studying the damage pattern zigzagged into the upper corner of the windshield in front of her. "Damn, I wish I'd caught that with the camera."

"How about you, Riley?" I called over my shoulder. "You come through that okay?"

"Yeah," the scribbler answered in an appreciative voice. "Fine and dandy, Jick."

"Good. Then open that notebook of yours to the repairs page."

The next morning there in Havre was the fourth of September, which also happened to be Labor Day—always the message that summer is shot and winter is at the door—and two full months since Mariah cornered me into the centennial trip. Sure, I thought to myself while easing out of bed onto my tender leg, which was feeling the change in weather, why not lump all dubious anniversaries into one damn Monday and frost it with Havre.

Mariah mentioned nothing at breakfast—not even my hotcakes alBago, doily-size but by the dozens—she and Riley poring over a map spread between them, him listing off towns ahead of us on Highway 2 and jotting them into his notebook with question marks after them while she cogitated out loud about photographic prospects, so I ended the meal fed up in more ways than one. A High Line breeze whined insistently in the overhead vent of the motorhome. Riley's pen tippy-tapped monotonously in his notebook. I peered out to see what kind of weather was in store, but no luck there either, Havre being down in a hole so much you can't even begin to see to any significant horizon. The day had me disturbed, even I will admit. Try as I did to rein in my mood, I suppose a bit of it worked loose in my general remark:

"Whatever in hell you two eventually manage to come up with, I hope to Christ it's got some mountains somewhere around for a change. This country where there's nothing to lean your eyes on is getting me down."

Riley's pen quit tapping the notebook, and when I glanced over at the unaccustomed welcome silence, he had the pen angled like a pointer onto a spot on the map. Mariah's index finger was there from the opposite direction. Both their faces were lit up as if they had hit the same socket at the same time.

It was Mariah who gave me a thankful grin and said, "Great minds run on the same track."

"What, me and you two?" I said skeptically.

"Better than that," Riley chimed in. "You and Chief Joseph."

On the map, out beyond Havre a backroad dangles lone-somely south from the little town of Chinook. Down it, across miles and miles of grassland being swept by the wind and at last almost into the Bearpaw Mountains, we pulled in at the Chief Joseph Battleground.

The Joseph story, actually the Nez Percé story because he was but one of several chiefs who led their combined bands—not just their fighting men but women, children, their old people, their herd of horses, the whole works—out of the Wallowa Mountains in Oregon in flight from the push of whites on their land, I'd of course read the basics of: that after a dodging route of seventeen hundred miles and several successful battles, the Indians were cornered into surrender here only a few more days' march to sanctuary in Canada. What I saw now, at history's actual place, was that the Nez Percé in that autumn of the last century had two more horizons to get over. Up onto the brief rise above this Snake Creek bottomland where they'd pitched camp. Then over the wider rim of skyline ridge to the north and across the boundary into Canada. The small horizon, suddenly deadly with cavalry and infantry, had been the one that doomed them.

Our threesome sat within the protection of the motorhome and studied the ground of battle, across the somehow wicked-looking little creek of wild rose brambles and stunted willows.

After a bit, Riley tested the air with his cocked-to-one-side tone of voice. "Custer was a loser, and he's famous as hell. Chief Joseph fought longer and harder and didn't get his people killed wholesale, and all he's got is that plaque on a rock over there. Why'd it turn out that way?"

Whether or not Riley really expected an answer, I turned and gave him the one that needed no words—simply rubbed the back of my hand, the skin there.

We stepped from the Bago into a wind just short of lethal, Mariah and I stepping right back in and swapping our hats for winter caps and pulling on heaviest coats. But Riley must have been in some kind of writing fever because he braved the wind in just a jacket to hustle over for a look at the Joseph plaque. By the time we joined him at that—there actually proved to be three memorial markers, a plaque apiece in honor of the U.S. soldiers, the Indians, and the Chinook townsman who'd helped preserve the battlefield; about as democratic as you can get about a combat site, I suppose—gusts were whistling even harder out of the west and Riley had to give up on his polar bear act. Borrowing the Bago keys from me, along with my look that said I hoped he wasn't going to keep diddling around in this fashion in weather like this, he scooted back to the motorhome to don a saner coat while Mariah and I ducked behind a little wall of shelter put up to keep visitors from being spun away like tumbleweeds.

Hunched in out of the gale, she blew on her fingers to get ready for shutter action. I blew on mine simply because they were cold. Both of us scanned the battleground in front of us across the brambles of Snake Creek. Everywhere out there the dead grass flowed identically in the wind, coulees and brief benchlands merging into each other as just slightest dents and bulges in the grass-color of everything.

"What year was the battle?" I asked above the whoosh of the wind.

"1877," Mariah raised her voice in turn.

"This place still is in a bad mood," I observed.

Mariah said an eloquent nothing. I recognized why. I am not a cameraperson but even I could see that for her photography purpose, this site was hiding its face.

"Not nice," Riley reported meteorologically as a gust propelled him behind the windbreak wall with us.

"In more ways than one," Mariah shared with him out of her contemplation of the tan smudge of battlefield. "This is going to take some real figuring out to shoot." So saying, she automatically reached up and reset her winter cap with the bill backwards now over the neckfall of her hair, to keep the brim out of the way of her camera.

"I sympathize," the scribbler responded. Not in any smartass way, but as if he might actually mean it, which made me wonder what was getting into Riley Wright lately. "I need to tromp around out there a while myself," he sped on. "The wind just lends a little atmosphere, hmm?"

Atmosphere was one way of putting it. I expected prickles at a place like this, and they came at once. Spirits hovering in their old neighborhood are not something I can bring myself to believe in. But I do figure there could be sensations left over in us—the visitors, the interlopers—from tribal times, from cave times; maybe our hair roots go deep into that past and it rises up out of us as the prickles at such a site as this battlefield.

Wanting to stay out of the way of Mariah and her lens as she bowed her neck and started stalking for any photo chance, I stuck with Riley when he began his own prowl along the little ridge at the south edge of the battle site. Up as we were, I could see that the country here was higher than the Milk River Valley where Chinook lay, these surroundings gradually stairstepping into the rounded small summits of the Bearpaw Mountains. The nicest ranching country I'd seen yet on the High Line, actually; snowdrifts would last and last in the gullies on these north slopes, and other water surely awaited in springs tucked here and there. For livestock, a promising enough place. For a life-or-death encampment, no. As we tromped around, hunching in that wind, every sense told me what nasty country this was to fight in—the creek bottomland dangerously unsheltered yet all different levels of land around the site like crazy stairs and hideyholes.

Riley had the order of battle, to call it that, down pat from his research while we were driving from Havre. The slightly higher ground we were on was where the Nez Percé had been able to flop down in cover and drive back the white soldiers' first attack. The U.S. troops lost an immediate twenty-two men and two officers in that opening charge against the ridge, and about twice

that many wounded. Some of the Nez Percé were killed that
night by their own warriors who mistook them for Cheyennes
allied with the white soldiers. Both sides dug in and it dragged
on into a kind of sniping marathon from trenches and rifle pits. In
all, Riley said, five days of such mauling took place. Near where
we stood Chief Looking Glass was the last man killed, picked off
by an army scout. Over there, Riley pointed out, the body of
Chief Toohoolhoolzote had lain unburied because of the field of
fire from the white soldiers. Down here below us, a howitzer
shell caved in a shelter pit on a Nez Percé woman and her child.

In no time at all of that chilly trudging and standing, my achy
shin felt like fire. Yet it never crossed my mind to retreat to the
Bago.

Even the clouds were askew here, scattered fat cottonwad
ones with perfectly flat bottoms as if skidding on the top of the
wind. Every so often, a floe of cloudshadow would blot across
the battlefield and I would see Mariah frown upward from her
camera.

Riley was spieling something I had wondered about, how the
Indians kept track of their casualties. *"Alahoos, an oldlike man
who was still strong, made announcement of all incidents and events
each day,"* he read off what he'd copied in his notebook earlier.
*"All knew him and reported to him who had been wounded or killed
in battle, who was missing or had disappeared."*

I'd stayed silent until something made me ask. "What was the
weather like during the fighting here?"

"Cold, rainy, windy, generally shitty," Riley named off. "It
ended up snowing about half a foot." This quicksilver battlesite
in white, a first sift of snowfall halfway up the long grass, the
bald brows of the hills showing through, I could readily see.

Then I recognized this day's weather. As much so as if the
wind had put on a uniform and the chilly air assumed a familiar
mask of ice.

It was blowing from May 18, 1943. I was eighteen and suppos-
edly a soldier. After enlistment and basic training I was shipped
to find my war in a part of the world I had barely even heard of,
the Aleutian islands. If you look hard enough at a map they are
a line of stepping stones in the North Pacific between Asia and
Alaska, and the Japanese were using them in just that way in
World War Two. In the fighting on the island of Attu my platoon
was sent out hours before daylight the morning of our attack on

Cold Mountain. We were to sneak into position where we could work over a Japanese emplacement of heavy machine guns, at least three of the goddamn things. That mountain was cold, all right. Ice on the tundra as we climbed the slope, and the wind trying to swat us off the face of the earth. Just in the earliest minute or so when it was getting light enough to see we spotted the first enemy, a sentry about fifty yards away. I guess he was not the greatest of sentries, because he was standing up there against the skyline shaking out a grass mat. Our lieutenant motioned the rest of us to take cover under a cutbank. Then he laid down in firing-range position with his legs carefully spraddled and shot the sentry. I have wondered ever since if that is pretty much what war is: some ninny stands up when he shouldn't and some other ninny shoots him when he shouldn't. What I do know for definite is that our prescribed plan of attack, to grenade those machine guns, was now defunct before it even started because we were way too far away to throw. Yet, for whatever reason, all at once here came four or five Japanese soldiers and an officer with a sword, kiyi-ing down in a bayonet attack on us. Our BAR man opened up, the Browning Automatic making that kind of regretful *tuck tuck tuck* sound as it fired, and that took care of the bayonet proposition. While the Japanese were thinking matters over, our lieutenant's next brainstorm was to send some of us out around to a little knoll so we could pinch in on the machine gun position. I was the third guy who had to scramble across there, running hunched down for maybe forty feet from the end of the cut bank to the cover of the knoll, and I was only a step from having it made when a bullet smashed my left leg not far above the ankle. I fell and rolled a long way down the mountainside. Not that I know an awful lot about it, except for the skinned up and bruised places all over my body later, because I'd immediately lost consciousness, but the other men of the platoon assured me I'd been the deadest-looking guy they ever saw, flopping down the slope like a rag doll.

That was my combat career, quick. Over with except for the piece of my leg where the ache lay under the bullet scar, my Attu tattoo. I—

No. Not over with. Not here, not this day. Peace of mind was splintered too by that bullet of forty-six years ago.

With a gulp I reached down and wildly rubbed my shin, trying to scrub away so much more than that boneload of pain. Oh

sure, it served me right for traipsing around to these sorrowspots
with this duo of Montanologists. Maybe my herder Helen had
the right idea: go and live with rocks. Goddamn it all to hell
anyway, how long did we have to stay here being augured by
the wind? Mariah, I saw, had finally sorted her way across the
deceptive levels of the battlefield and was at the far side mar-
shaling a picture of the bust of Chief Joseph within an iron spike
fence. I turned to strongly urge Riley too into finishing up this
yowling site.

Riley was gone.

Gone where, gone how, there was no sign whatsoever.

I squinted against the wind and tried to get a grip on why he
would up and vanish. My swoon back to the Aleutians surely
hadn't taken long enough for him to walk off over any of the
ridges or back to the Bago. And I could see along the entire
creek and all the battlefield to where Mariah was working. But
abruptly only the two of us in this welter of geography.

A new crop of prickles broke out on me. Aggravating as Riley
could be with his presence, to have him subtracted this way was
uncommonly spooky. As if my Attu memory of brushing against
oblivion had brushed Ri—

Not forty feet from me, his tall figure suddenly rose from the
ground. Oh sure, scribbling. Where the hell else would Riley be
extant? He had lain down in a little dip, most likely a rifle pit
dug by one of the Nez Percé, to belly into that sense of conceal-
ment and now here he stood again, telling his everlasting notebook about it all.

> . . . *in a pock in the earth. In a disease scar older than*
> *smallpox or any other.*
>
> *But craters of war heal over, don't they? Why else the bronze*
> *calm of plaques, the even-handed attestations to both sides who*
> *fought here in the narrow bottomland of Snake Creek in 1877? The*
> *grass has grown back as thick as flame. The brow of the hill to the*
> *east wears strips of farming like a cheerful striped cap. Sunshine*
> *dodges the clouds, uncurls flags of light on the hills.*
>
> *By now the only echoes at this battlesite are poetry. The sen-*
> *tences of surrender by Joseph, just the surviving chief of several who*
> *jointly led the Nez Percé almost magically through seventeen hun-*
> *dred miles of hostile territory and several battles before Snake*
> *Creek, were interpreted by one of General Howard's staff, tran-*

scribed by another; scrawled in a report to the Secretary of War, the surrender speech was merely a knell for one more band of outgunned Indians. But Joseph's words want to be more than that.

> *I am tired of fighting.*
> *Our chiefs are killed.*
> *The old men are all killed.*
>
> *It is cold and we have no blankets.*
> *My people have run to the hills,*
> *and have no blankets.*
>
> *Perhaps I shall find them among the dead.*
>
> *I am tired: my heart is sick and sad.*
> *rom where the sun now stands,*
> *I will fight no more forever.*

Combat pits nowadays are greatly deeper in the prairie south of the Bearpaws, where the Nez Percé ghosted across the center of Montana on their route to defeat. Concrete burrows, complete arsenals underground. Missile silos, we let the Department of Defense (née the Department of War, 1789–1947) call these most deliberate of craters, as if what they store is lifegiving. Two hundred Minuteman missile silos across Montana. More of these fields of nuclear warheads in the Dakotas and Wyoming, Nebraska and Colorado and Missouri. Enough gopherholed megatonnage to incinerate people by the million.

So, no, warpox does not heal. It merely scabs over with the latest materiel. And so we are still pitted, now with nuclear snipers' burrows. Maybe the one nearest you is for Kiev; if Mutual Assured Destruction has been calibrated cleverly enough, maybe the one siloed in Kiev is for here. (It is cold and we have no blankets.) In any case, the combat pits still are dutifully manned. On highways crisscrossing the heart of the West today, you can meet the next shift-change of missile crews in their Air Force vans, blue taxis to Armageddon.

So time came and went, there along Snake Creek. On Aleutian wind agitating battle earth in Montana. Through summer into colder calendar. Into Mariah's camera and Riley's notebook and out as scene and story.

In me. In the arithmetic that if you add to an eighteen-year-

old wounded soldier the years now since his bullet, my birthday—
this day—was my sixty-fifth.

"Got it finally," Mariah declared, ruddy from the wind but an
exultant grin on her, as she coalesced with Riley and me at the
footbridge. She'd earned grinning rights, because what she'd
done in her picture to go with Riley's piece was put that weather
to work—the flat-bottomed clouds, each drifting separate against
the sky, in the same sad lopped way that the sculpture of Chief
Joseph's head seemed based in the air amidst them. Mariah
hugged herself for warmth. "Brrr, let's get in out of this."

The wind put up a final struggle as we trudged head-on into it
the last couple of hundred yards to the motorhome, which I
forthwith went to unlock. Then remembered. "Oh yeah, I gave
the keys to you, Riley."

"Hmm? So you did." He reached a hand into the side pocket
of his coat and froze in that position. Next he cast an uh-oh look
at Mariah where she was jigging in place trying to keep warm,
then finally one toward me.

"Christamighty!" I yelped. "What'd you go and do now, lose
the goddamn keys?"

"No, no, of course not," Riley piped with a swallow. "They're,
ah, just in one of my other pockets, is all."

"So dig them out," I urged with vigor. "It's colder than the
moon's backside out here."

Riley's gaze at me turned sickly. "The pocket of *that* jacket,"
he admitted, indicating toward the Bago. The jacket he'd changed
for a heavier one. The jacket he'd left in the Bago. The jacket
he'd locked in the Bago.

Right then I could have gladly mangled him. Riley Wright
Ground Sausage, Handmade on Snake Creek. But Mariah put
herself between us and headed me off with multiple adjurations
of "Whoa now, that isn't going to get us anywhere!" and eventually I cooled down—in that wind it didn't take all that long—
enough to agree we had to do something drastic.

And it is a drastic amount of effort to break out a motorhome's
safety-glassed rear sidewindow, above head height, with a rock at
the cold blowy end of a miserable day, just as it is an even more aggravating chore to pluck and dig all the shards of glass out of the win-
dowframe, as we stretched and shivered and did until at last the frame
was safe for Riley and me to boost Mariah up to shinny through.

After she unlocked the doors and the keys were retrieved and I'd revved the heater up to full blast to start thawing us out, Riley assured me he knew precisely what to do next.

"Do you," I said icily. "Isn't it kind of late in life for you to start in on growing a brain?"

"We'll just swing by the hardware store in Chinook and patch some weather glazing over the window until we can get it fixed," he outlined. Under my continued stare he added, "Ah, which reminds me," and flipped open his notebook to the page of the buffalo-bashed grill, the AWOL hubcap, the pheasant-cracked windshield and dented chrome, and added the rear sidewindow to Accounts Outstanding.

When we reached Chinook, Riley's bright weatherizing idea proved to have missed only one detail: the hardware store was closed up tight for the holiday.

"Pull in here," Mariah directed before I could start on Riley again, pointing with great definiteness at the IGA foodstore. In she marched while the window assassin and I sat in mutual polar silence, although the wind howled merrily in through the surprise aperture it found at the rear corner of the Bago, and in a jiffy she was back with a roll of freezer tape and a box of bags made out of some kind of clear crinkly material, remarkably stout. Riley and I piled out to help her tape the bags over the window. I can testify there is some justice in life, because he was the one who gave in to curiosity and asked her, "What are these anyway?"

"Turkey basting bags," Mariah told him.

Then she surprised the daylights out of me.

"Your main present is that I held off mentioning what day this is until right now," she addressed to me as soon as we were back inside the bandaged Bago, "knowing how owly you always get about your birthday. And now that we've faced the issue, I'm taking you out to birthday supper. And here's a little something to add to that, even."

Mariah produced out of one of her ditty bags a small package with a major bow on it and delivered it to me with a kiss, without even any daughterly comment about the risk her lips were taking on my whiskers.

This was more like it and I was much touched, sure, but could easily have stood not to have Riley within a hundred miles of our family moment. He too looked as if he wished himself absent, but contributed a semigruff "At least you picked a day with enough wind to help you with the candles."

A western tie, one of those bolo ones that hangs like a large locket, lay in the small box I'd unwrapped. Its centerpiece was a polished oval of stone set in a broochlike clasp. The stone was darkest green, so intensely so it approached black, but full of sparks of color, reds, golds, grays; like a night sky of stars of hues never seen before.

"Isn't this nifty," I not much more than whispered, overcome with the star-specked beauty of the gift after this mortally awful day. "Thank you, honey, my God, thank you." I breathed tenderly on the gem and rubbed it on the sleeve of my shirt, brightening the amulet's constellations of sparks even more. "What kind of stone—?"

"It's jasper," Mariah said, her gray eyes bright. "Helen found it for me on the North Fork, in that coulee that leads down to the McCaskill homestead. You really like it?"

"Do I ever."

"Then let's dude you up in it." Mariah came over and slipped the bolo loop over my head and critically slid the oval gem into place at the base of my throat; most painless way in the world to dress up, all right. "There now, look at you."

And for once she even asked. "How much would you mind having your picture taken, just for the occasion?"

"I guess it wouldn't necessarily be fatal," I allowed. "Bang away."

She shot a variety of me in my new neck adornment feeling swave and looking debonure, but didn't radically prolong this camera session. "Okay, you both got your faces set for supper?" she asked with the last *click*.

"Why don't you two go ahead," Riley suggested, reason personified for once. "I'll stay here and write the piece from today, get it on in to the evil elf."

"If you do that, I have to race back here and run film through the Leafax yet tonight," Mariah objected as if Riley had peed in the path of her parade. "What about that back-up piece you sneaked in? What does that need on it, anything I can send in quick?"

Even I admit, Riley was showing the frazzle of the day as much as any of us and obviously could stand a square meal and a night off. He rubbed his eyes one at a time, first the blue one left showing and then the gray, like he was dimming down even as we watched. "Let me think. Yeah, it's just a thumbsucker, any number of your shots of country you've already sent in will go okay with that one."

"Then come on," Mariah urged. "Let's go birthdaying."

So we were not spared Riley for the occasion, but all else seemed auspicious enough at the moment, Mariah's thoughtfulness, my new jasper dazzler, evening dining ahead along the Milk River. Chinook was a tidy town, some nice logic to it—its block of bars, just for example, was a concentrate of western oasis nomenclature: Mint, Stockman, Elk, right there door by door by door. Where we headed, though, was out to the edge of town to a blue-painted rambly enterprise Mariah had singled out for this birthday shindig of mine. By now the day was losing the last of its light, so the place's high old neon sign out front was like electric paint against the onset of night: a giant long-stemmed glass, in which was seated the representation of a curvy woman in fringed skirt and bandanna and high-heeled boots—she too was long-stemmed, one shapely leg cocked over the edge of the martini glass and the other extended fully into the air—with her head thrown back and her arm up, tossing her cowgirl hat into the sky. When the sign blinked, the leg kicked in frolicsome fashion and the hat sailed high.

THE LASS IN A GLASS, the red-tubed wording underneath I guess not unexpectedly said, and spaced beneath that ran the enumeration of *Bar, Lounge, Supper Club, Coffee Shop, Bus Depot* and *Motel*. Riley evidently figured he was back in my good graces now that we were amid my birthday celebration—he could not have been more mistaken—and gandering up at those neon announcements he commented: "Wouldn't you think they'd go all the way and add a maternity ward and a funeral parlor?"

As soon as we were inside, Riley did the dutiful and employed the lobby phone long enough to coax some functionary in Missoula—despite that earlier elf crack, the BB naturally was nowhere to be found on the newspaper premises over a holiday—into just going with the back-up piece and picking a nice one of Mariah's file photos to illustrate it with, happy fucking Labor Day to him too. The day's wind must have sharpened all our appetites, for without even any debate we then bypassed the bar and lounge and set ourselves for supper.

*   *   *

Our exit occurred a considerable while later, the three of us
stuffed with soup, salad, fondue and breadsticks, prime rib,
baked potato, two or three vegetables, and chocolate cake—when
this place said supper club it meant it—but Mariah lighter by
quite a few dollars. I thanked her a kabillion for the birthday
feast, but if I thought I'd had an eventful enough day to hold me
for another sixty-five years, I had another think coming.

Riley of course was the culprit. We were harmlessly on our
way out of The Lass in a Glass enterprise, headed for the
motorhome ready to tuck in for the night, when he made the
uncharacteristic error of trying to be nice.

"Tell you what, Jick. Just to show you my heart's in the right
place," patting his rump pocket where his billfold resided, "I'll
buy you a birthday drink."

"Naw," I demurred as civilly as I could, "it's been kind of a
hefty day. I think I'll turn in early."

Say for Riley, he didn't smart off with anything about somebody my age needing his sleep. Instead, worse, he turned to
Mariah and invited, "At least I can keep my reckless generosity
in the family. Buy you a round, can I, Mariah Montana?"

"Best offer I've had since Shelby," she responded, surprisingly full of cheer. Then to me: "You don't mind if we hang on
in here a little while, do you? We'll let ourselves in the Bago
quiet as we can."

"Actually, the night is still a pup, isn't it," I resorted to,
letting my gaze rest on Riley. "Where's that drink you're
financing?"

The bar of this Lass in a Glass emporium was an average
enough place. A Hamm's clock above the cash register, Budweiser
lampshades on the dangling overheads, other beer signs glowing
here and there for general decor. The jukebox had Willie Nelson
and Waylon Jennings singing to each other about various toots
they'd been on. Wherever the Labor Day crowd was, it wasn't
here; only a handful of customers in ballcaps and straw Stetsons,
plus a wide young woman behind the bar who looked like
she could handle any of them with one hand. Remembering
the floor warriors of the Whoop-Up in Shelby, I hoped that was
the case.

Mariah and I each ordered our usual and Riley put in for his usual unusual, you might say, by summoning up a Harvey Wallbanger.

"Whup, wait a minute here!" I jumped him triumphantly. "You already had one of those on the trip. In Ennis or Dillon or someplace back there."

"Jick, a man never wants to let himself get reliably unpredictable," he told me, whatever that meant.

No sooner were Willie and Waylon done songstering than a color television started droning in the corner. I wonder if someday somebody will invent silence.

It for sure won't be Riley. He started right in yammering to Mariah about what piece they—*we*, he kept phrasing it with what he must have figured was a generously inclusive glance at me—ought to press on to next, Fort Peck dam maybe? I'd for damn sure press him onward, I thought to myself, right out of the vicinity of the McCaskills if I but could.

Fort Peck I knew a little something about from when I was a kid during the Depression and construction of that earthen dam across the Missouri River was a relief project which Montanans believed Franklin Delano Roosevelt had sent from heaven. Enough to inquire innocently, "Doesn't the dam kind of look like a big ditch bank about four miles long?"

Riley cut me a look, not the inclusive sort this time. "That's one way of putting it."

"Sounds real photogenic," Mariah met that with. "Riley, don't you know any history that isn't horizontal?"

She said it in a way that could be taken as teasing, though, instead of lighting into him like I'd hoped she would. By the time the bar lady brought our fluids, Riley was right back to being his obstreperously curious self.

"That's some sign out front," he broached to her. "How'd this place get its name?"

"You don't know the half of it. Everybody here in town calls her"—the bar lady indicated out into the night where the neon maiden was kicking up her heels—"The Lass With Her Ass in a Glass. Story is, the guy who opened this place was from back east somewhere. He liked his martinis and he liked a girl he met out here, so he put them together on his sign."

"Eat your heart out, Statue of Liberty," Riley said over his shoulder eastward after the bar lady trod off.

"Don't ever say they aren't poetic souls in this town," Mariah reflected. "Anyway, on to celebration." She hoisted her glass to me, and I automatically reciprocated with mine, and Riley had to clink in too. My daughter flashed the grin her mother customarily had at so many of my birthdays, but the words of her toast were Mariah's own. "Mark this day with a bright stone."

All in all, then, as we settled into sipping and conversing— most of it back and forth between them, who seemed to have discovered they had a surprising amount to say to each other tonight—my evening of entry into senior citizenship could have been a whole lot worse thus far. I was going to have to cash us in early for the night to keep Mariah and Riley from getting too frisky with one another, and toward that end I yawned infectiously every so often. But all seemed under control until a funny impression came over me, the feeling that the three of us were about to be joined by somebody else, even though nobody had newly come into the bar. I could have sworn I kept hearing a half-familiar voice. None of the few partakers strung along the bar was anyone I recognized, though, nor did they look like logical discussants of . . .

". . . eating dust and braving the elements," a tone like that of God's older brother resounded in a break in the bar conversation.

Mariah and Riley and I swiveled simultaneous heads toward the corner television.

Sure enough, Tonsil Vapor Purvis was in the tube in living color, not to mention a high-crowned cowboy hat.

"This centennial cattle drive is a true taste of the Old West," Tonsil Vapor was declaiming. "Twenty-seven hundred head of cattle are being driven by twenty-four hundred riders on horseback, while the world watches." The television picture changed from the mob of beeves and drovers to a traffic jam of communications ordnance, rigs with TV uplinks on top and all-terrain vehicles ridden by cameramen and reporters jabbering into cellular telephones. Abruptly the screen filled with a close-up of a bandannaed rider going *hyaah!*, either at a recalcitrant longhorn or Tonsil Vapor. The next instant, though, our news host was back, full-face-and-hat. "This trail drive means long hours in the saddle for these hardy cowpokes, but—"

At least Riley and Mariah's two-member reunion had been put on hold while they gawked disbelievingly at Tonsil Vapor in his buckaroo regalia and the rest. Indeed, I figured this was a heaven-sent, or at least beamed down by satellite, chance to further divert.

"Somebody tell me this," I postulated. "One sheepherder can handle a thousand sheep easy, but here they got a cowboy for every cow and a fraction. So if they call sheepherders dumb, where does that leave cowboys?"

"Now, now," Mariah purred as if running over with sympathy for television's mounted horde. "Don't be mean to those poor cowpokers."

"Hey, better to be a poker than a pokee," Riley got into the spirit by drawling in a croaky trailhand voice.

Mariah returned him a mock sultry grin, or maybe not so mock. "Oh, I don't know. We pokees figure there's a lot less strain involved for us."

Really great job there, Jick, of heading off the flirty-flirty stuff. Curfew seemed the only recourse. I cleared my throat and said, "If you two are done talking nasty, how about we head out to the Bago?"

"Jesus Christ!" Riley let out and sat straight up, gawking at the Hamm's clock and then back at Tonsil Vapor, who was going on and on. "They're giving him half an hour of airtime on this cattle drive! It's the *War and Peace* of cows' asses!"

"Horses', too," Mariah pointed out with photographic precision as Tonsil Vapor's visage again filled the screen, and I couldn't help but hoot along with my two tablemates.

Then before I could bring up the matter of adjournment again, the bar lady was serving us a reload on the drinks. "Who ordered these?" I inquired at large.

"I did," Mariah flourished a ten-dollar bill. "Anesthesia for watching Tonsil Vapor."

"You know, maybe this actually is a historic event," marveled Riley, critically cocking an ear as Tonsil Vapor intoned over pictures of cows, horseback riders, more cows, more horseback riders. "The biggest herd of clichés that ever trampled the mind. Bet you a jukebox tune he even manages to get in *ridin' 'em hard and puttin' 'em away wet* before he's done."

"You're on," Mariah took him up on it quick as that. I couldn't blame her. There wasn't much any of us would put past T. V. Purvis, but even he would need to outdo himself to call what was on the television screen heated cowboying. The way the mass of animals was strolling along through its media coverage, the only sweat that could pop out on the riders' ponies would have to be from stage fright.

So of course we had to watch the whole thing, during which another round of drinks evolved out of the residue of Mariah's ten-dollar bill, and wouldn't you know, just before the half hour was up and Tonsil Vapor was due to vanish into a blip, out spieled his observation that these Big Sky cowhands were ridin' 'em you-know-how and puttin' 'em away you-know-what.

"Hey, have you been moonlighting scripts for that bozo?" Mariah demanded of Riley with a nudge, although not as suspiciously as I would have.

"Faith is justified once every hundred years, is all that proves," Riley murmured becomingly of his powers of prediction. "Somebody owes me a serenade, though. Something besides Willin' and Waily for a change, okay?"

Mariah swigged the last of her current Calvert, fished out of her pile of change whatever coin a jukebox takes these days, and started to slide out of the booth to go pay off. But at the edge she paused, as if needing to make sure. "Vocal only?"

Riley blinked. Then said as if it was a new thought: "Doesn't have to be, far as I'm concerned."

I sat right there and watched as Mariah motated across the room to the jukebox and Riley unlimbered out of the booth after her and called over to the bar, "Okay if we dance, is it?"

The wide bar lady shrugged. "A lot worse than that's happened in here."

Mariah punched a button on the jukebox. Steel guitars reported. But after an overture or whatever it was, voice rode equal to the sound of the instruments, a slow song yet urgent, the woman singer of the Roadkill Angels confiding into the world's every ear.

> *"King's X," you said the last time*
> *we played this lovers' game.*

Mariah and Riley fashioned themselves to each other as those who've danced together do, her thumb hooked in a remembered kidding way into one of his rear belt loops, his spread hand in the natural place low in the narrow of her back.

RIDE WITH ME, MARIAH MONTANA

"Time out," you called just when
I'd chosen you by name.

Both tall, both more lithe-legged than you'd expect of a lanky couple, they circled together in the slow repeating spin of the song.

"No fair," I called out after
you changed the loving rules.

Mariah's shoulder-long hair moved with the action of their bodies, now touching one blade of her back, now the other. Riley held his head in slightly tilted orbit as if accommodating down to hers.

"Don't cheat," you heard the warning,
that's just the game of fools.

What true dancers know is to never forget each other's eyes. Mariah and Riley read there as if they'd been to the same school for it as they drifted with the music.

Marcella in my arms. Not many years into the past, yet forever ago. We had just finished whirling the night away, the Labor Day dance at the old Sedgwick House hotel in Gros Ventre. Now we were home after the early a.m. drive to the ranch, the dark already beginning to thin toward dawn. The music or the delicious sense of each other—perhaps it is the same flame—still had hot hold of us, wrapping us to one another as we reached our bedroom. Marcella moved first, as soon as my fingers alit at her top button; snap buttons, they sassily proved to be, her western shirt pulling all the way open *plick plick plick plick plick* when my glorious wife laughed and took that single slow essential half-step backward as if dancing yet. Then Marce moved to me again.

This time when we cross our fingers
Let's make it for luck,
Let's break the old hex,
Let's take back those words, "King's X."

With the tune's conclusion, Mariah and Riley separated orderly enough, but there still was a kind of cling between them as they came back to the booth. She startled me with a wink and the avowal, "I promise you the next dance, birthday kid," but established herself in the booth somewhat closer to Riley than she was before. He in the meantime was enthusiastically summoning to the bar for yet another visit by Lord Calvert and Harvey Wallbanger and Johnny Walker.

Talk about wanting to call time out. I'd have crossed all my fingers and toes too if that would have put a King's X of delay into the way this pair was romping. They showed every sign of spending the night on the town, cozier and cozier with each other, and where that led I didn't even want to—

The bar lady sang out, "Anybody named Wright Riley? Phone call."

"Can't the world let a man enjoy his Wallbanger in peace?" Riley said plaintively, but took himself off to the phone in the lobby.

He was back quick, with an odd expression on his face. "Actually it's for you, Jick."

Oh, swell. I figured it had to be Kenny, telling me some catastrophe on the ranch. Even the phone earpiece didn't sound good, full of those frying sounds of distance. Apprehensively I said into the mouth part, " 'Lo?"

"Hi, Dad. Happy birthday! If you'd stay home once in a while instead of gallivanting around, I'd have sent you a salmon."

"Lexa! Christamighty, petunia, it's good to hear you!" What I *could* hear of my younger daughter, that is, through all the swooshes and whishes across the miles to Sitka. "How'd you track me down?"

"I figured the newspaper would be keeping an eye on Riley wherever he was. Just where are you, anyway?"

I had to think a moment, which town by now. "In Chinook. In The Lass With Her A—uh, kind of an everything place. Riley broke down and bought me a birthday drink, would you believe."

Lexa gave a short snort of laughter, the proper response from a McCaskill at any notion of civility in the Wright brigade. Not that the one of us where it counted most, Mariah, was showing any similar sign of recognizing the ridiculous; from the phone I could see to the booth where she and Riley were paying each other necky attention. What differentiates how our children become? Take Lexa at the distant end of this phone line. Smaller, built more along her mother's lines than the lankiness of Mariah and me. Her hair more coppery than Mariah's, her face not so slimly intent, her chosen life more snug, moored. Yet those were the idlest of differences between my two daughters, they did not even begin to describe the distinction. I had not seen Lexa since she and Travis flew down for Marcella's funeral in February, yet I knew if she stepped out of that phone mouthpiece right then I would be surer of her actions than I was of any of Mariah's even after spending night and day of the last two months in her immediate vicinity.

"What's it like traveling with those two," Lexa was asking now, "the Civil War?"

"More like watching a bad dream start itself all over."

Distance hummed to itself while Lexa took in my news. Then she was exclaiming: "Mariah isn't falling for that mophead again? After the way they tore each other up in that divorce? She can't be."

"Honey, I wish you were right. But she shows every sign of doing just that."

"Tell her for me she needs her brain looked at. Tell her to go take up with the nearest sheepherder instead. I can't believe anybody, even that sister of mine, would—" Lexa's incredulity made way for a logical suspicion. "Dad, how many of those birthday drinks have you had?"

"I'm sober. All too."

And then wordlessness hung on the line between us, the audible ache of the miles between Montana and Alaska. Not just measurable distance was between us, but Mariah and Riley, the capacity for catastrophe the two of them represented. I remembered the expression on Riley when he said the call was for me. "Lexa, what was it you said to Riley when he answered the phone?"

"I just asked if he still was carrying a turkey around under his arm for spare parts."

Why couldn't that skeptical attitude toward Riley Wright be grafted onto Mariah? Judging from the ever closer conversation they were having in the booth, the sooner the better.

"I'm going to have to tackle Mariah in the morning about this Riley situation," I concluded to Lexa. "I'll keep you posted." I remembered that my son-in-law who hadn't turned out to be a dud was on the cleanup of last spring's *Exxon Valdez* oilspill. "How's Travis doing?"

"Sick at heart," Lexa reported in her own pained tone. "The whole wildlife crew at Prince William Sound is. New dead species all the time—the oil is up the food chain into the eagles now."

"I wish that surprised me." Where wouldn't that oilspill spread to, before things were done.

"Mm. Know what you get when you cross an oil executive and a pig?"

"No, what?"

"Nothing. There are some things a pig won't do."

Her bitter joke wasn't the best note to end on, but I didn't have any better. "Well, this is your nickel. Lexa, thanks for calling. It helps."

"Love you plenty. So long, Dad."

When I got back to the spooning booth, matters had quieted down, I was thankful to find. Mariah's arms were crossed in front of her with one hand up at the throat of her blouse, contemplatively fingering the point of her collar there. Riley was ever so lightly tapping the edge of the table with just the tips of his fingers, as if patting out some rhythm softly enough not to be heard. I had a moment of wondering how far gone they were; they'd each disposed of the drinks they were working on when I went to the phone, yet really neither one looked swacked. Quite the reverse. They both suddenly seemed keyed up and super attentive as I plunked myself down and passed along a few words of report about the Alaska wing of the family. What do they call a chance like this any more, window of opportunity? In any case, right now appeared to be the propitious opening for herding my birthday partygivers back to the Bago and letting things settle down overnight, and so I drank up fast before another round could happen or more dancing and carrying on, and gave the evening as casual an amen as I could.

"I'm gonna call it a day. You two look like you could stand to turn in, too. Ready?"

The gaping silence answered that before Mariah began to try.

"Jick. You go ahead. We, Riley and I, we're not going to be back at the Bago tonight."

I had a furious flaring instant of wanting to ask her, demand of her, where they were going to be instead; but that was senseless. I all too well knew. It was right out front, up in neon: M-o-t-e-l.

Once the desiring begins, all other laws fall. You know that whether you are fifteen or sixty-five or both added together. There in the motorhome the remainder of that night, I tried to fight through to longer thoughts than that first alarm about Mariah and Riley's craving for each other. Judiciousness. Forbearance. Parental declaration of neutrality. All had hearings with me, chorused their verdict over and over that whosever's affair this coupling night was, it was not mine. My stiff exit from the supper club had been correct deportment, giving the pair of them something to think over yet not making too much of what I was leaving behind. Definitely those two were adults, not to say veterans of each other. So what, if Riley was horny. All right, so what if Mariah was in that same condition. This happens and ever will, wherever people grasp enough about one another to fit onto and into.

And as regular as the basting bags taped over the Bago window flapped in the wind, I accepted every iota of their No Tell Motel linkup and still I sorrowed, fretted, all but wept.

Tonight, a single lightning night of them together, was no cause for bonedeep concern. Tomorrow and its cousins were. Any of the time ahead, the rest of this centennial journey or beyond, when Mariah might paradoxically backslide to Riley; with all the life that ought to be ahead of her, trapping herself into that again. I hoped against hope that what I was picturing was not about to happen. But as searingly clear as the flashes that had been coming to me from the gone years, I could see ahead to her and him failing with each other again. Their mutual season would not last, the solitude in each of them would win out, and they would break apart in anger and grief and worse again.

Some graft of time, I yearned for. Some splint of cognizance by which Mariah, Riley, the both, could be shown how not to repeat defeat. But all that was left of me seemed too used and brittle for any of that. Sixty-five years before, union between my parents passed existence along to me. On the Aleutian mountain battlefield in 1943, the poor aim of an enemy soldier lent me life from then until now. But what next. Or was this already the next. People do end up this way, alone in a mobile home of one sort or another, their remaining self shrunken to fit into a metal box.

I put my face in my hands and as if she could still be reached by such a clasp, I cried out:

"Marcella? Marce, what the hell am I going to do?"

Bread and ink making their morning rounds woke me.

The Eddy's Bakery truck looming in front of the windshield of the Bago took a minute to register on me when I foggily craned up out of bed to see what all the traffic at this campsite was. Everything came back too fast after that, however. This campsite the Lass in a Glass parking lot, Mariah and Riley inside between the sheets, the whole mess. By the time the news agent pulled up to replenish the newspaper boxes outside the motel and had let the lids drops, *kachunk kachunk kachunk*, I had some clothes and a mood on. Such sleep as I'd managed to get was ragged, tossful. All over I felt bony and bruised, as if I'd been slumbering on a sack of doorknobs. Oldlike. And the main matter still awaited with the daylight which was just starting to find Chinook, planetary capital of romance: how to induce a thirty-five-year-old headstrong daughter to take a reality check on herself.

Even the interior of the Bago seemed foreign this morning. Strange as hell, how a domicile so empty could feel so mussed. I shook my head in a yawn or at least some kind of a groggy gawp and gimped up front to an unbagged window for a peek at the day. If there was any balance at all to things, at least the weather would have to have improved.

The meteorological outlook, though, was not what hooked my gaze.

I did not want it to be what it was. I looked long and hard across the thirty or so feet from the motorhome to the newsboxes. I tried telling myself, huh uh, naw, they wouldn't, must be some other—yet newsprint does not lie, does it, at least not in this fashion.

Slowly I went out and dropped a quarter and a dime in the middle newspaper box. On either side of it the Great Falls *Tribune* and the Havre *Daily News* were reciting developments in Poland. The *Montanian* I plucked out hit closer to home than I'd ever dreamed print and picture could.

Center page, mighty, in splendid color, the photo of course was

Mariah's. Of the Double W gateframe, tall thick poles and crosspiece in angular outline like a doorway slashed into the sky. Under and around the flagrant gateway, the Two Medicine country of that month-ago evening on our way in to the centennial committee meeting: the night-rumple of mountains where the sun had just departed, the thin strokes of clouds still glowing above. One mercy—standing so stark and dark, the gateframe's lettered sign announcing WW, Inc. ownership could not be read. But the steer skull dangling just beneath more than made up for it, declaring there against the Noon Creek sky like a horned ghost.

TWILIGHT OF THE RANCHER? epitaphed the headline beneath. And beneath that, the words of Riley.

From a life spent under a Stetson, he has his divided mind written on his forehead, the tanned lower hemisphere where wind and sun and all other weathers of the ranch have reached and then above the hatline equator an oddly shy indoor paleness. When he was younger, that band of pearly forehead made him stand out at the Saturday night dances, as if a man needed to be bright-marked at the top to be able to schottische and square dance so nimbly. When he was that young, the fingers of his children traced there above his brow in wonder at the border between the ruddy skin and the protected zone of white. Now worry fits on at that line.

The rancher starts his day as usual now with a choice of frets. Looks at the weather and plays the endless guessing game of climate—an open winter coming, or another Alaskan Express? the droughtiness of the 1980s at last over (the numerals in his grandfather's identical thought were the skein from 1917 into the mid–1920s, in his father's they were the 1930s) or only stoking up for more years of grass-shriveling heat? Checks the commodities page and calculates one more time what the latest disappointment in livestock prices is going to cost him. (Of all of Montana's hard weather, the reliably worst has been its economic climate.) He plots out all that needs immediate doing and tries to figure out why hired help has become the rarest commodity of all. Runs on through the wish list to where he always ends up, damning his bones for their increasing complaint against the daylight-to-dark ranch life, yearning with everything in him for someone to shoulder all this after he soon can't.

If the legends of his landed occupation are to be believed, a century and more ago Montana ranching began heroically, almost poetically, splendid in the grass. Yet even then, here and there a rancher twinged with the suspicion that legends are what people resort to when truth can't be faced. In 1882, cattleman Charles Anceny contemplated himself and his neighbors in Montana's new livestock industry with just such skepticism: "Our good luck consists more in the natural advantages of our country than in the scale of our genius."

Old Anceny portended even more than he knew. Natural advantages have a habit of eroding away under spirited exploitation. And the spirit of the West, of Montana, of America, has been what the legends speak of as grand and truth has to call aggrandizing. The consolidating, the biggening, goes on yet and with consequences below; as economic structures become more global somebody has to become more granular, and the rancher is among those. The marketplace that is the land is slipping out from under him. If you possess your own television network or have the spare change to own a professional football team or are paid an anchorman's salary for your face or are commensurately compensated for your appearance on the big screens of the movies, yes, you can maybe compete with corporations and foreign buyers to own enough ground to be a Montana squire. But this rancher born on a few thousand family acres doesn't have those infinite pockets. Instead what he owns is a penchant for counting too much on next year, and the notion that he's not actually working himself to death because he's doing it outdoors. Well, those are possessions too. But not the marketplace kind.

The rancher goes back and forth in his mind—give it up, tough it out. The past stretches from him like a shadow, recognizable but perplexing in the shapes it takes. He knows too well he is alone here in trying to look from those times to this. He rubs at that eclipse-line across his forehead and wonders how he and his way of life have ended up this way, forgotten but not gone.

I felt as if I'd been stripped naked, painted rainbow colors, and paraded across the state.

I spun from the newsbox and went to search the building.

He was established at a window table in the not yet open

coffee shop, tippetytapping words into his processor. Flexing his fingers for his next character assassination, no doubt.

The newspaper page still was in my hand. Not for long. I wadded it up and hurled it in Riley Wright's face.

He flinched, but let it bounce off him without otherwise moving.

"The latest reader survey shows that the *Montanian* draws considerable reaction from sheep ranchers with a Scottish surname," the sonofabitch droned in the BB's tone of voice.

My fury was compounded of what he'd written about me, of how he'd resumed with Mariah, of everything this Wright character represented. Hours, years, could have been spent in the telling. But it shot out hard and quick.

"The stuff you do to people would gag a maggot."

"Jick, I think if you'd just simmer down—"

"I don't that much care a shit what you think. Just tell me this. Why do you keep giving the McCaskills so much grief?"

That got to him. At least something could. Dreadful squintlines of what I took to be anger pulled the skin white and webbed at the corners of his eyes. The torn look of a man seeing something he had hoped to avoid.

For once Riley searched a while to find anything to say. When he did, his voice was surprisingly husky, as if he was having trouble down in his throat, too.

"I'm not going to debate Mariah with you—that's between her and me, even if you don't want it to be. So let's just talk ranch."

"Yeah, let's," I snapped. "Now that you've written me up as such a supreme failure."

The goddamn guy would not give in to my gaze. He folded his arms across his chest and sighed. "Honest to Christ, it never dawned on me they'd slap that Double W picture on the ranch piece. As soon as I saw it this morning, I knew you'd come in here pissing fire. The only people who don't react to being written about are in the obituaries. But you're taking it entirely too personal. Jick, you're not the only one in that piece. Anybody trying to run a family ranch or farm, maybe any kind of a family outfit, is in that situation."

"Anybody, my rosy rear end. You might as well have plastered my name all over that description of—"

I stopped. The only face Riley had described was that of the situation, just as he claimed. Try mightily as I did, except for the universal hatline I could not point to where it wore a single identifiable feature of myself.

Riley said quietly, "Jick, there are only four of us in the world who know that piece fits you at all."

Himself and Mariah and . . . "Who're the other two?"

"You are. One version of you is as mad as if you'd found flyshit in your pepper. The other one of you knows what I wrote is the absogoddamnlute truth."

Right then I ached, in mind, in heart, worse than my Attu shin ever could. "You figure you even have the right to do my epitaph, don't you," I spat out at him. " 'Here lie the collected versions of Jick McCaskill.' "

Riley bailed out of his chair so abruptly I figured we were proceeding to fists, which suited me fine. By God, that suited me just fine. Sixty-five sonofabitching years old notwithstanding, extinction ordained for me in every goddamn copy of that morning's *Montanian* be as it may, I could still plant a few knuckles before Riley did me in.

But the slander merchant was snapping the screen down on his laptop and stepping back from the table carrying it at his side like the most innocent of appliances. See how the guy can't even be counted on to erupt when he ought to? Riley only said, "Not that this'll improve your disposition any, but I've got to get to a phone and send in this Chief Joseph piece. I'm sorry that other one happened to hit the paper today. If I'd done the Chief Joseph one last night instead of—well, just instead of, I'd have modemed it in then and the ranch piece wouldn't have run. But I guess that'd just be postponing the inevitable, hmm?" And with that he walked away, squaring those broadloom shoulders, out of the coffee shop toward the mutual motel room.

I slumped into a chair at the abandoned table. How long I stared out along Highway 2 at the Lass in a Glass sign, extinguished now, I do not know, but she found me there after the morning light had flattened into that of day.

"Hi. Up early, same as ever, I see," Mariah imparted too brightly, swinging her camera bag down and herself into the chair opposite me that Riley had vacated.

When I made no response, she took in a breath and tried some more of the obvious: "I was out shooting the country while the nice light lasted. The Bearpaws are a different set of mountains today."

"I imagine."

She glanced at me, then down at the table, then off into various corners of the comatose coffee shop. "They ought to be opening up here pretty quick and we can get some breakfast."

"Swell."

"How about a machine cup of coffee until then?"

"Why not."

On her way back from the coffee machine in the lobby she managed balance all the way to the table before the two Styrofoam cups slopped. "Shit," she said. Then while she was mopping at the spill with napkin after napkin, her voice took on another rare tone, a tinny one of every word having been rehearsed. *Mariah, Mariah,* ran in my mind, *what you're doing to yourself.* What she was letting be known now was:

"Actually, you were right about that deal you tried to make with me at the start. We can just borrow the rig to do the rest of the series and you can be shed of us, how about. I can drive you home to the ranch this morning, right now, while Riley pokes around town."

"Naw, that's okay," I said pleasant as pie but thinking, to hell with this noise, daughter of mine. No way are you going to cut me out of the picture so you can fall heart over head for Mr. Wrong again. Overnight is one thing, every night is another. "I'm kind of growing used to the Bago life. I'll just stick with you and Romeo until you're done. No problem."

Mariah swung her head the little bit to sway her hair away and clear a look at me. "No, really, we—I can get by okay."

"Mariah, I wouldn't dream of leaving you in the lurch. Besides, there's a lot of Montana left to be seen, isn't there, which I'd hate to miss, wouldn't I." I gave her a steady gaze before adding, "Then there's the other thing."

"Which other thing?"

"That if you're going to make a fool of yourself over Riley a second time in the same life, you're goddamn well going to have to do it in front of me."

Mariah reddened as if my words were a slap. But I kept on, I had to. "That's what you originally brought me along for, isn't it? To ride shotgun against your inclinations to regard Riley Wright as a worthwhile human being? So that's exactly what I'm going to do."

"Jick . . . Dad . . ." she sorted nervously. "That, last night. Riley and I were just . . . feeling frisky."

I continued to look squarely at her. I hadn't thought it was a mutual yen for a night's deep sleep.

She moved her eyes from the path of mine and tried to maintain, "I don't know that I'm making a fool of myself over Riley."

"You're giving quite an imitation of it."

"This isn't like what happened before," she essayed in what was surprisingly like a plea but failed to convince me one least bit. "Riley and I, this time we're not, mmm"—to my horror, she was conscientiously sorting out in that flaming head of hers which way to translate to me the fact that they were scratching the bed itch; my God, I thought, does their generation have an entire warehouse of expressions for it?—"*taking up* with each other. We're just *seeing* each other."

Speak of the devil, Riley right then stalked back into the coffee shop, spied Mariah and marched grimly over, calling out:

"That'll teach me ever to go near a fucking telephone. Can you believe this, that sonofabitching—"

Tension must have grown pretty dense in the vicinity of Mariah and me, because Riley stopped as if he'd walked into a glass wall.

"Uh *huh*," he evaluated. "A family conference. I'll just wait outside until the blood quits flowing."

"Why don't you hang around?" I offered. "You might learn something definitive about yourself."

"Depends on the source," he replied with extreme wariness as he regarded me and then my daughter the paramour.

"He thinks we're crazy to . . . be with each other," Mariah minimally summed up my views for him.

"Never heard of try, try again, hmm?" Even though the words pittered out of him as syruplike as ever, Riley looked drastically serious. "Jick, it wasn't anything intentional, last night. You know better than anybody that Mariah and I both came into this despite each other."

"Then why in goddamn hell didn't you keep it that way?" I erupted. The majority of parents my age were wildly worried about their married kids breaking up. Why was I the one to have to throw a fit that mine were getting back together? "You both were managing to get done what you wanted to, without having to tumble"—into bed, into the jungles between the legs, into an old fever newly risked—"all over each other just the way you originally did. I don't understand why you're willing to set each other up for grief again."

"Last night didn't remake the world," Mariah protested in a perplexed tone, drawing a startled glance from Riley. "I don't know that we're—"

Riley held up both hands as if stopping a shove. "This must be the ultimate definition of the morning after," he growled to Mariah. "We've got Cupid's conscience right here on our case and the BB waiting his turn."

"The BB," Mariah echoed, her perplexity giving way to something a lot worse.

"The very guy," Riley exhaled wearily. "He wants to see us back in Missoula again. Yet today."

Missoula was a whale of a drive from Chinook. What did this Beebe so-and-so think, that he could just reel us in whenever he felt like it? Or as I stated it now: "Can't that guy ever say what he wants to say on the telephone?"

Mariah and Riley exchanged cloudy looks. He was the one who at last said, "The BB is a Bunker Hill type of boss. He likes to see the whites of the eyes before he fires."

Past lunchtime but still lunchless, the roadweary three of us trooped into the *Montanian* building.

A ponytailed young man carrying camera gear similar to Mariah's slouched out of the BB's office as we approached it. He looked like he'd recently been pinched in a tender part. Mariah greeted him and asked how the BB's mood was. Ponytail responded, "He's chewing sand and shitting glass, if that gives you some idea," and stalked off.

So, braced is the basic description for the *Montanian* centennial task force as we entered the presence of Baxter Beebe. All during our drive from Chinook, Mariah and Riley had tried to think of how to save their skins this time. Without any result, for as Mariah put it, "We don't even know if this is a fresh mad or the same one he was in last time." I'd been bending my brain to the BB problem too, for the one thing I didn't want now was Riley and Mariah cast loose into the world together, without a chance for me to somehow cure her of him. I mean, this just really frosted my ass; finally wanting the centennial trip to careen onward and here the BB was about to grant my original wish and X-out the expedition.

The BB or Bax or whatever sent the two of them his average steely stare as we filed in, but in my case he bounced out of his chair and came and gave me the pump-handle handshake while declaring, "Great to see you again, Jiggs. I wanted you to hear this, too." Huh. Maybe they were fired and I was hired.

With that, Beebe circled back to his chair, seated himself again, clasped his hands as if glad to meet himself, and gazed at us ranked across the desk from him. When he figured enough time had passed, he pronounced:

"I have bad news for us all."

He eyeballed the trio of us as if he'd always known three was an unlucky number. Then he shook his head gravely and said:

"I lost out on a goat permit in the state drawing."

Mariah and Riley swallowed in chorus. For my part, I looked carefully around the tower walls at the dead menagerie again, trying to think of any other animal to ante in, but no luck.

All three of us waited for the BB to lower the boom on the centennial series. Instead he again singled me out for his approximation of pleasantry.

"But that's all right. We can try again next year, Chick."

Now I didn't know which to be more of, puzzled or alarmed. Nor it seemed did the pair beside me. If I was bonded to the BB as hunting crony for another year, where then did that leave Mariah and Riley? Did this mean he hadn't even hauled us in here to ream out about—

"The centennial series."

The depth of the BB's tone dashed all hope there. "I have something to tell you about that."

He gave us another going-over with his gaze, one by one by one. Then intoned very deeply:

"It's a bull's-eye."

The identical thought was in all three of us who heard this: hadn't the BB gotten his mouth mixed up, actually intending to tell us the centennial series was some other bull stuff than the ocular part? But no, huh uh, he was going on and on about how Mariah and Riley were finding the true grit of Montana and what a service to readers to provide them something more flavorful than the usual newsprint diet.

Now this was news. The letters to the editor that had been showing up in the *Montanian* were saying pretty much the same as when our buddy Bax here was chewing the inside of his mouth to tatters over them. Only a few days ago there'd been one that started off, *Why does your so-called writer Riley Wright dig up old bones like the Dempsey-Gibbons prizefight when the Real Issue is taxes?* and signed, *Mad As The Dickens On Southwest Higgins.* I noticed that Mariah and Riley, though both surprised within an inch of their capacity, were staying on their guard. Riley in a funny way even looked a little disappointed, I suppose at having his work so palatable to the BB.

After a lot more salve of that sort, the BB focused on Mariah and, to my surprise again, me.

"In other words, I just wanted you to know what a very good job you've been doing. Now, Mariah and Nick, if you would excuse us, there's something I have to convey to Riley."

As soon as Mariah and I were out of the tower, I asked: "What the hell is that little scissorbill up to?"

"Don't I wish I knew," said she in bewilderment. It wasn't like Mariah to look left out, but right then she seemed the occupational equivalent of orphaned.

"Maybe he just wanted us out of there so he could stuff Riley and put him on the wall," I speculated. "Which would be the best use of—"

"Why don't you wait here," she stated rapidly, "while I go check my mailbox," and all but galloped off out of range of further conversation.

Mariah was back a lot quicker than I expected, though, with one piece of mail sorted out of the sheaf of memos in her other hand. "For yoo-ou," she singsonged, holding the envelope out to me with her pinky suggestively up.

The handwriting with merry little o's dotting all the i's probably rated that, but I tried to make it look like a business matter as I thumbed open the flap thinking, what the hell now?

It was one of those greeting cards showing two little creatures, mice or rodents of some kind, wearing great big sombreros and doing, what else, a goddamn hat dance. Inside, the printed message was:

SO NOW YOU'RE A 'SENOR' CITIZEN! COME JOIN THE FUN!

The one in the giddy handwriting below was:

Happy birthday, Jick! Everybody *misses you! Affectionately,* Althea.

"So?" my snoopy daughter asked with an eyebrow up. "You got a secret admirer, birthday boy?"

"Uh, Howard Stonesifer," I alibied casually and jammed the card in my hip pocket.

Mariah's other eyebrow now was up too, just as if she'd never heard of an undertaker dispatching birthday greetings to prospective customers. Right then, though, the door of the BB's office sprang open and out shot Riley grinning like a million dollars.

By now even I was plenty curious, not merely about how the BB had taken a shine to Riley but how anybody could. The sly so-and-so warded off even Mariah's intense questions, insisting "This is so terrific, we've got to go make an occasion of it. I'll tell you over lunch. I'll even buy. Even yours, Jick."

Depend on Riley, the lunch place was called Gyp's and was just big enough for a counter and a fry grill. I ever so imperviously slid onto the stool that put me between Mariah and Riley. Behind the counter was a bony cook who, according to the wall's autographed photos of him posing with Mike Mansfield and Kim Williams, was Gyp himself.

"Ain't seen you for a while, Riley," Gyp said affably. "Been nice."

"Hi, Gyp. The Health Department hasn't had you assassinated yet, hmm?" responded Riley as he plucked up a menu, opened it and slapped it closed without having looked at it. "White cheeseburger, fries, and an Oly."

"Same," said Mariah, eyes fixed on Riley.

"Same again," I said, eyes fixed on her.

Our beers came instantaneously, but before I could get mine lifted Mariah was leaning a bit in front of me to look with exceeding directness at Riley and he was peeking around me with a sweetheart grin at her. I felt like a sourball salesman at a Valentine party.

Mariah broached it first. "Okay, Chessy cat. What was that all about, the BB wanting to see you alone?"

Riley somehow increased that grin, his mustache almost tickling his earlobes. He announced:

"They want me in California."

At first I thought it was sarcasm of some kind. In the pause after Riley's words, I took a drag of my beer and inquired in kind, "What for, rubber checks? Or just general personality flaws?"

Then I noticed how utterly still Mariah had fallen, frozen in that same position of peering around me at him. As still as if gone brittle; as if the flick of a fingernail would crack her to smithereens.

In a stunned tone she finally managed to say: "At the *Glob*, you mean."

"The *Globe*, yeah," Riley responded.

"A column?"

"Yeah, a column."

Was it possibly so easy? Abracadabra or whatever the California equivalent is, and Riley vanishes off into the palm trees? A fatherly fraction of me felt bad about Mariah looking so stricken. But the overwhelming majority of me wanted to turn absolute handsprings.

Gyp slapped down our cheeseburgers in front of us. I spooned piccalilli on mine in celebratory fashion while Riley began ingesting french fries.

Mariah, though, pressed the question that I figured Riley had as much as answered with his proud announcement of California's desire for him. She choked it out as, "So what did you tell the BB?" Really, it was a crying shame she had to be put through this from the absconder, but how else would it ever get hammered home to her that Riley Wright's only lasting partner in passion was himself?

"This seems to be getting kind of personal," I noted. "Do you two want me out of here?"

"Sure do, just like always," vouched Riley in what was maybe a half-assed attempt to be funny.

"No," said Mariah in her same tight voice.

"Tie vote," I interpreted to Riley. "Guess I'm staying."

"Suit yourself." He took his time about eating a fry, then washed it down with a long guzzle from his beer. "I told the BB yes, naturally, but that we don't want to until after the centennial series is done. He phoned down there and the *Globe* agreed to stagger along until then."

"Who's 'we'? You got a frog in your pocket?" It was the most elderly of jokes, but the way Mariah said it, it carried all the seriousness in the world. And not just for her. I put my swissburger down on the plate and began wiping away the piccalilli I'd squeezed out all over my hand when I heard that pronoun of Riley's.

The incipient Californian was gazing steadily back at her, past me. "Mariah Montana, my notion is for you to come too. As my wife again."

EAST OF CRAZY

> . . . *Wind is the ventriloquism of Montana's seasons. In utter summer it can blow in from the west, the mountains, and convince you November is here. The other way around, the truly world-changing recital: the chinook breathing springtime into deadest winter. In just such a toasting wind-from-another-time we found my father, slumped onto the steering wheel of his pickup after the exertion of putting on chains to navigate the instant new mud from the Shields River calving shed to home. . . .*
> —RILEY WRIGHT'S NOTES, EN ROUTE TO
> CLYDE PARK, SEPTEMBER 6, 1989

IT HIT me like a kick in the heart.

What is the saying?—life is one damn thing after another, and love is two damned things after each other. Both parts pertained in the instant after Riley's double-barreled ambush, oh, did they ever. Bad enough to me, the prospect of Mariah going into marriage misadventure with Riley again. But on top of that, the searing feeling of simply her *going*. California is the American word for away, and I knew perfectly well the declension of it. As if by rote, a time or two a year a visit would be staged, daughter dutifully back for some ration of days or father descending south to clutter up the routine there for a mutually uncomfortable span. Periodic phone calls, *Hi there, how you doing?—Good enough, how about yourself?*, because letters are not habit any more. But beyond such dabs of keeping in touch, absence across distance. The formula of the young for moving a life from what it came into the world attached to. No parent can say it is anything but the history of the race, tidally repeating, yet each time the pain comes new.

At least I wasn't alone in being caught off guard in the cardio quadrant. Mariah stared lidlessly past me and my strangled cheeseburger at the author of this remarriage proposal or marriage reproprosal or whatever it constituted.

"I suppose this is a little bit of a surprise," Riley said around me to her in his ever sensitive fashion. Still leaning far forward onto the counter, he seemed poised to plunge as far as it would take to convince Mariah. Cupid's own daredevil, all of a goddamn sudden. "But why wait with it?" he charged onward. "Mariah, this *Globe* job is just what we want to make a fresh go at life. It's like winning the lottery when we didn't even know we had a ticket."

Blinking at last, Mariah made herself respond. "Quite a change of geography you've got in mind." Quite, yeah. Somehow Mariah California didn't have the same ring to it.

"But don't you see, that's just exactly why we ought to do it," Riley hurried to expound. "New territory, new jobs. New—"

"Job*uh*," she placed into the record to rectify the *s* he'd plotched onto the word. "You're forgetting, the *Glob* only invited you."

"A shooter like you," Riley assured her in revivalist style but obviously also meant it, "can latch on in no time, at the *Globe* or somewhere else if you want. Or if you want a chance to freelance, or to just do your photography for the sheer utter fun of it for a change, that's in the cards now too. Bless their sunglassed little heads, the *Globe*'s going to be paying me more than enough for both of us to live on. How's that for a deal, hmm?"

He paused to see how that went down with her. I eyed her too, but with a different question in mind. How Mariah could even entertain the notion of retying the knot with Riley was beyond me. I mean, after our too-green marriage blew up, you could not have paid me enough to get me to marry Shirley a second time. Talk about double jeopardy. Yet here was this otherwise unfoolable daughter of mine, sitting there not saying no to this human bad penny, which pretty much amounted to a second yes by default.

By now Riley had backtracked to where he'd been heading before her reminder of job singularity. He could get wound up when he half tried.

"New us again, Mariah, and I don't only mean being married another time. By the time we get through with this series we'll have done about everything we can, and maybe then some, at the *Montanian*. First thing it'll be right back to me trying not to write the identical columns I did a year ago or five years ago or ten, and you'll be back at shooting Rotarians and traffic lights being fixed. The Zombies Return to the Dead Zone, is what it'll be."

A would-be luncher came in the door, took one look at the madly gesticulating figure with a different color in each eye, and went right back out.

"You know as well as I do it's a fucking wonder that the BB and the bean counters let us do something like these centennial pieces even once in a hundred years," Riley resumed. "I've—"

"What about your perpetual book about Montana?" I thrust in on him.

"I was coming to that. I've finally savvied there isn't going to be any book. Every motherloving thing I know how to say about Montana, I've already put into the column or will put into this series." Back to his main audience, Mariah. "Okay, I grant that it's not quite the same for you and your camera. The one thing this state is always good for is to sit and have its picture taken. Photogenic as a baby's butt, that's ol' Montan'. But think what a change of scene would do for your work too, Mariah, hmm? Everygoddamnwhere we look here," Riley made a wild arms-wide gesture as if to grasp Montana at each end and hold it steady for us to see, "somebody or someplace is just trying to hang on by the fingernails, trying to figure out how to make some kind of a go of it against all the odds—a climate that's forever too cold or too hot or too dry or too fucking something else, and never enough jobs and wages that're always too low and somebody else always setting the prices on crops and live-stock, and the place full of bigshot assholes like the BB who think the state is their personal shooting gallery, and people like us can't even do our work right without having to beg help from our relatives, and—"

The expression on me stopped him. "Look, Jick, if you don't want to hear this—"

"Who says I don't want to hear it? Rant on."

He did worse, though. He looked squarely at Mariah and as if breaking the news to her said quietly:

"Montana is a great place to live, but it's no place to spend a life."

I couldn't just sit there and take that. "What, you for Christ's sake think California *is* the—"

"California," Riley overrode me, "is America as it goddamn is, like it or don't. Nutso one minute and not so the next. Mariah, this is a chance to go on up, in what we do. I know you want to be all the shooter you can, just as I want to be all the writer I can. To do that we've got to get out of a place that has as many lids on it as this one does." Ardent as a smitten school-boy, he reached for what to say and found: "There's just more, well, hell, more California than there is Montana to the world any more."

"We'll count up after the earthquake and see," I put in just as rabidly.

Riley's eyes and mine held. Good God Almighty, how had I misread him yet again these past weeks? All the while I was fretting about Mariah drifting toward him, he was cascading back into infatuation with her. He hadn't been just having a randy night in Chinook, he was all too genuinely putting himself into that motel prance with Mariah. This goddamn Wright. You couldn't even rely on him to be deceitful.

From my other hemisphere Mariah was saying: "Riley, are you really sure about all this, I mean, California and . . . all? An hour ago we were both scared to a dry pucker that the BB was going to can us, and now you're—we're the ones deciding to pack up and pull out?"

"Life happens fast when it gets rolling," Riley coined. "And we can't possibly go as wrong the second time married as we did the first, right?" He must have noticed me opening my mouth to say not necessarily—World War Two had followed World War One, hadn't it?—for he rapidly resorted to: "Or maybe let's just start the count from now instead of then." He dropped his voice into the rich tone of an announcer: "Together again, for the first time!"

There was a moment of threefold silence then, the two of them regarding each other past me as I perched there stewing.

"So?" Riley at last inquired. He gawked at the floor ostenta-tiously enough to draw the cafe owner's attention. "Do I have to get down on one knee? I kind of hate to, given Gyp's housekeeping."

"No," Mariah answered tightly. "I heard it all right from where you are." She put her hand on my arm as if to say *wait, don't go*, as though I was the one invited off to the land of quakes

and flakes instead of her. Then she went around me and gave
Riley a kiss that would have fused furnace metal.

The Bago by now could almost guide itself in the groove it had
worn into this part of the universe, to Missoula and from Missoula, and the next day I drove rather absently, letting the
motorhome and the freeway hum away the miles together while
everything else was on my mind.

In the passenger seat Mariah too seemed to be on automatic,
watching the weather—more rain; the spigot this year seemed to
be stuck open instead of closed—and the country as we headed
east, past Drummond, past Garrison, the twin paths of the
freeway swinging south through the tan Deer Lodge valley and
then reverting east again, halving Butte into its old hillside
mining section and the shopping malls on the flats below, all the
route until then a running start up to the Continental Divide;
and quickly across and down to the headwaters of the Missouri,
past Three Forks, and onward through the fine fields of the
Gallatin Valley, past Bozeman, past the Bridger Mountains. I
noticed that all the while her camera stayed inactive.

Those road hours Riley spent at writing something—not a
Montanian piece, because he and Mariah hadn't talked one
over—the *pucka pucka* rhythm of his laptop as intermittent as
the mileposts rolling past.

> . . . *In the seasons before the chinook, hunting magpies with our
> .22s my brother and I played at being Lewis and Clark along the
> swift small river they named for one of the enlisted men of their
> expedition. A captaincy apiece, we insisted on—neither of us ever
> bothering to imagine back into 1806 to be a startled and proud
> Private Shields putting his footprints beside water that still carries
> his name—for boys settle for momentary glory. . . .*

Not until just beyond Livingston, when he let me know "It's
this exit" and I swung the Bago north onto the suddenly thinner
route of Highway 89 up the Shields River, did Riley put aside
his wordbox and join the other two of us in watching the land.

The Shields River country was a new Montana to me. Accustomed as I was to the Two country's concentrated force of the
Rocky Mountain Front along a single skyline, here I was surprised by piles of mountain ranges in all directions: the Absarokas

to the south, the Castle range to the north, both the Bridger and the Big Belt ranges to the west and northwest, and to the east, over Riley's home ground, the high and solitary range called the Crazy Mountains.

My pair of passengers stayed as mute as the ranges of stone. Neither Riley nor Mariah looked forward to this chore, as I could readily understand. I was not, however, what could be called sympathetic. This reunification notion they had mutually lapsed into still seemed to me as crazy as those mountains up there. My one ray of hope was that the two of them at least hadn't hotfooted it off from Gyp's lunch counter yesterday to the marriage license bureau. "If we're going to go through with this California business," Mariah had managed to stipulate when the kissing let up, "let's do it all new down there. Get married there, I mean."

Riley pretended to count the weeks to *Glob*hood on his fingers, then consented. "I guess I can stand that. Maybe a change of preachers is a good idea anyway."

There in Missoula when the love doves eventually had to find their way back to the matter of the centennial series, something did develop that made me perk up.

After a final swig from his beer bottle and futile reconnaissance for any more french fries, Riley popped out with: "I dread to, but you know what I better do? Swing by the home place on our way east and break the news there."

Mariah gave her head a little toss and regarded him with extreme steadiness. "Break the news? You make it sound like a car accident."

"Joke, J-O-Q-U-E, *joke!*" Riley protested, but I had my doubts and quite possibly Mariah did too. However, there in Gyp's she let him get away with the explanation that he'd of course meant the news of the California job, the kind of thing that took a little getting used to for parents, sorry to say, with an ever so innocent glance in my direction.

Now Riley had me turn east off 89 at Clyde Park and head dead-on for the Crazies. The Shields River valley must have been a kind of geographical basket of good ground, because there was farming right up to the base of the mountains. Nice tidy ranches, of the cattle variety, were regular along the road.

The Wright family's ranch was up on a last ledge of fields before the Crazy Mountains stood like vast long tents of white.

The place could be read at a glance as prosperous; the original clapboard house with a pleasant porch all the way across its front, the newer lower domicile where Riley's brother's family lived, the white-painted cattle sheds and pens, the nice grass of the tightly fenced pastures beyond. Country this orderly, you did wonder how it produced a guy like Riley.

Who, as we approached the driveway, cleared his throat and suggested to Mariah, "It might be best if you let me break the—tell about us."

She said with forced brightness, "Okay, sure, words are your department, aren't they."

I became aware of a heavy stare from Riley. "Who, me? I wouldn't even dream of depriving you of the chance to make the same wedding announcement twice in the same lifetime," I reassured him. "Besides, it ought to be highly interesting to hear."

A yappity pup careened across the yard to challenge the Bago. I braked just in time to keep him from becoming a pup pancake.

The canine commotion brought a woman out onto the porch of the older house. Plentiful without being plump, in blue jeans ageworn to maximum comfort and a red-checked shirt with a yoke of blue piping in emphasis across the chest, she still was wearing her hair in a summer hank—it sheened whiter than gray, grayer than white—more abbreviated than a ponytail, to keep it off her neck in back. Somewhat leathered and weathered, she nonetheless had a well-preserved appearance; time simply paid its respects to a face like that. She stood deliberating at the motorhome while the kiyi chorus of the pup reached new crescendos, until Riley slid back the sidewindow and yelled out, "Call off your dogpack, Mother, we're relatively peaceful."

"Here, Manslaughter," she spoke to the barking guardian and patted a denim thigh for him to come to her. By now the woman had recognized Mariah's red hair as well as Riley's vocal presence and she came down off the porch striding quickly, in a kind of aimed glide, toward the Winnebago as if she had something vital to deliver. But when the *Montanian* duo stepped out of the motorhome, followed by me, Riley's mother halted a good distance away and somehow managed to gaze from one to the other of them and both of them at once while saying diagnostically, "I

217

saw by your performances in the paper that you two are tangled together again."

Riley, trust him, cupped a hand to his ear and asked, "Did I hear a 'hello' or was that thunder?" Then he brassed on over as if doing a major favor by delivering a kiss to his matriarch.

"It would help, Riley, it really would, if you'd keep me informed as to when you're on speaking terms with her," his mother gazed indicatively straight at Mariah, "so I can stay in step. Couldn't you have it announced on the radio or something?"

A watcher of this didn't have to be rocket-swift to pretty speedily realize that Riley's mother had as much peeve built up at Mariah as I did at Riley and for the one and same reason, the crash of their marriage. Why this surprised me any I don't know—just one more case of an in-law flopped into an outlaw—but it did.

Mariah looked like she'd rather be juggling hot coals, but she said to the silver-haired woman, "We maybe both better get in practice on our terms, how about."

Riley's mother eyed my daughter skeptically. Then perhaps registering the echo of McCaskill boneline in Mariah's form and my own over Mariah's shoulder, she cast her first full look at me. A moment was required to decipher me under the beard and then her eyes went wide.

"Jick!" she let out with her blaze of smile. "Hello again."

" 'Lo, Leona."

Half a century it had been, since I first said that. Since Leona Tracy, as she was then, all but married my brother Alec.

I cannot say that oldest storm from the past swept through me again, as I stood now in the yard of Leona Wright's ranch, because the memory of that summer of 1939 has never really been out of me. The June evening it began, when just at supper-time at our English Creek ranger station Alec and Leona rode in, I can recall to the very sound of the quick extra stick of firewood being rattled into the stove by my mother as she set at generating an already-cooked meal for three into ample for five. Looking up from the Forest Service paperwork he'd been trying to contend with, my father watched through the window as my brother and the goldhaired girl, the fondest of arms around each other as they ambled, crossed the yard from their saddle horses. "Glued together at the hip, those two," he reported.

"Safer that way than face to face," my mother stated.

He looked around at her, startled. She always could surprise him more than he cared to admit. Then Alec and Leona arrived, more like alit, into the kitchen with the other three of us, and the summer of war began. For it was during that suppertime, well before the butterscotch meringue pie that I'd been dreamily counting on for dessert, when Alec announced that he and she intended to be married, that the college years and engineering career my parents had foreseen for him were nowhere in his picture, that he was staying on as a wage hand at the Double W until he and Leona could afford a preacher and a bed that fall. Nineteen years old, him, and seventeen, her, and they believed they had all the answers to my father's increasingly biting questions, to my mother's clamped silence which was worse than her saying something. Admittedly, that was not the first blowup ever to occur within our family, but the one that happened that night with the TNT of Leona added in knocked the absolute socks off us all. In my not quite fifteen years of life until then, there had been what I assumed was the natural McCaskill order of behavior; occasional eruption under our roof but always followed by a cooling down, a way found to overlook or bypass or amend, to go on in each other's company, which seemed to me the root definition of a family. But then and there, with lightning suddenness my brother had gone into bitter exile. And never lived long enough, due to war, to retrace his way from it.

The preamble to all that was Leona. I suppose her beauty simply ran away with itself, spun beyond the control of the teen girl she was. That spring of 1939 she'd dropped Earl Zane—not that I can fault anyone for choosing a McCaskill over a Zane any day of the week—and her romance with Alec got hot and heavy in a hurry. Maybe he was overly taken with the, what can they be called, natural resources of a seventeen-year-old beauty. But there was always this about it: Leona could have switched Alec onto simmer merely by telling him she wanted to finish high school that next year, that they'd do well to see how their passion stood up across a couple of seasons. She did not say such, or at least did not say it until late in the summer—too late—after Alec had declared independence from our family and could not bring himself to retreat. Shape it as fairly as I can and it still comes out that my brother got hit coming and going by Leona Tracy, first bowled over by her and then left flat in the dust of her change of mind.

*   *   *

Leona Wright, as she faced me now. It costs nothing to be civil and I had managed to be so the time or two I'd crossed paths with her in our grown lives, at Gros Ventre's town centennial where Mariah and Riley first veered to each other, then at their eventual wedding, and did again here, to the best of my power, as she said how sorry she'd been to hear about Marcella's death. That over, I drew into the background—Riley and Mariah were all but tooting with impatience—but couldn't help studying the once girl of gold who had gone silver. As the younger onlooker during Alec's courtship, I'd regarded the Leona of then as the bearer of the eighth and ninth wonders of the world. Now she was stouter with the years, weatherlines at her eyes and mouth, but still a highly noticeable woman.

And still a formidable smiler. Her face stayed wreathed in what seemed utmost pleasure even as she swiftly got down to basics with her visitational son. "What's the occasion? Have you used up all the rest of Montana in what you've been writing?"

The pup was running himself dizzy in circles around us. For his part, Riley looked like he was being rushed to his own hanging. Nor did confession seem to be good for the soul in this case, for he didn't appear any less uncomfortable after his recital of: "Mother, I'm switching jobs. They're giving me a column."

Leona lifted one silver eyebrow. "I thought you already have a column."

"This one's located in California."

Had the mother of Riley deigned to glance in the direction of her ex–daughter-in-law just then, the expression on Mariah would have told the rest of it, somewhat to the tune of *And if you think that's something to swallow, chomp on the news that your son and I are going to get married again, you old bat.* But Leona only gazed at Riley and switched to another smile, a measure of sadness in this one, before saying:

"In California? Riley, is that supposed to be an advancement?"

An evening such as this, with the peaks and fields of the Shields River country as fetching as Switzerland, a person did have to be more than a little screwloose to talk about living anywhere else. Riley drew in a mighty breath and performed his explanation to Leona that at the *Globe* he'd have twice as many readers as the entire population of Montana, that the salary there made the *Montanian* look like the two-bit outfit it was—I

waited for him to get to the part about California being a better
Petri dish of the world than Montana is, but he never did.

Mariah most notably was waiting too, for her rebetrothed to
find his way around to that other announcement. Her earrings,
sizable silver hoops, swung constantly, as if sieving the air, while
she intently followed Riley's words and Leona's if-a-mother-
won't-be-kind-about-this-who-will? mode of listening.

The declaimant still was on California and not yet even in the
remote vicinity of matrimony, however, when ecstatic yips from
the Manslaughter pooch directed attention to a heftier version of
Riley making his way across the yard from the new house to our
powwow.

"Hey there, Morg, you're just in time for the family reunion,"
Riley greeted him in what was at least distraction if not relief.

Giving Mariah a nod of surprised recognition and me a more
general one, the other responded in a tone that eerily echoed
Riley's voice, "What's going on, Riler?"

I could see Riley barely resisting some crack such as *Don't beat
around the bush that way, Morg, just come right out and ask.* He
somehow forbore and resorted to manners instead. "Jick, you
ever meet my brother Morgan? This is none other."

Morgan Wright and I shook hands and mutually murmured,
"How you doing?" As soon as that was accomplished, Riley
repeated his bulletin about going to the job in sunfunland.

Morgan stood spraddled, thumbs alone showing from the
weather-worn hands parked in his front pockets, as though it
might take all the time in the universe to hear this matter out.
Then he asked Riley with concern, "Has California voted on this
statewide yet?" which proved to me they were full-blooded
brothers.

With a merry growl the pup at this point attacked a cuff of
Mariah's bluejeans in a spontaneous tug of war. Standing on the
besieged leg as methodically as a heron, Mariah lifted her other
foot behind her and gave Manslaughter a firm crosskick in his
furry little ribs. The pup let out a surprised *wuh!* and backed off
to regard her with abrupt respect.

The Wright family conclave didn't even notice, what with
Riley giving Morgan the whys and wherefores of California
while Leona took it all in again with the same regretful
smile. Suddenly she turned toward Mariah and me as if utmost
revelation had hit home. Mariah tensed defiantly, and I con-

fess even I braced a little in genetic sympathy, before Leona said urgently:

"Have you had supper?"

For whatever reason, Leona addressed that straight to me, as though the two of us were still responsible for the care and feeding of these giant tykes, her Riley and my Mariah.

"Naw, but that's okay, we'll nuke us up some frozen dinners in the Bago, it'll only take—"

"You will not, John Angus McCaskill," she said in the distinctive Leona voice. "You'll come in the house and have something decent."

I do have to say, the venison steaks and new potatoes with milk gravy and fresh biscuits with honey and garden-pea salad with tiny dices of cheese that Leona served up to us will never be equaled by anything under tinfoil.

During food, which I have always liked to believe is inspirational, I finally figured out Riley's case of topical lockjaw. The expression on him, which I can only liken to the look of the proverbial man in such crisis he didn't know whether to shit or go blind, I knew I had seen before, but when? Twice, actually. Most recently, there in the Medicine Lodge at the centennial committee meeting when he realized I'd sprung Good Help Hebner on him. But more vitally, that day of spring three years ago, when Riley palely delivered himself to the sheepshed beside Noon Creek to tell me he and Mariah had broken up.

Could it be, though? Such a garden-variety emotion behind Riley's evidently extreme quandary? A diagnosis can be simple yet complete. No, I now knew: more than anything, more than fear, fire, flood or blood, Riley Wright hated to look like a sap.

Hoo hoo hoo. Because that condition inevitably awaited him here whichever guise he chose to put on. Trotting around with an ex-wife, as though he couldn't get away from the situation Mariah represented, plainly stood out to Leona as highly sappy. But the instant he tried explaining that Mariah and he now saw the error of their divorce, Leona naturally enough would want to know why they wadded up their marriage in the first place then—and what answer was there to that but sappiness?

Meanwhile as Riley in his flummoxed state awaited some magical moment when Leona would welcome a defunct daughter-in-law back to her homey bosom, Mariah maintained a silence astonishing to me. I would have bet hard money this daughter of mine could not keep her lips hermetically sealed for this length of time under this amount of provocation.

By the time we had supped and pied and coffeed and been shooed into the living room by Leona, quite a number of moments passed but none of them were noticeably magical between Leona and Mariah. The closest came when Leona said with extreme neutrality, "I've been seeing your pictures in the paper. What was that one of the girl's head in a beer glass?"

Oh, for the simple green jealousy of that Kimi night, hmm, Mariah? She stiffly informed her once and future mother-in-law, "That's what's called an interpretive shot."

Leona looked as if she agreed that it needed interpretation, all right.

I was having to divide my attention between the living room contestants and outside, because through the big picture window toward the Crazy Mountains I could see a palomino mare frisking in a pasture next to the cattle lot. Beautiful lightish thing there in the dusk, its mane blowing like flax. Morgan Wright long since had excused himself from us by saying that as much as he hated to miss any further details of Riley's future, he and his Mrs. had to go in to a centennial committee meeting tonight in Clyde Park. (I told him there was an awful epidemic of that going around.) Even if that ostensible master of this ranch had been on hand, Morgan was not the one I would have asked about that horse. Somehow I knew that lovely bright mare could only be Leona's.

"So do you still ride?" I inquired, then wished I had the sentence back to makings, because that way of putting it also asked *or has age caught up with you too much?*

"Some," Leona replied, her eyes following the path of mine to the palomino but no smile finding her face this time, just a considering look. "When we're moving cattle I still help out. I tell Morgan that when I can't ride any more he may as well haul me to the dump."

The entire fifty years previous I would have thought, of course that is the case; Leona Tracy Wright was put into this world to enhance its saddle ponies with her golden—and later, silver—form, and when time ended that it indeed might as well conclude her, too. Life is temporary, after all, and the girl version of Leona had gone down its road at full gallop. But here on this ranch, on Leona's earned earth, I was beginning to see

what more there was to her than that. The perfection of fencelines
and thrifty pastures and leisurely cattle in the dusk, butterpat
fat—she and the late Herb Wright must have worked like twin
furies to build such an enterprise. And she had stayed on in
evident working partnership with Morgan. And she had endured
a decade or so of aloneness since her husband's death, a sum I
found enormous after my, what, eight or nine months since
Marcella's passing.

Still. Her icepick treatment of Alec, and all it led to. Would
some version of our McCaskill civil war have happened anyway, between Alec and my parents, between Alec and me—
a brother outgrowing the other or one staying with the logic
of bloodline while the second felt the need to yank free—even
if Leona had not been blondly there to precipitate it? Possibly,
quite possibly. We are a family that can be kind of stiffbacked.
But Leona was who precipitated it, and the best I have ever
been able to do with that fact is to keep a silence about
it. Plainly enough Leona, by lack of mention to Riley and
Mariah when they first met, when it would have been the
easiest chance ever to say *Isn't this funny, now? I used to
go with a McCaskill myself, but we . . .* , she herself wanted
nothing said of that long-ago fling with Alec, of the McCaskill
family mess it caused.

My pondering along these lines was interrupted by simultaneous blurts:

"Leona. Riley and I—"

"Mother. Mariah and I—"

The annunciatory duo also halted in the same breath, each
tongue waiting for the other to do the deed.

"Maybe you want to take turns at it," I suggested, "a syllable
or so at a time."

Riley scowled at me and huffed that that wouldn't be necessary, and as if he was reciting from memory a manual on
dismantling bombs, he apprised his mother that he and Mariah
had nuptial intentions again.

Even Leona couldn't come up with any kind of smile to cover
her reaction to this.

"But then why ever did you—" she of course launched, causing Mariah and Riley to concurrently roll their total of three
gray eyes and one blue one. I'd already done the route Leona
was raking them along, so I gazed again at the outer world. The

pup Manslaughter went tearing across the yard in pursuit of a magpie fifty feet above his head.

When his mother's invocation of their breakup was completed, Riley in turn lodged the protest, "That's neither here nor there." Which when you think about it was a sappy remark even for Riley. The point exactly was the attempted union of him and Mariah *there*, in the none too distant past, and now *here* again; the two of them just would not let the goddamn notion go away.

"Okay, now everybody knows," Mariah surprisingly broke her self-imposed silence to summarize. "Why don't we talk about religion, sex, or baseball instead?"

"California," Leona uttered, as if that fit the bill for an extreme topic. "I have trouble imagining you there, Mariah."

"Maybe I'll get used to it," Mariah answered edgily.

"Neither one of you got used to your marriage the first time, though," Leona essayed. "I'm curious. Aren't you, Jick?" Downright purple with it, although I didn't say anything because Leona was doing just fine. I could see where Riley got his knack for getting under the skin. Leona studied the uneasy pair of intendeds with boundless interest and concern as she asked, "What's going to be different this time?"

"This time we'll know better than to both get mad for more than a month at a time," Riley floundered out.

"Leona," Mariah decided she'd better try, "maybe Riley and I did go ape, a little bit, in that divorce. You're welcome to blame me, if you want." At least that would balance things across family lines, given my attitude toward Riley. "But that doesn't change our getting back together," Mariah went on at a rattling pace. "This centennial trip has made us feel we want to stay that way." She snapped her head around to Riley so quick her earrings blurred. "Right?"

"Could scarcely have said it better myself," the wordsmith corroborated.

All of a sudden, from somewhere rang out a little *ding* and then a man's voice, as cultured as caviar, intoning: "*Kahk vasheh eemya ee otchestvo?*"

Riley, pretty much goosed up anyway even before this vocal development, catapulted out of his chair. "Who the f—?"

His mother flapped a hand at him and instructed, "Shush now, Riley, I've only got ten seconds to answer in."

Now Leona could be seen to be concentrating with every

mental fiber, her thumb and forefinger pinching together in an intent little *o* as if practicing to pluck from the air. Then she threw her head back and recited firmly: "*Ya Leeona Meekhylovna.*"

"*The question in Russian was,*" the celestial male voice resumed, " '*What is your first name and your patronymic?*' *If you were not able to translate it and answer in the allotted ten seconds, please do so now.*"

Leona smiled triumphantly and marched across the room to snap off a tape player and a gizmo plugged in beside it. "I set the lessons on a timer," she explained, "to catch me by surprise. It seems more lifelike, that way."

Riley gazed at her as if counting slowly to himself. After what maybe was an allotted ten seconds, he began: "Mother—"

"*Mahts,*" she promptly identified for him.

"Whatever. In plain English, in little words so I can try to get this—what are you doing studying Russian?"

"We're Sisters of Peace," Leona informed her son. He continued to look at her as if she'd declared she was Queen of the Williewisps. "Our women's club here along the valley, it's our centennial project," Leona went on. "We're a sister group to women like ourselves in Moscow. *Muskvah.*"

Kind of needlessly, it seemed to me, Riley did check: "I take it you don't mean the one in Idaho."

"Spoof if you want," Leona responded in a style that suggested he'd be better off not to. "I just thought it would be nice. To know how they talk. We're going to send them a videotape of the Clyde Park centennial day doings. Jeff is going to be our cameraman." Leona looked over at Mariah as if just remembering her existence. "Cameraperson." I was recalling that Jeff must be Morgan's son, hard to think of anybody having Riley for an uncle. "I volunteered to learn enough to say a few things to them in Russian, on it," Leona went on as if Cyrillic from Clyde Park made perfect sense. I confess, in spectating Riley's reaction to his mother the sexagenarian rookie linguist and Mariah's reaction to her *and* him, I'd lost track—maybe it did.

"My mother the peacenik!" Riley gabbled to Mariah in some mix of being perplexed and resigned and wary and proud.

"Mmm," Mariah responded ever so neutrally.

"I might as well be doing something with myself," Leona concluded. "I have the time, after all." She smiled around at the three of us in equal allotments, her blue eyes steady within the

fine wrinkles reaching in at their corners, then soberly focused
on Riley and Mariah again. "Where are you headed next?" Her
inquiry could just as well have meant what next plateau of folly
they aspired to after rematrimony and California, but that son of
hers chose to answer in Bagonaut terms, that we'd wheel east
from here, out into the big open of Montana away from the
ranges of the Rockies. Both he and Mariah, I was sorry to see,
were beginning to look like they might come out of this evening
intact after all.

I let Riley finish with the travel orientation and start to make
what he obviously hoped were evening-ending indications. Then
I spoke what I hoped were going to be the magical seven words.

"Whyn't you ride along with us, Leona?"

Leona looked pleasantly startled. Mariah looked as if I'd
invited a Tartar into the tent. Riley looked as if I'd poleaxed
him.

"I mean it," I went on cheerfully. Did I ever. There was no
forgiving Leona that hurtful yearling romance with Alec and the
consequences it walloped the McCaskills with, but this was no
time to be pouty about that. What needed priority was the
situation here in the room with us. Riley already was plainly
provoked; he was in for a lot more aggravation if I had anything
to do with it. I'd had my say, such as it was, to Mariah and this
secondhand swain of hers after their Chinook night of ecstasy,
hadn't I? A steady stout dose of Leona couldn't hurt as the next
remedy to try on them, could it? "Come see some country," I
spieled to her with enthusiasm. "I can guarantee you this about
it, traveling with Riley and Mariah is the kind of experience you
never even dreamed of before. Besides," I couldn't help giving
Mariah an innocent look, "you can't beat the price. The
newspaper's paying for it all."

"What a kind offer, Jick. But I'd just be in the way," Leona
demurred with a dazzling thanks-anyway smile.

I assured her, "No more so than me." Quite possibly more
effectively so, though. "These offspring of ours keep awful busy
with each other," I sped on. "At what they're doing, I mean.
Majority of the time, Leona, the two of them more than likely
won't even notice you're around." Interesting that my tongue
was capable of stretching itself so. The last person not to notice
Leona must have been blind, deaf and on the other side of a lead
door.

"You wouldn't mind, really?" Leona swung like a turret to the newspaper pair.

"No, no, no," Mariah managed with a swallow. "Not a bit."

"Entirely up to you and the Bagomaster, Mother," Riley got out, cutting me a *now you've gone and done it* glare from the corner of his blue eye.

"Jick?" Leona addressed me as if I was the next question. "This will teach you to make an offer like that."

"Snoose Syvertsen," Leona announced out of nowhere as the Bago purred past the Crazy Mountains and eastward along the Yellowstone River. "You remember him, don't you, Riley?"

Directly behind me at his writing station in the dinette where his laptop output was sounding slim this morning, Riley grumpily confirmed he remembered.

McCaskills in the forward seats and Wrights amidship, we had embarked down the Shields River valley from Leona's ranch an hour or so before. Outside, the day for once was rainless and fresh, the clawed-out peaks of the Crazies as clear as could be in dazzling first snow. Weather within the motorhome, though, was heavy and electrical, just as I'd hoped. In the passenger seat Mariah was noticeably squirmy and kept her eyes resolutely on the Yellowstone River as if seeking a spot deep enough to sink a mother-in-law in while Riley, as I say, was promisingly grumpy.

"Snoose was our choreboy a while, years back," Leona not unnaturally chose me as audience, "until he started herding sheep for a Big Timber outfit out on these flats. He'd go in to Livingston a couple of times a year to drink up his wages and whenever anybody asked him where he herded, he'd point off in this direction past the mountains and say, 'East of Crazy.' "

I chuckled and commentated, "At least the guy had his bearings," as if there were others in our vicinity, such as directly behind me and immediately beside me, who did not.

"I didn't get around to asking last night, Jick," Leona's words kept wafting distinctively to me as I drove. Hers was what I can only call a woodsmoke voice. It came as if tracing its way through the air to you, certain wisps more pungent than others. A voice, it had always seemed to me, that perfectly well knew it could embody as casually as it cared to because main attention would ever be on Leona's fierier attractions. So in essence, the listening side of a conversation with Leona was a matter of catching her drift. "Sheep," I heard loft from her now. "You're still running them, are you?"

"Still am," I admitted. "After about forty years they kind of get to be a habit."

"Morgan has us running breeds of cattle I've hardly even heard of," came her comparable report. "Red Angus, and some Simmentals. He figures we've got to try different kinds every so often to see how they'll do."

Yes, I thought savagely, that is the very thing a ranch needs: a Morgan Wright to dab around with new notions, to try out new fashions of livestock and crops. To put fresh muscle into the land. Which is exactly what my ranch has had no prospect of ever since Leona's other son, the knotheaded one behind me at that moment, turned down my offer.

"I'm surprised Riley hasn't brought you home some buffalo from Moiese to raise for hood ornaments," I lobbed over my shoulder.

"Buffalo?" Leona asked, puzzled, looking back and forth from me to her determinedly utterly silent progeny.

"Riley can explain it to you sometime when he's got his tongue along with him," I said. "Rest area coming up," I noted the announcing blue sign ahead by the side of the Interstate, "everybody get in the mood."

Riley was so ticked off at me that he violated the first principle of freeway lavatories: don't pass up any chance to go. I hummed off by myself to the men's side and on into the stall while Mariah and Leona, as silent toward each other as nuns with a vow, betook themselves into their side of the pleasant bungalow-size brick convenience. So far, so good, on this Leona deal. Riley already was significantly twitching. Keep applying his mother to one end of him and his ex-wife fiancée to the other and maybe he'd bail out to California early just to rescue his nerves. My definite hunch was that nothing, no known force, could peel Mariah away from finishing the centennial series; so if Riley called it quits, while she refused to—second thoughts about mushing their lives together again might be seeded right there, mightn't they? At least it gave me a somewhat promising prospect to mull while I had to be sat.

Walls in a public facility have their own topics they're insistent on, though. I could not help but notice, in fairly neat small penciling directly in front of me on the stall door, one lone unillustrated epistle. Leaning forward as much as was prudent, I just could read:

THE DEBRIS OF HUBRIS IS THE CHASSIS OF GENESIS.

I was contemplating my way through that when footsteps arrived.

"What'd we ever do before all these rest areas?" came a voice entering. "Just turn loose alongside the road? You know what they say, though. 'Pee by the side of the road and you get a sty in your eye.' But I don't remember that many styes, do you?"

"What all I don't remember would fill Hell's phone book," testified the other. As the duo zeroed in on the urinals, peeking under the stall wall as best I could I saw identical sets of streamline-striped jogging shoes—both pair of which, I would bet, were off the same sale table at the K Mart—blossoming out the bottom of very veteran bluejeans; by the sounds of their voices, these guys aged radically pore by pore upward from those zippy shoes.

"Hullo, what've we got here?" the first voice was saying. "Somebody left us a love note."

"I hope like the dickens it don't say, 'Smile, you're on Candid Camera.' "

"No. Huh. Huh. I'll be damned."

"Ain't that something, though? How do you suppose people get theirselves into the fixes they manage to?"

Whatever they were reading above the waterworks had not caught my eye on my way in, but it seemed to be something fairly sensational, because now several other guys were arriving— they were all of a group, at least from the evidence of universal speedstreak jogging shoes—and the note was the immediate topic of roundhouse debate.

"It says *what*? I never heard of no such thing." "Take a look for yourself, would you." "Let me get my reading specs on here. Any more I can't tell whether I'm on page nine or it's something by Paganini." "Suppose the guy who wrote this is on the level? What do you think, Bill?" "What am I, the expert on lying? Don't answer that." More reading, to the accompaniment of assorted trickles. "Hell if I know. Funny damn kind of a situation he claims he's got himself into." "I can see how it could happen." "I don't." "There's this much for sure. These days, anybody'd who'd pick up a hitchhiker ought to know better." "Ought to, yeah, but maybe he was trying to do somebody some good. You can't fault a man on that, can you?"

I emerged from the stall into the debating group. There in a cluster, seven familiar faces and I gawked at each other.

"We come across you in the goddamnedest places!" exclaimed Roger Tate, who I remembered was the seniormost of the Baloney Express car corps. "How you doing, Jick?" All the others heartily chimed in their greetings, old home week to the point where little Bill Bradley gestured in the pertinent direction and asked, "You seen this note on the wall here?"

"No," I admitted, "but I been hearing a lot about it." I moved up close enough to take my turn at examining the document.

BROKE AND BAREFOOT

Mine is a long story, but to put it short as can be, I picked up a hitchhiker yesterday when I left Coeur d'Alene, and after we reached here, and I got too sleepy to drive any more, I told him he had to get out, and go on on his own, while I caught some sleep. He did, get out that is, and I locked myself in the pickup, and stretched out on the seat, but when I woke up this morning, my shoes that I had taken off, and all my money, were gone. I am stuck here, until somebody can help me out. Any money you can loan me, would help me buy gas and food to get home to Fargo, and I will take your name, and address, and mail it back to you, quick as I can. I am in the GMC pickup, red in color, at the east end of the parking lot. Thank you.

You hear all kinds of stories of people begging in wheelchairs or whatever, then as soon as you're out of sight they hop up and stroll off to buy drugs with the money you just gave them. Evidently what people won't resort to hasn't been thought of yet. Naturally my mental question was the same as the Baloney Expressers: was this broke-and-barefoot note the newest kind of cheat?

Another round of democratic Roger-Bill-Nick-Bud-Julius-Jerome-Dale debate produced the idea of actually going and taking a look at the guy in the red pickup. I was either born curious or became that way a minute later, so off I set with the investigating committee.

As we were cutting across the parking lot past the fleet of clunkers my companions were ferrying to a used car lot in Billings, Riley popped around the hood of an idling Continental Freightways semi. "The women were starting to wonder if you

fell in," the knothead loudly addressed to me as he strode up.
Then he recognized the company I was in. "Don't tell me. The
Methuselah Hot Rod Club is on the loose again. Watch out,
world."

Inevitably the Baloney Express gang greeted Riley with ver-
dicts on his piece about them that, coming from them, he regarded as high praise. Then I explained to him our mission to
the east end of the parking lot and he glanced nervously over his
shoulder in the direction where his mother and Mariah were
waiting for us in the Bago, precisely as the two women emerged
around the semi in search of the searcher they'd sent scouting
for me.

The sight of the seven geezers whose collective rumps she had
presented to the reading public made it Mariah's turn for wariness, but they unanimously assured her that photograph of hers
had presented their best side to the world. Her first grin of the
past forty-eight hours broke out on Mariah as she asked what the
occasion here was. Leona meanwhile was in an all-purpose smile
while trying to get a handle on any of this, and after the Baloney
Expressers' sevenfold explanation about the *Broke and Barefoot*
note and I'd introduced Leona to each of them in gallant turn
and the entire general scrimmage of us had started moving
toward the pickup in question, she dropped back beside me and
wondered in a whisper, "Jick, do you know everybody in
Montana?"

"That's pretty much getting to be the case," I acknowledged.

"You want to watch out," she whispered again, "or you'll end
up as Governor."

The vehicular description "red in color" proved to be a wish-
ful memory of the beat-up pickup's faded appearance, and the
young guy in it didn't look like much either. When our delega-
tion drew up around him and he cranked down the window on
the driver's side, the face framed there was one of those misfitting
ones with not enough chin or mouth but a long thin nose and a
wispy blond mustache, scraggly, really. His eyes were red-rimmed
and darted around miserably among what must have looked to
him like a posse from an old folks' home. Treed in a sapling
about to snap, was the impression he gave.

But any con man worth the name would know precisely how
to appear so simultaneously victimized and embarrassed, wouldn't
he. The Baloney Expressers clustered around the driver's side

window, as attentive a jury as they had been while watching Riley wrestle the Bago tire two months ago.

Roger Tate spoke the doubt of everybody. "One thing that's hard to savvy, Mister, is how somebody could get at you that way in a locked pickup."

"For the longest time I couldn't figure that out either," the young guy confessed tiredly. "I knew goddamn good and well I'd locked both doors. But what the bastard did, I finally caught on, was he unlocked his wing window while I wasn't looking" —the pickup was so old it did have those vent windows with a little catchlock that moved about half an inch for opening them— "and after I fell asleep he must've snuck back and reached in through it and got that door open. And took off with my money and shoes." The guy swallowed and looked like he was about to bawl, but seemed to feel he had to tell it all: "Didn't even leave me my socks."

The congress mulled that testimony. One of the Walker brothers, Julius, remarked: "You're quite a sleeper."

"Mister, I know it sounds fishy. I almost can't believe it myself, what happened. And nobody until you guys would even come near me to hear about it. But jeez, it's the truth," he concluded, his face saying the awful realization of how much predicament his life's quota was.

Nor was his situation eased any when two or three Expressers simultaneously asked whether he'd called the highway patrol or sheriff yet. The young guy squirmed and looked away from all our eyes, down at the steering wheel. "Can't do that. My license plates are out of date. Couldn't afford this year's." A majority of the Baloney Expressers at once investigated at the rear of the pickup and verified that the North Dakota *Peace Garden State* license plate was 1988's.

In the kind of tone a district attorney would use on a pickup thief, Bill Bradley wanted to know: "You say you're from Fargo, what were you doing all the way over in Coeur d'Alene?"

"Looking for work. I come from Coeur d'Alene originally. When there wasn't any jobs there, I got on driving tractor for my wife's uncle outside of Fargo. But he got droughted out again this summer, same like last summer, and he had to let me go." This chapter of his story poured out of him, either well-rehearsed or from the heart. "I hoped something maybe'd opened up, back home there. But jeez, all there is in Coeur d'Alene any more is

changing bedsheets for tourists and they don't want people like
me for that. Logging's down. Mining's gone to hell. Farmers and
ranchers can't afford to hire. What am I supposed to do?" That
last word broke out as a rising note toward wail, do*ooo?*

I stood staring past the silent elderly heads at the wispy-
whiskered specimen of woe and his faded illegitimate pickup.
Curious no longer, I now was furious. When I was not much
younger than him, other pickups were on the road, passing
through the Two Medicine country from the droughted-out farms
of the High Line with the bitter farewell GOODBY OLD DRY
painted across their boxboards, and families of the Depression
crammed aboard with whatever last desperate possessions they
had managed to hang on to. The human landslide set loose by
auction hammers cracking down. Two rages balanced in me: that
here fifty years later there still was no goodbye to that grief of
being driven from the land, or that a clever beggar would play
on that memory of misery to coax money from us.

Out of that bloodsurge of the past, I called sharply to the
pitiful or conniving face in the pickup window:

"There in Coeur d'Alene, did you ever know somebody named
Heaney?" Leona was a little distance from me, and out the side
of my eye I saw her stir at that remembered name.

"Mister Heaney? Sure." The young guy lost a little of his
complexion of despair as he found something definite to offer. "I
used to mow his lawn. Ray Heaney? In the insurance business?"

The Baloney Express totality swiveled to watch my reaction.
In my mind now was the Heaney house on St. Ignatius Street in
Gros Ventre, Ray and I sprawled beneath tall cottonwoods on
that lawn of another time, our boyhood best friendship now
thinned to lines jotted on Christmas cards exchanged from his
insurance agency to my ranch . . .

I nodded, which brought a chorus of "Well, hell, okay then"
and "Good enough" from the group awaiting my verdict. Roger
Tate swung around and told the young guy, "We got to have a
little conference over here. You just sit tight."

Eagle-beaked old Dale Starr proved to be the fiscal lobe of
Baloney Express. While the others looked to him to decree a
sum that would get a man enough gasoline and meals to carry
him from the middle of Montana all the way across North Dakota to Fargo, plus putting something on his feet, Dale in turn
squinted at Riley and asked, "You in, Shakespeare?" Riley said

he supposed he was. It seemed to be just assumed I was a donor, so Dale inquired next: "Ladies?" Without looking at each other, Mariah and Leona each nodded inclusion into the ante. Dale promptly announced, "Okay then, nine bucks a head."

After we'd all dug down in wallets or pockets or purses for Dale, he in turn riffle-counted the sheaf of bills, nodded, and handed the money to Roger Tate. Who led us back to the pickup and told the young guy, "Here's $99 to see you home. Take care."

The guy choked out several versions of thanks and promises to repay, then started the clattery pickup and headed out onto the Interstate. None of the eleven of us said anything as we watched him go. He had a lot of miles ahead of him yet to Fargo, and still faced walking into a shoe store in Billings barefoot.

After that not particularly restful stop, we let the freeway go on to Boston while we sideroaded north. Naturally I reverted to watching our retread lovers deal with Leona's flagship presence. Jangled but not yet to the point of disintegration, was my reading of Mariah and Riley's mutual mood so far. They were taking refuge in their work insofar as they could. True, no *Montanian* piece came to light from our excursioning through Rapelje and Harlowtown and Shawmut and Judith Gap. But shooter and scribbler kept reminding each other in earnest that they absolutely utterly just could not afford to flummox around the way they had at the outset of the trip; as one or the other of them phrased it at least once a day, "We don't have time for a scavenger hunt." And it sounded to me as if both Mariah and Riley actually grasped that, this time; these two were educable about anything but themselves.

It wasn't many days into this Leona phase of the trip before we came to an intersection, close to the exact middle of the state, where the sign pointing south said one hundred miles to Billings and the sign pointing east said one hundred miles to Jordan. The *Montanian* twosome chose east, and so we Bagoed onward into country where a hundred miles to anywhere seemed a highly conservative estimate.

Keep your eyes on the horizawn was in a song that came around fairly often on Melody Roundup on the Bago's radio and the landscape surrounding us now was much like that, a kind of combination of horizon hypnotically the same and the earth letting out a stretching yawn as it drew its edgeline against the sky. The Big Dry, this prairie region out ahead of us was called, partly because Big Dry Creek traces across it but also for the general precipitation picture. Not this year, though. After the drought of the past couple of summers, even this gaunt midriff of the state had received decent rain this year. I would bet that it was green years of this sort which fooled the homesteaders into settling out here in the first place. This was a neighborhood where I had never set foot but yet felt I knew something of. When I was a kid during the Depression, one of the country school systems somewhere out east here got so strapped for funds that the only musical instruments that could be afforded were harmonicas, and so harmonica bands were formed. Fourth of July solemnity, graduation day, any of those type of functions featured mouth organ musicians en masse and for a few years there I devoutly wished our own Gros Ventre high school would either go broke enough or sensible enough to forget about stuff like trumpets and put us all on harmonicas. I mean, wouldn't it be something to hear *Pompous Circumstances*, as my father called it, orchestrated by a schoolful of harmonica kids?

People were not many out here any more. Now that it was after Labor Day, as we drove we regularly saw the bumblebee colors of schoolbuses moving along rural roads. But even that scene scarcened here at the onset of the Big Dry country.

Pucka pucka pucka, Riley's wordbox began to tune up as we rolled on.

> *In the red schoolhouse of his head, Jefferson, great Tom, calculated the doubling of America westward. He knew that miles in chunks could be whittled into dreams, farms, nation, and out of that Jeffersonian box of mind came an orderly arithmetical survey system which put the pattern of mile-square sections on the land; came his 1803 bargain with France for the Louisiana Purchase, the frontier expanse all the way from the Mississippi Valley to the western side of what is now Montana; came his instructions to his enigmatic young personal secretary Meriwether Lewis to find a cohort—the steady William Clark, he turned out to be—and explore up the Missouri River into this new dreamscape.*
>
> *In the presidency of Lincoln, Abe who had built farm fences, came the Homestead Act. That broadstroke of legislation in 1862*

*and its cousin laws proclaimed: come west, come into the Jeffersonian
vision, come gain yourself a piece of the earth by putting your
labor—your life—into it for this little sum of years.*

*Into Montana, mostly in the first fraction of the twentieth
century, came scores of thousands of homesteaders in the greatest
single spate of agricultural migration in American history. . . .*

We pulled into Winnett for the night. A grocery store. A
couple of bars, one doubling as a cafe. A gas station out by the
highway. Highway sheds, grain elevator. A school, nice and
modern. Some houses that were being lived in, but not as many
as there were empty ones and vacant lots. What was saddest to
see, though, was not just the proverbial grass growing in the
street but little jungles of morning glory vines snaking out.

And that was pretty much the town except for the courthouse.
You might not ever think so if you didn't know, but Winnett,
population two hundred, is the county seat of Petroleum County.

"Which," Riley announced out of the books he'd been looking
stuff up in as I drove us along the scanty main street, "has a
total population of—brace yourselves, gang—*six* hundred, in an
area, hmm, bigger than the Los Angeles Basin."

"There he is on California again, Jick," Leona shared with me
as if we were on a mutual quest for an antidote. She had taken
off her Walkperson headset that had been reciting Russian into
her and was gazing around Winnett as if she'd always been
meaning to pay it a visit.

"Maybe you two want to put some of this elbow room in your
suitcases for *Glob*land," I in turn suggested to Mariah and Riley
as I aimed the Bago into the otherwise empty Petrolia RV Park.
"Sounds like you could sell it by the inch down there."

The *Montanian* team ignored our parental remarks and scanned
out the window at trafficless and pedestrianless Winnett. "Let
me guess," Mariah eventually intoned to Riley. "What we need
here is a photo of Jefferson rolling over in his grave, right?"

I will say for Riley that he was bright enough to immediately
pack himself off uptown, so to speak, out of range of Mariah's
photo-thinking mood. Myself, I figured she and her camera
would charge right out and tackle the challenge of Winnett, but
this daughter of mine could still surprise me. When Leona offered to come out and help me hook up the utilities, Mariah slick
as a wink told her no, no, she'd be more than glad to help me at

that herself, she knew Leona had lots and lots of Russian to pipe into her head yet.

So out we went, Mariah and I, around to the side compartments of the Bago. She had been waiting her chance to get hold of me alone. "Thanks a whole hell of a bunch, Daddio," she let me know in a tone that would have peeled paint.

"What, for my general sainthood or something specific?"

"You know goddamn good and well," she said, yanking the electrical hook-up cable out of its cubbyhole a mile a minute. "For inviting the Duchess of Moscow along."

"Figured you'd appreciate having some female company on the trip for a change," I responded with an extreme poker face. "The benefit of an older wiser woman and all that."

"Benefit, sure, you bet," Mariah bobbed her head as if bouncing each word at me. "Now any time I get a craving for it I'll know how to order borscht."

"In California," I cautioned, "they probably call it liquid essence of beet."

That headed her off on Leona, at least. Mariah eyed me as if debating whether this next issue was worth taking to war. "You really don't want me to go to California, do you."

I bent to fasten the Bago's water intake hose into the campground spigot. Not that I'd entirely intended it, but this left Mariah with the honey hose—the toilet drain—to gingerly drag out and handle.

"What I really don't want, Mariah, is for you and Riley to carve grief into each other, the way you did the first time. California is only the wrapper that comes in."

McCaskills, daughter and father, looked at each other over the utility hookups. We both were so taut that a breeze would have twanged notes out of us.

Mariah at last shook her head.

"Nice try, but this," she indicated with a lift of her chin toward Leona's chesty silhouette in the Bago sidewindow, "isn't going to change anything between Riley and me."

"Then you got nothing to worry about, do you," I asserted back to her. "You and Riley can practice at marriage again by each having a beloved in-law around."

In this promising outlook for disruption, that night after supper I figured a game of pitch might be just the thing to help matters along.

Remembering his trouncing when we'd played at Three Forks, Riley sent me a narrow look and stated: "Huh uh. I don't participate in blood sports."

But just as I'd hoped, Leona was not about to let him squirm out of it. "I don't see any competing nightlife in Winnett, do you?"

It didn't take much doing on my part to contrive the next, either.

"Why don't you and me take them on, Leona? Show these heirs of ours how the game is played, why not."

Riley of course had things so backwards he was actually relieved to be partnered with Mariah rather than me or his mother; it was Mariah who twitched at the generational pairing, but what could she say? No way around it for her, which T-totally suited me. If she figured she was going to remake life with this Wright guy, first let her consider the mess he could make of merely a hand of cards.

Pearl Harbor with playing cards instead of bombs, is the nearest description I can give of what ensued. Leona and I played circles around the other two. Mariah bid tersely and Riley extravagantly and by the end of the second hand we led them six to one in the hole. I had to start to worry a little that Leona and I would have the game won before Mariah's agony of playing partners with Riley had been sufficiently prolonged.

Leona, though, helped. While Riley was deep in ponder of an untakable trick, she maternally observed to him:

"You must have left your luck outside tonight."

"Hmm? Oh. Right, Mother."

Riley's problem was, he thought through the cards and out their other side. When he should have been calculating trump, he was off beyond in contemplation of whether the queen of diamonds had her hair in a wimple or a snood, and why jacks came to be called jacks instead of knaves, on and on until he was somewhere out in the forest that surrendered the woodpulp that the cards were made from. I suppose that is the literary mind, but it is pitiful to see in a game of pitch.

It was during the next hand, while we once again waited for Riley to play a card, that Leona remarked she had something she'd been wondering about.

"How do you two," she coolly included Mariah in her inquiring gaze, "decide on what story you're going to do?"

Riley stroked his mustache rapidly. "It varies, Mother," he said and tried to run his jack of trumps past me, which I had saved my queen precisely for.

"I've been trying to watch how you work together," Leona went on, "but I guess I don't quite savvy it yet. Do you match the pictures to the words or the words to the pictures?"

Mariah blinked as if she'd been asked to explain nuclear physics. "Uhmm, both, kind of."

And often neither, I felt like adding about their periodic dry spells on the centennial series. Instead I observed to Leona, "You know they warn a person about ever watching sausage being made. It's a little bit like that with this newspaper stuff."

Leona just smiled. I'd begun to notice, though, that she had different calibres of smiles. The broad beaming expression that seemed to welcome all of life—the Alectric smile, I thought of it as, for I had first seen it on her when she and Alec were sparking each other, that summer of fifty years ago—shined out most naturally. You could read a newspaper by the light of that facial glow. But there was also a Leona smile that her eyes didn't quite manage to join in; the smile muscles performed by habit, but there was some brainwork going on behind that one. And then there was one that can only be called her foolkiller smile; when you got it, you wondered if you'd been eating steak with a spoon. Mariah got that one a lot.

With Mariah nicely on low boil, the next logical mission of the evening was to lend Riley some aggravation. As a former child and now an all-too-veteran parent, I pretty much instinctively knew what would do the job.

"I bet you're like me, Leona—never imagined, when he was a snip of a kid, Riley would grow up to be such a leading citizen. I know with Mariah, there were times when I wondered how the world was ever going to be ready for her." From the corner of my eye I knew Mariah was giving me a murderous stare, perfect to my purpose. Riley was just pulling his head out of his latest mystical contemplation of his hand of cards when I delivered the opening to Leona. "Funny to think back to what they put us through when they were little, huh?"

"Funny is the word for it," Leona brightly informed us as Riley uneasily held his cards in front of him like a tiny shield.

"He was a holy terror when he was little. The summer he was four, his dad started taking him with, out to the cattle. Here the next thing I knew, Riley was refusing to pee in the bathroom. The only way he'd go was outside—his little legs spraddled like he'd seen his dad do out on the range." She looked fondly at Riley as if exhibiting him at the county fair. "He killed off my entire bed of daisies that summer."

"Mother, will you for God's sake lay off my urinary history and—"

"Must be something about their generation, Leona," I put in remorselessly. "Maybe the doctors in those days fed them orneriness pills before they sent them home with us as babies from the hospital, you suppose? Mariah now, the story on her is—" and I of course proceeded to tell about the time she was in grade school and every recess Orson Zane would pester the daylights out of her but always was sneaky enough to get away with it until finally the day Mariah carefully spit down the front of her own dress, presented the damp evidence to the teacher as Orson's, and got him the curative spanking he was overdue for.

Leona laughed as mightily over that as I had over Riley taking a cowboy pee in the posies, our offspring meanwhile stewing in silence. Eventually, though, Riley glumly thought out loud for our benefit: "You know, folklorists just put numbers on stories that crop up time and again. Number 368, The-Chihuahua-Who-Took-One-Nap-Too-Many-In-The-Microwave-Oven. Parents ought to do that. Just call out the numbers. Save yourselves the trouble of doing the telling."

"But Riley, hon, the telling is the fun of it," Leona told him instructively.

"Besides, numbers don't go high enough for all the stories parents save up as blackmail," Mariah noted with a censorious glance my direction.

"Speaking of numbers," I glided to, for we'd played out the hand in the course of the conversation, "what'd we make, partner?"

Leona turned over the tricks she and I had taken and counted out high, low, and jack. "*Tree*," she reported with satisfaction, which by now we all knew was Russian for three.

"We treed them again, did we?" I thought that was pretty good, but nobody else seemed to catch it. Mariah was intent on my scorekeeping from the treasury of kitchen matches, to see how bad her and Riley's situation was by now. They'd actually scored a point, which wiped out their deficit—Leona's and my total now had reached nine—and I congratulated Mariah on their advance up to nothing.

"Gosh, Dad, just what I always wanted, a goose egg," she said in a dripping voice. "When I get done with it, what part of the goose do I stick it back in?"

Riley had gravitated off to the refrigerator and fetched a can of beer for each of us, plus his latest inspiration. "You ever hear that old Country-and-Western sermon about how a deck of cards stands for life?" He dropped into a deep drawl. *"Thurr're fifty-two cards in the deck, don't yuh see, one fer every week a the year. The four suits, hearts an' diamonds an' clubs an' spades, reperzents the four seasons a the year. They also mean the seasons a the human heart, love an' wealth an' war an' death. Add up all the spots a all the cards, along with the ever-prezent joker of life, an' they come out to three hundred sixty-five, one fer every day a the . . ."*

He paused at the expression on the other three of us. "You heard it?"

"Yes," stated Leona.

"Lots and lots of times," said I.

"Mmm hmm," even Mariah put in delicately.

"Oh." Riley busied himself picking up the cards he'd long since been dealt. "Whose bid?"

Now that there were four of us, commotion kicked off each morning in the Bago. The minute there was enough dawn, Riley was Spandexed up and out running the ridgeline. Mariah got down and Janed on the floor between the cab and the kitchen nook. Leona tucked herself behind the table there in the dinette, put her headset on like a tiara, and ingested Russian. I meanwhile did breakfast duty and tried to stay out of the various lines of fire.

Funny, what will bug a person. So as not to fill the ears of the rest of us with constant Moscowese, Leona performed silent recitation; that is, simply moved her lips in Russian to answer the headset questions. Myself, I considered it downright thoughtful of her and probably so would have Mariah, if she hadn't had to pop up in her exercise repetitions and every time see Leona wordlessly mouthing something—one exertion by Mariah would meet with a mute appeal about the way to the train station, her next contortion would have as backdrop a request to pass the salt. I noticed Mariah's workouts grow grimmer until she finally had to stop in midtummywork and ask:

"Mmm—Leona?"

The older woman blinked down at her, lifted off the headset and automatically palavered: "*Puhzhahlistah, puhftuhreetyeh vahpros yeshcho ras.* 'Please repeat the question again.' "

"Uh huh, right," Mariah said with a careful breath. "What I'm wondering is, how can you learn to say a word without *saying* it?"

Leona smiled interestedly while she considered. Then unloaded: "I suppose the same way you can put yourself through Jane Fonda's exercises without being Jane Fonda."

. . . The voices remember and remember. It was the second summer on the homestead, one of the early innocent years before the dry part of the weather cycle scythed across these arid plains, and the June rain had granted them a blue lake of crop, the blossoming flax that homesteaders sometimes resorted to until they could work the sod sufficiently to attempt wheat on it. The husband was out and away on some chore, as he always seemed to be, and the wife was at the stove, as she always seemed to be, when the three-year-old daughter called from just outside the door of the shanty.

"See my snake, mommy."

"Janie, hon, I don't have ti—See what? Janie, show me!"

"My snake. He mine. I killded him."

There in the yard the child had taken the garden hoe and hoed the rattlesnake in half. . . .

Road, road, and more road was the menu of this day as we headed east toward Jordan.

We passed prairie creeks in their deep troughs of flood-cut banks.

Dome formations poked up on the horizon like clay bowls upside down.

Fenceposts became more spindly and makeshift, crooked and thin as canes out here so far from forest.

Between Mosby and Sand Springs we met a Bluebird Wanderlodge with Minnesota plates and I could imagine that motorhome coming on a straight line, on cruise control, the 750 miles from the Twin Cities.

"A jackrabbit must have to pack a lunch through this country," I eventually couldn't help but observe as we went on through more miles of scantness.

"Those bunnies better put on their helmets and flak jackets," Riley said from his perch behind me. "The latest notion of what to do with this out here is to bombard the living shit out of it."

"Why's that?" I asked in honest surprise. A glance over my shoulder showed Leona looking at him with her eyebrows raised, too. "Montana isn't at war with anybody I know of."

"Tell it to the Pentagon, Jick." I heard him flipping in his notebook. "The military wants eight million more acres in the western states for tank maneuvers and artillery and bombing ranges. A million of those acres are up here around Glasgow. The other day an Undersecretary of Defense said—how's this for using the language bass ackwards?—these open spaces out here are 'a national treasure.' What he means is, they'll make terrific target practice."

The slap of Riley closing his notebook was the only sound for a while. His news about forthcoming bombs and tanks and artillery shells bugged the hell out of me. This country of the Big Dry did not appeal to me personally. Yet why couldn't it be left alone? Left be empty? Instead of the human creature finding one more way to beat up on the land.

Gas stations had grown so scarce that I pulled in at the one at Sand Springs—the gas station pretty much was Sand Springs— and crammed every drop of fuel I could into the Bago and religiously checked the tires and the air in the spare. Out on these extreme empty roads, you could die of car trouble.

The station attendant and I had been gabbing wholeheartedly— people out here in eastern Montana were as open as their plains— and while we did he noticed Mariah and Leona and Riley one after another emerge from the motorhome to stretch their legs or utilize the restroom or, in Mariah's case, just unlimber her camera on Sand Springs. When we settled up, along with my change he handed me:

"Traveling with your whole family, eh? That's nice to see, these days."

It surprised the daylights out of me, the notion of the four of us as a brood. I was briefly tempted to tell the stationman that yeah, we were just your normal vanilla American household these days; the silver-haired lady and I weren't married, at least to each other, but she'd once almost married my brother before thinking better of it, whereas the younger two, she mine (by my second wife) and him hers, *had* been married to one another but weren't any more, although they intended to be again. Family tree, hell. We were our own jungle.

Mariah found her picture that afternoon. Leona was the one, as we roved down from Jordan toward Cohagen, who noticed that some of the sheds on the ranches we were passing had chimneys and window sashes and for that matter, regular front doors: homestead houses that had been jacked up and moved after the sodbuster families "took the cure" and abandoned their claims in some final dry year. Mariah pored over one of those old shanties for what must have been an hour, and the photo she finally chose was a close-up of its siding, the wood weathered to the rich brown of a relic.

As long a day as it had been, prowling around the Big Dry country for Mariah and Riley to work on their piece, that night after we pulled into the campground on the outskirts of Jordan, pop. 450, I simply nuked up some frozen dinners.

Leona tasted the first forkful of hers and asked clinically:

"Excuse my asking, but what is this guck?"

Mariah was in her absent rhythm of tackling the food with a utensil in one hand while she messed around in a stack of proof sheets with the other, and Riley and I pretty much per usual were mauling away at our plates without much thought either, I suppose.

"Soybeans Incognito, would be my best guess," I theorized to Leona, although the label announced veal patties a la something-or-other.

"You people," she uttered more in sorrow than in anger, "eat like Gypsies."

"That's funny," Riley answered and gawked out at bare gray hills beyond the campground, ashen distance surrounding us everywhere. This will sound like I'm pouring it on, but honest to God, out there at the side of the road was a sign that read: HELL CREEK, 15 MILES. "You suppose maybe it might be because we *live* like Gypsies, Mother?"

Protocol when four people are packed into a motorhome and none of them are married to any of the others is tricky. Leona was up to it, though. She smiled from Riley to Mariah to me, then simply proposed it at large:

"Would anybody mind overly much if I took on the cooking?"

Our next encampment was at Circle, which Riley couldn't resist pointing out was a bigger dot on the map than we were used to; the town had about 800 population. This particular morning, while Leona and I held the fort at the Redwater RV Park, he and Mariah had gone downtown to the Big Sheep Mountains Retirement Home in search of more rememberers for their homestead piece. Old folks' home, such places used to be called. I wondered if I was going to end up in one of those. I hoped not. I hoped to Christ not.

For the time being, I actually had the Bago to myself while Leona was out doing her daily walk for exercise. The motorhome seemed suddenly expanded, big as an empty bus. Just me and a third cup of coffee and the rattle of the pages of the day's *Montanian* I had settled down with. EASTERN EUROPE in one headline, COCAINE in another. What the news seemed to add up to was that people were evaporating out of East Germany as fast as they could, leaving everything behind to bravely try to better their lives, while a sizable proportion of this country sat around trying to figure new ways to put conniption powder up its collective nose. I don't know. I try to be as American as anybody, but the balance of behavior looked pretty far out of whack at our end.

It was a relief, then, when Leona came back in from her constitutional and mentioned that she'd stopped by the phone box and called Morgan to see how things were at the ranch, and I said yeah, I was going to have to do the same to Noon Creek pretty quick, and we made conversation along that line for a while.

Leona hesitated, but then brought it up.

"Riley tells me you're thinking about selling your ranch."

I managed not to say he'd be the one to know, he was a major reason for that. Instead: "Thinking about is as far as I seem to get."

"It's always hard, isn't it," she answered. "When Herb and I married in '44 he'd already taken over the place from his folks, so all those years until Herb died, our ranch just always seemed to me as permanent as the Crazy Mountains. But that's not really the case any more. Morgan will run the place until his last breath. But after him, I just don't know. Jeff''—by now I knew that was her only grandchild, in college at Bozeman—''doesn't seem that interested. He's a quiet boy. So far, he won't even look at a girl.'' Leona turned aside to glance at her reflection in the window above the nook table, as if the answer to young Jeff might be there. ''No, I'm not at all sure the ranch is in his future. He maybe takes after Riley.'' She swung a smile my way. ''Don't even say it, Jick.''

In truth, it was hard not to burst out at the contradiction of a nephew emulating Riley yet not chousing after the female of the species. But the eventuality in what Leona had just told me was outechoing that. So even the prospering Wrights were only postponing, staving off for one more generation, the question of what would become of their ranch.

Suddenly the ranch topic lost its appeal for both of us and Leona said she'd better put in a session on her Russian flashcards. I offered my services, figuring I could riffle cards in any language, and she brightened right up. ''*Spaseebo.* Thank you. It'll make the situation seem more real to have you trying me out on the words instead of doing it myself.''

I flicked and flipped to the best of my ability, springing stuff like *What time is it now, please?* on her until she said that was about enough vocabulary for any one day.

The topic that had been in my own mind while she'd been practicing *pah rooskee* had to come out. ''Something you mentioned earlier, Leona. I'd kind of like to talk to you about it, if you wouldn't mind too much. All those years you spent with Herb—a lot like what I spent with Marce.'' I worked my throat overtime but managed to get the next words out. ''What can you tell me about—this.''

She knew what I meant. About being a widow, a widower. About being the one who lives on alone.

Leona's hands fiddled with the box of flashcards. The same little crimp of concentration she'd shown while I quizzed her on vocabulary appeared again between her silvered eyebrows, but her eyes stayed steady into mine. ''You still miss Marcella something fierce, don't you.''

I swallowed heavily and said, ''That's still the case, yeah. I guess really that's what I'm wondering from you. Does it ever get any easier?"

"In some ways." Leona paused. "Maybe it has to, or we wouldn't be able to stand it. We'd crush down until there wasn't anything left of us either. But it . . . the grief, the worst of it anyway, eventually does"—I could see her search as she sometimes did for a Russian phrase—"space itself out some. Every now and again, something pops into memory that hurts as much as ever. And there are days you wish you could take off the calendar forever. Herb's birthday is always hard for me. And our anniversary. And the start of calving time, because that's the time of year he died. But," she found a smile to encourage me, "that leaves a majority of days when a person can get by okay, I suppose is how I look at it."

"Leona, if this is too damn personal, just up and say so and we'll skip it. But—how come you never remarried?"

She flushed a little and looked down at the table, but did tackle my question. "I've had a couple of chances. Not as many as you maybe think. But every time it seemed like such an effort. To get used to someone all over again. I suppose I'm set in my ways, and at this—stage of life, the other person is bound to be, too."

"Yeah, I seem to be finding that out in myself. Old dogs bark the loudest." Immediately I wished that hadn't spouted out. Leona was, what, two years further into age than I was.

That inadvertent crack put her to looking squarely across at me again. She said, though, as if going right on with her catalogue of why she hadn't gone the matrimonial route with anybody in the years since Herb Wright's death: "Besides, you know my history, Jick. I don't seem to marry easily."

Huh. So she would at least allude in that direction. To Alec. Her jilt of him. The blond bolt of lightning she was for the McCaskills, back there half a century ago.

I didn't want to get into that with her now, given the missionary work she and I had ahead on Mariah and Riley and their marriage propensity. Instead I kept on the course I'd started with the remarrying question. "There's a real reason I'm trying to get a line on this. See, one thing I'll be going home to, after our newspaper aces finish off the centennial, is somebody who's got herself convinced she and I ought to get together." Althea Frew probably right at that moment was humming around Gros

Ventre red-circling on every calendar in town November 8, Centennial Day and the return of widower/bachelor/eligible-male-at-loose-ends-and-not-yet-utterly-decrepit, one J. A. McCaskill. "And at honest to Christ moments I wonder if she might just be right." Or as the Althea matter formed itself in the whispers in my mind, *My God, am I going to end up having to do that? If I am, I've got some overhauling to do on my thinking about that woman.* And soon. Centennial Day was not that far down the pike now, life beyond Mariah and Riley and the steering wheel of the Bago was fast coming at me, and if I was going to try and follow widower logic—admittedly, it was there—then pairing up with Althea would at least cure what loomed ahead of me at Noon Creek after that eighth morning of November, the aloneness. Loneliness.

"Oh, sure, she has plenty of things about her that kind of bug me," I summed Althea to Leona's smile of encouragement, "but she can probably double that in spades about me. We could likely iron each other out enough to make a marriage work, more or less, if it came to that. And that's what I'm wondering. Whether it's maybe worth it, not to have to try the rest of life"—the last of, we both knew I was saying—"all alone. But pretty plainly you've decided it's not worth it, huh? From your side of things, I mean."

That other side of things, I genuinely did have a long curiosity about. In the skin of a woman, how does life seem? I could remember speculating that about my mother, when I was still only a shavetail kid, fifteen or so: ranching and the Forest Service, male livelihoods both then—what did Beth McCaskill think of her existence in that largely man-run scheme of things? Certainly I'd had the occasions to mull McCaskill women since, too. Lexa, taking herself off to Alaska. Mariah—God, you bet, Mariah. And even though I felt we knew each other to the maximum, sometimes even Marcella had stirred that skinwhisper question.

"Maybe it's not just a matter of that," Leona was saying now, "the worth-it part, that is. Maybe it's more a matter of getting up enough nerve for it. I seem to have spent my nerve for—mating, whatever you'd say, on Herb."

Thinking how complete my version with Marcella had been, I could understand that too. "Uh huh. Could be that our share of enthusiasm for hearing wedding bells over and over again got parceled out to these kids of ours instead."

She laughed, looking a little relieved at the excuse to. I figured now was as logical a time as any, to start putting our heads together about Mariah and Riley and the flopperoo marriage they were determined to repeat.

"That's something I been wanting to get to with you, too, Leona. I don't have a whole lot of sway with Mariah, where Riley is concerned. But I wondered if there's any way you can work on him—or hell, *her,* for that matter—to keep them from going off the deep end again."

Leona gave me a smile, of a calibration I hadn't seen before. And delivered:

"Jick, you couldn't be more wrong. I think Riley and Mariah should get married again."

My ears about fell off.

While I was gaping at the woman, trying not to believe I'd heard what I'd heard, she was piling more on. "You're looking at me *kahk Srehdah nah Pyahtnyeetsoo.* Like Wednesday looks at Friday. But I'd think you, as Mariah's father and all, would be the first person in the world to want them back together."

"Togeth—? Leona, that first marriage of theirs didn't just come apart! Pieces of it are still flying through the air, it blew up so goddamn bad! Why in the name of anything holy should they make the exact identical mistake again?"

"Maybe they've learned how to do better."

"Or maybe they're only going to be better at how to make each other miserable. They weren't a couple of skim-milk kids when they got married, that first time. Now they're even more— well, indegoddamnpendent, is about the most polite way to put it, the both of them."

She still toyed with a small smile, which did nothing to improve the rotten humor this suddenly had me in.

"So you're not really for people remarrying either?" she tried on me, I suppose apropos of the Althea theorizing I'd been doing.

"I'd be a thousand percent happy to see Mariah and Riley remarried," I protested. "Just not to each other."

"Jick, it's their choice."

"I *know* it's their choice." If it was mine, there'd have been no chance of a repeat performance by those two. "I also know neither one of them is dealing with a full deck when it comes to deciding about the other one." How to render this politely. No, to hell with polite. "They get hot to trot, out on their job all the time like they are without any other candidates around to button their bellybuttons to, and then while they're at it, so to speak, they figure hey, wow, they're magically back in love. But Leona, that'll only last as long as the bedsprings squeak. Then they'll be dishing out hurt to each other again, which is what I dread for them. And I don't see why you aren't leery of that, too. For Riley's sake, if nothing else. Maybe I've been misreading, but I somehow got the impression Mariah is not your favorite person in the universe."

Leona stood her territory.

"I have my differences with Mariah, that's all too true. We all side with our own children when a marriage of theirs breaks up. After all, we're parents, aren't we, Jick, not neutral peacekeeping forces. But I'm not the one who wants to try married life with Mariah again, am I. Riley is. I know you think he's gone loco about this"—understatement of the century—"but Riley's instincts are generally right. Usually more right than mine." Her expression suggested the not remote possibility that they might be righter than my own, too.

If she expected that to get a rise out of me, it did.

"Let's back up here a goddamn minute. Didn't I just hear you putting remarrying out of your own picture? If that's true for you, why in all hell isn't it true for Mariah and Riley after they've already flubbed the dub with each other once?"

"A difference in Vitamin G level, I suppose," wafted across the table from her to me.

"Huh?"

"In guts, Jick. I said 'nerve' before, but I guess we're into speaking plain, aren't we. My time of life, my way of—getting through, isn't anywhere near the same as Riley and Mariah's. Their generation has its own agenda and it should have. I know you can't help but feel Riley and Mariah are being scatty about this, but Jick, they've got so many more years ahead of them they can afford to take those chances, can't they? If they possess the guts to try to make a go of life with each other again, good for them."

Like the kid starting his third year in the second grade, it was beginning to dawn on me how much ground I was losing. Good God in sweet heaven. Here I'd invited Leona Tracy Wright along as an ally against the tendency of our offspring to get dangerously smitten with each other and she turns out to be their head cheerleader.

So I wasn't one bit better at getting through to her at this farther end of life than I'd been at the early part, was I. The realization knocked every blossom off me. Why was it, the consequence always had to be the same where this person was concerned? I had believed I was putting aside the past between Leona and the McCaskills, shelving that oldest grudge of her having been too good for my brother, spending these Bago hours getting to know her as she was now instead of a disruptive memory, but no. I still didn't have the shadow of a clue to the real Leona, any more than that other time I had tried to be at my social utmost with her.

Probably she wouldn't even remember that time; there wasn't any great reason for her to. The Fourth of July rodeo, that summer when Leona and Alec were going at romance hot and heavy. I could see Leona yet, her silver hair returned to gold, the half-century gone to leave her magically at seventeen again, there in a clover-green blouse with good value under it, perched on a car fender by the arena fence. Alec was entered in the calf roping and he glommed on to me to go over and entertain his lady love while he spruced up to compete. It promptly emerged, though, that besides keeping her company Alec wanted me to keep her occupied; he didn't want Earl Zane, Arlee's equally bigheaded older brother, to come strutting around and cut in on his progress with Leona.

I was just in the midst of telling Alec nothing doing, that my not-quite-fifteen-year-old-yet repertoire of life didn't include anything on how to handle hearts and hand-to-hand combat, when Leona revolved in our direction, patted the car fender beside her, and of course beamed me in with a smile the way a moth would head for a lamp.

Well, okay, maybe, I thought to myself as I zombied over to her leading my horse. The horse, my father's big gray saddle mount named Mouse, which he'd grandly lent me for the holiday, actually was my best hope with Leona, for she was such an avid rider she definitely knew horseflesh.

In one way of looking at it, my subsequent brief stay with Leona on that fender did serve Alec's purpose of repulse: Earl Zane never showed his ugly face, nor did any saber-toothed tigers. On the other hand, entertaining Leona was an uphill battle every moment. Things reached their ultimate dead end just after I had told her a joke she didn't get, which is infinitely worse than no joke at all, when Mouse chose that moment to unroll his business end and proceed to take a world-record leak in front of my horrified eyes and Leona's evidently interested ones. Honest to God, the tallywhacker on that horse looked like a firehose in action and Leona studied it like it was the newest thing in hydraulics. Mouse's golden stream washed away what little composure I had left, and by the time Alec showed up and asked Leona how I did as company, she in all too much truth reported: "He's a wonder."

Her current opinion of me probably wasn't even ankle-high to that. She was the same calm Leona, dentproof as her smile, but her voice had a different bearing than when we'd been rushing Russian into her.

"Jick, really, I'm sorry we don't see the same way on Riley and Mariah getting together again, but—"

"Forget it. I need some weather in me." I quickly got up and jammed on my hat and coat and went out the Bago door.

Wouldn't you know, the afternoon had turned as blustery outside as in. Clouds needed to come a long way to these eastern Montana plains and they always seemed to mean business by the time they got here. There already was rain monkeying around to the west and a gusty wind was clearing the way for it into Circle. I wished I'd grabbed my winter cap instead of my Stetson. Not that I've had that much experience at domestic strife, but one of its drawbacks evidently was being dressed wrong for stomping out.

Misery and company. I was forging past the RV park office, head down, when the manager pottered out and called to me.

"You're site five, aren't you? Mr."—he checked the sheet of paper in his hand—"McCaskill?"

When I said I supposed I was, he handed me the piece of paper. "This just came in for you."

"Came in?"

"Sure, by fax. Got our machine right there in the office, in case you want to send something back."

By now I had taken a look at the last line of the facsimile, *Yours with every fond thought* followed by the emphatic signature *Althea,* and in my current mood the reply that popped to mind was the legendary telegram to headquarters we used to joke about in the Forest Service, the fed-up ranger wiring his forest supervisor: *Fuck you. Strong letter to follow.*

However, not knowing the law on transmitting imaginative language by fax, I declined the campground manager's eager offer and dragged a lawn chair over behind a Lombardy poplar for a bit of shelter from the wind and sat to see what was to be contended with in Althea's missive.

Jick, dear—
Not that I ever need an excuse to keep in touch with you, but those of us on the committee who are not off glamorously wandering the world (just joking! you know me!) have been arranging our Dawn of Montana ceremony, and as you are our orator I'm sure you will appreciate knowing the schedule.
5:00–5:30 a.m. Gather at the Medicine Lodge; musical interlude
5:30–6:00 Pancake breakfast
6:00–6:45 Dawn dance
6:45–6:50 Assemble at the centennial flagpole
6:50–6:52 Introduction of centennial speaker Jick McCaskill
    (Penciled in: by you know who!)
6:52–7:10 Centennial speech by Jick McCaskill

There was more, you bet there was—Althea could have given lessons to Cape Canaveral on countdown—but I skipped past the rest of the schedule to see what she'd tamped in to her last pair of paragraphs.

It's hard to believe our centennial celebration is almost here. I'll have to find something to do with myself after November 8. But then I'm not the only one in that situation, am I?
Kenny, who of course kindly told me where you are at this very moment (isn't fax such an advance!), says he'll see you in a day or two when you ship your lambs. I'll give you a jingle.

In Glasgow the day after, Riley and I went to a car agency so he could jimmy onto the expense account a rental means of transportation for me—I made damn good and sure it was going to be a Ford Taurus instead of a Yugo—and I scorched road home to the ranch. That next morning at Noon Creek, events kept on at about the pace of a catfight in a rolling barrel. Typical of shipping days, a bonechilling squall swirled down off the

mountains and we didn't even have the lambs started into the
trucks before Shawn Finletter drove up and said his bosses
back east just could not understand why I wasn't ready to sell.
Right then, with sleet sifting down the back of my neck and a
thousand lambless ewes blatting and Helen's dogging in the lamb
pen rending the air with barks and Kenny profanely trying to fill
the loading chute with lambs who had decided they were afraid
of the color of the truck, I could not understand why either.
At suppertime, Darleen informed me she and Joe Prentiss of the
Gros Ventre Mercantile were no longer on speaking terms, even
to argue, but before achieving that state of affairs Joe made it
known that the Merc would no longer carry us on a monthly
credit account and all groceries hereafter were strictly cash basis.
I was still digesting that fiscal turn when Althea Frew was on the
line—plain telephone, this time—offering herself as audience for
me to rehearse my centennial speech on, and I had to freehand
invent that I'd left my only copy back in the Bago, which even
as we spoke was being driven by Mariah and Riley to a remote
site on the Missouri River where Lewis and Clark had once
camped, thus regrettably out of range of fax.

And the morning after we shipped the lambs, Helen departed
from her herding years with me, riding beside me in the rental
car as far as the Amtrak station in Shelby where she gave me a
last remembering look through the blowing web of her hair and
boarded the train for Oregon and gemology.

Back at Glasgow, at my earliest chance I innocently asked
Mariah how everybody had gotten along in my absence.
She retorted with her camera, saying as she snapped me for
the kabillionth time on the trip: "Riley would be easier to
remarry if he were an orphan, I'll say that much."

Toward me, Leona behaved as if we'd never been at logger-
heads at all, asking how my lambs had weighed out and how the
grass prospect looked in the Two Medicine country now that
some rain finally had found Montana, ranch talk that was our
equivalent of church Latin. Yeah, well, sure, I told myself,
she'd had lifelong practice at sailing smoothly on, hadn't she.
Yet I was surprised to find that my snit at her kept cooling off
and off, I suppose because I didn't have time to maintain a mad;
there was the hour-by-hour matter of the centennial trip and

getting done what we were supposed to, all four. What a size life
was these days. A person had to get up twice in the morning to
begin to fill it. Across county after county I put on the miles,
Leona put on the meals, and Mariah and Riley kept on scouring
that upper righthand corner of the state. All navigation was
straight on those roads, one dead-ahead run after another. The
gray grain elevators of town after town we passed—Culbertson,
Froid, Scobey, Flaxville—with the high plains all around farmed
in brown plowed strips next to straw-colored fallow ones. Sometimes the yield of our miles would be a picture of Mariah's—the
water tower of the town of Frazer hanging just above the planetary rim of the plains like a tiny balloon on a string. Sometimes
what worked was a scene Riley and his tape recorder found in
someone.

> *"We had to pack up and pull out of here in '32,"* the woman
> remembers while revisiting Plentywood for the centennial celebra-
> tion. *"Just walked away from our place, that summer, and never
> came back. It was so dry the corn didn't sprout, the potatoes barely
> came up, the pasture was awful short. My dad and older brother
> had gone on ahead out to the Coast, to Everett, Washington, where
> we had relatives and tried to get any work they could there. Then
> while my mother went around the countryside until she finally
> found somebody to trade our farm machinery to for a secondhand
> Model T Ford, my younger brother and I—I was thirteen at the
> time—we got on our horses and started moving our handful of
> cattle to the stockyard here in Plentywood. It was an overnight
> trip, Millard and I slept on the ground, then the next morning the
> cattle were anxious for water because they hadn't had any since
> noon the day before. But Big Muddy Creek here was so low there
> was deep mud and Millard said, 'Mary, we've got to push them on
> past that water or they'll bog down in there and we'll be in
> trouble.' I was almost in tears to leave our cows so thirsty, but
> Millard was right.*
> *"When we got home to the farm we loaded the Model T—Mother,
> Millard and I, and a yellow cat—and started for the Coast. We
> lost the cat on the way but the rest of us made it.*
> *"Our horses we just left there on the range."*

Miles City. By now we had roved into October. Mapwise, we
were back south out of the farmed plains into cattlegrowing

country again and Miles, as the pleasant brick-faced little city was called by ranchers who described their places as "forty miles from Miles," came as a kind of oasis to us all, the big cottonwoods at the Roche Jaune RV Park greeting the Bago like a home grove every time we drove in from one of Mariah and Riley's daily delvings.

This day, though, Leona and I had set them off afoot downtown—the *Montanian* pair had come up with the bright idea of studying what Riley called "bucklelaureate ceremonies" and so they were at a westernwear store seeing just what belt buckles, cowboy boots, rangerider big hats and other regalia walked out of the store in the course of a business day—and she and I headed on toward what she'd spied in a Miles City *Star* ad, a horse auction at the CMR Livestock Auction Yard. Myself, I could take or leave horses, but I knew Leona's interest in them— did I ever—and so I figured, well, hell, what's a few hours of horseflesh to put up with.

The auction sale ring was actually a half-circle, a tier of seats for those of us in the audience arcing around it, with the auctioneer's pulpit centered there against the wall where the livestock was hazed in through one gate, had its moment of being bid on, and hazed out the other gate back into the stockyard. FRIDAY—FEEDER CALVES SATURDAY—SLAUGHTER ANIMALS announced a large red sign above the auctioneer but a person pretty much knew by nose the livestock traffic through here: the mingled smell of cattle and horses was heavier, less pungent than the iodine-and-lanolin fragrance of sheep that I was used to.

Regular buyers had front row moviehouselike seats with their nameplates on them, but Leona and I tucked ourselves onto an ordinary bench high at the back of the arena. As usual I looked the crowd over for anybody I might know but the only such spotting this time was by Leona.

"I see Ozzie Breckenridge is here," she pointed out a long-drink-of-water guy about our age perched at the far end of the arena arc. "He runs a dude ranch, down by Absarokee. Herb and I used to deal horses with him a little." The dude herder noticed Leona too, traded her a nod and obviously wondered who the Methuselah in a Stetson next to her was.

"And ready and we go," the auctioneer chanted and the hazers brought the horses on, one at a time. Roans, pintos, piebalds, Appaloosas, bays, duns, you name it, the equine pa-

rade went on for a couple of hours. It seemed to me there was a
serious oversupply of horses in the Miles City country and the
bidding reflected that too, the auctioneer about having to work
himself into a lather to get each animal sold off. In fact, the
auction wound down to the point where the regular buyers had
got up and left and the rest of the crowd was thinning rapidly
too. Throughout it all, though, Leona was rapt.

As we still had chores to do around town, grocery shopping
and so on, I finally suggested we stir. But Leona said, "Let's just
watch this one last one, Jick. That's not a badlooking horse."

Neither was it a goodlooking horse. At best the thing was only
about okaylooking, a sorrel gelding no more than fourteen hands
high, shaggy and a little swaybacked, with the scar of a bad
barbwire cut across its chest; the one pleasant distinction was a
nice blaze of white on its face. Obviously Leona saw more in the
animal than I could, and I sat back to learn.

"All right, folks," the auctioneer began as the blazeface trot-
ted a tight circle in the sale ring, "we're here to sell. Who'll give
me six fifty to start it off? Six hundred fifty, fifty, fifty, anybody
six fifty? Six hundred then, anybody six, six, six, who'll say six,
horsehorsehorse helluvahorse swelluvahorse horsehorse gottasell-
thishorse, six hundred, anybody?"

"It's a crime," Leona said softly to me, referring to the fact
that the horse would be cut back into the cannery slaughter
herd, which meant his destiny was to become dogfood, if nobody
bid on him. "He's no canner. Look how he handles himself in all
this commotion." True enough; the sorrel seemed alert to its
weird confinement without getting panicky. Leona went on in
the same soft tone: "That old fool Ozzie could use him in his
dude string, if he just would."

Thinking of horses I had known, particularly an assassin
packhorse named Bubbles, I started to nod in agreement that
this one by comparison might be a decent equine citizen, but
caught myself just in time. The auctioneer was spieling so desperately that I figured if I so much as twitched, I'd have bought
myself a steed.

"Folks, remember, you're getting the whole horse here," the
auctioneer admonished, "so isn't that worth at least five hundred
fifty dollars? You can barely buy a big dog for that. Five fifty
will start it off, five hundred fifty, fifty, fifty, ponyponypony
onlypony nothingphonypony ponypony ownthepony, five hun-

dred then, five, five, anybody, five? Where's the money, folks, where's the money? Will anybody bid five hundred dollars for this animal?''

Nobody would. The auctioneer's microphone voice took on a sweet fresh reasonableness. "All right, where do you want to start it then?''

Silence ensued. The only motion in the auction house was the blazeface slowly moving his head in wariness of the audience.

"Just one donor of green blood, that's all we need," the auctioneer sounded desperate again. "How about four fifty? Anybody, body, body, any bid, bid, bid?''

Leona had been fingering the top button of her blouse as if to make sure it was secure. Now she tapped the button with her index finger, just obviously enough that it was not missed by the auctioneer.

Oh, swell. Just what every motorhome household needs, an auxiliary horse.

But if Leona's signal alarmed me, it translated immediate new life into the auctioneer.

"Four fifty, I see bid! All right, it's more than I had. Now who'll say four hundred seventy-five, seventy-five, seventy-five, five, five, five—I have four seventy-five!''

More by osmosis than anything I could actually discern, I somehow knew that competing bid had come from Ozzie Breckenridge. He seemed to be casually eyeing in our direction, but I was pretty damn sure those gimlet eyes had taken in Leona's bidding method.

"Five now," the auctioneer raced on, "anybody, five hund-" —Leona tapped her button—"I have five hundred!''

Expensive as those taps were getting to be, I figured I'd better alert her to oculatory Ozzie. "Uh, Leona, that other guy can see you bid.''

"I know," she said, finger delicately on button. "I want him to.''

"Five fifty? Five fifty?" The auctioneer was putting it to Breckenridge, who was rubbing the back of his neck uneasily while he studied the sorrel from withers to nethers. "Five fifty? It's only double nickels. Five fifty?" Breckenridge continued to inspect the horse as if it was some hitherto unknown species. "It's a nifty for five fifty. Damn near a gifty. Why not bid a thrifty five fif—I have five fifty!''

Breckenridge's movement had looked to me more like a squirm than a bid, but maybe it was both.

"I have five fifty, now seventy-five, sev—I have five seventy-five!" Again Leona had wasted no time with her fingertap.

"Now six hundred, anybody six, six, six, who'll say six?" I saw Breckenridge sneak a look at Leona to make sure she still was eagerly fingering that blouse button. By now he had the appearance of a man who'd sooner give up several of his teeth, but at last he made whatever indication it took and bid the six hundred dollars.

Instantly the auctioneer launched his spiel anew, but Leona just as promptly had dropped her finger from the button and was shaking her head no, with a little smile. Within seconds the auctioneer banged his hammer down *whammo*, declared "It's all done, it's a sold one!" and the considerably startled Oz Breckenridge was in possession of a horse.

Riley, though. I had to admit he was more immune to his mother than I'd hoped.

Try as I did to find signs that life with Leona was making him unravel, he seemed pretty much the selfsame goddamn specimen. Take the very next morning, when I innocently pulled into a gas station to feed the Bago on our way out of Miles City. Mariah and Riley were in a mutual work trance, finishing up their westernwear piece to transmit into the *Montanian*, and Leona had retreated into earset Russian, so I climbed out to do the gassing up by myself. I was topping up the air in the tires when Riley stuck his head out the side door of the Bago, to clear his so-called brain I guess, peering over me and the airhose while he did.

"Shit oh dear!" he let out in an old maidy voice. "Everybody knows that's only the half of it! Two elements short is a lot even for Montana. Those old Greeks would be ashamed to death of us, Jick buddy."

From where I was kneeling at the front tire I glanced up and down the main street of Miles City for anybody who looked approximately Greek. "What the hell are you yakking about now?" I addressed Riley, but he had pulled back into the motorhome, where I could hear him asking Mariah for something.

Next thing, he bounced out and past me, and I was happy to have him out of my hair while I finished tending to the tires.

Not until I went to hang the airhose back onto its stanchion at one side of the service station did I discover that where the sign there read

AIR & WATER

Riley had just finished block-lettering beneath with Mariah's biggest blackest grease pencil:

EARTH & FIRE

"Jesus H.—Riley, you want to get us all thrown in the clink?" I wildly checked around for the service station owner.

"Hmm?" Riley stepped back to admire his handiwork. "Naw, we're doing this guy a favor. See, now all he has to do is hang up a new logo under his gas sign: NATURAL PHILOSOPHY WHILE YOU FILL."

"If they hang anything around here it's liable to be us, because of you, goddamn it. Come on, climb in the Bago and let's get the hell out of here."

A hundred coal cars on a railroad siding, today's resource wagontrain from the prairie to elsewhere. . . .

As early as Plentywood, it had become a common sight for us to see oil pumps working away in the farmed fields. The rocking-beam kind, that were like washerwomen dipping and rising as they scrubbed clothes on a washboard. But when Leona had cited them to Mariah and Riley once and wondered if they were ever going to do a piece about the energy business in this end of the state, the two of them simply shook their heads and chorused: "Colstrip."

The gigantic draglines skin the soil away to get at the coal. Longnecked, mammoth, lumbering, they are oddly technological mirages of the dinosaurs who earlier roamed these plains. . . .

Even the weather was getting to me, on that drive from Miles City down to Colstrip. Warmish and heavy, considerably too much so for this time of year. About the time you think you have seen everything this climate can possibly do, some new wrinkle comes along. Snow for the Fourth of July, or April hailstones big enough to knock out chickens. And now a sultry day in the middle of October, when the year ought to be gearing down toward winter.

"Must be getting into the banana belt," I commented.

"Tropical southern Montana, sure, you bet," Mariah more or less automatically responded from her watchful gaze out at the passing countryside.

Leona came in late on the conversation, just having shed her headset. "Isn't this nice-looking grassland, though?" she appraised the broad swales we'd been driving through for most of an hour.

"Now you've done it, Mother," Riley quit tapping at his laptop and pointed into the sky ahead.

Mariah had seen it too and already had her camera up.

Riley went on in his Movietone voice: "See there—the Power God heard that and is throwing thunderbolts at us."

The aircraft warning strobe lights on the smokestacks of the Colstrip power plants did seem like steady blinks of lightning in our direction. Even before I'd seen anything of this coal-stripping enterprise, I didn't like what I was seeing.

> *There is no muss to the town of Colstrip. Everything looks laid out according to plan, all the neighborhoods new, the downtown area that was installed with the power plants sprigged up with trees and lawn and other landscaping.*
>
> *Talk about landscape work, though. Just out from Colstrip, the strip-mining takes hundreds of acres at a time and sorts that ground into towering heaps, the grayish overburden of soil and stone clawed aside from the pits in dunelike processions and the black pile of coal so high that a bulldozer atop it looks the size of a hornet. The extracted coal is carried for miles by a huge pipeline-like conveyor to the power plants in town, where electricity is generated and then goes into the transmission lines to VCRs, Jacuzzis, neon signs, all the rest. The smokestacks here above the mined prairie are the tailpipes of our electrical luxury.*

A day of contemplating coal-stripping put all four of us ready for a drink before supper, you can bet. On Riley's insistence that the places on the edge of town are always more interesting, we pulled in at the Rosebud Bar just off the highway before Colstrip. "We get in on the indigenous this way, too, gang," he maintained as we trooped up to the door of the enterprise, by which I guess he meant that Rosebud Creek was just about within shouting distance.

Inside, the decor was relentlessly roses. Color photos of them beaded with dew. Vasefuls of red fabric versions on every table. A blimp shot of a stadium, which it didn't take me too long to figure out as the Rose Bowl. A very nearly life-size picture of Gypsy Rose Lee stripping for action, so to speak. Standing in a corner was a kid's sled with a you-know-what decal on it.

"Who do you suppose got hold of this place," Mariah wondered, "Gertrude Stein?"

"All right, tell me," Riley implored, stopping just inside the doorway with his back to it and covering his eyes with a hand. "There's a varnished plaque over the door that says *Gather ye rosebuds while ye may*, isn't there."

The other three of us turned and gawked up. Sure enough, there it posed: in fancy script with painted roses twining out the ends of each *y*, no less.

See what I mean about goddamn Riley—he could even floor his own mother. While Mariah whooped and gave him a vigorous tickle in the ribs, Leona perplexedly looked back and forth from the quotation to her son and asked, "How'd you ever know that?"

"Just unlucky, I guess."

A barmaid considerably beyond the bloom of youth came over as soon as we'd established ourselves at a table. "Hi, kids. What's it gonna be?"

I observed to her, "Quite the scheme of decoration."

"Isn't it, though," she said with a sigh. "They absolutely ruined this place when they went and redid it. They ought to be taken out and shot."

"What was it like before?"

"It looked like a whorehouse. The walls were red, all the chairs and booths were red velvet—we even had red lampshades. It was real pretty."

When we managed to get down to the business of drinks, Mariah of course had her usual Lord C and I my Johnny, and Leona's version had turned out to be forthright Jack Daniels and water. As the three of us entered the company of those gentlemen, though, Riley was brought a white production in a clear glass goblet.

"What in the name of hell are you drinking now?" I had to ask. "Rattlesnake milk?"

"Naw, it's a White Moccasin. Want a sip?"

"I'd rather parch," I let him know.

"Honestly, Jick, he was raised better than that," Leona frowned in reproof at her son's frippy concoction.

The barmaid saw it was six o'clock and turned the television set behind the bar on. If it proved to be T. V. Purvis I damn well was going to ask her to click it right back off, but the commercials eventually gave way instead to sportscasters, who seem to come in triplets.

"Well, well," Mariah contributed after craning around to check the screen scene as the players came on, "a bunch of high-paid hot dogs showing us their buns. My God, are they *still* playing that stuff?"

"You bet," I said. "The World Series, petunia."

"Or at least the California one," Leona said with a least little smile as the Oakland and San Francisco lineups electronically materialized on the screen.

"It comes to the same, I'm sure, Mother," maintained Riley, who I knew didn't give a hoot about sports except for cantering across the countryside.

"What beats me about having three guys on there to tell us what we're looking at, though," I started in, "is—"

"THERE'S AN EARTH—" one of the sportscasters declaimed and the television picture went blooey.

You didn't have to be a seismic scientist to fill in the rest of the word. For the next hours, when the TV people found a way to get back on the air, the four of us sat fascinated watching what the earthquake had done to the San Francisco Bay area. The collapse of that freeway, motorists crushed under slabs the size of aircraft carriers; the broken Bay Bridge; fallen buildings in Santa Cruz; all of San Francisco spookily lightless in the night except for the one neighborhood where apartment houses were burning; my God, I felt as sorry for people in that quake zone as if they had been bombed. And along with it, the overwhelming thought of how much worse it could have been. Candlestick Park with the World Series crowd of sixty thousand in it had not crumbled.

"Holy shit, think of it!" Riley said in genuine awe as a blimp camera panned down on Candlestick. "Fifteen hundred sportswriters at that ballgame and every one of them trying to transmit the same lead: *On this beautiful afternoon beside San Francisco Bay, God chose to shake the 'Stick.*"

"Helicopters," Mariah uttered wistfully, like a kid pointing out toys in a catalogue, as pictures of the gap in the Bay Bridge taken from midair came onto the screen. Both she and Riley erupted every time the coverage cut away from on the scene. "You fucking talking heads!" Riley roared at the set when a guy at a network desk somewhere began speaking with the Governor of California who had been caught on a sojourn in Germany. "Piggyback on what KGO is showing! You bunch of dumbfucks, let the local guys do the story in the streets!"

Eventually earthquake experts began coming on and saying this wasn't the Big One but it was a Pretty Big One. By then Leona and I had looked at each other a number of times with new understanding. A new feel for the distance between us and this avid pair glued to the coverage, maybe say. Neither she nor I would have willingly lived where such quakes kept happening if you deeded the whole of California to us. But if Riley and Mariah could have hopped on a plane and joined the newsgatherers right in the middle of all that earthquake mess, they instantly would have.

Billings begins a long way out from itself. Scatterings of housing developments and roadside businesses and billboards full of promises of more enterprises to come began showing up miles ahead of the actual city. The Bago and we four were rolling in on the freeway that runs shoulder to shoulder with the Yellowstone River, then the Yellowstone shied out of the picture and snazzy profiles of hotels and banks against the rimrocks became the feature.

"The Denver of the north," Riley crooned in an oily voice as downtown Billings came up on us. "The Calgary of the south." He waited until we were wheeling past a petroleum refinery that was obviously functioning much below capacity. "The Butte of tomorrow?"

"Mmm, though, look what the light is doing," Mariah put in. There in the late afternoon sunlight, the cliffs rimming the city were changing from baked tan to a honeyed color. Then and there I formed the opinion that held for the rest of our time in Billings, that if you had to have a city this was an interesting enough place to put it.

"No, honest to Pete, it's the truth, Jick, if I can call you that.

Just about the highest place you can drive in Delaware is the overpass on Route 202 where it goes into Pennsylvania."

"Aw, come on, Carl. How do you keep your heads above water back there?"

We'd been in the Energy City RV Park most of a week while Mariah and Riley were out toiling away at the implications of Billings—not to any avail that I could see yet—and Leona and I were getting to know the couple in the Bago next door. Retirees from Wilmington, Carl and Harriet DeVere were out here tasting mountain country, and inasmuch as they were going to drive the alpine Cooke City highway into Yellowstone Park this afternoon, by nightfall they might have their fill of mountains, all right.

The DeVeres now said they hated to break up our coffeeklatch but they had to go food shopping, did we want to come along? It was a handy chance to do so because they towed behind their rig a Honda Civic—*Winnebago Shopping Cart*, a carved wooden sign on it said—and Leona volunteered while I said I had something else I'd better get at.

The shopping expedition hadn't much sooner gone out, though, than Riley came in. He plopped the Sunday editions of the *Montanian* and the Billings *Gazette* on the dinette table. "Holding down the Bago all by your lonesome?"

"Yeah. Nothing injurious seems to happen to it when I'm here by myself."

He gave me a two-toned look but let that pass. Before he could start pawing through the Sunday papers, I asked: "Where's Mariah?"

"Shooting my mother," he reported absently. "The DeVeres, too. They are kind of cute, the three of them peeling off out of here aboard their Japanese skateboard." He noticed my own endeavor. "What've you got there, your prayer book?"

"Aw, an old paperback I bought in Wolf Point. Figured I better get going on that centennial speech or—what the hell you looking at me like that for?"

"You do it deliberately, don't you."

"Do what?"

"Oh, come on!" He aimed a finger at the title of the book I was holding. *The Collected Eloquence of Winston Churchill*. Riley actually looked a little wild-eyed, in both separate-hued eyes. "*Winnie*, in the *Bago*? If that isn't a weird sense of—"

"Riley, a walking word game like you doesn't have any right to—"

The side door popped open, and the camera bag and then Mariah alit inside with us. She stood there a moment, straight as a willow, and studied Riley and me. "Sipping herbal tea and discussing Zen, guys?"

"Just practicing for the union of our families again," I let her have.

"Actually, our agenda at the moment is to just read the Sunday papers," Mariah addressed back to me. "Do you suppose that can be accomplished without hand-to-hand combat?"

Riley still looked snorty and I maybe was a little that way myself, but we clammed up. They put their noses into their literature and I into mine.

Never in the field of human conflict was so much—Churchill was hard to keep concentration on, though. I was bothered, not to say baffled. My eyes kept drifting first to Mariah, then to Riley, each of them busily mauling through a newspaper. Was that love? If so, how had it come out of the ash and salt of their first try together? Was I ever going to savvy what, when, how, why? Some great record so far, mine. Plainly I had underestimated Riley. I had misestimated Leona and what I figured would be her natural reaction against our offspring falling for each other again. And after my thirty-five years as her father, Mariah still went up, down, and sideways in my estimation practically all day long. Maybe reading other people's heads was not my strong suit.

I shut Churchill. Newsprint was more my speed at the moment, too. All that was left of the Sunday *Gazette* from the rummaging those two were doing of it was the section with astrology, crossword, and wedding couples. A little leery of learning what I might be on the cusp of, and not much one for killing time crosswording either, I examined the fresh faces of the couples, each wearing the smile of a lifetime. *Kimberlee This and Chad That said their vows to each other at the . . .* There were seven or eight such enraptured pairs pictured and I read the particulars on each, trying to divine any logic in Mariah and Riley repeating this process of matrimony. Pretty hard to make parse: *Mariah McCaskill and Riley Wright have announced their betrothal, again. Parents of the couple are Mrs. Leona Wright of the Shields River country and, against his will, Mr. Jick McCaskill of*

*the Two Medicine country. The bride-to-be graduated from Gros
Ventre High School and Illinois Institute of the Arts, and is a
photographer who does not have a lick of sense beyond her camera.
The incipient groom graduated from Clyde Park High School and the
University of Montana and has been a Missoula inmate ever since.
Ms. McCaskill will retain her maiden name, just as she did the first
time they attempted the wedded state and royally screwed it up. Upon
saying their vows one more time, the rewedded couple will go to
California to have permanent lunch with the future.* No, try as I
might, I couldn't credit these two with as much perspicacity as
the eighteen- and twenty-year-olds radiating out of the wedding
pictures.

"Funny place they pick to do it, though," I thought out
loud.

"Who do what?" Mariah asked from where she was competi-
tively sizing up a *Gazette* color photo of a Crow Indian fancy-
dancer.

"Newlyweds."

Both she and Riley shot quick hard looks at me.

"Where they get married, I mean," I hastened to explain.
"Not much church to it any more, I guess, huh?"

Now they glanced at each other. On their established principle
that each of them was the wartime ambassador to his or her
respective parent, it was Mariah who inquired of me in a combat
tone:

"Is this leading up to another sermon against our getting
married again? Because if it is . . ."

"It is not," I answered chillily. "I am only making the observation that it's kind of interesting that of this week's wedding
crop here in the paper, three of the couples got hitched in one
church or another, but there's four other pair who went and did
it at—"

The Holiday Inn was quite the extravaganza, whether or not
you were about to get your nuptial knot tied there.

Walk in as the four of us were doing and the lobby vastly
soared all around you; in fact, that cubic center of the enterprise
at first encounter seemed to be universally lobby, a hollow
square the entire six stories to the roof and equally out to the
perimeters of the half-acre carpeted-and-plantered space. You
had to wonder whether the architect remembered to put on

motel rooms, until you discerned that the half dozen beige fac-
ings that ran all the way around this atrium at equal heights
apart like the ribcage of the building were actually balconies,
with room doors off them. The place had a lot of other ruffles,
too. Up one side of the whole deal shot a glassed-in elevator
shaft outlined with sparkly dressingroom-like lights the full alti-
tude to the ceiling. There, natural light descended through a
skylight, I suppose for the sake of the trees—some of them fairly
lofty—in eight-sided containers, beige, plunked near the middle
of the atrium. At the far end of the expanse was a waterfall, no
less.

I fingered my bowtie. A tuxedo was a new sensation for me.
Beside me as we trailed the Mariah-Riley vanguard into the
assemblage, Leona behaved like she went to weddings in the
atrium of the Holiday Inn every day of her life.

True, she had been a little surprised to come into the
Bago with the groceries and be informed by Riley we were
going to a matrimonial function. "But I thought you two were
waiting for the privacy of California. I don't have a thing to
wear and—"

"Mother, it's not Mariah and me, it's"—he consulted his
notebook—"Darcy and Jason."

Which didn't help Leona get her bearings any. "Do we know
them?"

"That never matters with these two," I edified her about
journalism.

Riley now did bring us to a halt at the edge of where the guest
chairs and the altar and the food tables and all the rest were set
up for the wedding and the reception after, the first sign of
restraint he'd shown in any of this. That Leona and I were here
at all was due to his cockeyed inspiration that this could serve as
a kind of substitute function—a surrogate wedding, to quote him
exactly—for our not being on hand whenever he and Mariah did
their deed in California. Next he must have used a chisel instead
of a pen to get the rental of formalwear for Leona and me as well
as for him and Mariah onto the expense account. I do have to
say, on Riley the money looked well spent. Those wide level
shoulders of his filling out the fit of the tuxedo like a ship under
full sail, his mustache and curly spill of hair a handsome topping
to the regalia below, the guy looked slick as an ambassador.
Hard to believe this was the identical yayhoo who once cracked

to me, back in that living-together period of theirs before he and Mariah got married the first time, "Jick, in the immortal words of Robert Louis Stevenson, marriage is a sort of friendship recognized by the police."

"Okay, crew, people are going to be gathering for a while yet," he was briefing Leona and me currently, "and I've got to go locate the bride and groom, see what their last words are." Meanwhile Mariah was chewing the inside of her mouth as she gauged the airy acreages of the atrium, so it was plain that finding a photo was going to occupy her for some time to come. That left two of us at loose ends, and when I questioned Riley about what role Leona and I were supposed to perform here where we were perfect strangers to everybody, his set of directions was, "Mingle."

As the *Montanian*eers invaded the wedding party, Riley off to corner the wedding couple and Mariah just off, I admitted to Leona: "I don't really feel like wading right in. I'll just hang on here and watch things for a while. You go ahead and circulate, why don't you." With a quick understanding smile she said yes, she'd wander and see who was who, until it came time for the ceremony.

Is it just me, or does such an occasion inevitably prompt a lot to think about? Oh, sure, Mariah and Riley's forthcoming repeat performance—what do you suppose the California custom is, holding the wedding in a swimming pool?—was prominent in those thoughts, but so was the wife I wished was beside me. I hadn't missed Marcella so much in weeks and weeks. Anybody's start of married life I suppose can't help but remind you of your own. Up toward the altar, where there was an archway of flowers, I could see Riley was now interrogating today's nuptial couple. The bride Darcy was a looker, a dark-haired young woman with an outdoor tan that set off priceless teeth and quick eyes. The groom Jason, there was hope for; he was at that boy-man age that teeters on the Adam's apple and perhaps before he quite knew it he'd be a full-throated husband and father. Even though the two of them had agreed happily when Riley phoned about him and Mariah doing a piece on their great day, I hoped they had some inkling of what they were in for when put in print. But probably not even Riley Wright could dent them today.

"Sir?" I heard and realized it referred to me. What this was, a waitress had come by to prime me with a cup of punch or a glass of champagne, and of course punch wasn't even in the running. I sipped at the bubble stuff and as I did, the tail of my eye caught a motion down behind where my elbow had been.

Taking a peek over my shoulder, I discovered a bronze statue about a foot and a half high levitating past. Then another appeared and vanished, and by the time I'd blinked at that, a third one silently circled in.

I backed off to where I could view the entire revolving trio. Huh. Elvis Presley, all three of him. Coming and going as a slowly spinning turntable revolved the triplet statuary. Huh again: in each stage Elvis was in full pelvic deployment, but otherwise these were three distinct ages of him, at the guitar-whanging start of his career, then in summit, and lastly in pudgy decline. Hound dog, top dog, and pound dog, I guess could be said.

The Elvi in orbit behind me, I was just getting my attention back onto the wedding crowd when Leona detoured out of it toward me.

"See what you think of this," she instructed and handed me a dainty cracker loaded with a tapioca-looking substance.

I tried it. "Not bad," I assessed, "particularly with a chaser of champagne."

"*Montahnskaya eekrah!*" Leona reported in jubilation. "Montana caviar!"

"Yeah? Where's it come from, up on the High Line by Kremlin?" I asked, which I thought was pretty good.

But Leona only shook her head seriously and informed me, "Over by Glendive. It's sturgeon eggs, out of the Yellowstone River." Having imparted that, she swept back to the crowd to delve further into wedding matters.

I supposed it was time I got into motion a little, too. So my champagne and I took a stroll around the outside of the throng, nodding when nodded to, sizing people up without being over-obvious about it. Everybody was dressed to the hilt, gabbing in knots of relatives or friends. I wouldn't have predicted so, but the young men displayed higher fashion than the young women. A number of groomsmen had those porcupine styles of hair they fuss together with gel someway. Highly interesting. As to the other hair situation among the males, a few mustaches besides Riley's could be counted but mine was the only beard in evidence. He and I were safely in the spectrum with our formal apparel, though; starting with the groom, every man there was tuxedoed up in some shade between maroon and purple like ours. I wondered whether Althea Frew knew of this current color scheme. Doubtless she already had the matter planned out, me in a plum-colored bib and tucker, she in exquisite mauve tulle, tweeting out vows to each other in the flower-arched foyer of the Medicine Lodge.

Uneasily I shook off the thought of Althea, and checked around to see how my *Montanian* companions were progressing here.

Riley, the damn chameleon, appeared to be utterly in his element at this event, cruising through the crowd as if personally fond of every cummerbund and pleat. Leona, too, with her freshly done-up silver hair and a blending dress looked classily in place.

Mariah, though. Mariah was in—well, I believe the term for what she was in is hot pink.

Against the general maroon of the tuxedo populace and, for that matter, the similar rich tone of the atrium rug, she looked like something that had ignited. At the formalwear rental shop that morning I hadn't paid any real attention to the women's end of things, the prospect of myself in soup-and-fish duds already plenty on my mind, but I did notice Leona a couple of times open her mouth as if to say something and then not. At the time I figured she was just running Russian through her head. But I now knew that those unvoiced remarks had to do with Mariah's selection—too strong a word, honestly, because shopping was nowhere on Mariah's list of priorities and she had simply grabbed out a dress and tried it on enough to be sure it wouldn't fall off her and said "Okay, this'll do, let's go"—of an eyestinging pink outfit. I wonder, what is the Moscow phrase for *If that color was any louder it'd be audible.*

Nor for that matter was any other woman at the wedding carrying an Appaloosa camera bag the size of a satchel as an accessory to her outfit. Really, to capture the main sensation of these nuptials Mariah should have been shooting herself, for in those high heels and her pink number and her deeper-than-red hair she stalked among the wedding-going youngsters trailing every kind of reaction behind her. Multiply Kevin Frew's calfish gape at her atop the rodeo arena fence, back there on the Fourth of July, by about twenty and you have the general expression of the groom corps. The bride's maidens on the other hand seemed divided between disgust at such electric fashion and wishing they'd thought of it themselves.

After Mariah had parted the crowd waters all the way across the room and ended up at the revolving Elvi, I felt so sorry for her I sifted over to try and hearten her.

"I haven't seen you so dolled up since your high school prom, petunia."

"This get-up." She kicked off a high heel and massaged that foot against the other one. "I feel like a pink flamingo on stilts."

"Well, you look like society to me."

She fired a glance to the far end where a particular regal silver head and complementing aquamarine dress stood out resplendent against the atrium's cascade, as if Leona had magically enclouded there out of the sprays of blues and silvers off the spilling wall of water.

Mariah said with more rue than she probably wanted to admit to, "Not nearly as much as some. How did she manage to coordinate her dress with that goddamn waterfall, I ask you."

"Leona would look dressed to the teeth with nothing on but her birthday suit," I attested, which drew Mariah's eyes immediately back to me.

Well, I had given words a try. "How about a snifter of this seasoned water?" I offered her my champagne glass.

She considered it longingly, but shook her head. "Thanks, but not until I figure out some kind of a picture of this circus. Then I'll be ready for a swimming pool of that stuff."

"So," strolled up a swank specimen of plummy tuxedo which of course was Riley. "Quite a shindig, hmm?"

Mariah put her hand on his elegant shoulder to steady herself while she shed her other high heel shoe and massaged that foot. "My God, this is a tough sucker of a shoot," she let out along with her breath. "Everybody keeps looking right at me, right down the old lens hole. It's all going to come out like driver's license photos."

"Maybe you should have worn blue suede and a guitar and blended in as Elvis Number Four," I suggested to her.

"Come on, shooter, you can do it," Riley dismissed her photographic fret with the world's most unworried smile and leaned in and gave her a smoochy kiss alongside one ear. At first I figured he'd been too deep into the champagne, but no, this beamy kissy version was merely Riley rediscovering wedded bliss, even when it wasn't his own, quite yet.

I yearned for the old days of Moiese and Virginia City when Mariah would have handed him his head for that kind of canoodling. The worst she could summon currently was to cock a look at him and ask with just enough of a point on it, "How're you coming with your part of the piece?"

"Got it writ," Riley said to her surprise and mine too. "I've turned Biblical."

> . . . Let him kiss me with the kisses of his mouth . . .

She wanted him ever since Algebra. Alphabetized beside each other there in third period desks, x and y doing their things on the blackboard, maybe it simply was a case of possibilities put side by side. From day one she knew he spent that class hour peeking sideways at her results—not just the paper kind—but she didn't quite know why she one day was fond of that angle of gaze on her and wanted it forever.

He wanted her in every one of the eternal ways of the Song of Solomon. But along other Bible lines too, of course. Those that say things like dwell. Abide, *which seems to be a little bit different but no less awesome.* Esteem. Worship. Beget. *Words that send you a little dizzy, thinking about all they promise and ask.*

> . . . Honey and milk are under thy tongue . . .

Her favorite is anticipation. All her life she has liked to plan, imagine ahead, see how it turns out. It has just always seemed to her that's the way to make matters come out right, especially the big steps. Like getting married.

His is the avalanche approach. Now is timelier than later, you gain a lot of ground if you don't put off and put off but just up and do it. That way, you're sure you aren't wasting life on the small stuff but are honed in on what counts. Like getting married.

> . . . His left hand is under my head, and his right hand doth embrace me . . .

He's a little spoiled, she grants that, coming from the mother he does. And she wishes the little thinning place in his crownhair didn't mark the spot where his father is as bald as a dead lightbulb. But genes aren't everything. (Are they?) She still feels right, too, about deciding to keep her own name, even though his mother told

*her she'll give up on that after the first time of having to do
Christmas cards with their two separate names. (Will she?)*

*She's swifter than he is, he knows that much, and there's always
been a breath-catching little lag between when she says something
funny and when he gets it. But women are like that. Okay, okay,
he realizes you can get the pud beat out of you for saying stuff like
that these days. But isn't it some kind of biological fact? That
girls, women that is, grow up faster and all of a sudden—well,
develop into Amazonian princesses?*

. . . There will I give thee my loves . . .

*They don't give a fig, this wedding couple, about odds or
obstacles or second thoughts or a million possible frets, is what it
always comes down to. Not this day, not at this altar, which is an
old, old word for a place of fire.*

. . . For love is strong as death.

Riley still had something monumental on his mind as Mariah
balanced against him to grimly work her feet back into high
heelery. The moment she was shod again, he gave out another
big goofy smile and said:

"You know, we could make this a doubleheader."

Witless witness though I was to Riley's sudden new shenani-
gan, I caught his drift before Mariah did, her photographic
attention already focused back into the wedding throng like a
riverjack trying to figure out just where to dynamite a logjam.
Doubleheader, hell, the recognition hit my dismayed brain, *there
went the ballgame.*

The object of Riley's intentions tumbled rapidly enough, however, to what had just been put to her. Her head jerked around,
eyelids fanning, as she a little wildly sought verification in his
face. "Get married, you mean? Here and now?"

"Yup, now and here," he corroborated with utmost good
cheer. "All we'd have to do is arrange for the minister to hang
around until Darcy and Jason scoot off to their honeymoon.
Why, we've even got dear loving family on hand," he dispensed
along with a generous wag of his head toward me and then one
in the general direction of wherever his mother was mingling.
"How about it, Mariah Montana?"

I honest to God had the impression, right then, that even
Elvis in triplicate stopped spinning, for that longest of moments,
to watch whether Mariah was going to endorse Riley's inspira-

tion to hightail to the altar. So much for my campaign against. No, reason and history and minimum common sense never stand much chance against the human impulse to dart off and do it.

"N-No, no I don't think this is the time and place," Mariah declined nervously, to my surprise, not to mention Riley's. "Getting married in this"—her eyes did a loop-the-loop to indicate the infinite reaches of the Holiday Inn lobby—"while we're doing a piece here would seem kind of, mmm, tacked on, don't you think?"

What *I* thought, not that anybody was running a poll for my opinion, was that now they could derive a sample of what they were letting themselves in for by remarrying. Blow up at her, left, right, and sideways, I mentally urged goddamn Riley: insist it's now or never, matrimonially, because that way you'll come in for a nice reminder of the spikes that spring out when Mariah stiffens her back. Jump him, the dressed-up motel romeo, for treating marriage like the decision to go get an ice cream cone, I similarly brainwaved Mariah. Get out the big augur, each of you, and remind the other of how you caused the wind to whistle through the holes of that first marriage.

But see how Riley can't even be trusted to be his normal aggravating self? He fixed his two-tone gaze on Mariah and, in the same soapy mood as when he'd strolled up, grandly allowed: "A woman who knows her own mind, just what I've always wanted. California is fine by me, for us to get official." And off he went to sop up some more mood of the occasion, humming a little Mendelssohn.

For her part, Mariah threw me a don't-think-this-changes-anything-just-because-I-don't-want-to-get-married-wearing-hot-pink-in-a-glorified-blimp-hangar look, shouldered her camera bag purposefully, and headed out to do lens war with the wedding-goers again.

With the help of a sip of champagne I assessed where I had come out at from this Riley-Mariah close call: gained nothing, but lost none either. Could have been worse. Probably would be.

"Sir, would you care for some?" a waitress made a courtesy stop at me with a platter of hors d'oeuvre tidbits.

"No thanks," I explained, "I prefer big food."

I still can't account for the next event. I mean, there I was, dutifully keeping my nose out of Darcy and Jason's event, trying to blend my plum-tuxed self into the maroon backdrop of the atrium rug, when the bald guy emerged from the crowd and came straight at me as if he was being led by a dowsing stick.

Actually, the guiding instrument sat on his shoulder. The videocam in fact might have been mounted permanently there, the way it led the guy shoulder-first as if he was doing some kind of walking tango across the floor.

"Hi, I'm Jason's uncle, Jim Foraker. You must be from Darcy's side of the family."

"Just mildly acquainted, is all."

"I'm making a video for the kids," he said, bombardiering through the camera eyepiece onto my visage. "When Jason and Darcy get up into the years a little, it'll be kind of a kick for them to look back and see who all was at their wedding, don't you think?"

Especially when they try to figure out who the hell I am. Before I could retrieve my tuxedoed bearded self from posterity's lens, however, Jason's videoing uncle let drop: "I've got the sound package on this machine too, so how about saying something? Just act real natural. Tell the kids maybe what it was like at your own wedding?"

Which one? tore through my mind first. Shirley, when our young blood was on perk day and night. Marcella, everlasting but lost to me now too. My God, it gets to be a lot, to have to publicly pick and choose among sorrows. Darcy and Jason replaying on their golden anniversary in the year 2039 will have to be the ones to report whether I flinched, tottered, trembled, or just what. But whatever was registered by the videotape constituted only an emotional fraction. I felt as if I was coming apart, the pieces of my life I most prized—Marcella, the ranch, our life there together, our astonishing offspring Mariah and Lexa—cracking from me like streambanks being gashed away by rising water: yet at the same time I needed to hold, to not buckle under even to those heaviest thoughts, to somehow maintain myself in the here and now. Atrium extravaganza or not, other people's occasions deserve their sorrowless chance.

So. I had it to do, didn't I. Squaring myself in Jim Foraker's frame of lens to the extent I could, I began.

"Every wedding is the first one ever invented, for the couple involved. So I won't go into any comparison of this one with my own. But I can tell you a little something about after. I don't know whether a shivaree is still the custom"—some manner of mischief was; out in the parking lot I could see young guys tying a clatter of tin cans on behind a car with JUST MARRIED! DARCY ♥ JASON soaped all over it—"but after Marcella and I got hitched, everybody in the Two Medicine country who was mobile poured in to the ranch that night."

Cars and pickups all with horns honking, it was like a convoy from the loony bin. People climbed out pounding on dishpans and washtubs and hooting and hollering; you could have heard them all the way onto the other side of Breed Butte. Of course the men laid hands on me and the women on Marcella, and we each got wheelbarrowed around the outside of the house clockwise and tipped out ceremoniously at the front door. Then it was incumbent on us to invite everybody in for the drinking and dancing, all the furniture in the living room pushed along one wall to make enough floor for people to foot to the music.

Luckily there is no limit to the congratulations that can be absorbed, and Marce and I were kept giddily happy by all the well-wishers delivering us handshakes and kisses on the cheek. Leave it to our fathers, though, to carry matters considerably beyond that. Lambing was just starting, and under the inspiration of enough wallops of scotch, Dode Withrow and Varick McCaskill formed the notion to go check on the drop band for me; as Dode declared, "Mac and me all but invented the sonofabitching sheep business." It was a mark of the occasion that Midge Withrow and my mother did not forthwith veto that foray, but just gave their spouses glances that told them to come back in somewhat more sober than they were going out. First Dode and my father had to flip a coin as to which of them got my working pair of overshoes to wear to the shed and who got stuck with two left ones from the discards in the corner of the mud porch, and then there was considerable general razzing from the rest of us about how duded up they were to be lamb lickers, but eventually the two of them clopped off, unbuckled but resolute, toward the lambing shed. Busy as we were with our houseful, Marce and I lost track of the fact of our sires traipsing around out there in the Noon Creek night, until we heard the worried blats of a ewe. Coming nearer and nearer. Then the front door flung open and there stood the volunteer overshoe brigade, muck and worse shed-stuff up the front of both of them to their chins—Dode had been the one who drew the two left overshoes, and it had been that awkward footwear that sent him sprawling face-first; my father, it developed, simply fell down laughing at Dode—and a highly upset mother sheep skittishly trailing them and stamping a front hoof while they wobbled in the doorway declaring, "By God, Jick and Marce, you can't afford not to hire us," each man with a lamb held high, little tykes still yellow and astonished from birth: the first twins of that lambing season.

Finishing that telling, I sought how to say next what it still meant to me, that shivaree of almost forty years before.

"I suppose there must have been a total of a couple of thousand years of friends under our roof, Marcella's and mine, that shivaree night. A lot has happened since; the toughest part being that Marcella isn't in this life with me, any more. But that shouldn't rob what was good at the time. Our shivaree was utmost fun, and by Christ," I nodded emphatically to make sure the lens picked up this part, "so is the remembering of it. Darcy, Jason," I lifted my champagne glass, just a hummingbird sip left in it by now but any was plenty to wish on, "here's to all you'll store up together, starting now."

Jason's uncle thanked me for my videocam soliloquy and I told him it'd been my pleasure, and next thing, it was ceremony time. I found where Leona and Riley were saving a seat for me. No sooner was I sat than Riley said, "Here you go," and proffered me a little packet of the sort I saw everybody had.

"What've we got here?"

"Birdseed," he defined. "You throw it at the bride and groom when they head out the door to their honeymoon these days— it's better for the birds than rice is."

Take progress any time you can find it, I guess, so I tucked away the birdseed for later flinging and sat back to watch matrimony happen. The waterfall had been switched off so that it wouldn't drown out the minister's performance. For that matter, the entire huge cube of the atrium had quieted down. Arriving guests and the desk clerks stopped in midtransaction to watch. Waitresses paused lest a swinging door emit a sound. By the time the groom was escorted by his best man down the ramp past the glass elevator and the bride made her entrance from the videogames area, you could have heard a Bible page drop.

The wedding was almost to climax in rings and kisses before I realized. I leaned toward Riley and whispered, "What became of Mariah?"

He murmured back, "She's shooting this."

I inspected every farflung corner of the atrium and behind the potted trees and even cast a glance under the grand piano, but no Mariah.

I whispered again, "Where the hell from?"

This time Riley's murmur was forceful. "You don't want to know."

With that I did know, though. Which is why, in the *Montanian*'s photo of the Darcy-Jason wedding taken from overhead, the bride a white blossom and the groom a plum sprig beside her and the minister's open book and the dot rows of the heads of the wedding-goers as if seen from the ceiling of a cathedral, the solo face gaping directly upward six stories to the atrium skylight—and Mariah and her camera—is my bearded one.

That was Billings, and the day directly after the wedding experience our trend was east again, one last time, another three-hundred-miler to somewhere that hadn't realized it'd been waiting a century for Mariah and Riley.

And so even after we had reversed the long angling freeway journey along the Yellowstone River all the way to Glendive, this time we still continued east, as if pellmell to see North Dakota.

Shortly before the Dakota line, though, at Wibaux, behind me Riley announced "Make a right here and keep on going until you hit the South Pole" and although he overstated it a bit, I aimed us down the quantity of miles ahead to Montana's south-eastern corner.

Away from the green settled valley of the Yellowstone, counties in this part of the state are whopping maps with a single pin of town in each. The fact was, this was almost off the map of any of the four of us. I was the only one who had ever been anywhere into this emptiest corner, and that a long time ago. We might as well have been a carload of Swiss trying to sightsee Mongolia. Grassland with sage low and thin on it ran to all the horizons—cattle in specks of herds here and there—and a surprising number of attempts had been made to scratch some farming into this barebone plain, but what grew here mostly was distance. Except for an occasional gumbo butte or a gully full of tumbleweeds, out here there were no interruptions of the earth extending itself until bent by the weight of the sky.

Really pretty quiet all four of us stayed, throughout this long country. Leona spent time cramming Russian through her headset. Mariah mostly appraised the horizontal endlessness outside, occasionally fiddling with an earring, today white daisies as if this vicinity could stand a bit of bouquet. I idly wondered how I'd gotten so expert at miscalculation; if anything, Mariah and Riley acted more allied, alloyed, whatever, than before I'd applied Leona to this journey to split them. Mariah's only rival in the cosmos seemed to be Riley's word processor, going *pucka pucka* now but only sporadically, none of his long runs that said he was getting somewhere with the words.

> *The terrasphere now . . . space travel, this, except it's on the ground . . . the highway the orbit . . .*

Running down, maybe we all were. The centennial was only a handful of days away now. This had to be Mariah and Riley's last piece until they hit Gros Ventre for our dawn ceremony. Between now and then, once they finished in this final reach of the state, I was to drop them in Billings so they could rent a car and scoot to Missoula to begin closing down their lives there, then I'd leave Leona off at her ranch and hustle myself home to the Two country. Humongous agenda, as Mariah would have put it. So, maybe ahead preoccupied us. Maybe we were each a little hypnotized by the capacities of the plains; the full eighty miles down from the Wibaux turnoff, this road lined away as straight as the drop of a plumb bob. The only hint of deviation came after we passed through Baker, when the land began to rumple just enough to make the ride like a long slow roller coaster.

Even the roadkills were different from what we four mountain Montanans were used to; over the crest of any of the little rolly humps, the Bago was apt to intersect the angular length of a run-over rattlesnake.

Ekalaka has had to declare itself as best it can in such a circle of horizon. The little town is beside as much of a hill as it could find and has put a big definitive white letter of initial on that promontory. But what interested me as we gradually—everything out here seemed gradual—drew closer to our destination was that instead of the E a person would naturally expect for some place named Ekalaka, this civic monogram unmistakably read C.

"What, are they working their way up through the alphabet?" I prodded Riley, as my chances to do so were about to run out.

Ever clever, he explained the landmark C had to be for Carter County. Indeed, Ekalaka as we pulled in demonstrated itself even more as a conscientious county seat. Unusual for a Montana community, it possessed a town square, made up of a white-painted wooden courthouse, a jail, and a funeral parlor. Maybe you had to travel a ton of miles to reach this town but basics were here when you needed them.

So were three bars, not bad for a populace of 632, and a couple of grocery stores, and a hospital, and a small motel, and a Wagon Wheel Cafe, and an enterprise that declared it was a clothing store *and* a liquor store, and a bank and a propane plant and so on. By description alone, I know it does not sound like enough of a place to willingly make a six-hundred-mile roundtrip to visit. But not so, at least for me. I couldn't have said why, because Ekalaka tucked as it was into the southeast corner of the state was literally the farthest remove from Gros Ventre, and the two communities didn't bear any ready resemblance. But something about this hunkered little town quite appealed to me in the same way that Gros Ventre's concentrated this-is-what-there-is-of-it-and-we-think-it's-enough presence always had.

Now what? was always the question after Mariah and Riley hit a locale, and after a cruise of town and figuring out where to site the motorhome overnight—anywhere—we held a four-way conference on strategy for the rest of the day. Riley had spotted a Bureau of Land Management office and said he'd better get up there before closing time and find somebody to talk to about this area's yawning surpluses of, well, land. Leona said she wanted to stretch her legs and so she'd go with him and shop around town some while he gabbed. Mariah had her camera eye on the courthouse with its cupola that sat atop like a little party hat, but would stay and take stock of things until the afternoon light deepened better for shooting. For my part, I sighed and decided I'd better stay planted in the Bago too, needing to get myself organized toward my now not very distant centennial oration. So off Riley and Leona went, Mariah and I warning them not to get lost in the six-block-square expanse of Ekalaka.

For the first time in a long time, then, we were separated into the Wrights and the McCaskills, and maybe it was this almost inadvertent siding up into families that finally did it.

I admit I was a bit keyed up, with a speech to put together and all. It didn't take much of that to give me a sneaking admiration for Riley, even; this jotting stuff down wasn't as simple as it looked. Still, if Mariah hadn't done what she did, I would not have flown off the handle, now would I? All in the world I intended was to take a little break and administer some caffeine for inspiration. So, as I was about to nuke a cup of coffee in the microwave, I turned my head to ask if she wanted one too and found myself gazing into an all too familiar *click*.

"Mariah, goddamn that camera! You've about worn the face off me with it! You must have a jillion sonofabitching pictures of me by now, what the hell do you keep shooting them for?"

She of course could not resist snapping yet another one while I was right in the middle of that. Probably she captured me looking mad as a wet hen: white-bearded kid in a tantrum.

But then the camera did come down from her eye, and Mariah was giving me her own straight gaze. But through a glisten.

I blinked, dumbfounded. There was no mistaking. Her gray eyes were verging on tears.

Then Mariah said:

"Because I won't always have you."

That dropped on me like a Belgian brick. It had never occurred to me—how could it?—to regard myself as some kind of memory album for Mariah. Photographic shadows of myself that would pattern across her days after I no longer do.

I managed to say, "Petunia, I don't figure on checking out of life for a while yet."

"No, and don't you dare," she instructed me fiercely. Like mine, her voice was having trouble finding footing in the throat.

Talk about earthquakes being abrupt. Daughter and father, we this suddenly stared across the shaken up air between us.

"Mariah. I didn't know, it just never occurred to me that— that was on your mind." The way her mother was on mine; the way the ones we love ever are.

"I suppose really that's why I dragged you into this trip," she said with an alarming quiver in her voice. "And now we're about out of trip, aren't we."

"All good things must you-know-what," I tried, to see if I could jack her out of this choked-up mood. And won the booby prize at consoling, for now two distinct tears carried the glistening down Mariah's cheeks.

This was the exact pain I had wanted to keep her from. Loss. The gouge it tears through you. What I had been so sure would be incurred in her by Riley Wright, incurring instead from me.

Hard to know, though, how to be reassuring about your own time ahead in the green bed. I knew nothing to do but gulp and try from a new direction.

"I'll tell you what. When the time comes for me to go to the marble farm, you and Lexa just give me the Scotch epitaph, how about. The one I read about in trying to come up with something for this goddamn centennial speech. They used it there in the old country when somebody special to them went out of the picture ahead of time, so to speak. What they'd do was put on the stone: 'Here lies all of him that could die.' "

The words hung as clear between us as if spelled out in sharpest black and white of one of Mariah's photos. Our eyes held. After a bit I was able to provide what I knew from the storms of memory these past months. "Mariah. Just because I'm going to be dead someday doesn't mean I won't be available."

Mariah blinked hard, then gave a shaky grin. "You've got a deal, Daddio. I'll scratch that epitaph of yours into the rock with my fingernails if I have to." Her voice firmed as she went into stipulations: "But not until a long time from now, you hear? You at least have to match that old fart Good Help Hebner."

"Gives me something to shoot for," I agreed with an answering grin and figured we had come out of it to the good. Mariah, though, gave her hair a toss and looked at me in her considering-the-picture way—her eyes were thinking—but without her camera in between and I knew better.

"That's in the long run," she delineated. "Now what about your immediate future, Mister Jick."

"Well," I said in what I hoped she would think was earnest, "I was going to have a cup of coffee and then try to write a speech."

"I don't mean this very minute," she overinformed me. "What I do mean is the ranch and you and your mood when you get back to the Two country for good in a couple of days. The deciding you've got to do about things." Things, yeah. She hadn't even counted Althea Frew into the enumeration.

"Depends."

"On what?"

"Lots of things."

"Name a few."

"Don't you have something to go take a picture of?"

"That can wait. Right now I'm trying to talk to my father about the rest of his life."

"Let's find some prettier topic."

"No, let's don't. For a change, let's try to look at Jick McCaskill after this trip is over. After you make your speech. After you decide about the ranch."

"If you're going to be in the business of afters, Mariah, don't leave out the main one."

That threw her off, for a few seconds. Then she took a monumental breath. "All right then. After Riley and I—"

"Mariah, it's okay." I had to attempt this, finally, even if I didn't know how to say it, maybe never would know the right words for it. Nothing ever prepares you for speaking what you most need to, does it. "What I mean, it's all right about Riley and you. About you and him and marrying again and California, the whole works. It's okay with me now."

"Since when?" shot out of her in astonishment.

"If it needs a birth certificate, how about from right now," I told her and more than meant it.

It cost me a lot of my heart, but this needed doing. No time like—when you're about to run out of time. Minutes ago I had tried my utmost to show Mariah how to make loss into change, to accept that they for a while will seem to be the same, until a healing, a scarring over, whatever works, can manage to happen. Now to make it begin on myself, where my unholdable daughter was concerned.

"Christ knows, I can't guarantee I can always act as if Riley as a retread son-in-law is just fine and dandy with me," I set forth to her. "But I've played out the calendar on trying to change your mind or his. People can regulate each other only so far, huh?" And then they must do what I was now, gaze acceptingly at Mariah in what she chose for herself and tell myself without flinch, *This is how she is.*

"I suppose I've had some help realizing that, lately," I had to

go on, my voice thinner than I wanted it to be. If I forced myself
to do this I could. I would. I did. "Leona wouldn't give you the
sweat off her saddle, yet it's fine by her for Riley to marry you
again as many goddamn times as he can manage to. So if she can
think that way from her side of things, why can't I from mine,
right?"

Now Mariah really blinked. "You keep on and you're going to
have me telling her thanks. *Spassyveebo* or whatever the cockeyed Russian for it is."

"Yeah, well, you're maybe better off in English."

My daughter studied me. She said at last: "What I can tell
you is, I appreciate this. All of it. Even the hard time you gave
me over Riley. I can see why you did it. Riley and I aren't
exactly a prescription pair, are we."

"No, but I guess there are other kinds to be."

She pulled her camera to her abruptly, but just when I was
resigned to being fired away at, she went to the side door of the
Bago instead and peered out. "The light's nice now," she reported huskily. "I'd better go get shots of the courthouse."

"Before you do," I said. "What you were asking about me
in—the short run. I'm working on it all, Mariah. Honest to
Christ, I am working on it."

"I figured you were," she said and now gave me the full grin,
the Mariah and Marcella grin. "You're entitled to a cup of coffee
first, though."

Morning brought the next. Morning and Riley.

We were supposed to pull out of Ekalaka by midmorning,
which would just get us to where we each were supposed to be
that night; Mariah and Riley relaying on into Missoula from
Billings by rental car, myself home to the Two country after
dropping Leona off at her ranch. Quite a number of miles ahead
for all involved and no time for dillydallying. Which Riley now
came down with a severe case of.

He broke out with it to Mariah when we were amid breakfast
in the Wagon Wheel Cafe, first putting down his coffee cup as
delicately as if it contained nitroglycerin. "Got a little confession
to make, shooter. I don't have my part of the piece yet."

"Mmm," she responded and stabbed up a next bite of hotcake.
"Well, that's okay, isn't it? There's time yet. You can finish it
up before we pull out." Leona and I attended to our food.

Actually the listening I wanted to do was to the next table, where a habitual bunch of town guys were gabbing and coffeeing up for the day. "This Eastern Europe thing is a growing thing, I'm telling you," one with a *Sic 'em, Carter County Bulldogs* ballcap told the others. "See, what I'm saying is, what the hell is old Gorbachev gonna do if those countries keep this up, if you see what I'm saying." Even locutions seemed long in this stretched part of the state.

Not Riley's. "I don't have the piece started yet."

Mariah and Leona and I all looked at him.

"You mean," Mariah said as you would to an invalid, "really not started yet, not even anything jotted down?"

"Oh fuck yes," he responded, drawing a wince out of his mother. "I've got stuff jotted down until it won't quit. But I don't have the piece. The idea." He reflected. "Even any idea about the idea."

At any point in the trip until then I would have lit into Riley unmercifully. I mean, Christamighty, he had picked one hell of a place to be skunked. It was just about shorter to the moon than what we had to drive yet that day, and for him to do any dithering would just royally screw—but I kept my peace.

For a mother with a California-bound son who didn't seem to know how to aim himself out of downtown Ekalaka, Leona too was comparatively restrained. "Are we talking hours or days, that it's going to take you to think up something?"

But Mariah still was Riley's point of focus.

"I want to get this piece right," he said quite quietly to her. "This last couple of pieces, here and Gros Ventre, before we quit Montana—I want to do them up the way they deserve to be." He gave Mariah the diamond-assessing look he'd done in Helena when he saw her fresh print of the Baloney Express bunch and asked, *How good are you going to get, shooter?*

Breakfast dishes between and spectating parents on either side notwithstanding, I more than half expected Mariah to go straight across the table and kiss him his reward. The way Riley would tackle anything and anybody in his work was something terrific, even I had to admit. Mariah as much as said so with the savvying grin she gave him now, but she only reached for her camera bag and agreed in teammate fashion, "Okay, word guy, let's go find out how good there is."

* * *

"Jick?" Leona asked with surprising shyness when she and I were back in the Bago waiting for Mariah and Riley to finish rummaging Ekalaka for their piece. "Would you mind, do you think—could I practice my talk to the Sisters of Peace on you?"

I assured her I didn't overly mind. "As long as there's nothing physical or mental to the job, I'm probably capable." Besides, who knew, maybe some of her Centennial Day spiel to Moscow would rub off on me.

Across the dinette table from me, Leona drew herself up, the piping across the chest of her yoke shirt squaring itself impressively, and gazing at me as if I was the video camera, she broke out with an international smile and spouted:

"*Zdrahstfooyte, Syohstrih Meerah!* Greetings, Sisters of Peace. *Mwih ochen rahdih bwit vahsheemee droozyahmee.* We are very glad to be your friends. *Myehnyah zahvoot Leeona Meekhylovna Riyt.* My name is Leona Michaelovna Wright . . ." Gorbachev ought to have signed her up on the spot.

During one of her pauses to linguistically regroup, I asked something I'd been curious about, even a little leery for Leona's sake. "This sister group—I don't imagine they're ranch women, there in Moscow. So just who are they, do you know?"

"They're wives of soldiers killed in Afghanistan," Leona said in a voice carefully level.

My eyes followed hers, out and away from that mention of dying young in a war, to the hill with the big white C. Figuring we could contemplate the general landscape out around Ekalaka only so long without becoming too obviously oblivious to each other, I rose and headed for the jar of instant coffee and the microwave. "Get you something from the nuclear samovar here, can I?"

Both Leona and I jumped when the motorhome's side door opened and that son of hers yelped in, "Got it!"

I appraised Riley as he bounded in but confined my response. "Yeah? Where?"

"There." He nodded to the window his mother and I had just been scrupulously attentive to.

We swiveled to see what we'd missed.

"The C hill," said Riley. "The white alphabet."

White shadows of the towns, these initials on the nearest hill, trying to imprint community, constancy. To cry out in a single

*capital letter that these painted stones are not yet as abstractly
abandoned as tepee rings. . . .*

And from that C hill I did see. In my mind, I saw all the way
to white letters above English Creek, the outlines in painted
rock on the benchland south of another hunkered town, my own
town: GV, for Gros Ventre. For more than that. The devout
abbreviation my grandfather Isaac Reese made sure to sprinkle
through his letters to Denmark had been DV, the express wish of
his world and time: *Deo volente,* God willing. These little towns of
the land, the Ekalakas and the Gros Ventres, I believe are
written onto time in letters that similarly say their hope and fate.
GV. *Geo volente,* The earth willing.

Mariah was the next one to bollix up the departure plan. At
least she spilled it right out:
"Riley and I have to stay."
Leona and I looked at each other, then at our contributions to
journalism. Mariah had brought it out, so I was the one to inject:
"What, are you two going to take up residence here?"
"Just overnight," Mariah maintained and explained her desire
for morning light tomorrow to shoot the best picture of the C hill.
"But you two don't have to stay just because we are," she
summed up, sweet reason personified. "We've got it all worked
out, huh, Riley?"
He now had the same cloud-of-bliss atmosphere he'd had
throughout the nuptial event in the Holiday Inn. "Huh? Right,
yeah, all worked out. Here's the deal."
What it amounted to was that the local BLM man had to go
into Billings for a bureaucrat meeting the next day and he'd
gladly drop Riley and Mariah there, to continue their trip to
Missoula by a rental. Twenty-four hours more or less, they
claimed, probably wouldn't make much difference one way or
another with the BB at this late point in their *Montanian* careers.
So, no problem, Leona and I could hit on down the road without
them, right now.
"But if Jick and I go in the Bago," Leona lobbed into that,
"where'll you stay?"
"There's a, uh, place at the edge of town," Mariah replied
sunnily.
A place. Right. You bet. Also known as a motel. Chinook,

Ekalaka; these two were original in their romantic venues, at least.

The C hill and our theoretically adult children behind us, Leona and I scooted for home. Eyebrows had gone up a notch, Leona's among them, when I said before leaving that I guessed she and I might as well head west out of Ekalaka on the back road to Broadus and on across the Northern Cheyenne and Crow reservations instead of retracing all the way north to Wibaux and the freeway. Mariah and Riley of course had to put in their combined four bits' worth that driving back up to Wibaux was maybe longer but definitely a more major road, but Leona rose to the occasion. "If Jick wants to go this other way, that's jake with me," and that settled that.

West we went, then, for once in this centennial trip traveling in as straight a line as possible instead of a journalistic curlicue, across country new to Leona and so far into my past as to be almost new. When we pretty soon passed by a parcel of the Custer National Forest that consisted of chalk buttes and some scattered ponderosa pine, something telling did come back to me from that early time of mine as a shavetail assistant ranger in this corner of the world: how those of us stationed out here used to joke that maybe the Custer wasn't the biggest national forest we could be on but it sure as hell was the longest. Across about seven hundred miles, from the Beartooth District midway in Montana to the Sheyenne District on the far side of North Dakota, the Custer was a scatter of administrative islands of dry stands of forest or grasslands. This afternoon in the Bago, with the teeny Ekalaka swatch of federal forest fading behind us and sixty or seventy prairie miles ahead of us to the next district of the Custer, that joke seemed still valid.

You might think Leona and I would be talked out, after a couple of months of motorhome life together. But we did find things to say, whenever one or the other felt like it. She was good to visit with that way. I let her know that Mariah and Riley now had, if not my blessing, at least my buttoned lip. She smiled and said that was probably as much as they had a right to expect. After a while she wondered how I was coming on my centennial morn speech and I said fine, except for not knowing what the hell I was going to say. " '*Ostahlos nahchahts, dah koncheets,'* the Russian saying is," she provided me. " 'All there is left to do is begin and finish.' "

That first hour or so went that way, nicely, on the surface. But after we buzzed through Broadus, Leona seemed to sense that my mind was on something else than talk and we let conversation lapse. I drove remembering. Places coming back to me, places over here—communities that now probably were ghosts of themselves—that I'd never even heard of in my Two country upbringing, and I'd always thought I was good in geography. Sonnette, Otter, Quietus. The look of this terrain odd to me too in comparison with the Two Medicine land. No real elevation here but constant little rises. Bumpy country, it still seemed to me. The road, the arid hills; probably the lives of the people around.

I recognized King Mountain, ten or a dozen miles to the southwest, its hatcrown summit in the middle of flattish timbered ridges. It was all I could do to keep the Bago on the galloping highway and gawk at that odd but remembered country. Ever since the four of us headed into eastern Montana, I had hoped Mariah and Riley would not zero in on this particular area for one of their pieces. More of the fact is, I hadn't known how I could handle myself if they dropped a finger onto the map just here and said, let's go. And so, now that I was free of that, how do I account for having chosen this route myself? For what I all at once blurted?

"Leona, would you mind a little sidetrip? Just down the country here a ways. It won't take long."

Leona looked at me from the passenger seat as if wondering where in an outback like this it was possible to go on a sidetrip. Whatever was in my voice must have said more than my words. She immediately answered, "If you want to, Jick, that'd be fine."

I recognized the turnoff surprisingly well, although I remembered not a single one of the rancher names on their signboard that soberly listed extensive mileages to their places. The road south off the highway was another plummet-line route, cleaving across the terrain as straight and quick as possible.

Leona stayed quiet as we drove. My mind did not. The young man I had been, I met here behind my eyes, seeing again with him. The badlands here along Otter Creek had always spooked him, me. Dry gulches and stark buttes and the odd reddish tone of the ground might be expected in the honest deserts of Arizona or New Mexico, but to find country of that kind here, showing through the grass like the bones of the earth, made the younger me feel like a stranger in my home state.

Three Mile Creek we passed, then Ten Mile, then Fifteen Mile, with cattleguards markering the trafficless road between those streams. Then with a last *brrrump* the Bago rumbled across the cattleguard just before our destination, and I pulled into the driveway and shut the engine off.

The Fort Howes Ranger Station was little changed. The stockade-fence of pointed posts that had been out front was gone, replaced by a rail fence that looked more peaceable but less like the place's historic namesake, and some equipment sheds had been added, but the main buildings were the same as forty years ago, the ranger station like a shingle-sided cottage, the house its longer but similar mate. Their low-held roofs still were covered with fist-size rocks to absorb the heat of the sun, for it could get utterly broiling here in summertime.

Leona took it all in, the huddle of buildings each painted with the same federal red brush, the surrounding badlands with gray lopped-off slopes that duned down almost into the back doors. The rockfield roofs that even in the November afternoon chill looked like beds of rosy coals. "Different country," she said, with extreme curiosity in the gaze she turned toward me.

"Different guy, I guess I was, the last time I was here." She knew none of the particulars of my three-year career in the Forest Service here; nor, gone from the Two Medicine country into her own life with Herb Wright, had she ever heard of my first marriage. I told her it all. Of myself and Shirley, when I was assigned as assistant ranger here at the Fort Howes station and Shirley found herself in the unexpected role of Forest Service wife in what seemed the bare middle of nowhere—two Missoula campus hotshots abruptly out into the real world of rocks and routine. Of how, despite my determination to stand up under whatever job the Forest Service saddled me with, I never for a minute felt at home here; to me then, these encompassing buttes and rimrocks were as if the land had been cut down and these were the stumps. And of how, if I was uneasy here at Fort Howes, Shirley was entirely unhinged. *Quo vadis, hell*, was her reaction to my being assigned here.

Leona was listening as intently as I was telling it. I went on to the finale:

"As I remember it, Shirley and I passed the time by fighting. In those days we didn't have air conditioning and everything, and it could get pretty tough here in summer. I know the last time we got to arguing, Shirley pointed straight up at the roof and shouted at the top of her voice, '*Only snakes and bugs were meant to live under rocks!* ' "

It had taken forty years, but I laughed at that memory. Leona gave a kind of elegant giggle as if trying to contain herself, but then burst into outright laughing too. Which set me off all the more, happy with the surprise that I was at last able to do so, and that really got us going, a genuine fit of laughing, Leona and I infectious back and forth, snorting to each other and then at the hilarious accused rocks atop the ranger house and convulsing off into new gales. Rollicking applause, four decades overdue, for Shirley for that exit line from our marriage.

"And I can't say I blame her," I brought out when Leona and I at last managed to slow our chortling enough to get some breath back. "Not one damn bit. It was a case of double behavior. Both of us flung our way into that marriage. It wasn't just her doing."

In record time Leona's face went from the glee we'd been sharing to deathly sober.

She gazed at me, her eyes working to take in the recognition as they'd done that first full moment of look at me in the yard of the Wright ranch. I could see how much it took for her now to manage the words:

"You're saying that about another case too, aren't you."

"Yeah, I am." I made a half-fist and gently tapped the steering wheel of the Bago as I thought of just how to put it. "It's probably past time I should've said something of the sort about you and Alec. But that old stuff dies hard, doesn't it." I studied the ranger house, the now-quiet combat zone of Shirley and my younger self, for a moment more and then shifted around to face Leona. "I don't know what the hell it is, whether it's just easier to keep on being half mad than it is to ever get over it, or what. But anyway, I need you to know, Leona—I don't hold you responsible any more for what happened between Alec and the rest of us in the family." For both her and me, I lightened it as much as I possibly could.

"Probably you didn't have to hold a gun on him to keep him occupied with you."

She took her eyes from me and looked off at the chalk butte beyond the ranger station. Even yet, even sad, Leona's face fully hinted of the beautiful girl she was in those days. "No," she said as if from a distance. "No, I didn't have to."

The rest of the ride with Leona was a cruise across silk, as far as I was concerned. Ahead of me from Fort Howes, the landscapes and the moments unrolled as if carrying the Bago, bearing us like first guests across the miles, the autumn afternoon. Beyond the Tongue River and then the redstone hills of the Northern Cheyenne Reservation; at Lame Deer an Indian father in a down vest and big black hat was loping his horse in the barrow pit beside the pony of his maybe eight-year-old daughter, this evidently her saddleback lesson, the two of them watching each other without seeming to as they kept their easy but steady gait. Then mountains beginning to the south, the Rosebud and Bighorn ranges. Another hour of quiltpatch road and we were passing the Custer Battlefield, monument, straggle of Seventh Cavalry graves, wrought-iron cemetery fence. Studying the terrain chopped up by small coulees—you would have to go some to invent worse country for cavalry—Leona shook her head and said she never would understand what all the fuss over Custer was about. "A lot of better people have died in wars." I only made an agreeing noise in my throat, those World War Two storms of thought behind me too on the trip now, and headed us on. After Crow Agency the road sledding down into nice irrigated bottomland, sudden treeline at the far side of it, the Bighorn River hugging below benchland in a way to remind me of the valley of English Creek. Now through the western half of the Crow Reservation, long rolling miles toward Pryor while daylight went, before long the Bago's headlights picking out plywood signs with the spray-painted message CATTLE AT LARGE ON ROAD. No more so than me. Into full night before ever reaching the freeway at Laurel and then the twin lanes beside the Yellowstone River again, the motorhome and I and our passenger as if on comfortable automatic now, until Big Timber where we late-suppered in the Country Pride cafe. From there we had only the easy last hour home for Leona.

* * *

So I was surprised, to say the least, at how she spoke up after we were onto the ridge road from Clyde Park out toward the Crazy Mountains, minutes from the Wright ranch.

"Jick," she said in a strained voice. "Pull over. Please."

What, could she be carsick, now after damn near two months of Bago motion? Dashlight was all I had to diagnose by, but my instant glance across at her told me Leona most definitely looked peaked.

Making the best version of emergency landing I could, I nosed the motorhome onto an approach leading into a field and cut the motor.

She did not open the passenger door and bail out into the night air for recuperation as I expected she was going to. Instead Leona faced around to me and spoke beyond the capacity of expectations.

"That time. The night of that supper with your folks and you."

Of my brother Alec declaring as if it was the world's newest faith, *We got something to tell you, we're going to get married.* Of Leona wielding her smile that proclaimed *And nothing can dent us, we're magical at this age.* Of my mother and father as unmoving as the supper plates, more than half knowing the next to come, that Alec was going to say a college ladder into the future was not for him, now that he'd have a wife to support. I sat startled to be simultaneously at that supper scene again and in the halted motorhome. The woman of silver here who had been that invincibly smiling girl said:

"I'd told Alec I was pregnant."

"But then—"

"I . . . I wasn't."

She was having hard going, her voice throatier than in the most straining Russian lesson.

"But a girl could say that then and be believed," she managed to get it out, "before the pill and the foam and the whatever else they have these days. Men then didn't much understand female plumbing. Whether they do now, I wouldn't know."

Leona turned her head toward the windshield, as if the reflections of each of us in the night-backed glass needed to hear this too.

"In those days, we counted the days of the month," she kept on. At least that much I knew. Shirley and I had our own few months of calendar nerves, that long ago springtime in Missoula before we got married. "We'd been meeting out along the creeks, Alec and I," Leona's words remembered. "The old Ben English place right there across English Creek was standing empty then, that was one we met at. But it was awfully close to town, we had to be too careful there. Noon Creek was better for our purpose, all those ranches standing empty after the Double W bought them up—Fain's, the Eiseley place, the Nansen place. Alec and I both lived on horseback in those days and there wasn't any shortage of places to ride to and make love." Still facing ahead, she stopped and swallowed. Then resumed. "So it fit with—the way we'd been with each other, my telling him the calendar had played a surprise on us."

Sometimes you know a thing because even invisible it fills a gap. I asked anyway. "On the ride out from town that night, wasn't it. When you told Alec that."

Surprised herself, Leona swung to look directly at me again. "Yes. Jick, did Alec . . . have you always . . . ?"

"No, he never said a word of any of this to me. To any of us. I just remember there was something about you two when I watched you come over the rise." Alec with his head up even more than his customary proud riding style, Leona golden and promising even at too great a distance for details. Their perfect gait, horseman and horsewoman, down from outline against the June sky as I crossed the yard from a boyhood chore to that supper-time. One of those moments that is a seed of so much else.

"Alec was both scared to death and as happy as he could be," Leona spoke now as if we were both watching that saddle-throned figure of my nineteen-year-old brother. "You can be that way, when you're young and convinced you're in love. Right then and there, on the county road before we came into sight of the ranger station, he wanted to know if it was safe for me to be on horseback, would it hurt the baby? I laughed and told him he was getting away ahead of the game, worrying about that already." But that was Alec, wasn't it. All go and no whoa, as my mother always said of him. Beside me Leona was saying now: "It was happening sooner than he'd wanted, in one way—we still couldn't get married for a few months, until he'd saved up his wages and talked the Double W into some kind of living quarters for us. And in another way, he was thrilled pink with the idea he and I were going to have a child. I hope you see, Jick. It decided for us. A baby then meant the pair responsible had to get married, there wasn't just . . . living together. That was the thing about it: my telling Alec settled so much we were still trying to figure out. It made life seem so much—safer. And he wanted some kind of sure path as much as I did, something he could just latch on to and go with. You know how Alec was."

Yes. Alec McCaskill and Leona Tracy, I knew how they both were then. In memory the perfect two of them, another month into that summer of 1939, at the after-rodeo dance in Gros Ventre when Alec won the calf roping, my brother tall and alight with the fact that he was astraddle of the world, beside him Leona golden-haired in a white taffeta dress that flounced intriguingly with her every step. His armful of her as Alec advised my friend Ray Heaney and me, enough younger that the only company we kept at dances yet was the wall, *You guys better think about getting yourselves one of these.* That was the appearance, royal Alec and priceless Leona. In actuality, both before and after Leona, my brother stubborned his way into a life that did not lead to much of anywhere. And Leona there at seventeen, who looked like her life was on clockwork—smile; let her hair gleam in the sun; beautify whatever scene she found herself in, on the back of a horse or twirling in taffeta at a Fourth of July dance—in actuality, a seventeen-year-old head on a body with the collected urges of centuries in it, on it. No more than the figurehead is steering the ship under full sail was Leona Tracy in charge of herself then.

This next I didn't ask. Why the episode with Alec didn't come out the way she'd set it in motion. This she owed herself to tell.

"I couldn't go through with it," the Leona of now was saying as if still in accusation against herself. Her voice had the same crimp of hard—hurtful—concentration that I knew was pierced in between her eyes. "Pretty soon after the Fourth, I told him that . . . it was a false alarm, that I was . . . back in step with Mother Moon. Oh, I think Alec more than half knew what I'd done. Started to do. Especially when I went on and said I thought we had better hold off on marriage entirely, that I'd decided to finish high school and take a look at life then."

A person tends to think that the past has happened only to himself. That it's his marrow only, particular and specific; filling his bones one special way. The anguished look on Leona disabused me of that forever.

"It's there, isn't it, Jick. If I'd kept matters that Alec and I simply were going together, that I didn't want to get serious about marriage right then, he might've eventually listened to what your folks wanted for him." And gone to college and made the life that education could have brought him, I mentally finished the fifty-year-old family accusation against her. "Or if I'd gone ahead and shotgunned him into marrying me, we in all likelihood really would have had a child by the time the war came." And Alec would not have charged off and enlisted the week after Pearl Harbor, this new burden of proof against Leona ran. "Either way," she finished with difficulty, "Alec might not have . . . ended up as he did."

I felt a sting at my eyes, but Leona was nowhere near crying. There is a dry sorrow beyond tears.

She waited, there in the almost-dark of the motorhome cab.

Life is choices. I could go back to the long McCaskill grudge against her, fortified now by knowing that my parents and ultimately I were righter than we had even imagined, about her effect that family-tearing summer. Or. Or I could make as much of a start as I could in the other direction.

By saying, as I now did:

"Leona Tracy was somebody the McCaskills never knew how to contend with. So I think we're lucky to have Leona Wright take sides with us."

We pulled in to the Wright ranch at close to midnight, the yard light illuminating the tidy buildings and the cow corrals and a Chevy pickup with a considerable portion of the ranch on it as mud. Out from under the pickup materialized a half-grown dog letting out a nightsplitting woof.

"Morgan and Kathy will be wondering what Manslaughter has got treed," Leona said. "I'll go across and let them know I'm back in one piece." She sounded strangely shy, tentative, with the next: "You want to come with, come in for a little while?"

"Naw, I'm going to turn in pretty quick, thanks anyhow."

"I guess it's a rare chance in this rig"—she cast a memorizing look around in the motorhome, which suddenly was seeming as empty as an unloaded moving van—"to have some sleeptime all to yourself."

"Yeah, I guess," I managed to semichuckle.

"You'll have breakfast with us, surely," she stipulated.

"Actually I can't. I've got to pull out for the Two Medicine country real early. I need to get home and sort out the situation there."

"Then I'd better say thanks now, for bringing me back. And for everything else you did today, Jick."

"That's okay, thanks for riding along. Been nice having some company. Been interesting."

Leona leaned across from the passenger seat and gave me a no-nonsense kiss, surprisingly like Mariah's version, on my approximate cheek. She smiled, maybe still a little sadly, before she opened the passenger door of the Bago. "With my background, would you believe it's taken me sixty-seven years to kiss a man with a beard?"

DAWN ARTICULATING

*When asked what he thought of today's centennial
celebration, 89-year-old Garland Hebner, odds-on
winner of the beard contest, declared: "A time was
had by all."*

—GROS VENTRE WEEKLY GLEANER,
NOVEMBER 8, 1989

A HUNDRED hours later, which had seemed like a century,
the Noon Creek road was a dike through the dark as I headed
the Bago in from my ranch toward Gros Ventre and centennial
morning.

The only other creature up this early was at the crest of the
benchland, a jackrabbit that leapt in panic and ricocheted back
and forth in the tunnel of light cut by the motorhome's bright
beams. I switched onto dim and the skittering jack managed to
dart free into the barrow pit.

Otherwise, nothing but before-dawn blackness on either side
of the gravel embankment of road until the gateframe at the
turnoff into the Double W, high and logthick, came into the
headlights.

I flipped onto bright again, as if the increased wash of light
would bleach away that triumphal WW sign and the cable-
strung cow skull swaying beneath in the wind. Still no such luck.
Nearer and nearer the gateway drew, the motorhome's headlights leveled steady on it; my trigger finger itching as ever here,
both of my gripping hands feeling the shotgun rise in aim at the
hated goddamn fancy transom, my eyes sighting in on the welcome vision of putting an end to that plaything skull by blasting
it to bits.

But by now other conclusions, this final nightful of thinking
them through, shouldered that one away and I drove past.

*   *   *

Life was definitely awake when I reached town. The Medicine Lodge was as lit up as boxed lightning. Switched on in more ways than one, too, for music was blaring out of the radiant old saloon as I climbed down from the Bago. The municipal serenade hit a crescendo that sounded like a truckload of steel guitars rolling over and over and then a woman's voice boomed in amplification: "That was a little tune we picked up from a rock group called Drunks With Guns. So now you've had your wake-up music and can tackle the pancake breakfast these nice folks have got ready for you, and we'll be back shortly."

Yeah, well, I guess there are all different ways of feeling gala, and musical commotion of their sort must be one of them. I started to cross the street to the site of rumpus, not to mention breakfast, but had to wait for traffic, one lone van toodling through town from the south. I stood impatiently for it to pass, more than ready to scoot across and get myself in out of the chilly wind; November is not much of a pedestrian season in the Two Medicine country. The leisurely vehicle at last reached me and I started to get my thoroughly cooled heels into motion again. But right in front of me the van pulled up, blockading my path, and the driver tapped out on his horn *beep beepitybeepbeep beep beep!*

I remained there with my jaw on my shoetops while geezers in dress-up stockman Stetsons, the dapper low-crowned kind you don't see often any more, came stiffly climbing out both sides of the van. "How you doing, Jick? All revved up to go through this again in 2089?" "Jick, you Two Medicine people get up before God sends Peter out to the Gate." "Got your speechmaking pants on this morning, have you, Jick?"

The Baloney Express gang and I shook hands and slapped shoulders and conducted general hubbub there in the middle of the street until I managed to ask, "What, you mean to tell me you guys got up before the chickens and drove all the hell the way up here from Great Falls just for our ceremony?"

"How could we stay away?" Roger Tate responded from behind the steering wheel of the van. "Ain't we all been waiting most of a hundred years for this?"

"Besides, it's only ninety miles back to the Falls," Julius Walker chipped in. "The way Roger drives, it'll only take us half an hour to get home."

"Had to deliver this anyway," Dale Starr declared and presented me a five-dollar bill and four ones.

"What's this, you guys running a lottery now too?"

"Compliments of our Shoeless Joe from Fargo," explained Dale, about our broke-and-barefoot casualty in the rest area a couple of months ago. "Wrote that things are still pretty tough with him, but he's trying to scout up enough odd jobs to get by on."

Then the other Walker, Jerome, had me by an elbow and was steering me back to the side of the street I'd started from. "We got something to show you over here, too. Don't look so alarmed, we didn't bring none of those used cars with us."

He headed me toward the rear of my Winnebago, where a couple of the more nimble members somehow had slipped away to and already were standing there with full moon grins. Gingerly I stepped around to peer at the rear of the Bago, and there on the bumper blazed a sticker in Day-Glo orange:

HONORARY BALONEY EXPRESS RIDER

"We had it made up special," announced Bill Bradley, rocking back on his tiny heels as if nearly bowled over with pride.

I didn't know whether to laugh or bawl, and so likely did a mix of the two.

After I had thanked them sevenfold, the bunch said they realized I needed to gather my mind toward the speech I was going to make—"Say what you're gonna say good and loud, or at least loud," ran the general tenor of their advice—and off they hobbled toward the Medicine Lodge and pancakes and coffee.

A minute to compose myself was definitely required, and I moved to the side of the Bago that was out of the wind and stood looking at Gros Ventre. Like other Montana towns, no Easy Street anywhere in it. Instead this highway main street, born wide because freight wagons and their spans of oxen or work-horses had needed maneuvering room, the twin processions of businesses, dead and alive, now aligned along that original route, the high lattice of cottonwood limbs above the sidewalks. With all the cars and pickups parked downtown at this usually empty hour and only one building alight, Gros Ventre looked busy in an odd concentrated way, as if one behavior had entirely taken over and shoved all other concerns out of the way. Maybe that is what a holiday is. The dark up there beyond the cottonwoods was just beginning to soften, the first of the hourlong suggestion of light before actual sunrise. I gazed across the street at the

crowd of heads behind the plate glass window on the cafe side of
the Medicine Lodge. Bobbing amid them, in a rhythm of choosing and coaxing and focusing and clicking, was a fireball of hair
deeper than red. Mariah riding the moments as they came.
Riley was not in action yet. I could see him propped against the
cafe wall, arms folded, not even wielding his notebook yet.

I squared myself, ready at last to go across and be part of the
occasion. I wish you were here for this, Marcella. But you are
not. And so I hope I bring to this day the strength of what we
were together.

Gros Ventre entire seemed to be within the straining walls of
the Medicine Lodge when I entered. Never in the field of
human jubilee had so many so voluntarily got up so early. Some
were history-costumed, here and there frock coats and Lillian
Russell finery, elsewhere cowboy and horsewoman outfits complete with hats of maximum gallonage; even occasional fringed
leather trapper getups. Others were in common clothes. In whatever mode, conversation was epidemic, people yakking and visiting back and forth in a mass from one end of the cafe to the
other. The back wall was startlingly bare, the centennial flag
down now and in folded repose across a number of long tables
like a golden tarpaulin, ready to be taken out for hoisting when
the time shortly came. All other tables of the Medicine Lodge
and a borrowed bunch more had been pushed together in spans
devoted to pancake consumption.

But my policy had to be first things first, even ahead of
breakfast, so I made my way over to her.

Naturally Mariah was in midshoot of Amber Finletter, who was
wearing big goony glasses with blunked-out lenses like Orphan
Annie's eyes and a housenumber "1" attached off the side to
make the eyerig read as a 100. Such centennial embodiment
notwithstanding, I got Mariah aside and had the talk with her I
needed to have.

To my news she simply gave me a ratifying buzz on the cheek
and added: "What can I say? I was the one who kept at you to
get yourself going again, wasn't I. You don't vegetate worth a
damn, Jick."

Then it was her turn, of telling me what she needed to.

Four months' worth of words with this daughter of mine dwin-
dled to basics. I only asked:

"You're real sure?"

"I finally am," said Mariah.

Away she flew, back to work, and myself to breakfast. Sleepy 4-H kids were ladling out the food. I negotiated a double plateload of pancakes and swam them in syrup, further fortified myself with a cup of Nguyen's coffee, then went over and found a seat across from Fred Musgreave, who had surrendered his bar domain to the music posse.

Fred appraised my hotcake stack and asked, "Gonna build a windbreak inside yourself?"

"Uh huh," I acknowledged cheerfully and began forking.

A fresh gust rattled the plate glass window. "At least it isn't snowing," Fred granted.

"Shhh," I cautioned him against hexing the weather.

After pondering me and my steady progress through the pancakes, Fred concluded: "I gather you're saving up your inventory of words for your speech."

I suppose I was. But also, by now a lot of the essential had been said. Said and done. I forked on and watched Mariah aiming her camera at Bill Rides Proud, his Blackfeet braids spilling down his back.

When pats descended on my off arm, the noneating one, I didn't even need to look. "Morning, Althea."

"Oh, Jick. It's so nice to see you back for good."

A Mariah-style "mmm" was all I was willing to give that until I had the last of the hotcakes inside me. In something close to alarm, Fred Musgreave abandoned the chair across from me to Althea and she took it like a throne. This morning her sense of occasion featured turn-of-the-century regalia, a sumptuous velvet bustle-dress with matching feathered hat; it broke my eating rhythm a moment to realize that, feathers excluded, the plum color of everything on Althea Frew exactly matched that of my Billings wedding motif.

"What a nice bolo tie," she found to compliment on me after considerable inspection. I only *mmm*ed that too, all the help really that Althea needed with a conversation. Pleasant as fudge, she proceeded to give me a blow-by-blow account of our centennial committee's doings in my lamented absence and then on into every jot and tittle of this dawn event and beyond. "Then we'll have more dancing, then when the bells ring all over the state at 10:41, we'll start our parade. Then—" You could tell she could hardly wait to get going on the next hundred years; for that matter, Althea would be gladly available by seance when Montana had to gird up for its millennium.

Suddenly music met its makers in the bar half of the Medicine Lodge, the band tuning up thunderously cutting off Althea in midgush.

"Interesting chamber orchestra," I remarked for her benefit.

Althea flinched the least little bit as a new chorus of whangs and clangs ensued. "I put Kevin in charge of hiring the music. He told me they're a dance band."

"Depends on the dance, I guess."

Over the throb of the music she swung back onto that ever favorite topic of hers, me. "We're all so anxious to hear your speech."

I grinned, by far the fondest I'd ever given her, making her bat her eyes in surprise, before I said: "I kind of feel that way myself."

Mood music was not the term I ordinarily would have applied to whatever the band was performing, yet somewhere behind my grin was the amplified tune beating through my body in an oddly familiar way. Then the voice of the woman singer resounded:

"Somewhere south of Browning, along Highway 89!"

The singer interrupted herself to announce it was action time, everybody better find their feet and stomp a quick century's worth. Even without that I was already up, needing to go see, assuring Althea I'd connect with her at speech time. And yes, as I passed I gave her a pat.

"Just another roadkill, beside life's yellow line!"

National anthems I can take or leave, but the music put out by these Roadkill Angels now drew me as if it was the strongest song of the human clan. And was drawing everybody else in the Two Medicine country, judging by how jampacked the bar side of the Medicine Lodge suddenly was with dancers and onlookers. The players in the band, mostly armed with guitars of colors I didn't even know they made them in, held forth on a temporary stage that had been carpentered across the far end of the bar. Behind and a little higher sat a drummer in a black plug hat with an arrow through it.

Amid this onstage aggregation the woman singer didn't look like much—chunky, in an old gray gabardine cattledealer suit, her blond hair cut in an approximate fringe—but her voice made maximum appearance, so to speak. She sang, my God, she sang with a power and a timbre that pulled at us just short of touch, as when static electricity makes the hair on an arm stand straight when a hand moves just above it. Holding the microphone like she was sipping from it, she sent that voice surging and tremoring, letting it ride and fall with the cascades of the instruments but always atop, always reaching the words out and out to the crowd of us. She activated the air of the Medicine Lodge: the floorful of solos being danced in front of the Roadkill Angels band was magnificent, the 4-H kids especially shining at the quick-limbed undulations this music wanted.

Up near the bandstand I spotted Mariah and Riley in conference, I assumed about their coverage of this spree. But then he looked at her for a moment, smoothed his mustache before nodding, and stuck his notebook in his pocket while she went over along the wall to where Howard Stonesifer and his ancient mother were sitting, Howard watching the dancers, and his mother watching the dancers and Howard. To old Mrs. Stonesifer's astonishment and Howard's blushing agreement, Mariah with royal fuss hung her cameras one after another around Howard's neck for safekeeping. He sat there proudly sashed and bandoliered with her photographic gear as she and Riley found space on the dance floor.

This was not the slow clinging spin in each other's arms as it had been at The Lass in a Glass. But even while dancing apart as they now were, the two of them responded to each other like partners who have heard all possible tunes together. Again, as that night in Chinook, their eyes steadily searched each other's.

When the song ended, they headed toward me.

I favored Riley with the question, "So how would you describe this band?" He responded, "It definitely isn't elevator music."

Mariah, though, was the one with something on her mind. She stood in front of me, a bit flushed from her round on the floor with Riley. "Dad," she said, "how about dancing with me?"

"Mariah, I can't dance to this stuff. Parts of my body would fall off."

RIDE WITH ME, MARIAH MONTANA

She gave me a monumental grin and said, "I'll bet they can tone the music down just enough to keep you in one piece," and she flashed away to the bandstand to put in her request to the singer.

I started to take this chance to say to Riley what I needed to, but he beat me to the draw by digging into the front pocket of his pants. "Before I forget, here," and he handed me a folded wad of money.

Inquiry must have been written on me as large as the bankroll I was gaping down at.

"For Bago repairs, courtesy of the expense account," Riley droned in what was probably a bean counter voice.

At that I rapidly performed finger arithmetic on the currency and sure enough, dented grill—lost hubcap—assorted ailing windows—and what all, it was the whole damages. All this and the surprise remuneration delivered by Baloney Express. By God, business was finally picking up as Montana approached its second hundred years.

I had to ask. "What'd you make up to charge this much off to?"

"Helicopter rental," said the scribbler nonchalantly.

"Heli—? Christamighty, how are you ever going to get the BB to believe *that*?"

"By the note I stuck on that says we also used the flight to spot mountain goats up behind your ranch."

After that, I almost hated to give him my news. And at first it did stupefy him. Riley was resilient, though, and by the time Mariah got back to tow me onto the dance floor, we left him looking only somewhat fogged over.

> *"So we've survived*
> *the nicks of time . . ."*

The music still had enough steel in it to be sold by the metric ton, but the woman singer was almost gentle now.

> *"Done our best against*
> *the tricks of time . . ."*

Whatever Mariah and I may have lacked in grace as a dance

team we made up for in tall, our long McCaskill legs putting us
at an eyelevel above almost all the other couples'. There was a
privileged feeling in this, like being swimmers through water
controlling itself into small bobbing waves, hundreds of them but
each one head-size. I started to say something to Mariah about
the specialness of this a.m. guitar cotillion scene, but she was
immersed in it too, her eyes alight as our slow tour of the floor in
each other's arms brought us past what seemed the entire community of the Two Medicine country.

"They'll say of us that
we had a past . . ."

Elbow to elbow, wall to wall, the Medicine Lodge was a rainbow
swirl of twined couples. Dancers came in all varieties. A tall
young woman with a ponytail stared soulfully over the hairline
of her partner half a head shorter than her. Of the English Creek
contingent, plaid-shirted Harold Busby, with an Abe Lincoln
beard since I'd last seen him, twirled by with his wife Melody in
a swishing black skirt with white fringe.

"But we know our way
to now at last . . ."

Althea Frew freighted me a chiding look as she steered an
apprehensive Fred Musgreave by us. I felt a rump bump and
glanced back to find it was Kenny, his jeans tucked in the tops of
his boots, earnestly waltzing with his arms cocked wide and his
behind canted out, as if about to grapple with Darleen as she
tried to match steps with him.

But of them all, people in costumes of the past century, people
dressed in everyday, people with generations behind them in the
Two country, people newer to its demanding rhythm of seasons—of
them all, I concentrated on Mariah, her lanky form perfectly
following mine as we danced, her face intent on mine, on this
time together. I could not but think to myself, how did Marce
and I ever do it, give the world this flameheaded woman?

After the music, we rejoined Riley. He and Mariah talked
matters over a last time as I just listened. Before any too much
could be said, though, marching orders for all of us came from

Althea, commandeering the singer's mike: "It's time, everyone! Out, out, out!"

True to her words, the crowd did begin to sluice out of the Medicine Lodge into the street, Amber Finletter and Arlee Zane at the door handing out to everybody, man woman child whatever, gold-colored ballcaps with DAWN OF MONTANA printed on the front. Arlee and I somehow managed to thoroughly ignore each other even while he held out a cap which I took. Behind me Riley of course wanted to know if there were any with earflaps for the Two Medicine climate, but then clapped a cap onto his frizzhead insofar as it would go and trooped on out with the rest of us.

It was breezy and then some, I will say. Quite a swooshing overhead as the wind gusted around in the tops of the cottonwoods. But Two Medicine people are born recognizing the nearest windbreak, and the centennial crowd now divided almost exactly to bunch in front of either the Mercantile or the *Gleaner* office, the empty lot with the flagpole between them, in a way that reminded me of sheep on either side of a fast creek. Meanwhile Riley for once had an idea that was useful as well as bright. I reluctantly loaned him the keys and he hustled off and moved the Bago around to the alley behind the Merc and the *Gleaner*, parking it broadside across the back of the flagpole lot to block at least a fraction of the wind.

Before I quite knew it, Althea had herself and me up into the back of Arlee Zane's auctioneering pickup, our vehicular speaking stand for the occasion. Above, the ropes still sang in their pulleys on the flagpole, but Althea seemed to regard it as the most refreshing weather of the entire century as she bustled forward to the microphone setup to introduce me.

I only half-heard her toasty testimonial to me, occupied as I was with my own words to come, the shapes and shadows of all I had to try to articulate. When is a person ever fit to speak for his native patch of ground? Old Churchill must have been something beyond a human being. Too quickly, Althea's pertinent part was ringing out—"and it's my deep personal pleasure to present to you our Dawn of Montana speaker, Jick McCaskill!"—and I was up there peering out over the loudspeaking apparatus atop the pickup cab and having the microphone bestowed on me reverently by Althea.

There in the half-light, sunrise impending only a number of

minutes away, I could make out individual faces of the crowd. I could see Mariah's Dawn of Montana cap, backward on her head to keep the bill out of the way of her camera. I could pick out the screen glow of Riley's word processor where he'd perched it on the pickup fender down in front of me. For the first time, it struck me that words of mine here might pass into print via Riley. The *Montanian*'s last centennial story, me at his laptop mercy. The thought of that once would have scared me spitless, but now I simply smiled at it as fact. Ink outlasts blood.

So I began.

"I don't really have the best feet for it, but I'm following in my mother's footsteps here. Hers was a Fourth of July speech, back when Montana was only half this old—and some of us were as young as it was possible to be, it seems now. The idea, there at that holiday gathering of the Two Medicine country in 1939, was for her to commemorate the pioneer Ben English and the creek that carries his name for us."

Silent this morning within the greater rush of the wind, English Creek flowed at the edge of the town, of the crowd, of the amplified reach of the speaker's voice.

I held the pages of my speech firmly in both hands against the zephyrs both outside and within me. "Most of you knew my mother, at least in her last years, so you know that from Beth McCaskill you customarily got more of what was on her mind rather than less. I suppose it shouldn't have been any surprise" —although it mightily had been; I could yet see my father in breathless freeze beside me on the picnic grass as we heard her multiply that occasion up from mere ritual—"when she began to speak not only about English Creek, where my father's ranger station was at the time, but of Noon Creek, where she was born on the ranch I have operated for the past forty years."

I drew a breath and made it into those words of my mother's:

" 'Two creeks, two valleys, two claims on my heart,' she said on that day in 1939. And being Beth McCaskill she was not about to stop at that. No, she proceeded to call the roll of dead ranches along Noon Creek. Of the families who had to leave those places during the Depression with the auction hammer echoing in their ears. The Torrance place, the Emrich place, the Chute place, old Thad Wainwright's place. The Fain place, the

Eiseley place, the Nansen place." Places, all, she knew as vacant and doomed; but where my hotblooded brother and the Leona of then found spring shelter for what their bodies wanted. "Places that are still being added to, yet today, across the emptying parts of this state. A little while back you maybe read, as I did, how Riley Wright summed up a lot of this: 'Of all of Montana's hard weather, the reliably worst has been its economic climate.' "

Only the sound of the wind making the cottonwoods give followed into the pause of his words.

"There are goodbyes to be said today besides our farewell to Montana's original century," I spoke it out while watching the writing figure. "The person down here doing the story of our ceremony, the selfsame Riley Wright, is one of those who is leaving for a life elsewhere. What he's going to find to say about us this morning, heaven only knows and even it usually has to guess, where Riley is concerned." For that he cocked an applesauce eyebrow at me but kept typing. "Riley and I have not always seen eye to eye. But I'll say this for him: life never looks quite the same after Riley Wright has shown it to you."

I paused and peeked down at him as the crowd clapped a sendoff for Riley. It was hard to be sure under partial light, but the sonofagun may have blushed.

I made myself resume.

"The other leave-taking, the one that makes today's goodbyes plural, is geographically closer to home. This one—no offense to Riley, but this other one knocks an even bigger hole in me. This other one is my—"

My throat caught, and I looked out at my daughter in the crowd, Mariah with her camera down, giving me her validating grin; I swallowed as hard as I ever have and finished the saying of it:

"—self."

There was a stir at that. Of all the honors there are, that moment of the Two country's twinge toward me is what I will take.

"My leaving is of my ranch," I went on. "The Reese place, as it began. Part of it also the Ramsay place, the homestead of my grandmother's side of the family. The McCaskill place, I

guess since I had a moment of sanity about forty years ago and
came back to the Two country from other pursuits and married
Marcella and we settled in to work the place, our place. Now,
though. Now like so many others I've had to face the day when
the land and the McCaskill family no longer match up. It is no
easy thing to admit"—all of them within listening range knew so,
yet I had to tell them the specific hardness of it—"because I
have always believed, as the people before us did and as I'm
sure you have, that he who owns the soil owns up to the sky."

*His words climbed as he threw his head back to outspeak a gust
that rattled his pages, to send his voice higher, stronger. Language
is the light that comes out of us. Imagine the words as if they are
our way of creating earthlight, as if what is being spoken by this
man in a windswept dawn is going to carry everlastingly upward,
the way starshine is pulsing constantly across the sky of time to
us. Up through the black canyons of space, the sparks we utter;
motes of wordfire that we glimpse leaving on their constellating
flight, and call history.*

"So, when you've got it to do," I resumed like a man re-
solved, "you wrestle the question until you see where it falls.
The automatic answer is to let my ranch follow all the others on
Noon Creek. Go the way"—the Double W way, the conglomerate
way, I did not even need to say—"that such places economically
have to go, we all know."

I took an even firmer grip on the pages of my talk and headed
into what I had to say next.

"However."

Funny, how that lone word made Shaun Finletter suddenly
look as if his arithmetic had been smudged.

"The automatic way of doing things isn't necessarily mine,
any more," I kept at the matter. "I've maybe learned a little
something about being usefully ornery, from the company I've
been keeping these past few months." Mariah only paused for a
half-second in biting off the leader of an exposed roll of film in
her lightning reload of the camera. Riley gave me a gaze of
kitten innocence. "Anyway," I delivered the rest of it, "I'm
leaving my ranch, yes. But leaving it to . . ."

The Nature Conservancy guy on the other end of the phone

the night before had sounded simultaneously enthused and curious, as if he wished he could peer across the distance from Helena to Noon Creek and gauge me face to face.

"Naturally we're interested in a piece of country like yours, Mr. McCaskill. We try to keep real track of what's left of the original biology there along the Rocky Mountain Front, and those native grasses on the prairie part of your place qualify for the kind of preservation we want to do. We know how you've taken care of that land. What, ah, did you have in mind?"

When I told him for comparison what the Double Dub through Shaun was offering me, he responded: "We don't always have the dollars to pay market value like that, but there's a way of doing it called a bargain sale. What that is, the differential between the market value of a ranch such as yours and what the Conservancy can afford to pay qualifies as a charitable gift; it comes off your income tax load, you net out on it. Let me run some numbers by you, okay?"

After that trot across the calculator, I said to him:

"Good enough. The outfit is yours, if you can do a couple of other things for me."

"And those are?"

I laid it on him that Kenny and Darleen had to be kept for at least a year, given a chance to perform the upkeep or caretaking or whatever on the place. "They aren't either one exactly whiz kids, but they're hell for work." My figuring was that the two of them would be able to show their worth okay within a year, but also that it conceivably might take every minute of that span.

"We can stand them, it sounds like," the Conservancy director granted in a dry tone. "And the other thing?"

When I told him, his voice sat up straighter.

"Actually, we've been thinking about a preserve for those someplace on this side of the mountains, if we could manage to get enough land together out north from Pine Butte."

"It's got to be part of the deal," I made good and sure. "The name and everything."

Through the phone earpiece I could all but hear the land preservation honcho thinking *Holy smoke, we don't get many ranchers who are such a big buddy of* . . . Then with determination he said: "We'll do it."

I took a pleasant moment to cast a gaze east from the ranch house, out across the moonlit hay meadows and grass country between there and my fenceline with the Double W. If Pine Butte could be kept a fen, this ranch could be kept a range. After all, WW Inc. wanted to see maximum animal units on this piece of land, didn't it? It was about to have them. Buffalo. A whole neighboring ranchful. Right in here next to a corporate cow pasture would now be the Toussaint Rennie Memorial Bison range, original inhabitants of this prairie, nice big rambunctious butting ones. Let the sonofabitching Double W tend *its* fences against those, for a change.

The Nature Conservancy headman, trying to keep delight out of his tone, carefully checked to see that we were really concluded. "That's all the details of our transaction then, Mr. McCaskill? We sure appreciate your doing this."

"One more thing," I said into the phone. "Happy next hundred years."

"I guess I see this as giving back to the earth some of the footing it has given to me and mine," I told the intent crowd now. "If we McCaskills no longer will be on that particular ground, at least the family of existence will possess it. That kind of lineage needs fostering too, I've come to think—our kinship with the land."

Mariah, of course operating as if she and I and the camera were the only three for miles around, had come climbing up over the bumper onto the other front fender of the auctioneering pickup and was kneeling there for a closeup of me framed between the loudspeaker horns.

"Speaking of lineage . . ." I resorted to with a rueful glance down at this ambushing daughter.

When the audience had its laugh at that, I looked from the impervious lens of Mariah to them and back to her again before I could resume.

"Mariah here is going into the next hundred years in her own style, as you might expect. She begins it immediately after our ceremony today. With Riley leaving—our loss and California's gain, but they need all they can get—maybe the *Montanian* figured it might as well trade in Mariah's job too. In any case, her new arrangement is—I don't know what something like this is actually called, but Mariah is being turned loose on this state as the *Montanian*'s photographer at large."

* * *

When she and I came off the dance floor to him this morning, Riley looked at her as if he was seeing the last one of a kind. "I still think we could've made it work this time, Mariah Montana."

"I don't," Mariah said gently but firmly, "and that'd have been a fatal start right there."

"You know, that's the trouble with reality checks," Riley said as if he'd been asked for a diagnosis. "They fuck up the possibilities of imagination."

"Better that than us," she gave him back, keeping her tone as deliberately light as his. "Riley, you know what?"

"I hope you're not going to tell me this builds character," he said in the voice of a man somewhere between keeping his pride and facing loss.

"Huh uh, worse. What I finally figured out is that you and I love just some of each other, mostly the job parts. We collaborate like a house afire. If the centennial trip went on forever maybe we could too. But that's just it—beyond our work, we make trouble for each other. We didn't manage to wear any of the rough edges off each other in three years of being married, and trying it again would be just more of the same. New try, new place, new whatever, but we'd be the same." Mariah cocked her head as if it was her turn to diagnose. "We're each in our own way so ungodly focused."

"Spoken like a photographer," he couldn't resist intoning.

"What it is, Riley," she said as quietly as before, "we can't keep up with each other. I don't know anything to be done about that and I think you don't either." Still looking at Riley, Mariah inclined her head toward me. "Jick McChurchill here would probably say we're geared too different. You've got a definite direction of what you want to do, and it turns out I've got mine."

"I've got to point out, Mariah," Riley said with care, "staying put is a funny kind of direction."

"Mmm. I know. I'm maybe a funny kind." She looked at me in a way that made Riley do the same. "I come by it honestly, huh?" But then she turned to him again, her gray eyes delivering quietly but definitely to his gray and blue. "If I go to California because of your chance there, I'm tagging after. If you stay here in Montana because of me, you're tagging after. Riley, neither one of us is cut out for that, are we."

Riley had known ever since the motel in Ekalaka; Mariah was distinctive even in fashioning a goodbye. After that, the BB was undoubtedly the easier case, Mariah letting him blab on about how very unique her photowork in the centennial series had been until he found himself agreeing that her best use of talent would be to keep on picturing Montana as it struggled with Century Number Two, wouldn't it.

And so Riley for once didn't argue. There in the Medicine Lodge, waiting to do their last piece before it became Mariah's job to rove and his to transplant himself to the *Globe* column, he managed at least a semblance of his sly look as he said to her: "You may be right—we're maybe a little advanced to be playing tag." But for half a moment I felt sorry for Riley, going off to California with just his mustache for company.

"The last some months," the microphone carried my words, "I've been on the go in parts of this state of ours that I'd scarcely even heard of. A lot of my daily reading since the Fourth of July has been roadmaps, and it eventually dawned on me that Montana is the only state of the continental forty-eight that is a full time zone wide. Where the Clark Fork River crosses into Idaho it gains into Pacific time, and when the Missouri River flows across into North Dakota an hour is adjusted onto life from there to the Great Lakes—while we here beside the Continental Divide that sends those rivers on their way exist on Mountain time. And I wonder whether Montana maybe fills a span of time all to itself in more than just that map sense.

"An awful amount of what I saw across this state, what Riley wrote of and Mariah caught in her pictures, does raise the question of what we've got to celebrate about. Montana has a tattered side. You look at the blowing away prairies that never should have been cut by a plow and the little towns they are taking with them, you look at the dump heaps and earth poisons left by mining, you look at so many defeated lives on the Indian reservations, you look at a bottom wage way of life that drives our young people generation after generation to higher jobs elsewhere, you look at the big lording it over the little in so much of our politics and economy and land—you look at these warps in Montana and they add up in a hurry to a hundred years of pretty sad behavior.

"Then you draw a deep breath, get a little of this endemic fresh air sweeping through your brain"—the wind surged stronger than ever through the treetops, and members of the audience made sure they weren't beneath cottonwood limbs that could crash down—"and you look at the valleys that are the green muscles on the rock bones of this state, you look at the last great freeflowing river in the continental U.S., the Yellowstone; you look at people who've been perpetually game to outwork the levels of pay here because they can love a mountain with their eyes while doing it, you look at the unbeatable way the land latches into the sky here atop the Rocky Mountain Front or on the curve of the planet across the eastern plains—and you end up calculating that our first hundred years could have been spent worse.

"So, what I've come to think is that Montana exists back and forth that way. That this wide state is a kind of teeter-totter of time. Maybe that expanse, and our born-into-us belief here that life is an up and down proposition, are what give us so much room and inclination to do both our worst and our best."

Do they hear us yet, the far suns of the night? A hundred years may be only enough to start the waft of our words, the echo chorus of what we have been like. The voices wing up and up, trying to clock us into the waiting sum of time. A man on the roof of the Helena Herald *that morning an exact century ago, shouting down into the streets the telegraph news: "Statehood!" The accented cluck of a Danish-born teamster reining his horses around as they grade the roadbed of the Great Northern railway. A homestead wife weeping alone in her first days of cabined isolation, saying over and over "I will not cry, I will not" until at last she does not. The potentates of Anaconda Copper calculating the profits of extraction and the social costs of it not at all. Congresswoman Jeannette Rankin's unique double "No!" in the stampede votes for war, spaced apart by the years between World War One and World War Two. Grudges and fears, our tellings carry starward. Doubts and dreams and hopes. Eloquence of loss, a Montana specialty. Love's whisperings . . .*

Sounds of distance have changed with the years. I found so when I placed the other call last night, after settling the ranch matter with the Conservancy. No longer comes the silent stretch of time as you wait for the other person to be summoned to the phone. The phone miles now have a kind of fizz to them, a restless current of connection as if the air is being held apart to make way for the words back and forth. I have made other calls in my life that I thought were vital—Christamighty, I had just done one—but what I said into the phone now pulsed out of me as if I had been rehearsing for it forever. Maybe a person at last knows when he is ready. Maybe he simply can't stand being unready any longer. Whichever, I spoke it all into the humming listening miles.

"Jick, I didn't expect . . . isn't this sort of—quick?" Leona said at the other end.

"Not if you count from fifty years ago. I'd say we better get started and make up for lost time."

"Is this a proposal? Because you know I haven't been able to bring myself to remarry . . . and you said you aren't really sure eith—"

"A kind of one. Enough of one to get us started, how about."

At that, she was nowhere near as overcome with surprise as a certain son of hers had been. This morning when Mariah had gone off to the bandstand to modulate the music and I'd used that opportunity to tell Riley what Leona and I intended, he looked at me like Wednesday looks at Friday. Then asked in a stupefied way:

"Wait, wait, let me get this straight. Are you telling me you're marrying my mother?"

I couldn't resist. Actually, I didn't try overly hard.

"Who said anything about marrying? We figure we'll just see how things go."

Even over the phone I'd been able to feel the smile that came into Leona's tone after I suggested we simply try life together, preacherless. The two of us, spend some time here in Gros Ventre in the house I'd be buying with the ranch money, some time there on the Wright ranch if I solemnly promised to Morgan not to get in the way—or whenever we felt like it, do some Bago travel.

"Without being chaperoned by Riley and Mariah?" she came back at me with a laugh.

"We outlasted them fair and square, so here's our chance," I advocated.

She had to turn serious, though. We both did. Leona phrased it slowly, still more than a little afraid of it.

"Jick, is this because of Alec in some way?"

RIDE WITH ME, MARIAH MONTANA

I wanted that said, I needed for her to know the full terms. It
freed me to state the new truth:

"No. Finally, it isn't because of that."

The rest of my phone performance tumbled out fast. I told my
intent listener that the stirrings I felt were for her, Leona Wright
as she now was, and not some vanished girl who never married
my brother. That I knew we were both shaky about defining
love all over again at our age but I hoped she felt enough toward
me to give this a try. That the time we had already spent
together justified sharing some more, that we needed to see
whether it could extend into years. Into lasting together. The
gold ring kind of lasting if it developed that way, but any kind
that proved enduring was worth a whirl. That—

Leona quit listening and spoke back across the miles.

"Yes," she magically said. "Yes to it all. Let's be together,
Jick, and see from there."

We spent a delicious excited minute working out how and
when to start, then each fell silent, not wanting the goodbye.
After a bit Leona said in that woodsmoke voice of hers:

"Jick?"

"Yeah?"

"You are a wonder."

*All, all the spoken sparks we are capable of kindling, trying to
pattern us against the nightdrop. And reflecting back into us, as
this man is saying in the Gros Ventre near-dawn, as the afterglint
we know as memory.*

"Memories are stories our lives tell us," I went to now, seeing
Althea check her watch meaningfully. "I believe that you can't
come to a day such as this one, a gathering such as we all are,
without hearing those murmurs from within ourselves. One such,
in me this moment, is of seeing Lila Sedgwick on these streets,
when she was as old as I was young. Lila's own mind by then
had some better days than others, but no days were clear, any
more. Yet it was because of Lila, the unclouded Lila when she
was young in 1889, that we are at this ceremony this dawn.
When Lila's mind no longer could tell her the story of that
morning a hundred years ago, it lived on in another memory.
Toussaint Rennie told it to me, and I want to speak it now, to
pass it into your memories."

The cadences of Toussaint, the rememberer of the earlier Two country, began in me now.

" 'Way before dawn. Out to the flagpole, everybody. It was still dark as cats, but Dantley from the livery stable had a lantern. Lila says, "This is the day of statehood. This is Montana's new day." Sedge puts up the new flag, there it was.' "

Then in my own refound voice:

"As those first Montanans did, let's now put up our flag and, for as long as our eyes or our memories hold out, see what we can make our days bring."

As the applause resounded the flag-raising team set to business, the furled cylinder of fabric being carried to them at the base of the pole by many arms . . .

The next thing was, I was blindsided by Mariah, hugging and kissing me and declaring I had an entire new career ahead as a public spieler. I told her I hoped to Christ not, then held her just far enough away to gauge as I said: "Petunia, I hope you're ending up out of all this okay. I mean, without any—company?"

Mariah performed the little sidetoss of her head, the proud cascade of hair clearing away from her gray eyes as if offering me the clearest possible look into them, into her.

"You know how Missoula is," she stated with a grin. "Somebody interesting will come along." She swung her gaze just for a moment past me to the figure scrutinizing the flag ceremony and tapping steadily into his writing machine, soldiering on. "Riley did."

Now ready to hoist, four men take grips on the lariat-thick lanyard . . .

"So when do you have to head down the road?" Mariah issued next, her camera up and ready but not yet firing as we turned to watch the flag-raising.

"Right after this." By afternoon the Bago and I would be there at the other ceremony, when Leona and her women's club videoed the Crazy Mountains country for their Sisters of Peace to see.

"Tell your sweetie for me I hope her Russian pronunciation knocks their garters off in Moscow," Mariah instructed.

"I surely will."

The flag-raisers had their hands full. Shaun Finletter and Joe Prentiss and Kevin Frew and Larry Van Der Wende, strong men all, were hefting down hard on the rope, but only slowly did the flag do any significant unfolding, the attached end streaming up in a draggy thin triangle as more and more of the tremendous bundle lifted out of the holders' arms. They were going to have to go some to get it all the way aloft by sunrise.

Then, though. Then the streamer was high enough to reach the full wind, funneling over the Bago between the buildings, and the golden cloth caught at that force, bellying like a boatsail. The men pulled and pulled, the giant flag billowing out and out, writhing up through the air.

"Christamighty, listen to that!"

Why I let that out I don't know, for Mariah beside me plainly was hearing the same astounding thing. Everybody in Gros Ventre was, maybe everybody period. Now snugged against the top of the pole, up in that storm of air the blowing flag was making a sound that filled the sky, a roaring crackle like a vast fire blazing. Blizzard, chinook, squall, gale, I thought I had heard them all but never this. Ultimate Montana wind and great field of cloth, they were creating thunderous melody of flow over our heads.

The central emblem panel of THE TWO MEDICINE COUNTRY 1889   1989   GREETS THE DAWN OF MONTANA shimmered, as if in emphasis, every time the wind powerfully snapped the flag into another loud rumple.

But suddenly there was a new, quicker, dancier snap of rhythm within the flag roar.

The upper border of the flag, the sheep-cow-horse repeating design, was flying on its own, as if the livestock were bucking free of the heavier fabric beneath.

Then the panel below that, with the sewn-on representation of a Blackfeet chief's headdress, tore free and similarly flew from the flag rope on its own.

The crowd, stunned, awed, whatever, gaped up in silence until there came the vexed voice of Althea Frew:

"Oh, foo."

One by one the other sewn seams were freeing themselves there in the wild ride of the wind, the bottom border of forest and stream abruptly a separate wing of banner, next the stitchwork panel of Gros Ventre's buildings undulating independently as if the wind had lifted the entire town.

"Every part up there's got a mind of its own!" a voice—odds were it was one of the Baloney Express bunch—called out, setting off laughter.

"By God, this'll give us something to remember!" someone else shouted, and the laughter grew.

"Yeah, hell, we're getting all different kinds of flags out of this, for the same price as one!" issued from someone else, which set the crowd to really cheering and clapping, waves of sound to match the flapping symphony above.

Mariah had been clicking the overhead parade of banners as if motorized, but she stopped now and jiggled me in the ribs.

"What a zammo morning. We're next, Jick," she announced as keenly as if she and I were ticketed on the next ascension of wind.

So to speak, so we were: the mountainline of the Two country up over English Creek and Noon Creek that the two of us had stitched on came flapping free, Roman Reef and Phantom Woman Mountain and Flume Gulch and Jericho Reef dancing in the sky. I had to chuckle at that, the geographical pennant of the McCaskills, as Mariah

swiftly moved low to one side of him and captured the picture to go with these words, of Jick with his bearded head thrown back as he laughed upward at the multiplying banners of the centennial. As she clicked, day's arrival was definite, the sun articulating its long light onto the land.

ACKNOWLEDGMENTS

My ground rules for myself in this novel have been the same as in the first two books of this trilogy, *English Creek* and *Dancing at the Rascal Fair*: the heartland of the McCaskill family is the Rocky Mountain Front near what is actually Dupuyer, Montana, but the specific places and people are of my own invention. Similarly, except for a handful of irresistibly emblematic Montana institutions—the M & M in Butte, the Country Pride cafe in Big Timber, the Wagon Wheel cafe in Ekalaka, and the sign on the Elk Bar in Chinook—the RV parks, bars, eating places and so on that are my Bago travelers' ports of call across the state are not actual.

Again, too, a community of friends and acquaintances unflinchingly lent themselves to me and the making of this book these past three years: Mike Olsen, Ann McCartney, earring consultants Bryony Angell and Gilia Angell, Bob Simmons, Liz Darhansoff, Jud Moore, Laird Robinson, Michael Korn, Marshall Nelson, Lee Goerner, Sharon Waite, Richard Maxwell Brown, Barry Lippman, Hazel and Gene Bonnet, Barbara A. Niemczyk, Sue Lang, Pete Steen, Joy Hamlett and two generations of Bradley Hamletts, Bill Robbins, Merrill Burlingame, Ted and Jean Schwinden, Laurie Paris, Dorothy LaRango, Sven H. Rossel, Dore Schwinden, Thomas Blaine, Germaine Stivers, Marsha Hinch, Barbara Arensmeyer, Laura McCann, Tom Chadwick, Herb Griffin, Tom Stewart, Jim Castles, Brian Kahn of the Montana Nature Conservancy, Nancy McKay, Jean Roden, John Roden, Jim Norgaard, Vern Carstensen, Peter Haley, Dave Carr, Linda Foss, and Elizabeth Simpson.

Nor could a book of this sort have been done without these libraries and their helpful staffs: Great Falls Public Library; the Montana Historical Society at Helena; the Mansfield Library of the University of Montana at Missoula; the Parmly Billings Library; the Renne Library of Montana State University at Bozeman; the Shoreline Community College Library at Seattle; and the University of Washington Library at Seattle.

Throughout the decade of research I've spent on these books, I was rescued time and again by the extraordinary skills of Dave Walter, reference librarian of the Montana Historical Society. Among other things, this trilogy is a monument to Dave's patience.

My, and Riley's, versions of history have been derived and inspired from numerous sources, these perhaps main among them. The Indian quote about buffalo that "the country was one robe" is from *The Last of the Buffalo*, by George Bird Grinnell. For historical backdrop of Virginia City and the Alder Gulch mining era, and much else in Montana's past, I've gratefully relied on *Montana: A History of Two Centuries*, by Michael P. Malone and Richard B. Roeder. Butte's story is voluminously told, but specifics about mining fatalities were drawn from the annual reports of the Montana Inspector of Mines and "The Perils of Working in the Butte Underground: Industrial Fatalities in the Copper Mines, 1880–1920," Brian Shovers, *Montana: The Magazine of Western History*, Spring, 1987; about the Montana National Guard's 1914 occupation of the city from "Butte: A Troubled Labor Paradise," Theodore Wiprud, *Montana: The Magazine of Western History*, Oct., 1971; and about the Company's use of "rustling cards" from *The Gibraltar*, by Jerry W. Calvert. Detailed research on women's exigencies in the frontier environment is in Paula Petrik's chapter, "Capitalists with Rooms: Prostitution in Helena, 1865–1900," and elsewhere in her book *No Step Backward*.

My version of the process of relocating a grizzly bear is an amalgam of techniques and circumstances; I'm greatly indebted to wildlife biologist Michael Madel for his painstaking advice on my grizzly scene. It should be noted that according to the best available figures from the Montana Department of Fish, Wildlife and Parks, there have been two fatalities of grizzlies in more than two hundred bear relocations by that Department. Riley's account of the Dempsey-Gibbons fight in Shelby is drawn from avid coverage by national newspapers, and valuable background was provided to me during my Shelby visit by Theo Bartschi, Mabel Iverson, and the Marias Museum of History and Art. The detail of Tommy Gibbons disappearing to walk the hills at dawn is in a sidebar in *The New York Times*, July 5, 1923. In the scenes at the Chief Joseph Battlefield and the town of Chinook, the quote about Alahoos being told the Nez Percé casualties of each day is in *Hear Me, My Chiefs*, by L. V. McWhorter, and Charles Anceny's observation about luck-over-genius in the pioneer cattle industry of Montana can be found in the *Rocky Mountain Husbandman*, Feb. 9, 1882. *A Traveler's Companion to Montana History*, by Carroll Van West, was especially helpful in my sojourns into eastern Montana. For purposes of plot I've sometimes changed the locales, but I'm much indebted for quintessential episodes of the homestead and Depression eras to Mary Dawson, once of Sumatra; Fern Eggers, once of Vananda; and Lucy Olds of Butte. For historic photos and background before my visit to the Fort Howes Ranger Station, I wish to thank the Custer National Forest headquarters and Dr. Wilson F. Clark, author of *Custer National Forest Lands: A Brief History*.

The *Montanian* and the freewheeling way Mariah and Riley go about their journalism are a figment of my imagination, as much a vehicle for this novel as the Bago they resort to. But for basic lore and lingo of newspapering today, I was greatly helped by feature writer Kathleen Merryman, and by Steve Wainwright's tutoring of me in the newspaper technology of the moment. As for Mariah's habits of the camera, some are Carol Doig's, a few are even my own, and I learned bundles from the splendid lensman Chris Bennion letting me watch some of his shoots.

Kudos to Zoe Kharpertian, copy-editing virtuoso, for finding a way to keep the lilt of westernisms amid the logic of style.

To Linda Bierds, my deep thanks for looking over this manuscript chapter-by-chapter with her unique combination of ever-encouraging friendship and poet's insight.

Similar gratitude to Bill Lang, former editor of *Montana: The Magazine of Western History* and still a polymath of Montana and Western history.

Finally, all ultimate thanks to my wife Carol, for her photography from Moiese to Ekalaka and for her confidence and care toward this book from A to Z.

FOR THE BEST IN PAPERBACKS, LOOK FOR THE

In every corner of the world, on every subject under the sun, Penguin represents quality and variety—the very best in publishing today.

For complete information about books available from Penguin—including Pelicans, Puffins, Peregrines, and Penguin Classics—and how to order them, write to us at the appropriate address below. Please note that for copyright reasons the selection of books varies from country to country.

In the United Kingdom: For a complete list of books available from Penguin in the U.K., please write to *Dept E.P., Penguin Books Ltd, Harmondsworth, Middlesex, UB7 0DA.*

In the United States: For a complete list of books available from Penguin in the U.S., please write to *Dept BA, Penguin*, Box 120, Bergenfield, New Jersey 07621-0120.

In Canada: For a complete list of books available from Penguin in Canada, please write to *Penguin Books Canada Ltd, 10 Alcorn Avenue, Suite 300, Toronto, Ontario, Canada M4V 3B2.*

In Australia: For a complete list of books available from Penguin in Australia, please write to the *Marketing Department, Penguin Books Ltd, P.O. Box 257, Ringwood, Victoria 3134.*

In New Zealand: For a complete list of books available from Penguin in New Zealand, please write to the *Marketing Department, Penguin Books (NZ) Ltd, Private Bag, Takapuna, Auckland 9.*

In India: For a complete list of books available from Penguin, please write to *Penguin Overseas Ltd, 706 Eros Apartments, 56 Nehru Place, New Delhi, 110019.*

In Holland: For a complete list of books available from Penguin in Holland, please write to *Penguin Books Nederland B.V., Postbus 195, NL-1380AD Weesp, Netherlands.*

In Germany: For a complete list of books available from Penguin, please write to *Penguin Books Ltd, Friedrichstrasse 10-12, D-6000 Frankfurt Main 1, Federal Republic of Germany.*

In Spain: For a complete list of books available from Penguin in Spain, please write to *Longman, Penguin España, Calle San Nicolas 15, E-28013 Madrid, Spain.*

In Japan: For a complete list of books available from Penguin in Japan, please write to *Longman Penguin Japan Co Ltd, Yamaguchi Building, 2-12-9 Kanda Jimbocho, Chiyoda-Ku, Tokyo 101, Japan.*